UNWANTED

C.J. PETIT

Copyright © 2021 by C.J. Petit
All rights reserved. This book or any portion thereof may not be reproduced or used in any manner whatsoever without the express written permission of the publisher except for the use of brief quotations in a book review.

Printed in the United States of America

First Printing, 2021

ISBN: 9798754312616

CONTENTS

PROLOGUE 2
CHAPTER 1 10
CHAPTER 2 51
CHAPTER 3 77
CHAPTER 4 98
CHAPTER 5 133
CHAPTER 6 159
CHAPTER 7 238
CHAPTER 8 301
CHAPTER 9 346
CHAPTER 10 382
CHAPTER 11 433
CHAPTER 12 479
CHAPTER 13 504
CHAPTER 14 540
TRANSITION 581

… C.J. PETIT

PROLOGUE

March 17, 1862
Pleasant Hills, Missouri

The family stood with their heads bowed as Reverend Abernathy prayed over the unfilled grave. At the bottom lay a plain pine coffin containing the earthly remains of William Quimby.

Arranged in a gentle semi-circle were his oldest son, John who stood beside his wife, Elenora and their two small sons. Next to Eleanora stood the youngest Quimby son, Jeremy and beside him, the deceased's second son, Edward stood with his head bowed and his hat in his hands.

There were a few family members from neighboring farms grouped behind the preacher. The two gravediggers leaned on their spades nearby as they waited to shovel the dirt back into the hole. It was close to lunchtime, and they were growing annoyed with Reverend Abernathy's droning. Whenever they learned that he was going to preside over the burial service, they'd demand an extra dollar from Mister Winchell, but he never gave them more than a dime.

Standing by himself leaving a ten-foot gap from Edward was Joe Beck. He had his droopy brown hat in his hands, but his head wasn't bowed. Technically, he was family, but when he left the house with the others, John had made it clear that he wasn't to stand with the Quimby family when they buried his father. John had emphasized the words 'my father' when he warned him.

Joe knew that his oldest cousin wouldn't let him stay in the house very long, even though he actually lived in the barn. Even on the hour-long wagon ride to the town cemetery, he wasn't allowed to sit with the Quimbys. John drove with his wife sitting beside him and his two boys filling the rest of the seat. Jeremy and Edward rode their mules alongside while Joe sat on the tailgate with his feet dangling just inches from the ground. He was only surprised that John had expressed his intentions before the burial instead of waiting until they returned.

He stood hearing but not listening to the reverend's seemingly unending praise of the saintly William Quimby. He didn't hate his uncle but wasn't ready to award him sainthood, either. But his uncle was no longer his problem, and neither was John. Joe was taking advantage of the minister's pride in his oratory to refine his plans for what he'd do tomorrow when he no longer had a roof over his head.

Joe was deep in thought and was startled when Reverend Charles Draper Abernathy finally ended his tiresome eulogy with a flourish by shouting, "Praise be to God!"

While Joe may have been blasted back into the real world, the two grave diggers had a very different reaction. They had been eagerly waiting for the reverend's standard final exclamation. His shout was still echoing from the walls of his nearby church when they stood, pulled their spades from the ground and began shoveling the dirt back into the gravesite. They didn't even look at the family as they stepped around the Quimbys who were walking toward the reverend to thank him. Joe watched as they lined up to express their gratitude but thought it would be hypocritical for him to join the short queue even if John would have allowed it.

He still didn't return to the wagon until John and his family passed in front of him without giving him a glance. Even John's little boys ignored him. Joe waited until there was an appropriate gap before he began walking behind them. He waited until everyone was seated, and the wagon started rolling back to the farm before he hopped onto his tailgate seat.

Even before he did, he began to wish that he'd just started back on foot as soon as the ceremony ended. As the wagon bounced and rocked along the road, Joe knew he'd have to hurry to get to his space in the loft before Jeremy did.

Jeremy was the youngest of the Quimby boys but still two years older than Joe. He was four inches shorter than Joe, but a good twenty pounds heavier. Joe wasn't afraid of any of his cousins, but he wasn't concerned about being pummeled. In the last year, he'd caught Jeremy trying to steal his Model

UNWANTED

1841 Mississippi rifle twice. So, Joe had created a hidden space in the loft to prevent a third attempt. It wasn't difficult to find, but it would take Jeremy at least ten minutes to discover its location and Joe should be able to stop him before he left the barn.

He didn't need to turn around to look for the Quimby farmhouse and barn because he knew they were about a quarter of a mile from the access road. He always had to unharness the team almost as punishment. But this time, he would use it to his advantage.

After he finished with the mules, he'd just climb to his loft and start packing his things into the two burlap sacks he'd saved to use as travel bags. He wouldn't bother waiting for John Quimby to order him away but would leave as soon as he could. He'd walk back to Pleasant Hill and buy some supplies with his small stash of money before continuing north to Lone Jack. He wasn't going to stay in the small town but would build a shelter of sorts until he figured out what he'd do for the rest of his life.

The wagon soon turned left onto the access road and Joe was preparing to hop off just before John pulled it to a stop. When the wagon slowed, Joe dropped to the ground and started trotting to the mules to take their reins.

John leaned back on the reins, but before he set the handbrake, he looked at Joe and said, "Jeremy will take care of the mules, Beck. I wanna talk with you near the hog pen."

Joe glanced at John and thought about telling him that he was leaving but knew it wouldn't matter. He'd probably have to fight his way to the barn if he did. So, he didn't reply before he turned and started walking to the farm's large, malodorous pig home. He thought it was an appropriate location for what he knew would be an equally offensive conversation. But it was neither the spot nor the topic that bothered Joe. It was that he knew that now, Jeremy would be given his opportunity to find and steal his rifle. He was hoping that he wouldn't find it before John finished telling him that he was an unwanted appendage to the Quimby family.

He stopped on the upwind side of the hog pen which gave him some measure of olfactory protection then turned and waited for John to deliver his eviction notice.

John stopped four feet in front of Joe and stared at him for a few seconds before he said, "You know my pa only took you in 'cause my ma promised her sister that she'd take care of you. Before she died, she made him take a vow to keep that promise. He did, but I didn't promise anything to anybody. You ain't a Quimby and now that I'm the man of the family, I don't want you eating our food."

Joe didn't argue even though he'd been providing free labor to the family for six years and knew he'd worked harder than any of the Quimby boys. It wasn't that he was worried about starting a brawl with John, he just needed to get to his rifle before Jeremy found it.

UNWANTED

He didn't break eye contact with John as he said, "I won't take another bite of food, John. I'll just pack my things and leave."

Joe started to step away, but John grabbed his upper arm and exclaimed, "I'm not finished talking to you, Beck!"

Joe ripped his arm free of John's grasp and began jogging to the barn. There was only one reason for John's attempt to keep him from leaving. As he trotted away, he knew that John was probably just a few feet behind.

Joe reached the corner of the barn and slowed when he saw Jeremy carrying his Mississippi rifle as he headed to the house. Jeremy must have heard him coming, but never bothered to turn around as there was no reason for him to worry. There were three Quimbys and only one Beck.

As Jeremy entered the house, Joe was furious but didn't give John the satisfaction of seeing his anger. He took a deep breath and continued past the unharnessed wagon and entered the barn. He didn't care if John was still behind him when he began climbing to the loft. It was only when he neared the top of ladder that he looked back to the barn doors. John was gone and so was his precious rifle. He assumed that Jeremy had taken his ammunition pouch and powder horn as well.

He soon stepped onto the loft floor, saw the empty hole where he'd hidden his rifle then walked to where he'd left his two burlap bags. At least Jeremy or Edward hadn't helped themselves to the rest of his things. Granted, nothing else he had was worth much, but he wouldn't have been surprised if one of them didn't take his bags and burn them in some form of flaming exorcism. But as he began filling the bags, he prayed that during his search for his rifle, Jeremy hadn't found his only possessions that he treasured even more than his father's Mississippi.

He tied the bags together then hung them over his right shoulder before he draped his two woolen blankets over his left. He then stepped to the back of the loft and dropped to his heels. He pulled out his pocketknife and extended the long blade before using it to pry open a small board in the corner. After it popped open, he set it aside and removed a small leather pouch. He stuffed it into his coat pocket and was about to reinsert the covering piece of wood when he realized that it no longer mattered. He stood, took two steps to the opening and began his final climb down the ladder.

When he reached the barn floor, he took one step toward the barn door then stopped and turned to the tool bench. They took his rifle, so he didn't feel guilty for taking their hatchet. He slid the handle behind the cord that held up his britches then covered it with his coat. He expected John or one of the other Quimbys would watch him leave but didn't believe that they would bother searching him.

He never bothered to glance at the farmhouse as he walked across the front yard and headed for Pleasant Hill. He didn't

UNWANTED

know where he would create his temporary home or what he would do with the rest of his life, but he knew without question that he'd never set foot on the Quimby farm again. No one should stay where they were unwanted.

CHAPTER 1

August 16, 1862
Northwest of Lone Jack, Missouri

The sun was barely up but Joe was already sitting on the bank of the creek with his hook in the water hoping to inspire a catfish to join him for breakfast. He was staring at his line when his fishing expedition was disturbed by the distant sound of marching men.

He wasn't surprised after hearing the cannon fire yesterday. It came from the east, closer to Lone Jack but it was a good mile away at least. When he turned to see who was going to pass behind him, he saw a column of Confederate troops approaching. He stood, pulled his hook from the water and began winding the line around the two small branch stubs he'd left on the branch for that purpose.

Joe had just stuck the hook's tip into the wood when the leading elements of the column reached him. Most of the soldiers glanced at him and grinned as they passed, but a corporal pulled out of line and stepped closer.

He stopped and looked up at Joe who was noticeably taller than the grizzled soldier and asked, "What are you doin' here, boy?"

Joe glanced at his fishing pole before replying, "Just fishing."

"You got a rifle with ya?"

"No, sir."

"How old are you?"

"I turned fifteen in February. Is that important?"

"Only if you was a Yankee spy. You're mighty tall for bein' only fifteen and you got a good growth of beard, too."

"I can't help either of those things, Corporal. I don't have a birth certificate to prove it, so you'll have to take my word for it."

The corporal stared at Joe for a few more seconds before asking, "Did you see any bluebellies this mornin'?"

"No, sir."

"You ain't lyin' to me; are ya?"

"No, sir. I never lie."

The corporal grunted before asking, "If you see any, are you gonna tell 'em that we passed by?"

"Only if they ask me. I told you that I don't lie."

The Confederate NCO snickered then said, "You're either honest or stupid, but I reckon it don't matter now anyway. It's gonna get real noisy around here soon. You oughta find yourself a place to hunker down while we go lick some Yankees."

Joe nodded before the corporal turned and trotted back to rejoin his column. He watched as the long snake of soldiers marched past and knew that the corporal's prediction was probably right.

After the column turned east and disappeared over the nearby rise, he carried his fishing pole upstream to his shelter and pulled back the canvas door. He set his pole against the wall and disregarded the corporal's advice and returned to the spot where the column had crossed onto level ground. He cautiously climbed the grassy incline until he could peer over the top. He saw the column still marching eastward and wondered how soon it would be before they ran into Yankee soldiers.

He stepped a few feet to his right and leaned against a pine trunk to watch and didn't have to wait long for his answer.

As he watched, the column of Confederates that was now about a thousand yards away, wheeled to their left facing north. Then all hell broke loose when a mass of Yankee soldiers poured out of a gap between two low hills. The men in blue were soon engaged by another large formation of

UNWANTED

Confederates including cavalry. Cannons were being fired by both sides, but Joe could only see some of the artillery crews.

For the next thirty minutes the gunfire and cannon thunder rolled across the ground. Mixed in with the loud reports were rebel yells and screams of pain as men fell. Joe watched until he realized that the battle was moving closer. He was about to slink away when he spotted a line of Union soldiers coming around the western edge of the nearby hill. But he wasn't the first to notice their arrival. It looked like a company of rebel infantry was hurrying to prevent them from getting around their flank.

Joe was mesmerized by the pending clash and expected the two equally sized companies would soon unleash hell against each other. But suddenly, the column of Yankees realized that they weren't alone at the western end of the battlefield. They all stopped in their tracks, but their officer who was leading the column kept running. He was a good hundred yards in front of his men when he turned and realized that he was alone. But even as he exhorted his soldiers to follow, the rebels opened fire.

Joe watched him shout once more to his men but to no avail. Now the officer had a new problem. The Confederates had cut him off from his column and he soon recognized his dilemma. The officer didn't shake his fist at his men but turned and began racing directly towards Joe. A dozen or so rebel soldiers raced after him and Joe knew it was time to disappear.

He stepped away from the tree, but rather than return to his shelter, he found a much larger pine nearby and slid behind it. He kept his eyes on the small rise and wondered if the Union officer was going to use it as a redoubt to hold off the rebels until his men arrived. Even if he was able to live that long, he wouldn't be able to survive much longer. Even if he was carrying one of those new Spencer rifles, he wouldn't be able to shoot them all.

Captain Milton Chalmers didn't look behind him as he raced for the safety of the trees. He knew the rebels were close but hadn't fired yet. He'd reviewed the maps after yesterday's skirmish and knew there was a creek ahead. But it was the protection afforded by the bank that was important. He just needed to reach it before they killed him.

He was just twenty yards from safety when four of the Confederates fired a volley. Captain Chalmers felt one of their Minie balls slam into right upper arm and stumbled but kept his legs churning. He could feel his warm blood flowing past his elbow and knew he was finished. It wasn't a fatal wound but unless the rebs turned back to rejoin their unit, he had no way to defend himself. He couldn't use his precious Henry but could fire a few pistol shots using his left hand. He just didn't know if he'd be able to free his Colt New Army from his holster.

He reached the edge of the rise then just dove to the ground and let his momentum carry him a few feet down the grassy slope until friction took over. He could hear the rebel yell growing closer as he pulled his Henry onto his chest and waited.

Joe had been surprised that the officer had survived but when he saw the blood dripping from his arm, he didn't hesitate. He rushed out from his protection and raced to the injured officer. He knew that the rebel soldiers were getting close, so as soon as he reached the captain, he dropped to his knees.

Captain Chalmers didn't even see Joe until he knelt beside him. He immediately thought that he was a rebel and wished he could find a way to defend himself.

Joe quickly said, "Let me handle the rebels, Captain."

Milt was confused and snapped, "*What?*"

Joe loudly replied, "Let me borrow your Henry. Please."

If Joe hadn't said 'please', Milt wouldn't have let him take his repeater but had no real choice anyway. If the bearded youth wanted to shoot him, at least it would be with his own weapon.

He released his grip on his repeater and Joe quickly snatched it away. He wasn't sure if there was a round in the chamber but wasn't going to waste one if there was. He assumed the captain wouldn't go into battle with it empty.

So, he cocked the hammer and crawled to the top of the rise. He'd never fired a Henry before but knew it was powerful enough to be effective at this range.

When he stuck his head over the edge, he was greeted by another salvo of rifle fire. The ground on both sides erupted when their bullets drilled into the dirt. He thought they'd be closer by now, but they must have become cautious after losing sight of the Yankee officer. But while they may not have been as close as he'd expected, they were still well within range of the Henry. The soldiers who had just fired were reloading their rifle as four others aimed their rifles. Joe had to at least distract them, so he aimed at one of the shooters and fired. The repeater's recoil was nothing compared to his Mississippi's kick, but he didn't take time to do a full evaluation.

The rebel he'd shot went down and he cycled in a new round as three more rebels fired their muskets. He felt his old hat fly from his head as he fired his second shot, and another soldier fell. Two turned and ran back to reload as Joe began to make good use of the carbine's ability to send lead down its barrel.

He fired his eighth and final shot when one of them realized that the captain's company was about to cut them off. The survivors turned and raced away as some of the Yankees pursued them and others headed to help their commanding officer.

UNWANTED

Joe slid back down the rise and soon reached the captain. After he set the hot Henry next to the officer, Joe sat on his right side and began ripping away his jacket to examine his wound.

As he tore the heavy fabric, Joe said, "They're running away, Captain. I'm gonna take a look at your wound and try to stop the bleeding."

Milton looked at him and asked, "Who are you? Why did you help me?"

Joe was ripping off the blouse's sleeve when he replied, "My name's Joe Beck. I helped you because I could."

Joe began wrapping the removed sleeve around the captain's wound and was tying it off when the first members of the captain's company appeared over the rise. Because of the sounds of the nearby battle, neither Joe nor Captain Chalmers realized they were there.

It was only when Private Louis Bassett shouted, "He's tryin' to kill the captain!" that Joe looked up.

He didn't have time to utter a sound before he saw the bright muzzle flash then the world went away.

———

Joe slowly opened his eyes and groaned. He didn't stand but rolled his head left and right to see where he was. He was almost surprised to find that he was exactly where he was when he'd been shot. When that memory popped into his mind, he quickly began feeling the top of his head with his right hand. It was wet, so he pulled it back and looked at his palm but didn't see any red. It was damp with sweat but no blood. He let his hand do more exploring and discovered a large bump on the back of his noggin. It was sensitive to his fingertips, so he didn't press it very hard. He looked at his fingers again, but still didn't see any blood.

He couldn't understand how a shot at such a short range hadn't taken the top of his head off. He slowly sat up and felt woozy, but not too badly. He stayed sitting as he surveyed his surroundings. He could hear the sounds of battle in the distance, but none of the fighting was close. Then he remembered the Yankee captain and looked to his right. He spotted the patch of almost black dry blood, so at least it hadn't been a very realistic dream.

He wasn't sure it would be a good idea to try to stand yet, especially as he was on a slope. So, he rolled onto his hands and knees and began crawling like a baby to the top of the shallow rise. The sounds of the battle grew clearer as he neared the crest.

When he made it to the top, he saw the giant clouds of gunsmoke in the distance. There wasn't much wind, so it just hung over the battlefield like a fog. He didn't think that's what they meant by the phrase, fog of war. Whatever they called this manmade cloud was unimportant. He knew that the cloud was only there because soldiers were trying to kill each other.

After he spent a few seconds staring at the distant battle, he felt safe enough to crawl all the way to the top. If he saw any soldiers wearing either uniform, he'd roll back down the hill to the creek. But when he finally spotted soldiers, he knew that he wouldn't need to make a hasty retreat. He saw eight bodies on the ground and knew he had been the one who had killed them. He closed his eyes and asked God to forgive him but reminded the Almighty that he'd only fired to protect the Yankee officer who couldn't fire his Henry or his pistol. He assumed God knew what a Henry was.

He opened his eyes and was about to slide back down to the creek when he realized that there were no other soldiers nearby and he could see the Confederate's rifles lying on the ground. Joe slowly stood and felt stable enough to walk. He didn't trust his recovery enough to jog, but carefully made his way to the line of bodies.

Joe continued to scan for nearby, living soldiers as he walked but still focused on the rifles. When he was close, he stopped and turned in a complete circle to make sure he could make it to safety if someone came. He soon stood over the first dead rebel and examined his rifle. It was a Dickson smoothbore, so he left it on the ground and sidestepped to the next body. It was another Dickson, and Joe hoped that some of the others were issued different models. If they were all the same, he'd still take two back with him. After losing his Mississippi to Jeremy, he had been without any firearms at all.

After finding a Springfield near the next body, Joe was excited when he spotted a Mississippi rifle lying on the ground beside the next soldier. He quickly reached down to grab it, but when he bent over, he lost his balance and almost fell when a flash of dizziness reminded him of the knot on his head. He caught himself before he fell on top of one of the dead soldiers then grasped and quickly examined the rifle. It was a percussion model as his had been and fired the same .54 caliber ball. He was about to remove the soldier's ammunition pouch when he decided to check on the other rifles.

He was glad that he had when he found a second Mississippi that was a match to the first. With a rifle in each hand, Joe scanned the battlefield once more and didn't see anyone within a mile. He doubted if anyone was even looking west as each army's attention was focused on the other.

He turned and trotted back toward the creek and the protection of the rise. As he jogged along, he began thinking of adding much more to his supplies before a detail was dispatched to recover the bodies. By the sound of the ongoing fight, he suspected they wouldn't begin the morbid task for a few more hours, so he decided that he'd scavenge what he could while he had the chance.

UNWANTED

By the time he reached the rise and slid down the slope with his treasures, Joe had created two rules for his scavenging. He wouldn't take anything that touched skin and he'd avoid anything with a CSA mark.

After stopping his slide, he laid the rifles on the ground then spotted his hat a few yards away. He could see that it had been almost destroyed by one of the rebel's shots, so he amended his own rule to allow him to take one of their hats if it didn't mark him as a soldier.

He was feeling more like himself again as he scrambled back up the rise and barely looked for soldiers as he quickly returned to the bodies. His next priority would be the ammunition pouches of the two Mississippi rifle users, although he'd be able to use all of them. Before he began removing the first pouch, he quickly looked at the fallen hats and was surprised to find one that looked more like a Union cavalry officer's hat than one that would have been issued to a Confederate private. He picked up the hat and carefully placed it on his head. It was a good fit, but his skull still objected.

He ignored the complaints and began unbuckling the soldier's belts with the attached ammunition pouches. After gathering the first two, Joe continued until he had four, but knew he'd reached his limit. So, he hurried back to his grassy slope to deposit his supply of ammunition.

So began Joe Beck's ninety minutes of hurried scavenging runs. Other than the hat, he honored his rule about not taking anything that touched skin. Even though four of the bodies had boots that fit, and they probably wore socks, Joe didn't take them. Nor did he go through their pockets because he considered it stealing. Taking what they'd been issued wasn't.

The last items he carried to his impressive stack were the Fayetteville rifles. He had no intention of keeping any of the guns except the two Mississippi rifles. He'd wait a few weeks after the battle ended and carry them to Pleasant Hill and see if Mister Plummer would give him some ammunition or gun cleaning fluid and oil for them. He knew that the gunsmith would never part with cash for used army rifles. He'd also use them to trade for what he did need.

After safely reaching his pile of scavenged treasures, Joe pulled one of the backpacks from the stack. He opened the flap and after rummaging for a few seconds, found a ration sack.

He set aside the backpack and greedily opened the bag. He'd missed breakfast and lunch because of the battle and was grateful for the find. Missing meals was more the rule than the exception for Joe over the past few months. As he wolfed down some smoked sow belly, Joe guessed that his weight was down to around a hundred and thirty pounds. If he was five feet and four inches, that would be fine. But he was already close to six feet tall and looked like a beanpole.

He emptied the ration pouch but didn't bother searching for another. He needed to move his cache to his shelter. It was about two hundred yards north along the creek, but he should get it all safely stored within an hour or so.

———

It had taken Joe almost two hours to get everything stowed in his small shelter, but it left no room for him when it was all tucked inside. It really didn't matter until the weather turned cold and that wouldn't happen for three months. He'd be able to make a nice mattress of two or three of the bedrolls he'd scavenged.

He'd been adding to his shelter since he found the location the day after he'd been driven from the Quimby farm. It was a perfect place for a hideaway. He had the creek nearby and the sycamores and cottonwoods kept him hidden in the rare event that someone would pass by. Before that Confederate column had passed, he'd only seen two men and they'd been a few hundred yards away and on the other side of the creek.

It was late afternoon when Joe began searching through the backpacks. He'd keep what he found useful and either burn or bury the rest. As he pulled the one that he'd already opened in front of him, he hoped that he didn't find any letters from home. He didn't want to know the names or anything else about the men he'd killed. He needed to keep them faceless and nothing more than ghosts if he hoped to sleep without nightmares.

For another hour, Joe added items to three stacks. One was for keeping, the other for burning and the third for burying. He had only found two letters and without even glancing at the names, he crumpled each of them and tossed them into the creek. But the largest pile by far was the one he would keep. It was an immense bounty that might even provide him with the means to begin his journey.

Two of the nice additions to his supplies were a pair of cutting shears and a good shaving kit with a well-honed razor. He hadn't shaved for months, and his hair was already over his shoulders. If his beard didn't mark him as a teenaged youth, he wouldn't have bothered shaving at all. He was annoyed with his long hair, though. He'd tried to trim it using his pocketknife but had been close to slicing his neck in the process.

After being sent away, Joe had spent much of the time thinking of his future. He may have grown up on two farms, but he had other skills that would give him a choice in which direction that future would take. He'd used one of them to save the Yankee captain's life. When he thought about the officer, Joe wondered what had happened after his men arrived and tried to kill him. It didn't matter, but he was curious.

But now that he had trade goods that might earn him a cash stake, he'd be able to take the first steps down the road to his future. He had already decided that he wasn't going to stay in Missouri even before watching the chaos of the nearby battle. He would walk to Kansas City or Independence and see if he could convince some family heading west on the Oregon Trail to bring him along. The wagon trains wouldn't be departing again until spring, so he'd have to winter here.

In early March, he'd start walking northwest. He didn't know what he'd be carrying, but it would be a heavy load. He wished he could buy a horse or a mule, but the war was causing their prices to skyrocket. He'd seen Union and Confederate cavalry in the distance and was sure that there were already a slew of dead horses lying among the human bodies. The wagons, cannon and caissons all needed animals to move them as well. He couldn't fathom how many horses a unit the size of the Army of the Potomac would have.

He looked at the eight rifles he had leaning against two nearby trees and knew he'd have to clean them soon. He'd work on the Mississippi rifles first. He wasn't sure if he'd keep the bayonets, though.

After emptying another ration pouch, Joe carried the two Mississippi rifles to his shelter and began cleaning the first of its residue. After he'd oiled it, he reloaded the rifle and set it inside his shelter. When he checked the second, he found that it hadn't been fired, so he placed it beside the first. He wondered if his hat had been shot off his head by the soldier who had been issued the first one.

Before he cleaned any of the others, he took a close look at the blue cavalry hat and when he looked inside, he was surprised to see that it belonged to a Yankee lieutenant named G. Gillespie. It didn't have anything to mark it as property of the Union army, so he set it in his shelter until he could wear a hat again.

The sun was setting when he finished cleaning and loading the last of the rifles and was about to put it into his shelter when he heard someone shout in the distance.

"Hey, boy! Are you down there?"

Joe kept the Fayetteville rifle in his hand as he crept along the creek behind the trees.

Then the voice shouted, "If you're there, kid, my captain wants to talk to ya!"

Joe hesitantly stepped to one of the sycamores and peered around the wide trunk to see who was calling to him. He didn't think that he'd been spotted by the rebels, so he guessed that he was being summoned by a Yankee. His lack of a Southern accent added to his supposition.

He had been so busy discovering and sorting his treasures as the sounds of the distant battle drifted in on the wind that he hadn't even noticed when they had stopped. The battle must be over, and it sounded as if the Yankees won. He wondered if the rebels already collected the eight bodies.

UNWANTED

When he spotted the soldier standing at the top of the rise, he noticed that he wasn't alone. There were three other men in blue with him and Joe had to decide whether he should show himself. None of them had their muskets ready to fire and his curiosity made the decision for him.

He stepped from behind the tree and as he began walking toward the soldiers, he yelled, "Why does he want to see me?"

Corporal Jones was surprised that the kid was still there then was immediately surprised again when he saw him. Captain Chalmers just described him as a teenager, so Isiah Jones had expected that if he did find the boy, he'd be a lot shorter.

He shouted, "I reckon he wants to thank you for savin' his life."

Joe continued to walk closer but wasn't sure if he wanted to go to the Union camp so soon after the battle. He was still having his private debate when he reached the bottom of the rise and looked up at the four soldiers.

"Did you win?"

Corporal Jones was tickled by Joe's question and snickered before he replied, "Yup. It was touch and go yesterday, but we got a lot of reinforcements and sent the rebs home with their tail between their legs."

"How is the captain?"

"He's doin' okay. The butchers didn't even have to cut off his arm. He's in his own tent again and asked us to come fetch ya."

Joe exhaled sharply then began the short climb up the grassy incline.

When he reached the soldiers, the corporal said, "Our camp is about a mile away, so we gotta start movin'."

"Okay."

The soldiers stepped off at a rapid pace and Joe had no problem keeping up with his long legs. None of them seemed to care about his rifle, but he was relieved that the eight bodies were gone. He wasn't sure that they'd search this far from the battlefield but figured the men who ran back to their unit would know where to look.

Corporal Jones asked, "What's your name, boy?"

"Joe Beck."

"How old are you? The captain said you were a teenager but you're pretty tall for a young'un."

"I turned fifteen in February."

"You ain't just sayin' that so you don't have to go into the army; are ya?"

UNWANTED

"No, sir. I don't have a birth certificate on me, but there's one in the Johnson County courthouse in Warrensburg if you want to check."

Isiah snickered then said, "I reckon not. We'll be movin' out pretty soon anyway."

"How bad was the battle? I only ran afoul of those few rebs before it seemed to head east a mile or two."

"It was pretty bad all things considered. We lost a lot of good men but the rebs lost more before they run off. We only won 'cause we got more replacements than they did. It looked pretty bad yesterday, though."

Joe nodded as Isiah asked, "Where's your home?"

"I have a shelter down by the creek, but I'm planning on heading west in the spring."

"Are you an orphan?"

"Yes, sir."

Isiah ended his brief interrogation when the Union camp came into view.

Joe was amazed by the size of the encampment but knew it was much smaller than those built by the large armies. It was still impressive, and he could see scores of blue clad soldiers crowded around fires waiting to be served a hot meal. He could see several lines of horses just to the north of the line of tents and wondered how many lay dead on the battlefield. He could see large clusters of vultures circling in the red sky to the east and hoped that they were there only to feast on the four-legged victims of the fight.

Corporal Jones led Joe past two fires and turned down a line of tents. When he reached a large tent at the end, he put up his hand telling Joe to wait then pulled back the flap and ducked into the tent. As soon as they'd stopped, the other soldiers walked away, probably to get their hot food before it was all gone.

Corporal Jones soon popped out of the tent and said, "Go on in. I'll wait out here 'til you leave."

Joe nodded but before he entered the tent, he handed the Fayetteville rifle to the corporal just to prove he meant no harm to the officer.

Isiah grinned as he accepted the long gun then Joe pulled back the flap and bent over before he stepped inside. He found Captain Chalmers on his cot with two pillows under his head. His torso was bare, and his right arm was heavily bandaged.

But the officer smiled at Joe and said, "Have a seat."

Joe replied, "Thank you, sir," then lowered his thin butt onto the stool rather than the nice chair behind a small desk.

UNWANTED

Captain Chalmers said, "I know you told me, but I don't recall your name."

"Joe Beck."

"I'm very glad to have met you, Joe. I'm Milt Chalmers and I am indebted to you for saving my life."

Joe shrugged then said, "You're welcome, sir."

"My men told me that you killed eight rebels with my Henry and there were only eight rounds missing. One checked the bodies and each of them was hit within inches of the center of his chest. How did you do that?"

"They were pretty close, and they didn't move. But I hoped that they would just run away."

"I understand. But I am very grateful that you chose not to run away. I'm sure that when my wife reads my next letter, she'll be even happier knowing that I'll return to her and our two boys. That was an incredibly brave thing you did. I wish my men were as brave and as accomplished as marksmen. My whole company balked when they saw the rebels and I was cut off. That's how I got shot before I reached that rise. I was hoping that my men would then flank the Confederates before they caught me, but they hesitated. If you hadn't been there, I wouldn't be here. Did you get shot?"

"No, sir. One of them put a ball through my hat, though."

"I'll have the supply sergeant give you another one."

"There's no need, sir. I scavenged all I could from those eight rebel bodies, and one had a Yankee cavalry officer's hat, so it's in my shelter. I meant to ask what happened to me when your men showed up. I saw one of them fire then I blacked out. When I woke up, I didn't feel any blood but had a good-sized knot on the back of my head."

"You came close to losing a large chunk of your head. Private Bassett was the one who believed you were trying to kill me. But Private Potts was closer and was already swinging his musket when Bassett fired. The ball must have missed by an inch or so after Private Potts' rifle butt struck your head. His musket was ripped from his hands and the stock had a piece of wood taken out of it.

"It was a close call, and I can't tell you how relieved I was when Potts told me you were still alive. They had to get me back to the surgeon, so they left you there. The doctor told me I was lucky you stopped the bleeding, or they would have had to amputate. So, you not only saved my life; you saved my right arm."

Joe just nodded and wanted to return to his shelter now that the mystery of the bump on his head had been solved.

He said, "I'm glad I could help, sir. But I've got to get back to my place before it gets dark. I don't want to bump into one of your sentries."

"I'll have a couple of my men escort you back. But could I ask you a few more questions before you leave?"

"I guess so."

"Have you used a Henry before? You seemed to know how to use it and I'm happy that you did. I was just surprised because it's such a new design."

"I never fired one before, but I've been visiting the gunsmith in Pleasant Hill for a while. I do odd jobs for him, and he shows me his guns and how they work. I told Mister Plummer that I would rather learn about guns than get any money. I reckon he would have been happy just to show me anyway. He likes his job."

"How did you learn to shoot like that?"

"My pa taught me when I was eight. He had a Mississippi rifle and after he figured I was good enough, he let me do the hunting for the family."

"That's a nice rifle. But if you're living down by that creek in a shelter, I assume that you're on your own now. What happened? Don't you have any family?"

Joe glanced at the closed tent flap before answering, "We had a small farm northwest of Warrensburg. That's in Johnson County. Five years ago, we must have had some meat go bad because everybody got really sick. I wasn't too bad and was able to help everybody else. My little sister died first, then my two brothers. My father held on for two days, but my mother seemed to be doing better. So, I drove the wagon into town to have the bodies buried. When I got back, she was out of bed but was almost too weak to walk. So, I told her to lay back down, and I'd do all the chores. She went back to bed but told me to ride to Pleasant Hill to fetch her sister, my Aunt Mary.

"I thought she just wanted help, so I rode as fast as I could and told my Aunt Mary what happened. My Uncle William wasn't happy when she said she'd come with me to help my mother, but we left the next morning. When we got back, my mother was still in bed. It was only two hours later when Aunt Mary told me that my mother had died. I wanted to stay on the farm, but my aunt had promised my mother that she'd take care of me on their farm. So, after we buried my mother with the rest of my family, I took what I wanted from the house, and we took the wagon and our milk cows and other animals to the Quimby farm. That was my Uncle William's last name.

"They weren't pleased to see me but seemed happy with the wagon and animals. They took a wagon back to the farm and took what they wanted before they sold the farm. My Aunt Mary died from pneumonia in the winter of '59, but before she passed, she made my uncle agree to honor the promise she'd made to my mother. He did as she asked, but barely. I didn't live in the house but made my bed in the barn loft.

"I was already planning to go off on my own when my Uncle William died in March. His oldest son practically threw me off the farm but one of my cousins took my father's rifle. I was mad but couldn't do anything about it. I headed for Lone Jack and set up my shelter near the creek. So, that's why I live alone. Sorry I talked so much. It just came out."

"That's alright. I'm glad you told me the whole story. But before you leave, I have to reward you for saving my life."

Joe shook his head and said, "No, sir. I have all I need now. Like I told you, I scavenged everything useful from those bodies. I have too much now and can use some of it for trade."

"Then what will you do? Are you going to spend the rest of your life living in that shelter?"

"No, sir. I plan to head up to Kansas City or Independence next spring and see if I can join a wagon train heading west on the Oregon Trail. I don't know where I'll wind up, but I'll figure that out on the way."

"Are you sure you don't need anything, Joe? Your boots aren't in very good shape."

Joe looked down at his feet but didn't want to admit that he'd been tempted to take the boots from some of the bodies.

"I'll be okay, sir. Do I just tell the corporal outside that I'm leaving, so the pickets don't shoot me?"

"He would have done it without asking, but I still feel as if I haven't thanked you enough."

Joe rose from the stool and stood bent at the waist as he replied, "I'm just happy that you'll be able to see you wife and boys again, sir."

Before the captain could make another offer, Joe turned and waddled out of the tent and finally was able to stand straight.

Corporal Jones grinned as he handed him back the Fayetteville rifle and said, "I'll escort you back to your shelter, Joe."

If the sun hadn't set, Joe would have declined his offer, but didn't want to depend on another fortuitous clunk in the noggin to avoid being shot, so he nodded then began retracing his path back to his shelter. He hadn't been surprised to learn that the corporal had listened to the entire conversation he'd had with the captain. The officer may even have ordered him to eavesdrop.

As they passed the groups of soldiers enjoying their hot supper, Isiah asked, "How come you didn't let the captain give you somethin'? You sure earned it and most fellers woulda taken all they could get."

Joe replied, "I just did what I thought was right. I didn't want to be rewarded for killing those men."

Corporal Jones glanced at Joe curiously as they passed the sentries then continued walking into the shadowed fields.

UNWANTED

Joe looked to the east and couldn't see any vultures but wasn't sure if it was because of the poor light or they were all feasting on the horse carcasses.

When they reached the rise before the creek, Joe expected the corporal to turn around, but he didn't. As they made their way down the grassy slope, he began to worry that the Yankee soldier was going to shoot him to take what he had scavenged but quickly discarded the notion. He turned right then walked along the creek behind the sycamores and cottonwoods until he reached his shelter.

Joe turned and said, "Thank you for making sure I didn't spook your sentries, Corporal."

"You're welcome, Joe. You take care now."

Joe nodded and was surprised when Corporal Jones offered him his hand. After a firm handshake, Isiah turned around and marched away.

Joe stood watching him as he faded into the darkness then sighed and carried his Fayetteville rifle to his shelter. He set it with the other and didn't bother building a fire before he lay on top of his new double-bedroll mattress and pulled one of his new blankets over him.

He wasn't tired, so he just reviewed the incredible day. When he'd awakened that morning, he couldn't have imagined all that had happened in less than sixteen hours. Now he had enough trade goods to get what he'd need to make the journey west in the spring. He only had eight dollars and seventeen cents in cash, but maybe he'd be able to add to the amount by selling some of his scavenged treasure.

But his most important find were the two Mississippi rifles. While Jeremy still had his father's rifle, he was still happy to have them. He knew that Jeremy would happily trade his father's rifle for the two in his shelter, but he wasn't about to return to the Quimby farm.

After the armies took their war someplace else, he'd have plenty of time to consolidate what he'd keep before he started his trading expeditions to Lone Jack and Pleasant Hill.

―――

When Joe opened his eyes to the morning light, he spent almost a minute just listening. The Yankee army should be breaking camp before they marched to their next assignment. He would have asked the captain where they were going but didn't. It wasn't because he thought he'd be suspected of being a Confederate spy either. He just assumed that they'd be following the rebels. He hadn't heard the defeated army leave the field, so they had to have gone in any direction other than west.

But he didn't hear any man-made noise, so he tossed aside his blanket then swung his legs to the side and stood. After taking six strides to the edge of the creek, he added a tiny amount of depth and color to the water before he turned and stepped back to his shelter. He knew that nothing could have been taken, but he still checked his newfound treasures. Before he made himself breakfast, he decided to take a peek over the rise to see if he'd spot any marching columns. It was still pretty early, so he suspected that they'd be having chow before they assembled into marching order.

He had only taken three steps before he spotted a large canvas sack hanging from one of the sycamore branches about thirty feet away. It was almost six feet long and was swinging gently in the light morning breeze. He made a single revolution as he scanned the surroundings but didn't see anyone.

Joe trotted to the bag and when he reached it, he pushed it to check its weight. It swung away just a few inches, so it was heavy. When he noticed the US stenciled along the top, he realized that the captain had probably had his men leave it for him.

He examined how it had been suspended and smiled. It was pretty ingenious for such a simple task. One end of the rope was securely attached to the bag, but after tossing it over the branch, the loose end was threaded through a grommet and a bayonet had been inserted in the rope to keep it from slipping. Before he pulled it free, he returned to his shelter and grabbed two of the unused Confederate bedrolls. He carried them back and made a closer and softer landing spot for the bag. He didn't think that there was anything inside that was breakable, but why take the chance?

With his landing pad in place, Joe held onto the bag with one hand then yanked out the bayonet. The rope buzzed as it passed through the grommet then whipped around the branch as the bag dropped to the bedrolls and began rolling toward the creek.

Joe rammed his left foot in front of the escaping bag then took hold of the canvas to prevent it from making another attempt to go swimming. He left the bedrolls and after yet another glance behind him, began dragging the bag back to his shelter. He probably could have carried it, there was no reason to do it when pulling it along the ground was easier and safer.

When he reached his shelter, he left the bag without satisfying his curiosity and returned to collect his bedrolls. As he walked away, he tried to imagine what the captain had sent him. When he'd held it, he could feel a boot heel which would be a godsend. He just hoped the captain had noticed his big feet. There weren't many soldiers with larger feet than his and he suspected that in another year, they'd be even bigger.

He rolled up each bedroll before he plucked them from the ground and headed back to his shelter without bothering to look behind him. After storing the bedrolls in his shelter, he rolled the two bedrolls he'd used as his mattress and put them in his tiny home before folding his blanket and adding it to the stack. He wasn't being a Neat Nick, but it looked like rain might be in the offing and he wanted to keep everything dry.

UNWANTED

He slid the bag to his log chair and stood it up before sitting down. Joe grinned as he delayed the surprise. He hadn't had any gifts since he's lost his family and wanted to savor opening this unexpected bounty.

He took a deep breath but avoided blowing across the bag as if he was making a wish before he untied the drawstring and pulled it open. As soon as the light entered the bag Joe was stunned by what his eyes revealed. He slowly reached into the bag and took hold of the Henry's barrel and slipped it free. After the butt was clear, he studied the repeater. He knew it was the same weapon he'd used to stop the rebels. He looked at the magazine tube and found it full of .44 caliber rimfire cartridges. He'd check if one was in the chamber later.

While he was incredibly happy to have the carbine, he felt guilty knowing that it was the captain's primary weapon. He carefully leaned it on the log then looked deeper into the bag. He reached inside and pulled out two pairs of sturdy boots that were nicer than those issued to the soldiers. He guessed that they were officer's boots. What made him smile was when he noticed that one pair was slightly larger than his own old boots and the second pair were larger still. But despite their high-quality leather, they were still much heavier than they should be.

He set down one pair and soon discovered the reason for their added weight. Each boot had a box of Henry cartridges inside. He grinned when he did the math and realized he had ninety-six spare Henry cartridges. He left them in the boots for the time being then continued his exploration.

He didn't have to reach very deeply into the bag before his fingers told him they'd touched thick wool. He pulled out a heavy coat that may have been Union blue but was devoid of any insignia or markings. He laid it onto the log then stuck his hand back into the captain's gift and his fingers reported touching leather. He let them slide across the leather before he pulled it free and found himself holding a gunbelt with an ammunition pouch. But it was the covered holster that intrigued him. He opened the flap, pulled out the pistol and gasped.

He knew what he held in his hand but never thought he'd own one. It was a Colt New Army pistol that looked as if it had never been fired. He slid it from its holster and admired the weapon. All six of its chambers were filled with .44 caliber balls. He forgot about the rest of the bag as he caressed the Colt's grips and let his fingertips slide across the steel. He was frothing at the mouth to fire a few rounds but didn't want to draw attention to himself.

After returning the pistol to the holster, he set the gunbelt on his new heavy coat and pulled the bag closer. It was much lighter now, but it wasn't quite empty.

He smiled after he reached into the bag and pulled out four pairs of heavy wool socks. The last gift he'd received from his mother was a pair of woolen socks that she'd knitted for him.

UNWANTED

The last item in the bag was a large knife in a heavy leather sheath. He slipped it out and admired the sharpness of the long blade. It was ten inches long and an inch-and-a-half wide at the hilt. He hadn't told the captain that he didn't have a good knife and couldn't figure out why he'd decided to send it along. Whatever his reason, he was very happy that he'd added it to the bag.

He stood and began loading everything back into the bag except for the Henry before he dragged it closer to his shelter. After he reached his tiny residence, he set the Henry with the other eight rifles then began moving everything else into the shelter which filled it to overflowing. He thought about strapping the gunbelt around his waist but decided he'd do some reconnaissance first.

Joe trotted away from his modest home and headed back to the rise. When he looked over the top, he could see smoke from their cooking fires to the northeast but didn't see any movement yet. He thought about visiting Captain Chalmers to thank him but thought he might be too busy as his army broke camp and prepared to march.

He slid back down the dew-covered grassy slope and trotted back to his campsite. He'd have a cold breakfast then take more time to examine the captain's well-appreciated gifts.

As he made his way along the creek, he wondered if Captain Chalmers had included a note somewhere and he'd missed it during his initial discovery. If he had, Joe hoped he had included his home address, so he'd be able to write a proper letter expressing his gratitude. He hadn't bothered to learn the captain's unit, which he believed was almost embarrassing.

He reached his shelter then knelt before the opening and stared into the stacks inside the shadowed enclosure. He'd already checked the boots, and the only other place there could be a note would be in one of the pockets of the heavy wool coat. He had to move the bedrolls aside before he pulled the coat from the stack and carried it to his log seat.

After sticking his fingers into each pocket, he was disappointed to find them empty. He folded it again and was about to return the coat to his shelter when he noticed a flattened area that should be curved. He unfolded the coat, undid the buttons and laid the thick woolen coat over his lap. He saw a folded leather edge protruding from a long inner pocket then gripped it with his fingertips and slid it out.

It was a fancy, well-made wallet, and it wasn't empty. He had been hoping to find a note but knew that there were other papers inside the wallet. He still wanted to find a note as opened the dark brown wallet. He pulled the currency from one side but didn't count it before he extracted the contents from the other side where he finally found a small white sheet of paper.

He returned the greenbacks into the wallet then slid it back into the pocket. He finally opened the note and read:

UNWANTED

Dear Joe,

I know you didn't expect to be rewarded for all you did for me, but I needed to show my appreciation. Don't be concerned that I was being deprived of my weapons by sending my Henry and my Colt. I wouldn't be able to use either one for at least a month, anyway. By then my father-in-law, who owns one of the largest gun shops in St. Louis will have sent me replacements for both.

The boots, socks and coat were 'borrowed' by my sergeant at my request. I made it clear that none of them should have any US markings that could cause you difficulties.

Don't worry about the cash, either. As a captain, I'm paid more than a hundred dollars a month and don't really need the money. My father owns several businesses and is an important man. It's why I received my commission as a captain despite my lack of military training. I had a comfortable life and was given all the tools necessary to become the man my father expected of me.

But despite the little that life has provided to you and your fewer years, I believe that you are already the better man. I think that you have a bright future waiting for you in whichever path you choose.

We're leaving tomorrow, but I can't tell you where we're headed. But before we go, I wanted to wish you all the best as you follow your path westward. If you ever need anything, write to me or my wife at the following address.

**Milton or Alice Chalmers
1621 St. Charles Avenue
St. Louis, Missouri**

Godspeed and May the Lord protect you.

Your friend and indebted servant,

Milt Chalmers

Joe stared at the extraordinary letter. Before he opened it, he was hoping to have the captain's address, but was expecting nothing more than a list of what had been in the bag with an explanation and a brief thank you.

He'd been right about all he'd expected or hoped to find, but it wasn't just a quick expression of gratitude. While he still didn't see himself as a man, much less a better man than Captain Chalmers, he didn't deny the powerful lift it gave his soul.

He folded the letter, pulled the wallet back out and slid the white paper into one of the leather pockets. Then he began to count the currency. His eyes grew wider as he leafed through the notes. He'd never seen more than twenty dollars in one place before, yet now he had $245 in his hand.

UNWANTED

Joe automatically looked behind him as if someone was about to slam a hatchet into his head, but there wasn't a soul in sight.

He returned most of the cash to the other side of the wallet, and after sliding the leather bank back into the inside pocket where he'd found it, he stuffed the rest into the left pocket of his dirty britches. He stood, but before folding the coat and putting it back into his shelter, Joe tried it on. It may be the middle of August, but he'd be grateful for the warm coat long before winter arrived.

While the sleeves were a close fit, and his shoulder seams were where they should be, when he buttoned the coat, he thought he had enough room inside to fit a couple of turkeys. He had no idea how much he weighed, but now he'd be able to improve his diet and put on some pounds before he left for the Oregon Trail in the spring.

He unbuttoned the coat, folded it and set it on his stacks of supplies. As he looked at his shelter, he decided that he'd build another one to keep him dry and reasonably warm. He could afford to get wet in the summer months, but he wasn't about to let his treasures become either rusted or moldy.

Ten minutes later, as he ate his cold breakfast, he began to think of what he'd do on his next trip to Pleasant Hill. More importantly, he tried to figure out how he'd be able to keep anyone from stealing his things while he was gone. While he had few visitors, there were people in nearby Lone Jack who knew about his shelter. Joe decided that the best way to keep that from happening would be to employ a guard who could also become a useful companion. So, he decided that he'd look for a dog the next time he went to town.

By the time he finished eating, his earlier decision to build a second shelter had morphed into building it further north and out of sight. He'd still leave some of his things in his old shelter, but he'd keep what he would be taking with him in his new home.

October 24, 1862

Joe held his breath and let his finger slowly draw back the trigger. The Mississippi's butt pounded his right shoulder as the .54 caliber ball blasted out of its muzzle then flew across the creek and decapitated the unsuspecting turkey hen. The rest of the flock scattered into the air using every point of the compass as Joe stood.

He turned and exclaimed, "Fetch our supper, Newt!"

Newt had been waiting to be released and shot away from Joe then leapt into the creek. He dogpaddled across the twenty-four feet of flowing water then scrambled onto the opposite bank. After shaking the water from his black and brown fur, he climbed the other bank and trotted to the dead turkey. He snatched it by the neck with his strong jaws then carried it back to the creek with its tail feathers dusting the ground.

After recrossing the creek with his feathered prize, he dragged the wet bird to Joe and dropped it at his feet.

Joe grinned as he rubbed Newt's dry head and said, "Good boy. After I prepare this bird, we'll have a feast."

Joe handed Newt a piece of smoked venison to tide him over until supper was ready. It would be a while before the turkey was ready to eat, although he knew that Newt would be more than willing to eat it feathers and all. He had already begun cleaning his rifle while Newt had fetched the turkey, so Joe finished the job and reloaded the rifle before he started preparing the turkey for roasting.

The Mississippi rifle and its brother were the only two guns he had kept of the eight he'd recovered from the rebel bodies. But he'd kept most of the ammunition, so he had enough percussion caps and paper and ball charges for more than two hundred shots. He hadn't fired his Henry once because it hadn't been necessary. He had already tested its accuracy before Captain Chalmers had given it to him.

After the armies had gone, he'd been making regular trips to Mister Plummer's gun shop and other stores in Pleasant Hill and Lone Jack to trade his unneeded items, so his old shelter wasn't even half-filled with things he could afford to lose. While his new, larger shelter protected his valuable items, there was still enough room for him and Newt.

He'd traded one of the Fayetteville rifles for Newt at the end of August in Lone Jack. The farmer had a pack of coon hounds and was happy to make the swap. He hadn't asked the farmer why the hound bore his name as he needed to do more trading. But Newt seemed to be pleased to leave the farmer and the pack, probably because he wasn't the top dog.

But Newt had proven to be a great trade, aside from his usefulness as a hunting dog and guard. Joe hadn't realized how lonely he'd been until he started talking to the hound. Those conversations may have been monologues, but as he spoke, he invariably scratched behind Newt's ears or pet his short coat of fur, so Newt readily accepted Joe as his friend.

Even before he traded for Newt, he'd made his first productive swap when he exchanged the Springfield for a large cart and some spare boards. It had seen better days, but Joe didn't mind. He had spent a week overhauling and modifying the cart then began using it to transport his trade goods and return with supplies.

He still wasn't finished with his modifications. It was fine for carrying his trips to Lone Jack or Pleasant Hill, but he needed to add more features for the long walk that he intended to take in the spring and then the much longer journey across the western half of the country.

CHAPTER 2

March 13, 1863

Joe tightened his harness across his chest then turned to Newt and said, "I hope you're ready for a long walk, pal."

Newt had been excitedly running in circles since Joe had started packing the cart, but Joe figured that he'd lose his enthusiasm by the end of the day. The snow had melted away a week ago, but he'd waited until the ground dried out enough to keep his cart's wheels from sinking into the mud.

He had extensively modified the cart over the autumn and winter months, but the wheels were still narrow, and it was carrying a lot of weight. After he had finished all of his trading, he still had six bedrolls, eight backpacks, and the two Mississippi rifles and all of their ammunition. He'd kept some of the other rifles' ammunition as well, but only for the powder. He'd opened each of the paper-wrapped loads and filled a large crock with the gunpowder. He had no particular reason for doing it but thought it might come in handy during his long journey. He'd kept a couple of dozen spare percussion caps to replace those that might fail, giving him a total of a hundred and twenty.

In addition to his two most important trades, Newt and the cart, Joe was pleased with some of his other bargains. He'd gotten two large used canvas tarps and six stoneware jars for one rifle and its ammunition pouch. But the best part of that deal were the six small sheets of gutta-percha. He knew what they were and was amazed that the storekeeper was willing to include them in the trade. He guessed that he had received them in an earlier swap with a Confederate soldier. The flexible gutta-percha was an answer to one of the questions that had plagued him since he decided to follow the Oregon Trail. He had been close to cutting up two of the rain slickers from the backpacks when he traded for the gutta-percha which was much better at making the jars waterproof.

He hadn't needed to add much to his wardrobe after his afternoon of scavenging. He did part with some of his cash to buy a heavy, knitted woolen cap for the cold weather and hadn't worn the Union cavalry hat since November. He had even recovered his old hat that had been shot from his head by one of the rebel soldiers. He hadn't put it on his head again but saved it as a reminder to be more careful if someone was shooting at him.

He still had almost all of the cash that Captain Chalmers had given him and had stored the U.S. notes in one of the small jars, sealed it with a gutta-percha lid, then buried it in his can of axle grease.

Before he'd buried the jar of currency into the grease, he'd thought about putting his precious pouch beneath the cash but changed his mind. If some thief stole the money, he'd be angry but would still continue on his journey. If he stored his pouch in the same jar, then he'd have to hunt the thief down and kill him.

So, after hiding his money jar in the grease, he fashioned a gutta-percha cover for his pouch then tied it beneath the cart where the long struts connected to the front of the cart.

Many of his preparations were designed to keep his possessions dry. His biggest concern was having to cross rivers and deep, fast-flowing creeks. He knew that all of the big rivers had ferries, and some even had bridges, but it was the unnamed creeks that would be called rivers in much of the country that presented the biggest problem. The covered wagons could cross at marked fords without too much difficulty. They were not only much taller, but their weight would also keep them from being taken downstream, and their oxen or mule teams could pull the wagons up the opposite bank.

The bottom of his cart was barely a foot off the ground and while it would be heavy for him to pull, it wouldn't be able to resist the pressure of a fast-flowing stream. He wasn't sure he'd be able to pull it up the other side, either. But the gutta-percha had solved his problem of keeping things dry when he did need to cross a creek or stream. He'd have to accept that his clothes and bedrolls would get soaked but could be dried out as he pulled his cart.

There was no concern about the brass cartridges for the Henry, but he'd wrapped a sheet of the flexible, waterproof gutta-percha over the mouth of the jars to protect his powder and the paper-wrapped ammunition packets for his two Mississippi rifles.

The rifles themselves found a home in one of the bedrolls. After sliding the first rifle into the bedroll, he folded it over and inserted the second into the upper half. There was enough bedroll left to fold over the rifles' butts before he covered the bedroll with one of the slickers. It wasn't waterproof, but it would keep out the rain and the morning dew.

The long rifle bedroll was tied down on the left side of the cart and the Henry and its ammunition shared another bedroll on the right. He'd have his pistol for unexpected danger but would use the Mississippi rifles primarily for hunting. He'd only use the Henry if he was in serious trouble.

He'd kept all eight of the rebel bayonets as well as the one used to suspend the duffle of gifts because he found them to have many other, more practical uses. One was to use them as tent stakes. After trying a few different configurations, he settled on a simple, fast method of turning his cart into a tent. He had cut some branches to size and use them as tent poles at the front and back of his cart then tie off one of his tarps to the bayonet tent poles. It wasn't elegant, but it worked.

One of the things he'd done over the winter was to use his hatchet and knife to convert branches into more than three dozen poles of different diameters and lengths. He spent more time on one of them to create a nice walking stick and could use the others for fuel when the trees began to disappear.

As he began pulling his heavy cart north alongside the creek, he hoped to reach the Missouri River east Kansas City by the end of the day. He'd set up camp and tomorrow he'd search for the ferry to get across the surging river. He expected to reach the Kansas side of Kansas City within two days then hopefully, he'd be able to join a wagon train heading west.

He'd probably need to make more modifications to his cart as he pulled it along the Oregon Trail and discovered its shortcomings.

Newt had stopped racing in circles after Joe began tugging the cart away from their small home. He soon realized that his human friend was moving too slowly, so he followed his hound instincts and began a weaving, sniffing path a few yards ahead of Joe.

Joe had been using his cart for his trading trips to Pleasant Hill and Lone Jack, but he'd never had it fully loaded before and soon discovered the difference an extra hundred and fifty pounds made. He kept his eyes focused ahead as he worked to keep the cart moving. The ground may have lost much of its moisture, but the wheels still sank a good inch into the soft earth near the creek. So, he shifted another few yards to his right and found the going a bit easier. He still had to modify his timetable and hoped to reach the Missouri River by noon tomorrow.

As he pulled his cart further away from his shelter, he began singing Kathleen Mavourneen. It was his Irish mother's favorite song and she'd sing it to him and his brothers and sister each night.

He focused on Newt as he began to sing, "The horn of the hunter is heard on the hill…"

He didn't have a great voice, but at least it no longer cracked and there was no one but Newt to hear him anyway.

He'd been slogging along for almost an hour when he pulled up and stared ahead at something totally unexpected. Someone had built a bridge across the wide creek in a location that didn't make any sense at all.

Joe started his cart rolling again and kept focusing on the bridge. He didn't see anything that might pass as a road to account for its presence, but he soon was close enough to notice its crude, yet robust construction. When he spotted a line of stumps on the other side of the creek, he finally figured out who had built the bridge.

The Confederate column that had passed by before the battle must have been dispatched to flank the Yankees while the bulk of the rebel army had continued due east. They'd built the bridge to get their cannons and wagons across the creek.

UNWANTED

As he continued to draw closer to the bridge, he estimated that it wouldn't have taken them but a few hours to build it. Cut down two or three of big cottonwoods to serve as the base of the bridge, then split some logs for the flooring. He was curious if he'd see any ruts left by the towed cannons and wagons when he reached the bridge.

But just finding the bridge made Joe modify his plans. Instead of taking the ferry across the Missouri River, he'd cross the bridge and enter Kansas before turning north to Kansas City. It was an easy decision as he didn't even know the location of the ferry across the Missouri River. Then he'd have to take another unknown ferry to cross the Missouri again when he turned west anyway.

Joe plodded on for another forty minutes before he reached the bridge where he stopped and stared at the ground. There were still some old, deep ruts left by the passing of the heavy cannons eight months ago, but there were a large number of hoofprints going in both directions that were much more recent.

He may not have been trained as a tracker, but he'd been hunting since he was barely able to wield his father's Mississippi rifle. The one that Jeremy Quimby had stolen. He counted at least a dozen horses and estimated that the tracks heading west into Kansas were about a week old and the fresher tracks coming back into Missouri were made just a day or two later.

Newt had already trotted well past the trail of hoofprints, so Joe had to call him back before he tugged his cart to his left and started for the bridge. Before he reached the first crossbeam, Joe had to build up speed to get the cart moving fast enough so the wheels would be able to bounce over the raised edge of the bridge. He was grateful for the downslope as he began jogging then shortly after he hopped onto the bridge, his cart bounced and almost pulled him over the edge. He was saved by his harness, and after the stumble, he kept his momentum to make it up the upslope on the other side of the bridge.

The cart bounced again after leaving the bridge and its mass almost pushed him over the upslope until it slowed in the soft earth then challenged him to reach level ground. Joe struggled the last few feet, but the cart surrendered when he reached firmer footing.

He stopped and gulped for air as he watched Newt trot behind him then sit down and stare up at him with his big brown eyes.

"You're not even panting, Newt. I reckon you thought it was a lot of fun watching me almost fall into the creek; didn't you?"

Joe laughed then scratched Newt behind his floppy ears as he said, "I'm still glad we found the bridge, though. I think I know who used it a little while ago, too. Kansas is only about twenty miles west of here, and I reckon those riders were Missouri raiders out to pay a visit to some Jayhawkers."

UNWANTED

If he hadn't seen those hoofprints heading back to Missouri, Joe would have made a quick turn to the north, but his curiosity kept him following the trail.

He and Newt stopped for a break around noontime and after removing his harness, Joe gave his hound friend a piece of smoked possum then stretched and sat on the open end of his cart. He took a larger piece of meat from the backpack, ripped off a bite and tossed it to Newt before he began kneading his tight calves.

For the first time since he'd decided to follow the Oregon Trail, Joe began to have doubts of the wisdom of that decision. He'd probably only pulled the heavy cart ten miles so far and hadn't even reached Kansas yet. But he was already exhausted, and his legs were as hard as wood. His shoulders were sore from his harness and his back wasn't too pleased, either. He had towed the cart to Pleasant Hill and back without feeling this bad.

Joe looked back at his own ruts heading east and wondered if he shouldn't have waited at least another week for the ground to dry a bit more. He sighed as he stood and twisted to loosen his back then walked back to the front of his cart and put himself in harness.

Newt trotted past and resumed his snaking, sniffing scouting role before Joe started the cart rolling and mumbled, "If I waited, the spring rains would probably make it worse anyway."

Joe still followed the departing and returning hoofprints and wondered if there were any towns in that direction. He didn't think there were enough raiders in the band that had crossed the bridge to attack a town of any size. He suspected that they'd be content with wreaking havoc on a few farms.

He continued following Newt for another four hours and knew he was close to the Kansas-Missouri border. He'd had to cross two streams and hadn't had any problems, but both were just a few feet across and not more than a foot deep. At least he had been able to cross them without getting stuck in the mud.

It was almost sunset when Joe stopped, slid his harness from his shoulders and called to Newt who was about a hundred feet ahead.

As he stretched his aching shoulders and back, he scanned the horizons and didn't see anything moving at all, not even squirrels or rabbits. There were some crows and other birds winging their way across the sky, but there were no four-footed creatures moving through the quickly growing grass.

Newt arrived and sat nearby as Joe slid a slicker from the cart and spread it on some level ground on the left side of his cart. Then he laid out a bedroll on top before he pulled out a canteen and took a few swallows of water. He set one of the rebel soldiers' deep tin plates on the ground and filled it with water for Newt.

UNWANTED

After returning the canteen to the cart's bed, Joe sat down on the bedroll, then stretched out so he could massage his stiff leg muscles. As he kneaded his calves, Newt trotted close and flopped onto his side.

Joe looked at the coon hound and said, "All things considered, we did alright today, Newt. We might even be in Kansas now, but I reckon it's still a couple of miles west of here. Maybe we'll see a big white line letting us know we're crossing the border tomorrow."

He laughed then said, "I figure we'll reach Kansas City late tomorrow unless my legs fall off. When we get there, I'm gonna have to buy some supplies, and that'll make it harder for me to pull the cart. Maybe I should give up one of those Mississippi rifles to save some weight."

Newt didn't offer his opinion, so Joe stood and walked to the back of the cart to fetch their supper. After he tossed a good-sized chunk of smoked venison to Newt, he took out a smaller piece for himself and sat on the edge of his cart.

When he'd first decided to make the long journey, it had sounded like an adventure. He yearned to discover lands he'd never seen before and even thought of going all the way to the Pacific Ocean. But now, even before he reached a starting point of the Oregon Trail, he recognized that while it still may be an adventure, it would be much more difficult than he'd expected. And that was even more astonishing because he already knew it would be a challenging undertaking.

If he had anyplace to call home, he would have turned around. But he didn't have anything but his small shelters laying empty a few miles behind him, and he'd taken most of the wood. His parents, brothers and sister were all dead and the Quimbys didn't want him.

Joe stood, then turned and faced into the setting sun. He didn't know what was out there; or how far he would go, but he knew his future was waiting for him where the sun was still shining.

Joe was in harness early the next morning and Newt was out front with his nose near the ground and his ears flopping back and forth as he picked up scents that no human nose knew existed. Joe's shadow stretched a good fifteen feet in front of him as he towed his cart west, still following the bi-directional hoofprints.

His legs had been stiff when he started but after the first mile, they had actually improved. He'd been pulling his heavy cart for almost an hour now and Joe had developed a smooth gait that didn't put too much strain on his legs.

He spent most of his focus on Newt, but still scanned the surrounding landscape for signs of danger. He hadn't seen a single person yet and that surprised him. This wasn't the unexplored wilderness of the Great Plains, even if it was Kansas.

UNWANTED

It was midmorning when Joe spotted a man-made shape on the western horizon. It didn't look like a house or a barn, but there was one straight edge that Mother Nature would never create or tolerate.

He shouted, "What do you think that is, Newt?"

Newt stopped his sniffing then turned and looked back at Joe before he continued his snaking scent search.

Joe grinned but picked up his pace a bit to get closer to whatever was ahead. But those hoofprints led in a straight line to whatever it was, so he suspected that it was the remnants of a farm that the raiders had visited.

He almost turned north to avoid witnessing what they had left behind but seeing something standing triggered a desire to do some scavenging. Before he'd left his shelter, he wished that he'd extended the cart's bed another two feet or so but didn't have any boards that were long enough. He almost made another trip to Lone Jack but didn't want to delay his departure and thought he'd buy them in Kansas City. But whatever was still standing might provide the lumber he needed. He might have to use his hatchet to cut them to size, but it was better than buying the boards. He knew it was almost silly to avoid spending fifty cents on some nice boards and nails when he still had more than two hundred and thirty dollars. But he wouldn't be able to replace the cash until he settled down and found work, and that could be a year from now.

Around forty minutes later, Joe identified the shape. It was a half-burnt barn that had collapsed. He didn't know why the half that was still upright hadn't gone up in flames, but assumed it was because of a sudden rainstorm. The house was another fifty yards away and wasn't so fortunate. There was a fireplace, a few posts and some interior studs still standing, but the rest was reduced to charcoal.

As he drew closer, Joe decided that he wasn't about to do any scavenging in the house. He didn't want to find the charred bodies of the farmer and his family. He'd take his boards then leave and cut them to fit later.

When he was within a hundred yards of the collapsed barn, Newt suddenly lifted his head, stuck his sensitive nose in the air then turned and barked once before trotting toward the barn.

Joe followed and by the time he was close to the only corner that still stood, Newt had stopped and pointed at the wall. His tail was sticking high in the air, and Joe knew that he'd smelled something that was alive. He suspected it was a racoon or maybe a possum.

He slipped out of the harness then opened his holster flap and approached his coon hound.

He rhetorically asked, "What is it, Newt?"

UNWANTED

Newt didn't even look at him as he stared at the barn.

Joe began to wonder if one of the family had been in the barn when the raiders arrived and had managed to hide even as they set fire to the house.

He stepped close to the wood and shouted, "Hello! Is anyone in there? I'm alone with my dog and won't hurt you!"

Then, instead of a human voice, he was answered by a sharp bray. He looked down at Newt and said, "I guess we're gonna have to figure out how to get that critter out of there."

He didn't need to return to his cart for his hatchet but walked to the end of the upright part of the wall and pulled down a half-burnt board. It cracked in the middle and Joe tossed aside the two long pieces. The next one came down intact, and he had enough room to enter the dark space and soon found himself staring at an ass's ass.

Joe slowly approached the donkey and had to squeeze between his side and the barn wall to reach his head.

The donkey turned to look at him and brayed once again before Joe rubbed his head and asked, "How did you live through this, mister?"

He thought he'd be able to back the donkey out of the stall but was concerned that the desperate animal would try to make a panicked escape and take the rest of the barn down in the process.

He patted the donkey's neck and said, "I'm going to leave you for a few minutes. But don't worry, I'll get you out of here pretty soon."

Joe awkwardly slipped out of the stall as the donkey watched him leave without expressing any complaints and soon left through his newly created narrow doorway. Newt was waiting when he stepped back into the sunshine and walked to the corner of the barn. He spent a minute to choose the right board to begin creating an exit for the donkey. He pulled his big knife from its sheath and began shaving the adjoining board until there was enough space for his fingers.

After sliding his knife back into its sheath, he slipped his fingers into the new handhold and yanked the board away. As it fell to the ground, the donkey brayed, and Joe could hear loud creaks and bangs as the animal bounced in his stall.

He didn't waste any time to calm the donkey, but hurriedly pulled down the next two boards until he saw the animal's frightened eyes looking out at him.

"Okay, mister. Let's get you out of there before you pull it down on yourself."

Joe stepped into the opening, untied the donkey's halter from a post then led him outside.

The donkey snorted when he spotted Newt who was busy sniffing the air surrounding the bigger four-footed creature. Joe began his own examination of the young jack and found that his left hindquarter's brown coat had been singed, but only enough to leave a black mark without damaging the skin. He guessed that the donkey had been stuck inside the collapsed barn for around a week and was amazed that he had fared so well. Why he'd been tied up and not taken by the raiders would remain a mystery. But finding the strong jack was an answer to an unspoken prayer.

He smiled at his new cart puller and said, "Let's get you some water then let you enjoy some of that fresh grass."

He led the donkey to his cart and let him graze nearby while he took one of his canteens then filled Newt's plate and set it on the ground in front of the dog. He then emptied the canteen and all of the contents of a second canteen into his small cooking pot and carried it to the donkey who was devouring the sprouting shoots of grass.

As the jack shifted his muzzle to the pot, Joe asked, "I don't suppose you know what your name is; do you? As you're probably not going to tell me anyway, I'll give you a new one. I know that you won't have that black mark from the fire much longer, so I'll give you a name that'll remind you. How does Bernie suit you? I know you can't spell, so if you want to think it's spelled with a U instead of an E, then that's alright."

After the donkey tipped the empty pot over and resumed mowing the grass, Joe laughed then said, "Maybe you really can spell."

He snatched his pot from the ground, returned it to the cart and hunted down a piece of his smoked venison and tossed it to Newt. He hadn't planned on scavenging anything more than boards from the barn, but now that he didn't have to pull his cart anymore, he could afford to add more weight.

Newt dropped to the ground then held the meat between his paws and began to rip it apart as Joe started walking back to the barn. He doubted if the donkey was going to go anywhere. Even if he did, he knew Newt would bring him back.

He soon slipped through his first doorway and once inside, he waited until his eyes adjusted to the shadows before he began searching for anything that might prove useful. He found the donkey's harness on the floor but most of the leather had been burned. He still picked it up and hung it over his shoulder before walking deeper into the shambles that had once been a barn.

Joe didn't see anything worth taking, so he turned around to leave. But just as he neared his three-board doorway, he saw the top four inches of an axe handle sticking out of some burned debris. He grabbed the handle and tugged it free. He was pleased to find that it was a pickaxe and not a double-edged cutting axe. He wondered if there were more tools under the pile, so he used the shovel end of the pickaxe to start clearing the mess.

He grinned when he spotted the business end of a spade and soon pulled it from under the rubble. The handle was scorched but intact. He set the pickaxe aside and used the spade to start moving the loose material in the hope of finding more tools.

Joe giggled when he found a large crosscut saw that had been protected from the flames when the nearby sharpening wheel had collapsed on top of the innocent saw. He had to lift the heavy stone disc to free the saw but didn't even think of taking it along. Now that he had a saw, he'd be able to cut those boards to length and take some along for firewood now that he wasn't going to be the source of power for his cart.

He carried his new tools out to his cart where he set them down. Then he began to empty his cart to start his first major modification since leaving his creek shelter. In addition to making the bed longer, he decided that he'd convert the cart into a smaller version of a covered wagon.

Joe was whistling as he began to work.

Kansas City, Kansas

Faith had never felt so humiliated in her entire life. She had heard her father rail against slavery for as long as she could remember, but now she understood how those black people felt when they stood on the auction block.

She saw the line of covered wagons lined up nearby as the families carried their purchases from D.L. Johnston Supplies and Dry Goods. She couldn't see her father standing behind her but knew that he was getting frustrated after no one had even spoken to him. The wagon train was leaving tomorrow morning and she didn't know what he would do if no one took her today.

What was most embarrassing was the sign she wore around her neck. Her mother had printed the lettering because she had a good hand. But it was her father who decided on the wording.

It had originally read:

**FAITH GOODCHILD
WILL CLEAN AND DO LAUNDRY
WORKS HARD AND EATS LITTLE
PLEASANT AND QUIET
GOOD WITH CHILDREN
$60**

That was bad enough, but after the whole day without anyone even talking to her father, he'd crossed off the $60 and wrote $40. She was being discounted yet still no one had seemed interested.

Her father may have claimed that she ate little as a selling point, but she wished she had something to eat right now. She was tired of standing while trying to appear pleasant to would-be buyers.

Most of the people who passed by just read the sign and laughed or shook their heads, but one of the men had seemed to look at her more judgmentally. She'd just seen him enter the store a few minutes ago, and she was sure that her father had noticed his lingering examination as well. She thought she'd seen him before with his pregnant wife who had said something to him as they passed. She guessed that the man might be interested because they needed a nanny.

She didn't want to admit to herself how terrified she had been since her parents told her that they couldn't afford to keep her any longer. It was after her mother told her father that in a few months, there would be another mouth to feed. Faith had asked if she could stay for another few months until she was sixteen and could marry, but they refused. She knew most girls were already married at her age and some were wed when they were only thirteen, but her father was adamant that she waited until she was sixteen.

As she stood with that hideous sign hanging from her neck, she began to wonder if her parents had refused her request to marry because they hoped to make some money by sending her away.

She was still staring at the wagon train and its growing herd of animals when she heard a man's voice ask, "Has she helped with childbirth?"

His question confirmed her earlier suspicion, but she didn't dare turn to look as her father replied, "Yes, sir. She helped with my three youngest children. She's probably as good as any midwife."

The man huffed then said, "My wife is heavy with child and will need help with our three young sons."

"Faith will be a good companion for your wife and is very obedient. I'm sure she'd be able to relieve your wife's burden."

Faith closed her eyes as the man asked, "Will you take twenty-five dollars? That's all I can afford."

She hoped that her father would refuse but wasn't surprised when he said, "I can tell that you're a moral man and will treat her well. I'll accept your offer."

Faith opened her eyes and listened as the man talked to her father for a few more minutes and then counted out the cash.

Once he had the money, her father said, "Do not be afraid of using hard discipline if she gives you any trouble, Mister Moore."

Then Basil Goodchild stepped in front of his oldest daughter and said, "You do whatever Mister and Mrs. Moore ask of you, Faith."

She nodded then watched her father hurry away without so much as a goodbye before the man took his place in front of her. He was just a bit taller than her five feet and five inches, but probably weighed at least another thirty pounds.

UNWANTED

He glanced at her departing father before he looked at Faith and said, "Come with me, Miss Goodchild. I'll introduce you to my wife and sons."

Faith nodded and said, "Yes, sir," then removed the sign from her neck, threw it aside and picked up the cloth bag that contained all of her worldly belongings.

Joe stepped back, looked down at his coon hound and asked, "What do you think of my covered cart, Newt? I know it looks more like a rolling tent, but with the added length and the canvas tarp, we'll be able to stay dry underneath when it rains. There's enough room inside for more supplies, too."

Newt just stared back at him as Joe laughed then turned to look at the donkey.

"Do you think you'll be able to start pulling this tomorrow, Bernie? I modified my harness to fit you, so you don't get a vote anyway. At least you won't starve to death in that wreck of a barn."

Joe had inspected Bernie's joints and legs and found him to be in surprisingly good shape. He seemed to be content now that he'd spent hours grazing, so Joe was confident he'd be able to pull the longer tent-cart without a problem.

While he hadn't entered the charred remains of the house, he had searched the grounds nearby for any signs of the family, but all he found were hoofprints left by the raiders' horses. But it hadn't been a wasted search as he'd found a wooden bucket on the western side of the house. It was one less thing he'd have to buy in Kansas City.

After feeding his four-footed companion who enjoyed meat even more than he did, Joe used one of the salvaged harness straps to tie Bernie to a bayonet stake. He could pull it out if he had a mind to run off, but Joe suspected that he wouldn't attempt an escape. He knew that donkeys, just like their more prestigious equine relatives, were social creatures and any company was better than being alone. Especially after having spent a week or so in the dark corner of the collapsed barn.

With his updated tent cart now loaded with his new tools and other finds, Joe set his slicker and bedroll on the ground then pulled off his old work boots and slid inside. He hadn't worn the two pairs of boots that Captain Chalmers had given him even though one pair did fit perfectly. He didn't doubt that by the time he reached his destination, wherever that might be, all three pairs of boots would have holes in their soles.

Newt lay down beside his human friend and Joe rubbed his neck as he stared at the Milky Way that stretched between the horizons. He estimated that he was less than twenty miles from Kansas City and guessed that he'd find a town before he reached the city. When he reached Kansas City, he'd see if any wagon trains were waiting to begin their long journey on the Oregon Trail. He'd talk to the wagon master and ask if he could tag along. He had no intention of parting with any of his cash to join the wagon train but would offer his services as a hunter and added protection in exchange for nothing more than having company during the long journey.

Faith was under the large blanket between four-year-old John Moore and three-year-old Alfred. Their father was already snoring beside Alfred and his very pregnant wife, Mary, was sleeping on the end with their one-year-old boy, William in between his parents. She was the only one still awake as she focused on the bottom of their covered wagon. Mrs. Moore had explained her duties but little else. So, tomorrow morning, they'd start rolling west across Kansas and away from the only home she'd ever known.

When she'd made her heartbreaking farewells to her brothers and sisters, her mother couldn't even look at her. Now she wondered if her parents would sell Grace when she turned fifteen in four years. She knew that her father wouldn't part with Gabriel or Michael even though they were both older than Grace.

While she knew that she wasn't welcome in her family home, Faith thought about stealing away during the night and hiding in Kansas City until after the wagon train had departed. But she knew it was just a passing thought. Mister Moore had paid for her, and her father had said to do as she was told and suggested that Mister Moore should beat her if she disobeyed. She really had no other paths available to her. So, she'd be the subservient servant girl that she was supposed to be. Maybe she'd meet some young man in one of the other wagons who would want to marry her. She looked to her left and saw John's small, sleeping face and smiled. At least Mister Moore hadn't bought her to marry one of his sons.

CHAPTER 3

Joe didn't take long to start moving the next morning. After sharing a cold breakfast with Newt, he'd put Bernie in his modified cart harness then took out his walking stick and began his journey to Kansas City. The morning sun was casting long shadows that acted almost as a compass, so Joe knew he was walking north-northwest and hoped to pick up a roadway soon. It was a chilly morning with thick dew covering the fast-growing prairie grass which would have slowed him down if he still had to pull the cart. But Bernie wasn't having any problems, and he felt incredibly light as he followed Newt's winding path.

He'd already decided what he'd buy in Kansas City, but a lot depended on when the next wagon train was due to depart. If there wasn't one forming, he'd continue on to St. Joseph.

―――

Faith sat on the stool milking one of the Moore's two milk cows. It was the first task that Mrs. Moore had assigned to her. In addition to the two cows, they had one billy goat and five nanny goats. Four of the nannies had kids, so she'd have to milk the one who already lost her kid, too. Keeping the cows and goats moving and protected as they traveled west was also part of her new duties.

As she squirted the warm milk into the bucket, she heard a loud argument break out in front of the Moore's wagon. She continued to work the cow's udders as she looked to her left where she saw Mister Moore and two other men arguing with a tall man whom she thought was the wagon master just by his manner.

Faith heard the tall man shout, "I know I said we'd be movin' today, but one of my scouts ain't here yet. If he doesn't show up before sundown, we'll leave tomorrow. Okay?"

One of the other men snapped, "If he doesn't show up, we ain't payin' you the full price, Ferguson!"

Bo Ferguson was fuming as he replied, "He'll be here. But if he doesn't show up, I'll cut my fee by twenty dollars."

That seemed to settle the issue, so Bo watched them wander away before he headed back to the lead wagon which served as his rolling office. Chuck Lynch had arrived ten days ago, and he wondered where the hell Mort Jones was. He had cut it close before and wasn't a friendly sort either. If he wasn't such a good shot, Bo wouldn't have hired him again. But each day they wasted cost him money, and no matter how good he was with his rifle, this was the last straw.

He was still seething when he reached his wagon and found Chuck cleaning his Colt.

When his scout looked up at him, Bo said, "They ain't happy, Chuck. Do you know where Mort is?"

"Nope. But I reckon he'll drag his butt in shortly. Personally, I was hopin' you'd hire somebody else this time. He's a bit lazy and gets mad pretty fast, too."

"Yeah, I know. I thought about it, but this train was set up too fast for me to go lookin'. But he'd better get here soon. If he doesn't, we'll have to leave in the mornin', and it'll cost me twenty bucks. Then I've got to start scoutin' myself and that's not a good idea."

Chuck nodded then resumed cleaning his pistol. Even though things had been a bit rushed with this group, he still thought Bo should have spent a couple of days looking for another scout. He suspected it had more to do with the higher pay a better scout would expect. Mort didn't know that Bo paid him a hundred dollars more and wasn't about to tell him.

Joe was still moving at a good pace when he found a road just before midmorning. He hadn't seen the town at the other southern end, but it didn't matter. He had been surprised by Bernie's stamina after having been trapped for all that time. He began to wonder if he'd overestimated the age of the tracks left by the raiders. Whatever the reason, Joe was pleased that the young jack seemed to be doing so well, even with the added load of the tools and the tent extension. He'd added a few more pounds of split boards for firewood as well.

He stopped for a break around noon when they had to cross a stream. After temporarily satisfying Newt's constant hunger, he let Bernie graze while he munched on some really dry salted beef. It was already fairly warm, so before he resumed their walk, Joe swapped his heavy coat for his old, lighter jacket and decided to finally wear the Yankee cavalry officer's hat and took off his knitted wool cap.

After he'd donned his jacket and unworn hat, he picked up his walking stick and tapped Bernie's flank to let him know it was time to return to work. They crossed the narrow stream then continued north on the improving roadway. He still hadn't seen any traffic and wondered if it was Sunday. He'd lost track of the days a month ago because they didn't matter. He'd ask someone when he reached Kansas City which he expected to see by mid-afternoon.

It was just forty minutes later that Joe saw his first fellow traveler when he approached an intersection and spotted a rider coming from the east. He was moving fast, and Joe wanted to avoid a collision, so he stopped before the crossing roadway.

Mort Jones saw the tall kid leading his donkey cart and would have stopped to see if he had anything valuable but was more concerned that Bo might have already started moving the wagons. So, he barely slowed before he ripped his horse around the turn and raced toward Kansas City.

UNWANTED

Joe had been about to greet the first human being he'd seen in days before the rider rocketed past and then headed away leaving a large dust cloud. Luckily, Newt had already scampered from the roadway, or he might have been run down.

Joe looked at his donkey and asked, "I wonder why he was in such a rush? We'll give him a couple of minutes to get ahead and hope that a posse doesn't push us off the road."

The rider was just a dot when Joe tapped Bernie with his walking stick and crossed the intersection. He looked east and didn't see a posse or anything else on the road, so the reason for the rider's haste remained a mystery.

———

Bo Ferguson had spent most of the day either apologizing or arguing with the men who had their fully loaded wagons still standing in line. He had Chuck Lynch searching in town for Mort and began to suspect that his second scout was probably recovering from a bender.

He was passing the herds of stock animals when he spotted a rider coming from the south and recognized Mort's brown mare. His jaws tightened as he stalked in that direction to have a few words with his unreliable scout.

Mort had been relieved when he first saw the line of unmoving wagons but wasn't pleased when he noticed his boss striding angrily towards him. He had his well-rehearsed excuse ready and admitted that it wasn't a great alibi, but he knew that Bo had little choice but to accept it.

Bo Ferguson stopped, crossed his arms and waited until Mort pulled up and dismounted before growling, "Where the hell have you been, Mort? I told you two weeks ago that we'd be rolling today. I've got a bunch of pissed off settlers back there and I've got half a mind to let 'em decide what to do with you."

Mort took off his hat and apologetically replied, "I'm sorry, boss. I was headin' back yesterday when Belle threw a shoe. I had to go back to Independence to put on a new set."

Bo knew Mort was lying and could easily have proven it by checking his horse's shoes, but he needed his services for this run and let it go. He wouldn't use him on the next trip even if there was one. He figured that they'd start building that long-delayed transcontinental railroad as soon as the war ended, and the days of wagon trains would be over. He'd have to find a new job, maybe with the railroad.

He still glared at Mort as he said, "Go see Chuck and he'll tell you what you need to do. I'll give the good news to the families that we'll be leavin' tomorrow."

Mort nodded, then pulled his hat on and mounted his mare. He had been dangerously close to snickering and knew that it might have pushed Bo a bit too far. He set his horse toward the front wagon to find Chuck. He knew that there should be little work for him until the train began moving, but he wanted to find out about the families that filled those wagons, especially any unattached daughters or sisters.

Bo watched his scout ride away and shook his head before he headed back to the wagons. He could already see some of the men gathering and hoped they would just be pleased to be getting underway.

———

Joe had spotted the first of Kansas City's buildings twenty minutes after the rider had disappeared then just a short time later, he saw the line of wagons.

He grinned and said, "It looks like we won't be going to St. Joseph, Bernie."

He picked up their pace slightly before calling to Newt. Joe would rather have his hound close when they neared the wagon train. He could already saw the large mass of cattle, goats, pigs and sheep and Joe wasn't sure how Newt would react. If he wanted to convince the wagon master to let him tag along, the last thing he wanted was to have Newt chase down a chicken for his dinner.

Faith was minding the boys outside the back of the wagon and had seen the wagon master talking to the rider. She had seen Mister Ferguson's angry face and guessed that the newcomer was the missing scout who had delayed their departure.

After the rider had ridden to the front of the line, she picked up a distant shape coming from the same direction as the scout. At first, she thought it was a late-arriving covered wagon, but as it drew closer, she realized it was much too small.

She was squinting when four-year-old John pointed and asked, "What's that?"

"I don't know. It looks like a rolling tent."

"Can we stay to see it?"

Faith had William on her right hip and three-year-old Alfred was clinging to her left knee as she replied, "Alright, but stay close. Okay?"

"Alright."

She continued to stare at the strange-looking vehicle being led by a very tall man then noticed the dog trotting alongside and glanced down at John to make sure he didn't get excited and wander off. Mister Moore had warned her of severe punishment if any harm came to his sons while in her care, and she wasn't about to learn what form it would take before they even left Kansas City.

Joe had no idea how to find the wagon master but was pleased to see the large supply store just a few hundred yards behind the stock animals. He'd buy his supplies while the store was still open then try to find the wagon master.

UNWANTED

He was about to shift to his right to head to the store when he noticed a young woman with three children staring at him. She was fairly tall but needed to put some pounds on her thin frame. He knew he probably looked even thinner but didn't know how tall he was or how much he weighed. He knew that he'd grown an inch or so the past year because his britches and shirtsleeves were a bit short. He hoped that he had put on some weight too, but knew he probably still resembled a scarecrow.

After he'd gotten a bit closer, Joe noticed something odd about the young woman. She not only seemed almost girlish; she had blonde hair and blue eyes, yet the three boys all had dark hair and eyes.

As he wondered about the small mystery, without realizing it, he had continued walking straight rather than shifting his direction toward the store.

Faith was smiling at the odd sight and missed John's sudden escape. When she saw him trotting toward the floppy-eared dog, she felt helpless as she was encumbered by Albert and William.

She shouted, "John! Get back here!"

Little John ignored her as he raced to pet the dog.

Joe saw the tyke break away from the young woman he assumed was his nanny then tossed his walking stick away before he hurried away from Bernie to catch him before he reached Newt. This had the potential for being a bigger disaster than a dead chicken.

Newt's tail was already wagging as the small human raced towards him, but before John could even touch his cold nose, Joe flashed past his hound and scooped the boy from the ground.

John pointed at Newt and shouted, "I just want to pet him!"

As Joe carried him back to his nanny, he grinned and replied, "I'll let you do that after you have permission. Okay?"

John kept his eyes on Newt who was now trotting beside Joe as they approached Faith and her two small charges who were staring at the dog.

Joe still held John after he stopped and said, "I'm sorry, miss. My dog wouldn't hurt the boy, but I was worried he might get knocked over. If I put him down, he'll probably want to pet Newt. Little boys just like dogs, except maybe the little feller who's hiding behind your dress."

Faith was staring up at Joe as she hesitatingly said, "Um, thank you. They aren't my children. I'm just their nanny."

Joe smiled as he replied, "I kinda figured that out, miss. Do you mind if I put him down now?"

She looked down at Newt who was busy sniffing her feet and said, "If you're sure he'll be safe."

UNWANTED

"He'll be okay."

Joe set John onto the ground and as soon as his small feet contacted the earth, he began petting Newt's head then looked up at Faith and began giggling.

Newt was overwhelmed with the onslaught of so many new and different scents that he didn't even notice he was being rubbed, but Joe was now worried that his hound might bolt to the herds and flocks of critters who created much of those odors.

He sharply said, "Newt! Sit!" and the coon hound's butt dropped to the ground as John continued to giggle and rub the dog's head.

Faith was still staring at Joe when she quickly asked, "Do you live in Kansas City?"

He shook his head as he replied, "No, ma'am. I need to head to the store to buy some supplies."

She was disappointed but asked, "Where do you live?"

"Wherever I want to live. I was going to follow the wagon train but need to speak to the wagon master first. Do you know where I can find him?"

"You're going to join the wagon train? With that odd cart?"

"Not exactly, ma'am. I just want to tell him that I'll be following, so he doesn't try to shoot me."

Faith's disappointment vanished as she turned and pointed to Bo Ferguson who was still talking to a small group of men a few yards away.

"That's him. He's the tall man, but he's still a shorter than you. His name is Ferguson, and he uses the first wagon."

Joe marked the man before he said, "Thank you, miss. He seems busy right now, so I'll get my supplies and then go talk to him."

Faith nodded as Joe tipped his blue hat then said, "Come along, Newt."

He turned and headed back to the cart with Newt trotting next to him. He snatched his walking stick from the ground before he reached Bernie and tapped him on his left haunch.

After Bernie started walking, Joe turned him to the right to head to the large store and waved to Faith as he passed. She couldn't return his wave as she had to use her free hand to restrain John, so she just smiled and nodded.

Some of the men talking to Bo Ferguson noticed Joe's odd tent-cart and began pointing and laughing. The wagon master turned around, saw what appeared to be a miniature covered wagon and grinned.

Ben Smith snickered then loudly said, "I reckon a couple of our wagons done had themselves a baby while we weren't lookin'!"

UNWANTED

Joe heard the joke and their laughter but didn't mind. He knew how silly it must look, but it was practical and now that it was being pulled by Bernie, it was capable of making the long journey.

He pulled up outside of the store and tied off Bernie's reins and told Newt to stay at the open end to protect his valuables. No one could see his rifles or much else beneath the tarps but having Newt there would keep anyone from searching. He had more than enough cash to buy what he needed and to improve his wardrobe.

He entered the store and grinned when he saw a line of hand carts for customers' use. He grabbed the handle of the first in line and pushed it down the first aisle. As he added his selections, he marked the prices and kept a running tally. He noticed that they were higher than he expected and assumed it was because of its location near the Oregon Trail's starting point.

He loaded the essentials first: twenty-pound sacks of rice, corn meal, and dry navy beans, ten pounds of salt, a large jug of molasses, another of lard, a large bag of crackers, four boxes of matches, six bars of soap and four towels. He still had enough cash in his pocket to add two pairs of larger britches, two shirts, four pairs of socks and four pairs of underwear. He finally added a hairbrush so he could keep his hair in some semblance of order.

He was down to just two dollars and forty-five cents when he spotted large jars of sour pickles. The pickles themselves were worth the fifteen cents, but the reusable glass jars would be even more useful. He added four jars to his cart and pushed it to the long counter.

When he started to move his selections to the counter, the proprietor said, "Hold on, son. I can add 'em up where they are. Are you payin' in Yankee dollars?"

"Yes, sir."

"Okay. That'll cost ya $26.75."

Joe handed him the exact change which seemed to surprise the man, but he still smiled and said, "Thank you, son."

"You're welcome, sir," Joe replied before he pushed the cart out the door then to the back of his cart where Newt stood guard.

He glanced back at the wagons and noticed a short man standing before the blonde-headed girl and wagging his finger as he seemed to be lecturing her. He assumed that he was the father of the three boys and suspected that he and Newt were the reason for the scolding. He hoped he didn't get her into too much trouble as he began to unload his purchases and find spaces for them inside his tent-cart that balanced the load.

UNWANTED

Harry Moore hadn't even noticed Faith talking to Joe or his oldest son's race to pet Newt. He'd been focused on what the wagon master had been saying. It was Ben Smith who mentioned it just before Bo Ferguson headed back to his wagon.

By the time Joe had noticed, Harry was finishing his tirade as he said, "If you ever let John run away like that again, I'll make you walk all the way to Oregon in bare feet. Do you understand, Miss Goodchild?"

Faith nodded as she replied, "Yes, sir. It's just that I had my hands full with William and Albert."

"That's no excuse. I paid good money for your services, and I expect you to do as you're told. Don't make me use the switch."

"I'll do better, Mister Moore."

Harry grunted, then turned and walked back to the wagon to check on his wife. She still had another four weeks before the baby was due, and both knew that they'd been fortunate that their boys were all still with them and Mary had survived giving them life.

While they hoped that she'd have no problems having their next child while on the Trail, it had been Mary's idea to buy Faith as a contingency. But what even her husband didn't understand was that even if she lived through the childbirth,

Mary had no desire to conceive again. She'd let the skinny girl take her place in satisfying her husband's urges.

After he'd gone, Faith looked down at John and said, "Don't get me into any more trouble, John. Okay?"

"I'm sorry, miss. But the dog didn't bite me."

"I know, but he could have. What do you think your father would have done to me if the dog had bitten your hand?"

"I wouldn't tell him, miss."

Faith smiled down at John as she said, "You're a good boy, John. Just listen to me."

John nodded as Faith said, "Let's go back to the wagon. William is already napping on my hip."

"Okay."

Faith took one last look at the tall, skinny boy who was loading his cart and wondered who he was. As she walked back to the wagon with the Moore boys, she hoped that Mister Ferguson would let him follow the wagons. The Moore wagon was at the end of the line, and she'd be able to talk to him when she herded the cows and goats.

Joe pushed the empty flatbed cart back into the store then returned to Bernie and led him to a position a hundred yards or so south of the last wagon before he stopped. After telling

UNWANTED

Newt to stay, he began walking parallel to the line of wagons to talk to Mister Ferguson.

When he reached the first wagon, he found him talking to two men and recognized one as the rider who'd shot past him at the intersection.

He approached the wagon master and after he stopped a few feet away, Chuck Lynch grinned and said, "You got a visitor, boss."

Bo turned around and said, "You're the one with that odd-lookin' cart; ain't ya?"

"Yes, sir."

"You don't figure on joinin' this wagon train with that contraption; do you?"

"Not exactly, Mister Ferguson. But I do want to let you know that I'll be trailing behind. I expect nothing from anyone."

Bo studied Joe for a few seconds before asking, "Are you tryin' to avoid fightin' in the war?"

"No, sir. I just turned sixteen in February."

Mort snickered then said, "That don't mean nothin' even if you're tellin' the truth."

Bo snapped, "Shut up, Mort."

Then he turned to Joe and said, "There are a lot of fellers joinin' trains just to get outta fightin', but this ain't one of 'em. I can't stop ya from followin', but it's gonna be a long, hard trail. If you get hurt, we ain't gonna stop."

"I know, sir."

"You got a rifle?"

"Yes, sir."

Bo shrugged then said, "I hope you know how to use it. The Yankees stripped the western forts to fight the rebs and the Injuns are mighty pleased about it."

"I heard about that, Mister Ferguson. But when I hunt, if I shoot any big game like buffalo, I'll just take what I need, and the folks are welcome to the rest."

Mort snorted before Joe tipped his hat then turned and walked away. He marked Bo Ferguson as a good man but didn't trust the man he called Mort. He wasn't sure about the other scout. Joe hadn't volunteered any information about his number of rifles or the pistol he wore beneath his jacket as there was no reason for anyone to know about them.

When he reached his cart, Newt stood and began wagging his tail but didn't step away from his assigned position.

UNWANTED

Joe smiled and scratched behind his ears as he said, "Good job, Newt. I'll give you with a tasty piece of beef jerky as a reward."

The hound seemed to be expecting the treat and quickly turned to face the back of the cart before Joe finished talking. He watched intently as his human friend pulled a long slice of the dry, salty meat from one of his hidden pouches then handed it to him.

Joe stepped to the other side of the cart and studied the line of wagons. He could see a lot of the folks preparing their wagons for tomorrow's journey and some were among the large mixed herd of animals dropping hay for their critters or just making sure that they were still there. He didn't see the blonde girl but suspected that she was probably helping the boys' parents prepare the wagon.

He didn't want to set up his own camp so close to the store or the wagon train, so he pulled his walking stick from his cart then took Bernie's harness and led him southwest. When he visited Mister Ferguson, he had seen a small pond a few hundred yards in that direction.

When he reached the pond, he was a good four hundred yards away from the closest wagon. He let Bernie satisfy his thirst before having him tow the cart to a clump of river birch where he finally removed the donkey's makeshift harness. He attached a tie rope to Bernie's halter because he thought that his jack might decide to pay a visit to one of the wagon train's mares.

Bernie didn't seem to be frustrated as he grazed, and Joe checked his singed coat. He thought the darkened patch was already smaller and would probably be completely gone in a few more days.

He walked to the cart, removed the pickaxe and dug a hole on the side away from the wagon train to use as his private privy. After making quick use of the hole, he buried it and returned the pickaxe to the cart.

The sun had already set when he built a fire and cooked a basic supper of smoked venison and beans that he'd already cooked before leaving his shelter. As he ate, he could hear what sounded almost like a celebration being held on the other side of the wagons. He wondered how happy they'd be after a week on the trail. He had no illusions of the difficulties that lay ahead but was now more convinced that his destiny was somewhere out west.

―――

Faith sat in front of the fire listening to all the joyful talk about finding a better life in Oregon and thought about her own future. Her life had been so routine that she still found it difficult to believe that she was even here.

Her father had dominated her life for as long as she could recall and had expected that when she came of age, her parents would choose her husband and he would take charge of her life. She would just keep house and have their children. In all of her fifteen years, she hadn't spent a moment planning her own path because it wasn't necessary.

Now, after being sold for a pittance, she was being controlled by a man she barely knew. But he wasn't her father or her would-be husband. He was just a man who'd parted with twenty-five dollars to have her work for him. She didn't know what Mister Moore expected of her for his investment, but Faith didn't care.

As she stared at the flickering flames, Faith decided that for the first time in her life, she would be the one to decide her fate. She wouldn't let Mister Moore, or any other man or woman order her around like a servant.

She glanced at Harry and Mary Moore as they talked quietly just a few feet away. She knew that Mister Moore was worried about his wife, and she would help Mrs. Moore when it was time for the baby to arrive. But after that, she would do what she wanted to do. Until then, she hoped that she'd be able to talk to the tall, handsome boy with the odd-looking cart.

CHAPTER 4

Joe had been startled to hear a loud bell ring out in the predawn but was already moving west along the well-traveled ruts of the Oregon Trail before most of the families had even harnessed their oxen to their wagons. He may have told Mister Ferguson that he'd be trailing but knew that he'd only be able to find game if he was far out front. He didn't know how the wagon train functioned but suspected that the two men talking to the wagon master would be out front as well and either hunting or scouting for danger.

All he knew about the Oregon Trail other than its points of origin and its vague destination somewhere in Oregon was that after it crossed Kansas Territory and entered Nebraska Territory, it followed the North Platte River for a few hundred miles. Other than that, the rest of the path was a complete mystery to him, as were the Indians. But he hadn't been surprised when Mister Ferguson said that the tribes might be more aggressive after the western forts were either closed or reduced to a skeleton force. But despite Mister Ferguson's warning, leaving with only two scouts made Joe believe that even the more hostile tribes would be more likely to bargain than fight.

Even with that belief and with Kansas City still visible behind him, Joe had Bernie hold up. He stepped to the back of his cart and slipped one of his loaded Mississippi rifles from its bedroll scabbard, then rested it on his right shoulder before he encouraged Bernie to start moving again.

As he led his cart a few yards south of the deep ruts left by earlier wagon trains, he glanced back to see if the long line of wagons had started moving. He saw activity but they hadn't begun rolling.

He was almost two miles away when he noticed a lone rider heading towards him and recognized the horse belonging to the rude scout. He didn't focus on the man as he kept Bernie moving northwest looking for game of any sort. He didn't expect to find any large critters for a while but hoped to spot a large jackrabbit or a groundhog.

As he scanned the landscape, he kept his ears attuned to the sound of the approaching rider. Joe didn't expect any trouble but suspected that the man might be offended just by his presence out front of the unmoving wagon train.

Mort had been watching Joe since he passed their lead wagon almost an hour earlier and wondered what he had in that loaded cart of his. He'd seen him buy his supplies and figured he had to have more money somewhere. He didn't see the rifle the kid said he had and wondered if he was lying just to stick around, but he still hadn't spotted Newt.

He had saddled his horse then told Bo Ferguson that he'd go on ahead to check the condition of the Trail. It was one of his jobs, so Bo just nodded before he mounted and rode off.

Mort had just ridden away from the wagon when he saw the kid pull up then take his missing rifle from his cart. He slowed his gelding slightly as he watched Joe rest it on his shoulder before he began moving again. Mort kept his same pace which still cut the gap as he focused on the kid's rifle. It didn't take long for him to identify it as a muzzle-loader. Mort figured the kid was out hunting but believed the rifle was his only shooting weapon.

It was just a few seconds later when he noticed a dog about fifty yards in front of the cart and that changed a few things. He suspected that the dog was protective of the boy, and it would make it almost impossible to sneak up on him.

So, as he drew close, Mort decided he could afford to be patient. A lot of accidents happened on the Oregon Trail.

Joe heard him drawing closer, so he stopped and turned, but let Bernie continue knowing he'd pull up soon on his own. He left his rifle on his shoulder and still held his walking stick in his left hand as he watched the rider approach.

When he pulled up, Mort looked down and asked, "What are you doin' out front, boy? You told Ferguson you'd be trailin'."

"I wanted to hunt."

UNWANTED

"That's my job, kid. I ain't gonna be happy if you're out here scarin' the game and I reckon Ferguson will send you packin' soon enough."

Joe didn't see any reason to have an unnecessary confrontation, especially this early in the journey, so he just nodded and said, "Sorry."

Mort had expected to rile the kid but sat in his saddle and watched as Joe called Newt back then walked to the front of his cart and turned the donkey to his left.

Joe led Bernie south away from the ruts and was soon joined by Newt who began scouting ahead of the rolling cart.

Mort snickered then started walking his horse alongside the ruts believing that the kid was afraid of him. He looked at the cart as it rolled away and grinned. He'd ride ahead for a while because he'd told Ferguson he would.

Joe still planned on doing some hunting. He wanted some fresh meat and figured if he made a wide loop to return to the back of the wagon train, he should find an unsuspecting jackrabbit or maybe a small deer.

―――

Faith was hurrying back to the wagon with her heavy bucket of warm milk when she stumbled. She caught herself before falling but some of the milk splashed onto the ground. Luckily,

Mister Moore was sitting on driver's seat and Mrs. Moore was in the wagon dressing the boys.

She reached the open tailgate, set the bucket on the heavy boards then clambered into the wagon.

Mrs. Moore looked at her but didn't say anything as Faith took out five tin cups, then used one to fill the other four and set them on top of their small table. She waited until Mrs. Moore gave one to John then began helping William to drink his milk as Faith picked up Alfred and put the cup to his small lips.

When the boys were finished, Mrs. Moore drank her milk then said, "You may have the rest, Faith. We'll be rolling soon, and my husband wants you to herd the cows and goats."

Faith nodded then quietly replied, "Yes, ma'am," before she used the fifth cup to drink the last of the warm milk.

The wagon lurched forward as she was drinking and almost spilled her breakfast but managed to avoid the disaster. She only had one other dress and wasn't keen on doing the laundry so soon. She'd already been told that doing the wash was one of her tasks but at least there were only five Moores. She'd been doing the family laundry since she was twelve and there were eight members of the Goodchild family before her father reduced it to seven. Now it was probably Grace's job.

After the wagon was rolling, she took the tin cups and placed them into the bucket before sliding off the tailgate. She had to walk behind the moving herds to get to the stream where she could wash the bucket and cups. When she was close, she saw another girl about her age leaving the creek carrying a small crate filled with clean dinnerware. Faith hadn't seen her before, but she hadn't met any of the other families either.

The dark-haired girl approached Faith, glanced at the rolling wagons then said, "You'd better hurry."

"I will. I'm Faith Goodchild."

"My name is Marigold Smith, but everyone calls me Mary. I've got to go."

Faith nodded as Marigold trotted after the slowly moving wagon train then quickly jogged to the creek where she hurriedly washed the bucket and cups.

She finished in less than a minute then turned and headed back to the wagon. She'd watched Marigold carry her crate to the third wagon in front of the Moore's wagon and wondered about her status. She was probably a little older and definitely more physically mature, so Faith doubted if she was a servant. She was well-nourished, so Faith assumed she was the oldest daughter of the Smith family.

She didn't have to run to catch up to the Moores' wagon but did have to avoid the mass of moving animals. There were two young boys and three older women walking among the critters to control their own animals. She would soon join them after leaving the bucket and cups with Mrs. Moore.

Faith glanced at their two cows and six adult goats as she passed but didn't see the four kids among the taller animals. She wasn't concerned when she reached the back of the wagon and set the bucket on the tailgate.

Mrs. Moore stepped to the back, then wordlessly slipped the bucket into the wagon before Faith turned around to mind the cows and goats. Their cows were easily identified by their coloring, but each of the goats wore a yellow necktie of sorts made from one of Mrs. Moore's discarded dresses.

Faith reached the cows then turned and matched their pace as they walked behind the wagons but off to the right side so they wouldn't break an ankle in the deep ruts. She glanced at the goats before she began walking alongside the cows while watching the wagon train heading into the frontier.

She was thinking about what lay ahead and all she could imagine was more drudgery interspersed with times of peril. After her years of sedentary life with her family, she was actually hoping for some excitement, regardless of the danger.

Faith continued to walk almost in a daze as she ruminated, but after a few minutes, she realized that she hadn't checked on the kids. So, she turned then walked behind the trailing cow and found the five nanny goats dutifully following their lord and master, the bigger billy goat.

UNWANTED

She started to smile when she realized that there were only three kids trotting beside their mothers. She didn't panic but began walking among the other goats, sheep and pigs looking for a kid wearing a yellow tie. She found other kids, but none wore a tie and she suspected that one of the boys had removed the tie and added it to his animals. But even as she continued her search, she didn't think it was likely. The kid would return to his mother sooner or later, even though he'd been weaned.

Faith returned to the cows and scanned the open grounds to the south but didn't see the kid. It didn't help that there was nothing but tall grass just fifty yards from the ruts. The kid would be impossible to find if he'd run off into the tall grass to have himself a private feast. She continued to walk beside the cows as she focused on the tall grassland, hoping to spot the missing kid. She didn't want to have to tell Mister Moore that she'd already lost one of their precious goats. He probably treasured the kid more than he or Mrs. Moore valued her. She knew her worth…twenty-five dollars.

Joe had Bernie moving parallel to the ruts again. They were about a thousand yards to his left as he searched for something to shoot. He'd returned his walking stick to the cart, so he'd be able to fire quickly. He'd seen all sorts of small, ground-dwelling critters, but none of them would be more than a snack for Newt. He was surprised that the hound hadn't already snatched one, but figured Newt was already expecting his human friend to provide a bigger and tastier meal.

As he searched for a target, he'd take an occasional glance back at Mort who was already a speck on the horizon. He doubted if Mister Ferguson really cared whether he and his cart were out front or behind. He'd be doing the scout's job without being paid. Joe's poor opinion of Mort made him suspect that the scout was probably checking out his cart's contents to see if anything was worth stealing. He hadn't been able to see much if he did, but Joe knew he'd have to depend on Newt to warn him if the scout paid him a visit during the night.

Joe was almost to the front of the wagon train when he spotted something pushing aside the grass to his left. He was surprised that Newt hadn't alerted but the hound was already far to his right as he pulled Bernie to stop.

He cocked his Mississippi's hammer and raised it into firing position as he waited to see the animal that was still pushing the stalks of new grass aside. He was about fifty yards away and Joe was surprised that he hadn't bolted yet. He was upwind of the animal, and that critter should have picked up his scent long ago.

When the grass stopped moving, Joe still couldn't spot him, so he began slowly stepping closer with his sights on the last place he'd seen the grass shake.

UNWANTED

He began to think that the animal had managed to steal away without notice, which would have been almost impossible when he decided it must be a large possum who had decided to fake his death after smelling the human.

Joe was smiling as he stepped closer then suddenly stopped when he saw the back of what looked like a small deer. He was about to fire but held his trigger finger in place before he loudly said, "I'll shoot you if you don't run!"

He expected the fawn to race away, but it didn't. When it raised his head, Joe started to laugh when he saw a yellow strip of cloth wrapped around its neck.

He released his hammer then as he began walking to the kid, he said, "Your mama must have dressed you for school today, son."

The small goat bleated before Joe arrived and took hold of his yellow harness then called out to Newt.

As the hound bounded through the grass, Joe began awkwardly walking back to his cart. He was bent at the waist as he pulled the kid while still trying to balance his rifle on his shoulder.

He soon reached his cart and slid the Mississippi back into its bedroll scabbard before picking up the kid. He wasn't about to let the small goat loose among his sacks of corn meal, rice and beans.

He looked down at Newt and said, "Let's get this escapee back to the wagon train. I hope his owner doesn't accuse me of trying to steal him."

Newt didn't reply before he disappeared into the tall grass with only the white tip of his tail visible as he wound his way toward the wagon train.

Joe didn't bother retrieving his walking stick as his arms were full of squirming goat. Bernie simply pulled the cart behind him as Joe headed back to the wagon train.

———

Faith had already stopped looking south as it was nothing but frustratingly futile. She had searched the herds again and didn't find the missing kid before resuming her position beside the cows.

To stop worrying about the consequences for losing the kid, she let her mind drift to the tall boy she'd met yesterday. She had been disappointed when she hadn't seen him earlier and wondered if he'd already decided to just stay in Kansas City rather than follow the Oregon Trail. It was an almost depressing thought because he had been the only bright spot in her life since her father had announced his intentions. He could use all sorts of other, less despicable terms, but she knew what he'd done. He'd sold her as if she was nothing but one of the animals she was guarding. Maybe she should follow the kid's example and escape.

She smiled at the idea before she glanced to the south again then felt her heart skip a beat when she saw the tall boy and his cart. She didn't know why he was coming from that direction but was enormously pleased knowing that he hadn't stayed in Kansas City. Now she might be able to talk to him again.

Faith was still looking at him as he drew closer and soon noticed that he was carrying something in his arms. It took her a few more seconds before she realized that there was a patch of yellow contrasting with his dark jacket and whatever he was carrying was squirming. She couldn't believe that he had the missing kid but still left the cows and began walking towards him. Not for a moment did she think that he might have stolen the kid, but if he did, she hoped it was because he wanted to talk to her.

Joe saw the blonde-headed girl leave the herd of critters and was curious if it was because the kid belonged to her family or maybe she just wanted to talk to him. If it was because he was returning the young goat, he would at least be able to chat with her for a few minutes. He hadn't spoken to a girl his age since leaving the Quimby farm. He had met many older women and some small girls, but fate always seemed to deprive him of the company of teenaged girls.

Faith had finally recognized the kid the tall boy held in his arms and felt a surge of relief. Before she was close enough to talk to him, his dog arrived with his tail wagging, so she stopped and began rubbing his head.

As she scratched the hound behind his ears, she kept her eyes on the tall boy realized that she knew the dog's name, but not his owner's.

She smiled at the grateful pooch as she said, "Hello, Newt. It looks like your friend found my missing goat. I think it's time I introduced myself."

Before Joe arrived with the kid, Faith glanced at the wagon train to estimate how much time she could spare to chat then looked back at Joe. He was just a hundred feet away with his donkey-drawn cart following a few feet behind him.

Joe smiled as he approached the girl and when he was close, he asked, "I found this kid enjoying the grass about a half a mile away. Is he yours?"

Faith smiled as she replied, "I'm just supposed to keep them together, but he must have run off before the wagons started rolling."

Joe took a quick look at the wagons before setting the goat on the ground and saying, "We can let him walk back to his family."

As they began walking back to the herds, Faith said, "Thank you for finding him. I would have been in trouble if I'd lost him."

"That's kinda silly, miss. Why should you get in trouble if he ran off before the wagons started moving?"

UNWANTED

"Maybe Mister Moore would have accepted it as just an accident, but I don't think so."

Joe nodded then said, "My name is Joe. Joe Beck."

Faith quickly replied, "My name is Faith. Faith Goodchild."

Joe couldn't help but smile after hearing her name and Faith noticed before she asked, "Do you think my name is funny?"

Joe shook his head as he said, "No, ma'am. It's just that your last name has two more letters than all of my names put together."

"Isn't your name Joseph?"

"No, ma'am. It's just Joe and I don't have a middle name either."

Faith smiled as she said, "I guess you'll laugh if I told you my full name."

"If I do, you can't get mad at me. Okay?"

"I promise I won't because most people do laugh when I tell them. It's Faith Hope Charity Virtue Goodchild."

Joe didn't laugh but his eyebrows rose as he asked, "Was your father a preacher?"

"No, but he and my mother are very religious, and I was their firstborn, so they heaped those names on me hoping I would grow up to be virtuous."

Joe smiled and asked, "Did it work?"

Faith was going to answer with a quick yes, but replied, "I don't know."

Before Joe could ask another question, the kid began trotting south again, so Joe took one long stride to the small goat then nudged him in the opposite direction with his foot.

After the kid grudgingly trotted northwest toward the wagon train, Joe said, "I'll be right back," then turned and walked to the back of his cart.

He pulled out his walking stick then rummaged through his stack of debarked branches and found one that suited his purpose and slid it free of the pile.

He returned to Faith and handed her the new stick as he said, "Use this as a walking stick and to keep those goats from wandering. In a few weeks, you might need to use it as firewood, too."

"Thank you. Joe, you're the tallest man I've ever seen but you aren't that old; are you?"

Joe grinned as he replied, "My whole family was tall, but I only turned sixteen in February."

UNWANTED

"I'll turn sixteen in October. How tall are you?"

"I'm not sure. I think I'm a couple of inches over six feet, but I don't think I've finished growing yet. I need to put on a few pounds because I'm pretty skinny and spending all day walking isn't going to help."

"I don't think you're skinny. I'm not exactly fat either."

Joe smiled but before he could reply, he noticed the kid wandering the wrong way again, so he reached over with his walking stick and rapped the small goat on his left side to get him turned back toward wagons.

Then he said, "This one is going to give you trouble. He's a boy, and boys always seem to be troublemakers."

"Are you a troublemaker?"

Joe smiled as he replied, "Definitely."

As much as she wanted to continue the conversation, Faith knew she had to return soon, so she said, "I suppose I should be getting back."

"Okay. But if you ever need anything, I'll be setting up my camp on the left side of the wagons about a hundred yards back."

"Thank you, Joe. And thank you for the walking stick, too. It'll be handy to control the goats."

"You take care, Faith Hope Charity Virtue Goodchild."

Faith laughed then said, "You too, Joe Beck."

She then used her new walking stick to turn the adventurous kid back to his family as she focused on the Moore wagon wondering if Mister or Mrs. Moore had seen her talking to Joe. If they had, she was curious what their reaction would be. She almost wished they would be so angry that they'd toss her out but knew it wasn't very likely. Mrs. Moore was going to need more help with the three boys over the next few weeks and even more when she had her baby. If she had known of Mary's real plans, she would never have returned to the wagon.

Joe watched Faith herd the kid back to the other yellow-tied goats and hoped that he hadn't gotten her into trouble with the family. He assumed that she had been sent to live with her aunt and uncle after being orphaned, much like his situation. Joe assumed that Mrs. Moore was her mother's sister, just as his Aunt Mary had been Mrs. Quimby. He'd ask her about it the next time they spoke. Maybe she'd visit him after he set up camp.

He looked down to Newt who hadn't followed Faith or the kid and asked, "What do you think, Newt? Do you reckon she might want to visit later?"

Newt looked up at him, probably expecting a treat but was disappointed when Joe just said, "Let's see if we can't find supper."

Joe tugged Bernie's homemade harness and turned him south again then followed Newt as he returned to the deep grass.

———

Faith returned the kid to his mother and was relieved that neither adult Moore had seen her talking to Joe. It hadn't been that long, and Mister Moore was busy driving the wagon while Mrs. Moore took care of her boys.

She watched Joe heading southeast and thought about visiting him later. If Mister Moore tried to prohibit her from leaving as her father definitely would, she'd take her few possessions from the wagon and walk away. What would happen after that was in God's hands.

———

Joe had returned his walking stick to his cart and had his rifle in his hands as he stealthily approached a large collection of tall bushes. He was just a hundred and fifty yards from the family of white-tailed deer who were grazing on the fresh foliage. He could have fired much earlier, but his preferred target was an old doe who was mostly behind the bushes. The younger does had youngsters with them, and the large twelve-point buck was too handsome to shoot.

Newt hadn't moved since he first picked up their scent and was already a hundred yards behind him. Joe was shifting slowly to his left to get a good angle on the doe but if they saw him, he'd fire at the closest deer.

Each step revealed more of the doe until he saw her head as she reached her mouth to a higher branch. He settled his sights on the doe's neck and squeezed his trigger.

The Mississippi boomed and the doe immediately collapsed as the other deer bolted away. Joe turned and walked back to the cart as Newt trotted through the grass to guard the fallen deer from scavengers.

After returning his rifle to the cart, Joe led Bernie to the bushes then took a length of rope from the cart and walked to the deer. He looped the rope around its neck and dragged it to a nearby cottonwood.

It took him almost two hours to salvage most of the fresh venison then after rewarding Newt with a large chunk of fresh meat, he wrapped it in the fresh deerskin and carried it to the back of his cart. He salted each cut to keep it fresh before loading the heavy load onto his cart.

Joe set Bernie in the direction of the wagon train that was almost to the horizon by the time he started back. He'd still lose ground as he worked his way at an angle but knew they'd soon be stopping for their noon break. Then he'd cut the gap and continue to gain on them once he reached the ruts.

UNWANTED

As he strode through the tall grass with his walking stick, he was already calculating how much of the venison he'd give away. He could smoke some of it in his crude smoker but figured he could give half of the almost fifty pounds away and knew who would be the first to be offered the meat. Faith may not have been as skinny as he was, but she was certainly thinner than she should be. Maybe the venison would start to put meat on her bones. He'd given up all hope that he'd ever see the plus side of a hundred and fifty pounds himself regardless of how much he ate.

Joe understood that the growth spurts had been responsible for his lack of girth but hoped that would change when he stopped growing in a couple of years. Without realizing it, he'd already achieved his maximum height and had already begun adding muscle to his frame.

―――

While neither of the Moores had seen Faith talking to Joe, when the wagons pulled up for the noon break, Harry Moore noticed that she was carrying a smooth walking stick and called her over.

Faith stepped closer and asked, "What do you need of me, Mister Moore?"

"Where did you get that walking stick?"

Faith wasn't about to lie, so she replied, "Joe Beck, the young man who has that odd-looking cart gave it to me."

She was surprised by his sharp tone when he asked, "Why did he give it to you?"

She almost returned to her subservient role but after meeting Joe Beck, she decided that she had a new path stretching before her.

Faith stared back at Mister Moore as she replied, "One of the kids escaped and I chased after him. Joe saw the problem and used his walking stick to stop him then gave me one of his spares to help me keep them together."

Harry was close to ordering her not to talk to the boy again, but just looking into her fierce blue eyes warned him that it might drive her away and he couldn't afford to let that happen.

Instead, he just said, "Don't let one of them run away again."

Faith felt as if she'd scored a victory but didn't gloat as she replied, "I won't, sir."

"Help my wife with lunch then you can let John and Alfred walk with you for a while."

Faith just nodded in reply rather than to say what she wanted.

Harry turned and headed back to the front of the wagon while Faith stepped to the tailgate to help Mrs. Moore. As she walked to the back of the wagon, she glanced southwest and spotted Joe leading his odd tent-cart in the distance. Now that Mister Moore knew that she'd talked to him, she didn't think that he'd object if she visited him at his campsite after sunset. If he did, well that was his problem.

———

Joe was following the wagon train now, but off to the left of the sets of ruts left by the iron-trimmed wheels of this train and the others that had followed the Trail for years. Newt was out front sniffing the ground as if he didn't see the wagons about a mile ahead. Joe was chewing on his last piece of smoked duck and thought about opening the cask of crackers but decided to wait. It was only the first day and there were at close to another two hundred more before the wagons reached Oregon. He still had no idea of where he would go or what he would do when he got there, but he knew that he wasn't going to farm again. He didn't mind the work, but he wanted to do something different with his life now that he had the opportunity.

He wasn't ashamed to admit that he yearned for excitement and almost relished the thought of facing danger. When he'd stood up with Captain Chalmers' Henry and started firing at the rebel soldiers who were shooting at him, he'd experienced something he couldn't explain. It was as if a calming blanket had been draped over him and time slowed down. He could see their muzzles exploding in flame and smoke but didn't give a thought to where their Minie balls were going as he fired. After all of the rebels were on the ground, time returned to normal, but he never felt afraid or even confused. He knew what he had to do and just did it.

Joe didn't fall into the immorality trap as had many of those young men who marched into battle. He knew the risk and the likelihood that he might die. But he had never felt so intense as when he'd faced danger then felt the exhilaration of life after the threat was over. It was one of the reasons that he'd decided to head West. It was where he could prove himself.

Joe noticed that the wagons had stopped, so he picked up the pace slightly. Bernie didn't seem to mind. He hoped that they stopped before sunset because he had a lot of work to do. He had to clean his rifle before he began smoking some of the venison. He'd bring some to Faith before they started the wagons rolling in the morning unless she visited him later.

As he drew closer to the wagons, he noticed the other scout riding towards him and wondered what he wanted. He didn't slow and soon the rider passed on his left then turned his horse around and pulled up beside Joe.

Chuck Lynch looked down at him and said, "Mort came back a little while ago and said that you were gonna cause us trouble. Me and my boss know Mort isn't the most truthful feller, so he asked me to come back here and ask you what happened between you two."

Joe replied, "Not much. I was out front because I knew that no game would be found behind the wagons. He told me that it was his job and if Mister Ferguson knew I was out front, he'd make me leave. I didn't want to cause a problem, so I just said I was sorry and headed south."

Chuck snorted then said, "That sounds more like the truth to me. Did you find any game south of here?"

"Yes, sir. I found a small herd of deer and took an old doe."

Chuck grinned as he said, "Maybe the boss oughta hire you and get rid of Mort."

"I don't want to create any disruptions, sir."

"Disruptions? You sure use big words, kid. What's your name?"

"Joe Beck."

"I'm Chuck Lynch, so if you need to talk to my boss, see me."

"Thank you, sir."

Chuck waved then rode away to relay what Joe had told him. He knew that Bo Ferguson wouldn't be surprised to learn that Mort had lied, but also suspected that lying would be the least of the problems Mort would create for them on the journey. He also believed that Joe Beck might be the first victim of whatever troubles Mort would cause. But because the kid wasn't a paying member of the wagon train, it wasn't his or

Ferguson's problem. He hoped that Joe Beck could protect himself.

Joe watched Chuck ride away and marked him in the same class as Mister Ferguson. They may not be friends, but they weren't going to give him trouble. As he continued to close the gap, he looked at Newt as he wound his way northwest and was really happy to have him along. That incredibly sensitive nose of his had already proven its value as an early warning alarm and Joe always kept him close at night anyway.

The sun had set, and Joe had already fried a few venison steaks for his and Newt's supper and as leftovers for tomorrow. He'd had to use some lard as the meat didn't have any fat at all, but he wasn't about to toss the grease. After removing the last of the steaks, he began laying his corn dodgers onto the oily surface.

He had just flipped the first of them with his fork when he saw Newt alert and point back toward the wagons. He didn't growl, so Joe smiled before he turned and saw Faith stepping out of the darkness.

"Hello, Faith."

She smiled and as she sat next to him, she replied, "Hello, Joe. That smells good."

"Would you like some? I made enough for tomorrow anyway."

Faith had already eaten but was still hungry, so she quickly replied, "Yes, please."

Joe flipped the next corn dodger as he said, "I have two plates, but Newt can wait. These will be done soon."

"What are they?"

"These are my special corn dodgers. Those are venison steaks on the plate, so while these are cooking, why don't you toss one a few feet away so Newt can have his supper?"

Faith laughed then took a steak from the stack, flung it into the darkness and watched Newt fly away after his supper.

"Why didn't he just take one while they were stacked on the plate?"

"I taught him that it was ill manners to take food before it was offered. It took me a month or so to get it into his doggie brain."

Joe moved the hot corn dodgers from the greasy skillet and set them on the second plate before sliding one steak from the stack beside them.

"I only have one knife and fork, so I'll cut up the steak and we'll share the fork. Okay?"

"I don't mind."

Before he began cutting the steak, Joe leaned to his left, grabbed the jar of pickles and unscrewed the lid.

"Would you like a pickle, Faith?"

"Are they really sour or sweet?"

"I have no idea, but I really wanted them for the jars. I've never seen anything like them before. The lid just screws on and off. I wish I'd found these before I left Missouri."

"I've never seen them before, either."

Joe slid one of the pickles from the jar and after letting most of the liquid drip back into the jar, he took a bite and said, "They're pretty sour. Do you want a bite?"

"Okay."

Joe held it close to her mouth and watched as she took a fairly large bite. He expected to see her eyes pop wide in reaction to the very sour taste, but they didn't.

Faith smiled and asked, "May I have one? They're very tasty."

Joe grinned as he replied, "Yes, ma'am," then held the first pickle between his teeth before holding the jar out to Faith.

UNWANTED

After she selected her pickle, Joe screwed the cap back on and set it on his left side then set his bitten pickle on the plate near the steak.

As Faith began working her way down her pickle, Joe began cutting the steak into good-sized bites and said, "When you finish the pickle, try one of my corn dodgers."

Faith nodded then tossed the last piece of pickle into her mouth before picking up one of the warm corn dodgers.

Joe had finished cutting the venison when Faith took her first bite of his corn creation and said, "This is really good, Joe. How do you make them?"

Joe rammed his fork into one of the chunks of fried meat as he replied, "Corn meal, salt, lard and water. But what makes them different is that I add some molasses to add a little sweetness."

Faith was about to take another bite when Joe held the piece of venison out to her, and she snapped it from the fork.

Joe laughed then picked up his own corn dodger but ate a bite of steak first. As he chewed, he handed the fork to Faith and used his smaller knife to stab another piece of meat.

Faith swallowed then pointed to a small tipi-like tent and asked, "What's that? It's too small for you, but does Newt sleep in there?"

Joe grinned as he shook his head and replied, "No, ma'am. That's my portable smoker. I dig a firepit, then light the small fire and toss in damp wood chips. It takes a while to smoke even ten pounds of meat, but it works. I reckon I'll run out of wood chips pretty soon, so I'll need to improvise."

She stuck the fork in another piece of venison as she asked, "Is this deer meat?"

"Yes, ma'am. I shot her this afternoon. I have almost half of the meat left and was going to give it to you tomorrow if you didn't visit me after sunset. You can take it with you when you return."

Faith quickly asked, "Why don't you bring it by in the morning before we start rolling? I have to milk one of the cows anyway, and I can introduce you to the Moores."

"Okay. Why do you only milk one of them? You have two; don't you?"

Faith nodded as she chewed her venison then swallowed and replied, "There's no place to store the milk, but Mister Moore said that once we're underway, he'll let the Smiths milk the other one. I met their oldest daughter this morning when I was washing the bucket and cups."

Joe stabbed and made quick work of another piece of steak before he asked, "Is Mrs. Moore your aunt?"

UNWANTED

Faith had a mouthful of corn dodger, so she shook her head while Joe tossed the last of his corn dodger into his mouth.

Faith used the time spent chewing to formulate her answer, so when she swallowed, she simply replied, "No. I'm not related to them at all."

"Really? Are you an orphan?"

"No. Mister Moore, um…hired me to be their nanny."

Joe smiled as he said, "They probably pay you a lot less than you're worth."

"I suppose so."

"The reason I asked was because your name is different. When everyone in my family died over a few days in March of '57, I was sent to live with my Aunt Mary Quimby."

"How did that happen? Was it a fire?"

"No. I think it was bad meat. I got sick, but I was the only one to survive. My aunt's family wasn't happy to see me, and if my mother hadn't made my Aunt Mary promise to take care of me, they probably wouldn't have let me stay for a day. My aunt died a couple of years later, but she told my Uncle William honor the promise she made to my mother. I was told to leave the same day that they buried my uncle."

"Is that when you came to Kansas City?"

"That was a little over a year ago. Since then, I've been living in a shelter that I built near Lone Jack in Missouri."

Faith glanced at the cart-tent and asked, "How did you get the donkey cart and all those things?"

"It would take a while to explain, and I don't want to get you into trouble. We'll have plenty of time to talk before we get to where we're going."

Faith paused before she said, "I don't know where I'm going; do you?"

"Nope. I only know that I'm not going to be a farmer again."

"What will you do instead?"

Joe shrugged then grinned as he answered, "I have no idea."

Faith turned and looked back at the wagons before she said, "I think I'd better go back now. I'll tell Mister Moore that you'll be bringing some fresh venison in the morning. Okay?"

"I'll probably be waiting near the cows."

Faith stood then before she turned away, she looked at Joe and said, "I'll save some buttermilk for you."

Joe rose before saying, "I haven't had any in a while, so I'll be grateful."

UNWANTED

Faith smiled then said, "Goodnight, Joe. And thank you for the steak and corn dodgers."

"Your welcome, Faith. And thank you for visiting. Goodnight."

Faith turned then trotted away from the dying fire and Joe watched her disappear into the darkness.

After she'd gone, he sat down and finished his supper then emptied half a canteen of water before wrapping the two remaining steaks in deerskin and setting them in the steel bowl he'd used to make his corn dodgers. Newt had returned and looked anxiously at the hidden steaks, but Joe disappointed him by covering the bowl with one of the tin plates.

Joe smiled at his hound and said, "I'll share one with you in the morning, Newt," then scratched his head to let him know that they were still friends.

He added more damp wood chips to his smoke tipi, then began cleaning up.

As Faith walked back to the wagon, she wondered why she felt too ashamed to admit that her father had sold her for twenty-five dollars. She soon realized the reason. She may be thin, but she was still a young woman. Telling Joe that she had been sold would make it sound almost immoral.

She could see the wagon in the shadows and hoped to find Mister Moore standing at the tailgate with his arms folded and ready to interrogate her for visiting Joe. If that happened, she'd turn right around and head back to ask Joe for much more help.

But when she reached the wagon, she found Mister and Mrs. Moore in quiet conversation which stopped when they heard her approaching.

When she was close, it was Mary Moore who quietly asked, "Did you visit that boy with the cart?"

"Yes, ma'am. He shot a deer and he'll be stopping by in the morning to bring some venison meat."

Mrs. Moore looked at her husband before he said, "The wagons will be moving even earlier tomorrow. We need to get some sleep."

"Yes, sir."

As they prepared the blankets beneath the wagon, Faith wondered why Mrs. Moore hadn't seemed angry when she asked about Joe. Maybe they really were worried that she might leave.

Faith had no idea just how concerned the Moores were about Joe Beck. They couldn't afford to drive her away but had to figure out how to stop Faith from visiting him.

UNWANTED

Joe added some more damp chips to the smoldering fire beneath his bayonet-skewered venison before closing the flap and preparing for sleep.

After dropping off the salted meat to the Moores tomorrow morning, he'd head to that small creek where he'd seen an oak tree and fill a bag with more chunks of hardwood, so he could make more of the chips.

Before he packed everything away, he'd cleaned and reloaded the Mississippi and had another pickle for dessert. He already had plans for the vinegary liquid after he'd eaten the last pickle.

After he laid out his bedroll, Joe walked to the front of the cart and detached the gutta-percha wrapped pouch from beneath the bed and stepped back to the dying fire.

He took a seat then carefully unwrapped the protective gutta-percha and set it aside. He opened the pouch and emptied its precious contents onto his open palm before laying the leather pouch atop the sheet of gutta-percha.

Joe stared at the gold watch and admired his great grandfather's exquisite craftsmanship. He had carved the image of a deer with massive antlers proudly standing before a mountainous background. The watch no longer kept time as his father had lost the winding key before he'd been born. It didn't matter anyway as the sun's position was all that mattered out here. His great-grandfather had made it as a gift to his grandfather when he left Bern in Switzerland. His father was going to pass it on to his older brother William but all of them died within days, so now it belonged to him. He was determined to present it to his own son as he told him how it had reached America.

While it no longer was useful as a timepiece, it served an even more important role now. He huddled over the watch to block the breeze then opened the case.

Atop the watch's crystal was a lock of his mother's dark red hair. It had been just an impulse, but he was now enormously grateful for that sudden decision. It was a physical reminder of the woman who had given him life. He sighed, closed the gold lid and flipped the watch over. The perfectly carved German script read: *Go with God, Johann.*

As he returned the watch to the pouch, Joe began to softly sing Kathleen Mavourneen and heard his mother's voice.

CHAPTER 5

The sun had barely peeked above the horizon as Joe strode quickly toward the wagons carrying his deerskin pouch of salted venison. He had his walking stick in his left hand and Newt trotted behind him, probably hoping that a piece of meat might slip out of the sack.

Joe was hoping to see Faith already milking the cows but figured he was either too early or too late. He almost turned around when he spotted Mister Moore harnessing his four oxen, so he shifted toward the front of the wagon and approached Mister Moore. He could already hear the wails of young children from inside the wagon and assumed that Faith and Mrs. Moore were having an argument with at least two of the boys.

Harry Moore had seen Joe much earlier but acted as if he wasn't even there.

He was still pushing one of his oxen into position when Joe stopped on the other side near the driver's seat and said, "Mister Moore, my name is Joe Beck and I told Faith that I'd drop off some fresh venison for your family this morning."

Harry looked at Joe and said, "No, thank you. You can give it to the Smith family in the next wagon if you want to get rid of it."

Joe was surprised as fresh meat, even this early in the long journey should be gratefully accepted. He glanced at the noisy wagon and thought about waiting to ask Faith. But Mister Moore's terse response made him suspect that he'd just be causing trouble for Faith if he did.

So, he just nodded then headed for the next wagon in line thinking that he'd stop on the way back to talk to Faith. He saw a man he assumed was the head of the family harnessing their oxen to their wagon with the help of a boy who appeared to be a couple of years younger than he was and more than a foot shorter. He could already hear bustling noises from inside the wagon and from the other side.

Ben Smith waited for the tall youth to draw close before he asked, "You're the one with that odd-looking cart; aren't you?"

"Yes, sir. My name's Joe Beck and I just talked to Mister Moore and offered him some salted venison that I harvested yesterday. He wasn't interested and suggested that I offer it to your family."

Mister Smith's eyebrows rose as he asked, "He didn't want the meat? How much do you have?"

"I reckon it's around twenty pounds or so. Do you want it? If not, I'll just head back and cook it myself."

UNWANTED

Ben grinned as he replied, "I don't know why Harry Moore turned it down, but I won't. Just take it to my wife on the other side of the wagon. I appreciate it, Mister Beck."

"Call me Joe. I reckon that I'm only a little older than your son."

Ben glanced at Russell then said, "Russ turns fifteen in May. How old are you?"

"I'm sixteen as of February the eighth."

"You're sure tall for your age, Joe. You're taller than any other full-grown feller that I've ever met, too."

Joe said, "I need to put on some weight, though," then turned and headed to the back of the wagon.

He turned left at the tailgate and soon found Mrs. Smith with a dark-haired girl about his age cleaning up after breakfast.

Both Smith women turned when they saw him, and the girl smiled broadly before he stopped before them.

He held out the heavy sack and said, "Mister Smith said to bring this to you, ma'am. It's about twenty pounds of fresh, salted venison that I harvested yesterday."

Before she could reply, the girl stepped forward, accepted the deerskin pouch and said, "Thank you very much. What's your name?"

Joe flushed as she smiled at him and awkwardly replied, "Um, Joe…Joe Beck."

"My name is Marigold Smith, but everyone calls me Mary."

Joe nodded as he said, "It's a pleasure to meet you, but I've got to get back to my cart now."

Joe didn't have a chance to turn around before she asked, "How can we repay you for your generosity, Joe?"

"It's just a gift, miss. I didn't want it to go to waste."

Marigold said, "Then I'll just say thank you again," before Joe tipped his hat then spun on his heels and stepped away from Marigold with Newt trotting behind him.

He immediately noticed Mrs. Moore closing their wagon's fold-out table but didn't see Faith. He turned behind the Smith's tailgate then walked past the Moores' wagon without seeing Faith, so he thought she must be milking the cow. When the critters came into view, he spotted a few women and boys scattered among the barnyard animals but didn't see Faith. He continued walking until he reached the goats wearing their yellow neckties and looked at the two cows. It appeared that one had been milked, so he assumed Faith was giving the boys their buttermilk.

He glanced at the back of the Moores' wagon and thought about heading that way but decided he'd better harness Bernie first. He didn't need to hunt today, so he'd just walk the cart behind the wagon and figured he'd be able to talk to Faith soon.

———

Back near the Smith wagon, Beatrice looked at her daughter after she returned from storing the venison and said, "It seems as if you're smitten with that boy, Mary."

Marigold replied, "He's very handsome; isn't he, Mama?"

"He's also tall and skinny, Mary. Besides, we know nothing about him. He could be a deserter from the Union army. Did you even notice that blue hat he was wearing? Your Uncle Jacob wears one like that and he's a lieutenant in the cavalry."

"He's too young to be an officer in the army, Mama. How could he have deserted?"

"Just behave yourself. Besides, I thought you liked Luther Carlisle."

Marigold rolled her eyes before saying, "Mama! He's not even fifteen yet. He just follows me around."

"Well, I don't want you to talk to that Beck boy until we know more about him. Is that understood?"

Marigold then asked, "How can we know more about him if I can't talk to him?"

Beatrice knew her daughter well enough to modify her original prohibition by saying, "Alright. But you can't talk to him alone. Is that good enough, Mary?"

Marigold smiled as she replied, "Yes, Mama."

"Then let's get everything cleaned up before we start rolling."

―――

Joe had harnessed Bernie and waited for the wagon train to start moving before he tapped his donkey's butt with his walking stick. He was about two hundred yards behind the herds when he finally saw Faith emerge from behind the Moore's wagon. She was carrying her walking stick and had barely stepped into open ground before she waved.

He returned her wave then nudged Bernie into a faster pace just to get closer. Newt was out front again but was heading on a parallel course with the ruts while Joe had Bernie pulling the cart at an angle. He figured his hound would notice the growing gap before long.

As he led Bernie toward the moving herds, he noticed two men riding away from the front of the train and assumed that both scouts were heading off to do their job. Now that they were already around twenty miles from Kansas City, he understood the reason why both scouts took the point. While it was still unlikely, they could run into hostile Plains tribes before the day was done and would need the extra firepower.

UNWANTED

The wagons had already rolled more than half a mile before Joe reached Faith as she walked beside the cows with her walking stick.

When he got in stride, he said, "I didn't see you this morning, Faith. I hope you didn't get in trouble with Mister Moore."

"I didn't, but it was a bit odd after I returned."

"How so?"

"When I got back, I thought Mister Moore might lecture me about leaving, but he didn't. Mrs. Moore asked if I'd spoken to you, and I told her that I had and that you'd be bringing some meat in the morning. Then Mister Moore just said that we'd be leaving early and needed to get some sleep. Then this morning, he said that he'd milk the cow. Did you give him the venison?"

"I offered it to him, but he turned me down and told me to give it to the Smith family in the next wagon, so I did."

Faith's eyebrows rose as she asked, "He didn't take it?"

"Nope. I was kinda surprised because fresh meat is always welcomed, especially if it's free."

"That is a surprise. I wonder what's going on."

"I have no idea, but it doesn't matter. Do you think that he'll get mad if he sees you talking to me?"

"He didn't seem upset last night, so I don't think so. It really doesn't matter to you if he did get angry; does it?"

"Not to me, but I don't want to cause you any problems, Faith."

Faith smiled and replied, "I'm not worried. You said that you'd help me if I needed it."

Joe nodded as he said, "I will always help you, but I don't want to lose your pay just because of me."

Faith paused before she said, "I'm not…well, just don't give a second thought about money. Okay?"

Joe was close to asking Faith how much she was being paid but thought it was too personal, so he simply replied, "Okay."

Faith quickly asked, "Are you going to do more hunting today?"

"No, ma'am. I'll just bother you for a while. I have enough meat to last three or four days. When it runs low, I might do some fishing if I get the chance, too."

"You have fishing hooks and line?"

"Yup. I have a lot of things in my cart."

"You didn't get a chance to say where you got it. I'm sure that it's nothing bad. So, can you tell me now?"

UNWANTED

"Sure. It's not bad, at least it's not illegal. It was last August, and I was sitting by my shelter when a line of Confederate soldiers marched past…"

As Joe told her about the sequence of events, he kept most of his attention directed at the line of wagons and focused mainly on the front of the Moores' wagon. He knew that Mister Moore had seen him talking to Faith and suspected that he'd better be gone before the train pulled up for their noon break.

Faith listened as Joe conversationally described the almost terrifying story and was stunned when he mentioned that his hat had been shot from his head.

She knew that he wasn't exaggerating but sharply asked, "Weren't you afraid when you saw those rebel soldiers shooting at you?"

Joe shrugged as he replied, "I suppose I should try to pretend that I was scared to death but still bravely faced the danger, but that wouldn't be honest. I just felt as if it wasn't even me who picked up the captain's Henry and began firing. Besides, not all of them were shooting. Only four of them had their rifles aimed and only four of them had fired. They were reloading, so I took advantage of the repeater and began firing at the ones who still had charged rifles. After they were down, I shot the others because they had all reloaded and the rest took off. I was just surprised that none of them didn't drop to the ground and fire from a prone position."

"But they shot your hat off your head! Didn't that scare you?"

"No. I did get a bit peeved about it but didn't let it affect my aim. I have it in my cart if you want to see it."

"I believe you, Joe."

"I know. It's just that it's still pretty interesting."

Faith sighed then asked, "What happened after they were all dead?"

"I was helping the wounded Yankee captain when some of his soldiers arrived. I guess one of them thought I was robbing their officer because…"

Faith was transfixed as she listened to Joe's tale and thought no less of him when he began talking about scavenging what he could from the eight bodies, including the blue Union cavalry hat he wore.

He told her about being summoned to meet Captain Chalmers and the unexpected reward that had been left hanging from a branch. She smiled as he explained how he'd begun trading what he didn't need for the cart and Newt.

Before he reached the discovery of Bernie, she asked, "So, you have three rifles in the cart?"

"Yes, ma'am. I have two muzzle-loading Remington Mississippi rifles. You saw one yesterday. And I have the

Henry repeater and plenty of ammunition for all of them. I have the pistol in a holster under my jacket and enough ammunition for about twelve reloads. I can make more if I need them."

"Are you a good shooter?"

"I'm very good with the rifles because anyone who hunts jackrabbits and possums with a single shot rifle needs to be accurate. I've only fired the Colt once and I'm satisfied with my accuracy, but I'll only need it when I'm in serious trouble."

"I feel safer already. How did you get the donkey?"

"After I left my shelter, I found a bridge that the rebels had built but had been used by some Missouri raiders. I followed their tracks into Kansas and…"

―――

Harry Moore had expected that Joe Beck would soon be having a long conversation with Faith and already had a plan to put a stop to it. He knew he had no real control over her and suspected that if he tried to intervene, she'd probably just leave. And that was a totally unacceptable situation.

As the oxen pulled their wagon along the Trail, he occasionally glanced back to see if that tall, gangly boy was still there. He was getting more irritated by the minute but there was nothing he could do until they stopped for their noon break. Mary was in the back with the boys but was already resting. They even had to leave some of their things behind to leave enough room in the wagon for her to lie down now that she was so close to having their fourth child.

He thought that she needed the rest, and he began to regret turning down the kid's offer of the fresh meat. Mary could have used the extra food, but she was the one who had made the decision not to accept the venison.

After Faith had told them that he'd be stopping by in the morning, Mary had suggested that he turn down the meat and send him to the Smith's wagon knowing that Marigold might attract his attention away from Faith. Marigold was much more developed than Faith and if Beck was smitten with her, their worries about losing Faith would be over.

After Faith had gone to control their cows and goats, Harry was finally able to tell Mary that he'd seen Marigold flirting with Beck, and things looked promising. But now that he saw the boy spending so much time with Faith even after meeting Marigold, knew he'd have to talk to Bo Ferguson during their noon break.

———

Joe didn't get to talk to Faith much longer when Mrs. Moore called to her from the back of their wagon.

She smiled at Joe as she said, "I have to return to taking care of the human kids now."

"Maybe you should put yellow neckties on them and let them walk with the four-footed kids."

Faith laughed then said, "Mrs. Moore wouldn't want to destroy another dress to do that."

"I reckon not. Bye, Faith."

"Goodbye, Joe."

Joe waved and started back to collect Bernie as Faith walked to the Moore wagon.

Joe figured he'd head to the oaks that he'd seen earlier and collect more firewood for use as wood chips as he knew that there wouldn't be many trees of any kind in a couple of days.

After turning Bernie to the south, Newt plunged into the deep grass and began his snooting zigzag path ahead of Joe and the cart.

By the time he reached the trees, the wagon train was already more than a mile away and still rolling. He pulled up and replaced his walking stick with the hatchet and the saw, then walked to the thick oaks. There was a stream flowing a few yards away on the other side, so he'd be able to fill his canteens before heading back.

Joe removed his jacket, laid it on the ground and then set his hat on top before removing his gunbelt and laying it on the coat. He thought about taking off his shirt but figured he'd wash it in the stream when he was finished instead.

He picked up the saw and started his cuts at the base of a thick branch. After it fell, he moved to a second branch on the opposite side, and it soon lay on the ground.

He then worked his way down each of them removing smaller branches with his hatchet until he had two long, naked branches and a tall pile of smaller ones.

He cut the long branches into six-foot lengths then began to reduce them into foot-long pieces for firewood. But when he was about to saw the last six-foot section, he stopped, set the saw down and picked it from the ground. There was a large knot right near the top of the pole, so Joe decided to use it as a better walking stick.

After stripping the smaller branches of leaves, he began loading his cart with the oak. He'd remove the bark from the knotted pole later. After the wood was loaded, he removed his bucket then returned to the tree and began scooping up the oak chips from the ground. The bucket was almost full of the chips when he set it on the ground then strapped on his gunbelt, put on his hat and just grabbed his coat.

As he walked back to his cart, he noticed that the wagon train had stopped for the noon break, but it was almost two miles away. He'd clean up, fill his canteens, then head back before they started moving again.

UNWANTED

As soon as they'd stopped, Faith hurried, and Mrs. Moore waddled to prepare their noon meal while Harry checked the oxen.

But Harry only made a cursory examination before walking down the long line of wagons to talk to Bo Ferguson.

Chuck Lynch and Mort Jones had just returned and were reporting to Bo when Harry arrived.

The wagon master asked, "So, everything's clear ahead?"

Chuck replied, "Yup. We didn't see anybody and that creek ain't swollen too much 'cause we didn't get much snow last winter."

Before Bo could ask another question, Harry said, "Bo, I need to talk to you about that kid with the cart."

Bo turned around and asked, "What about him?"

"He's getting too friendly with my wife's nanny and the Smith girl, too. I don't want any incidents, Bo. I'm paying you to get us safely to Oregon and that includes my nanny. That boy isn't paying a penny and I don't want him anywhere close to my wagon."

Bo shrugged then said, "He don't impress me as bein' the kind of feller who would hurt your nanny or any other girl, Harry."

"He may not hurt her, but he's distracting her, and I won't have it."

"Alright, I'll tell him to stay out of sight. Is that good enough, or do you want me to shoot him?"

"Of course, I don't want you to shoot him. I just don't want to see him again."

"I was just jokin' about shootin' him, but I'll let him know."

Harry nodded then turned on his heels and quickly strode back to his wagon.

Mort quickly said, "I'll go tell him, boss."

Bo looked at his scout and said, "I'm not surprised. Go ahead, but if I hear a gunshot, then you may as well keep ridin' back to Kansas City."

Mort grinned then mounted his brown mare and set her to a medium trot alongside the wagons. It took him almost a minute to spot the tent-cart because he thought it would be closer to the back of the Moores' wagon.

As he headed toward the distant trees, Mort thought he'd have some fun with the kid, but didn't want him to turn around and head back to Kansas City. He'd try to convince him that he should stay out of sight, but ahead and to the north of the wagon train. Mort wanted to know where to find him when he decided to pay him a visit.

UNWANTED

Joe had filled his canteens and washed his shirt, hair and torso before donning one of his new shirts. After pulling on his coat and hat, he carried the damp shirt back to the cart and hung it on one of the branches that jutted out of the back.

He was about to share the last of the fried venison steaks with Newt when he noticed a rider coming from the wagon train. He immediately identified him as Mort and thought about taking out his Henry but just left his coat unbuttoned. He had no idea why the scout was looking for him and even suspected that the wagon master might ask him to do some scouting as well. He'd been surprised that they only had two scouts as they'd be passing though hostile Indian lands with little protection from the depleted forts.

He walked away from the cart as the scout's horse crashed through the tall prairie grass and Newt surprised him when he began to growl.

Joe turned and said, "Sit, Newt."

The hound lowered his butt to the ground as he stared at the oncoming rider. If he could have glared, he would have. Joe assumed a non-hostile stance and demeanor but wasn't about to appear overly friendly either, as it would be disingenuous. He then pushed the brim of his cavalry hat back as Mort pulled up and waited for him to tell him the reason for the visit.

Mort quickly dismounted and stepped closer before saying, "The boss said to tell you that he wants you to stay outta sight."

"Why?"

"'Cause some of the folks don't like you hangin' around, that's why."

Joe wasn't sure if Mister Ferguson had sent the scout or not, so he asked, "Can I talk to Mister Ferguson?"

"Nope. He said if we see you again, then he'd send someone to shoot your skinny ass."

Joe doubted that even if Mister Ferguson had sent Mort that he would have made the threat, but he wasn't about to give the scout any excuse to go for his Colt. Mort's pistol was in an open holster while his revolver was beneath its covering flap.

Joe shrugged then said, "Alright."

Mort was surprised by his answer then said, "If I was you, I'd ride outta sight but northeast of the wagons. That way, if you broke an axle or somethin', you could ask for help."

It was Joe's turn to be surprised but didn't show it as he replied, "Maybe I'll do that. Thanks for the advice."

Mort grinned as he said, "Just don't let anyone in the train see ya. Maybe I'll pay you a visit every now and then to make sure you're okay."

Joe nodded then watched Mort return to his horse, mount and ride away.

Newt immediately stood and growled before looking at Joe probably expecting a tongue lashing.

Joe smiled and scratched behind the hound's right ear as he said, "You've got a good judge of character, Newt. I imagine Mister Mort hopes I'll be out of sight northeast of the train so he can make use of his pistol and shoot the pair of us. I've got to cut that flap off my holster in a little while."

Joe watched Mort until he reached the distant wagons then returned to his cart and pulled out the last fried venison steak. He didn't bother taking out his knife but simply ripped it in half and tossed the smaller piece to Newt figuring he wouldn't mind.

As he chewed on the meat, Joe wondered if it had been Mister Moore who had complained to the wagon master. It could have been Mister Smith or even the pair of them. He wasn't about to take the northeast position that Mort had suggested, but wasn't about to return to Kansas City, either. He'd follow the wagons, but he'd be out of sight to the southwest where he was now. After the wagons began rolling again, he'd wait until he could only see the roof of the Moores' wagon before he had Bernie start pulling the cart.

As he waited for that to happen, he removed his coat and took off his gunbelt. His big, sharp knife made short work of the protective flap. It was designed to keep the pistol from being thrown out of the holster as the cavalryman rode into battle, but he wasn't riding, so it was an unwanted obstruction.

He noticed the wagons beginning to move, so after strapping his gunbelt back in place, he left his coat on the cart and removed the knobby oak branch to start stripping the bark.

Joe was carefully scraping off the bark as he leaned against the cart and watched the wagons heading northwest. He'd miss being able to talk to Faith, but it was going to be a long journey and he'd always know where she was even if she didn't know his whereabouts.

———

After the wagons started rolling, Faith was told to keep an eye on the goats, so she grabbed her walking stick and headed to the herds. She looked for Joe's tent-cart and couldn't see it anywhere. She assumed that he must be hunting or something but planned to visit him in his campsite later.

After she'd gone, Harry turned to his wife and said, "We won't see that boy again, Mary. Bo Ferguson sent one of his scouts to tell him to stay out of sight. I had the impression that the man he sent would tell him to go back to Kansas City or he'd shoot him."

"I hope he doesn't do anything so drastic, but I'm glad he won't bother Faith anymore."

Harry smiled and said, "He could have ruined everything."

Mary nodded then picked up little William and set him on her lap.

———

Joe had Bernie moving just before he lost sight of the Moores' wagon. He wanted to see if he'd be able to pick it up again if he stayed in the tall grass. He knew he'd be able to move faster if he followed directly behind the wagons, but still thought he'd be able to at least match their speed over the rougher terrain. He was using his new oak walking stick and the large natural knob created by the knot made it easier to handle. It was noticeably heavier than his first walking stick but thought it was a good tradeoff. He had Bernie moving at a steady pace as he focused on the northwest hoping to spot the top of the Moores' wagon. He was pleased when it first popped into sight after just thirty minutes or so, so he slowed Bernie to keep the roof in view without gaining.

The afternoon turned into almost a cat and mouse game as he'd lose sight of the canvas roof, pick up the pace, see it again, then lose it just a few minutes later. Part of the reason was that he couldn't maintain a straight path and had to avoid obstacles like bushes or small hills. But as he led Bernie, Joe kept about the same distance from the stream that paralleled the Trail. The trees were already thinning, but he should be able to stock up before they disappeared.

The sun was setting when the wagons stopped, and Joe turned Bernie south toward the stream. He could no longer see the tops of any of the wagons by the time Bernie dipped his muzzle into the stream and Newt ferociously lapped up the water.

After unharnessing Bernie, Joe set up his camp and decided not to build a fire. It wasn't because he wanted to conserve his wood supply because there were still a few trees nearby. He suspected that Faith might be searching for him and didn't want her to see the fire then walk so far just to talk to him. It would take her more than an hour and she'd probably get in trouble. Especially if it had been Mister Moore who had told the wagon master that he didn't want him around.

―――

Faith hadn't been searching for Joe but was worried when she hadn't even seen his tent-cart all afternoon. As she was helping Mrs. Moore feed the boys, she thought that she'd soon see the light of his campfire and after the children were put to sleep, she'd be able to pay him a visit. She had decided that she'd finally tell him that her father had sold her to Mister Moore for twenty-five dollars.

UNWANTED

Harry hadn't told anyone other than his wife about his complaint, so he thought that after a few days, Faith would forget about the boy. He hadn't counted on Marigold Smith, who was also very curious about Joe's whereabouts.

Faith and Mary Moore were cleaning up after supper when Marigold appeared out of the shadows and approached Mrs. Moore.

She smiled as she said, "We just had a very nice dinner with the venison that Joe Beck dropped off this morning and wanted to thank you for sending him to us."

Mary glanced at Faith before replying, "You're welcome. We just thought you could use it more as your family is larger and has older children to feed."

Marigold then looked at Faith and said, "My name is Marigold, but everyone calls me Mary. You seem to be too old to be a daughter, so are you related?"

Faith was surprised that everyone didn't know that she was bought and paid for, but replied, "No, I'm just their nanny. I'm Faith Goodchild."

"It's good to meet you, Faith. I've seen you often enough and I'm happy that I finally got a chance to talk to you."

"I'm glad to meet you too, Mary."

Marigold then surprised Faith when she asked, "Do you know where Joe Beck is camping? I saw him talking to you before the noon break."

Faith shook her head before answering, "He set his camp up a couple of hundred yards southeast of our wagon last night, but I haven't seen him since we talked."

Marigold ignored Mrs. Moore as she asked, "What did you talk about? Is he going to follow us all the way to Oregon?"

Faith could hear her obvious interest, so she replied, "Joe said that he doesn't know where he's going."

"He's awfully tall; isn't he? But he's quite handsome, too."

"He said that he's probably still growing but needs to gain some weight."

Marigold giggled before saying, "I don't think so; do you?"

"He had his coat on, so I don't know."

Then Marigold lowered her voice as if Mrs. Moore couldn't hear her before she said, "I saw that Mort Jones riding that way while we were stopped for the noon break. Do you think he might have been told to send Joe away?"

Faith was stunned for a few seconds before she replied, "I don't know why he would do such a thing. Joe wouldn't hurt anyone. If anything, he would protect us."

"I don't think he'd do anything bad, either. But Mort Jones is a stupid, evil man and I wouldn't be surprised if he threatened to shoot Joe just for talking to you."

"Why would he do that?"

"Haven't you noticed how he looks at you when he rides past?"

"No."

"Well, I've noticed how he looks at me and it makes me sick. I think that he didn't want Joe around because he didn't want any competition, as if he has any chance with me in the first place."

"I guess I should be happy that I'm so skinny."

Marigold smiled as she said, "You're not as bad as you think. You'll probably start filling out soon."

"Now that you told me about Mort, I'm almost glad that I haven't."

Marigold laughed then said, "The other scout, Chuck Lynch, isn't like him at all. He seems very nice. Anyway, I've got to get back. It was nice to meet you."

Faith replied, "I'm happy to talk to you too," before Marigold smiled at Mrs. Moore then turned and headed back to her family's wagon.

Faith didn't know what to make of Marigold but didn't think Mister or Mrs. Moore would mind if she and Marigold became friends.

Mary Moore would tell Harry about the likelihood that Marigold would discover why Joe Beck had been sent away then tell Faith. They'd have to devise a believable excuse for making the complaint before that happened. At least they wouldn't have to worry about Joe Beck again now that Marigold expressed an interest.

―――

Joe was still smoothing his new oak walking stick as he sat near the small stream. While he wouldn't be able to talk to Faith, or anyone else for that matter, at least he wouldn't have to deal with Mort again. He smiled when he thought of the scout's futile search for him northeast of the wagon train. By staying out of sight to the southwest, no one would know where he was.

So, as they crossed Kansas and entered Nebraska Territory, he'd be traveling alone with just Newt and Bernie for company. His only real concern was that if the wagon train ran into hostiles, he'd be too far away to help Faith. It wasn't a problem now, but soon they'd be entering Pawnee lands and then things could become dicey. He wished he wasn't so ignorant of the Indians and pretty much everything else west of the Missouri River.

CHAPTER 6

Joe didn't know if they had reached Nebraska Territory yet, but it didn't matter. For four days, he'd maintained the same on-again off-again pattern as he followed the wagon train. No one had paid him a visit and while he missed Faith, he appreciated not seeing Mort riding in his direction.

But the dry days were now behind them. He wore one of his three intact slickers as the clouds sent waves of showers from the sky. While he wasn't able to keep the same pace, he suspected that the heavier, loaded wagons would be even more affected by the muddy ground. He hadn't seen them yet this morning as his visibility had been reduced to just a few hundred yards in the rain.

Newt and Bernie didn't seem to care about being soaked, but he was glad that he still hadn't worn his new boots as his work boots were already sinking a good two inches into the mud. At least the cart was still rolling reasonably well. They'd crossed their first good-sized creek on the first day he'd remained out of sight and Bernie had managed to cross the twenty-foot wide and three-foot deep creek without a problem. Even though he'd wrapped his hidden pouch in the gutta percha, Joe still removed it and put it in his pocket before they crossed. He was grateful for his height as the water never reached the pocket. He'd also removed his three rifles and carried them across in his arms as if he was cradling a baby. It had taken two days to dry all his clothes and bedrolls.

He imagined that with all this rain, that creek was probably a foot deeper already. As he plodded along, he was thinking of a better way to protect his rifles and clothes before they had to cross deeper creeks or rivers.

―――

Faith had given up searching for Joe and believed that Mort had convinced him to return to Kansas City. Marigold had visited her when she was with the cows and goats and told her that it was Mister Moore who had complained about Joe and that was why he was gone.

Marigold hadn't asked why he'd made the complaint, but suspected it was because he didn't want Joe to talk to Faith. She did tell Faith that when she'd briefly talked to Joe, her mother had told her to stay away from him because they didn't know anything about him. Then she said that her mother had modified the restriction to allow her to talk to Joe but only with a chaperone nearby.

Faith had laughed but was more than annoyed when she learned that Mister Moore was the reason that Joe had gone. If she had any idea where Joe was, she would have taken her personal bag and gone to find him. But she didn't know and each mile they traveled would make it more likely that she would never see him again.

UNWANTED

But each day, she and Marigold walked together and were becoming friends. A fact that neither of the adult Moores seemed to notice or deem of any importance.

Today, she was riding inside the wagon with Mrs. Moore and the boys while Mister Moore sat on the driver's seat in his slicker as he guided the oxen. If it hadn't been for the rain, she might have spotted the tent-wagon less than two miles to the southwest. Joe had been gaining on the wagons without realizing it.

―――

The rain was still falling but had lessened to a little more than a mist when Joe pulled up for the evening. He hadn't started a fire since he'd been told to keep his distance but decided to build one now. He wanted a hot meal and needed the heat after the chilly, wet day.

He used two of his new poles, the bayonets and a tarp to build an open tent then dug a firepit at the end away from the cart. Newt had already claimed residence under the tarp as Joe began gathering makings for their dinner. He was down to the first jar's last pickle, so he set that on his plate knowing that Newt wasn't about to steal it. Dogs didn't seem to like anything green, much less something that smelled as sour as the pickle.

He used some smoked venison and the last of his prepared beans for supper and gave a big chunk of the meat to Newt as he set his frypan on the grid.

As his supper cooked, Joe returned to thinking about how to keep his rifles dry when they crossed a deeper creek. He knew the Henry could get wet and still immediately fire, but the Mississippi rifles would be an iffy proposition if any water snuck past the Minie ball that should block its passage. He could just leave them unloaded to avoid the issue, but he'd still have to clean and oil all of the rifles after crossing a stream.

By the time he finished eating, Joe figured that after he'd used each of the Mississippi rifles for hunting, he'd leave them unloaded but cover them with some of his axle grease to keep them protected until they were needed. If they crossed a deeper creek, he'd just hold the Henry over his head. It wasn't much of a plan, but it was all he could come up with at the moment. That was partly because his mind drifted to thoughts of Faith.

The rain had finally stopped, so he left his tent and walked to the front of the cart. When he looked northwest, he was stunned to see the light of a large fire. It had to be the common fire of the wagon train and he estimated that it was around a mile and a half away. He knew they couldn't see his fire because it was masked by the cart and his tent, but knowing they were that close gave him another problem. If he was still here when the sun rose, he might be spotted. Then it wouldn't be long before Mort would come riding his way.

UNWANTED

Joe thought about harnessing Bernie and leading the cart back east until the fire disappeared but immediately changed his mind. He'd stay put and watch the wagons until they passed from his view in the morning. They usually started rolling shortly after sunrise, so it wasn't likely that he'd be spotted. If he was and then Mort came riding his way, he'd be waiting with his Henry this time.

But as he stood looking at the distant fire, he began to think about paying Faith a visit. He assumed that she must have believed that he'd returned to Kansas City, so maybe he could at least leave her a note to let her know that he was still following the wagon train.

Then he figured that Mister or Mrs. Moore would probably find it first and wouldn't tell her anyway, so he discarded that idea before he returned to his tent that he'd share with his stinky hound friend. He didn't know that even if Faith had found his note, she wouldn't be able to read it. Her father only allowed her brothers to learn to read and write. She, Grace and Patience were girls and would only be taught what they needed to keep house. Faith had been able to recognize some words just by their context, but reading a full note was beyond her abilities.

When he returned to his dying campfire, he picked up the pickle jar with its vinegary contents and carried it to the back of the cart. Rather than dump it out, he added some molasses then screwed on the lid and shook it to mix the sweet and sour liquids. After removing the lid, he began scooping oak chips out of his bucket and dumping them into the jar. When it was full, he sealed it and set it in the bucket. He wondered if he'd be able to taste the difference in the meat that he smoked with the saturated wood chips. He'd have to do some hunting to obtain the meat first.

―――

Faith did believe that Joe had returned to Kansas City but wasn't about to forget him. He had been the primary topic of the conversations that she shared with Marigold as they walked with the herds.

While Marigold shared Faith's disappointment over Joe's disappearance, there was one other person among those heading westward who was also disappointed. Mort had expected to find Joe northwest of the lead wagon and after five days without seeing the kid, Mort believed that he had gone too far with his threat, and he'd returned to Kansas City. Unlike the two young women, Mort completely forgot about Joe Beck.

―――

When the sun rose the next morning, it was just a bright disk behind a gray curtain. The rain had stopped during the night, but it was a decidedly chilly morning. Joe even thought about wearing his heavy winter coat but figured his jacket and slicker would suffice unless it started snowing.

UNWANTED

It was already warmer when Joe watched the wagon train roll out of sight before starting Bernie through the muck. He imagined that it was much worse for the long line of wagons as they were following those ruts and probably added a few inches of their own. His cart left its own ruts, but the prairie grass helped firm the ground and probably absorbed enough of the water to make the surface somewhat firmer.

As he walked through the mud, he looked down at his feet and thought he might have to wear the first pair of boots that Captain Chalmers had given him. While his work boots were still functional, his toes were protesting each time he'd pulled them on. He'd abandoned the use of socks before he left Missouri, but his feet must have stretched a bit more because his toenails were threatening to cut their way out of the boots.

He looked at Bernie and asked, "Now aren't you glad you don't wear shoes?"

After a brief pause, he laughed and patted the donkey's haunch before he said, "I can't see any more of that singed hair, Bernie. I suppose I should change your name, but I don't want to cause you any confusion."

He snickered again before taking a few longer strides to get in front of Bernie. He had one of his Mississippi rifles over his shoulder as he walked and kept an eye out for game. There was just a mild breeze, and it was coming from the southwest, so he would be downwind of any unsuspecting critters.

While he still scanned for game, he made sure that he wasn't gaining on the wagons. He'd seen them once shortly after he started and renewed his game of hide and seek. They'd probably hear his gunfire if he took a shot, but that might reach Faith's ears, so it would be worth a possible visit by Mort Jones. Hopefully, he and the other scout would be miles out front by then.

———

The sun was beginning to win its battle with the cloud cover by mid-morning when Joe noticed Newt suddenly stop and alert as he pointed southwest.

Joe stopped Bernie then shifted his rifle into both hands as he stepped closer to Newt who stared into the thick grass. Joe couldn't see whatever creature the hound's nose had detected.

He continued his approach and soon reached Newt and followed his nose. He saw one of the largest cottontail rabbits he'd ever seen. It was about the size of an adult beaver. He was hunkered down and still nibbling on grass as Joe slowly cocked the Mississippi's hammer hoping that the loud click didn't alert the rabbit.

When it snapped into position, the rabbit suddenly stood on its hind legs and looked in Joe's direction but must not have seen him because he soon dropped back down and resumed grazing. Joe slowly brought his rifle level, set his sights on the giant rabbit's head and fired.

As he and Newt hurried to fetch the rabbit, the loud report echoed across the plains. It took more than a half a second for the dissipating sound waves to reach the wagon train. Most didn't notice it over the sounds of their creaking wagons, conversations or a host of other local noises. But Faith was walking in the mud alongside the cows when the compressed waves reached her left ear drum and caused it to vibrate. The tiny bones inside her ear then notified her brain and Faith quickly turned to the southwest.

She exclaimed, "Joe!" and luckily, no human ears were close enough to hear her.

She wished that Marigold was with her so she could confirm what she'd heard, but just that distant crack was enough to let her believe that Joe hadn't returned to Kansas City after all. It was a comforting revelation knowing that he and his silly looking tent-cart were close enough that she could hear him hunting. Not for one moment did she believe that it could be anyone else because that would be unacceptable.

She turned to the first cow and tapped her on her shoulder with the walking stick that Joe had given to her and laughed. She couldn't wait to tell Marigold.

———

After preparing the rabbit, Joe just salted it down for supper. Newt made short work of what he'd removed, so he already had his lunch.

As big as the rabbit was, he knew there wasn't enough meat to smoke but would make a big meal for him and Newt.

He cleaned and reloaded the Mississippi before returning it to its bedroll scabbard then took his new oak walking stick and began moving again. He figured the wagon train had moved no more than a mile since he'd pulled Bernie to a stop, so he'd be able to keep a reasonably fast pace over the drying ground before he spotted the wagons again.

As he walked, he began doing some calculations about the report from his rabbit-killing shot. He estimated that he was around three miles from the Moores' wagon, so the sound would have taken almost a second to reach the wagon. It would have been weak, but it would have still been heard at that distance. If Faith was out with the critters, then she could have picked up the distant sound. It was only a slim chance, but he hoped that she'd heard his shot and understood that he was still trailing.

Joe picked up the wagons again when they had stopped for their noon break, so he pulled Bernie to a stop and had a quick lunch of crackers and jerky.

As he leaned against the cart chewing on his jerky, he stared at the roof of the Moores' wagon and asked, "Did you hear that shot, Faith? I hope so. If not, then maybe you'll hear the next one. I kinda hope that Mort heard it and decides to pay me a visit, but I reckon he was a few miles northeast of the lead wagon with the other scout. I guess this will be the only way I can talk to you for a while."

He snickered then popped the last of the jerky into his mouth before he turned to check on Bernie. He briefly thought of changing his boots but decided to do that when he dressed in the morning. He'd finally get to wear one of his eight new pairs of socks, too.

―――

While Mort wasn't that far ahead of the wagons, he still hadn't heard the distant gunfire. The only one who'd noticed it was Faith which made it almost a personal message.

The reason Mort wasn't miles ahead of the train was that he and Chuck Lynch had spotted a band of eight Pawnee warriors riding from the north to the south and after the Pawnee had seen them, the scouts quickly turned and headed back to warn Bo.

The warriors hadn't followed them, but Chuck and Joe were concerned that they were heading back to their village to get more men.

They were arriving just after the wagons had stopped and everyone was rushing to prepare a noon meal.

Bo hadn't spotted them as he was talking to Ed Carlisle, who was the elected leader of the families.

It was Ed who first saw them coming then said, "Bo, Chuck and Mort are comin' up real fast. It looks like trouble."

Bo wheeled around, saw his scouts racing towards him and guessed what the problem was.

Without turning around, he said, "Stick around, Ed. I reckon they ran into some Pawnee. They'll probably wanna trade, but things mighta changed. We may need everyone to get back here with their rifles."

Ed stared at the rushing scouts as he replied, "Okay."

Chuck and Mort pulled up quickly and both horses slid a few inches before they hurriedly dismounted.

Chuck said, "We were about three miles out when we saw eight Pawnee warriors about a mile ahead of us cuttin' across the Trail. They saw us but kept headin' south. I reckon they were a huntin' party, but they could turn into a war party after they get more men."

"Alright. Let's not get too excited. You boys get somethin' to eat and me and Ed will meet with the other men."

Chuck replied, "Okay, boss," then took his horse's reins and led him to their wagon with Mort following behind.

UNWANTED

Bo and Ed soon gathered all of the family heads together before Bo explained the issue.

"Now, it's more likely that the Pawnee won't bother us, but they if they do show up, they'll probably ask for payment for crossing their lands. That's why we have those extra rifles. ammunition and ironware in my wagon. But those big herds of buffalo are gettin' scarce in these parts, so they might want some of your farm critters. If so, then it's up to you do decide how much you're willing to part with."

Ed looked at their concerned faces as he said, "If anyone can spare a cow or some sheep, he'll be reimbursed from the common fund."

Harry Moore said, "I'm not giving up my only two cows or any of my goats, either."

Others began muttering their objections before Bo loudly said, "You men should be more willin' to give up just a few critters if they ask for 'em. If you turn 'em down, you'd better be ready with your rifles."

Harry then snapped, "We paid you to keep us safe, Ferguson! You should have hired more scouts and given them repeating rifles."

Bo glared at Harry before he snorted and said, "Maybe you reckon havin' six scouts armed with Henrys would let you keep your precious cows, Mister Moore. But if they wanted to kill every soul in this wagon train, only a troop of cavalry could stop 'em...maybe."

Wilmott Schmidt said, "I'll give up one of my sheep," which prompted a few other men to agree to give up one of their animals knowing they would be reimbursed. Harry Moore wasn't one of them.

Bo nodded then said, "Alright. If it comes to dealin', I'll start with a couple of rifles, two ammunition pouches and a couple of pots. If they want critters, I'll offer 'em just one cow and two sheep, but no more than two cows, two sheep and two goats. Is that okay?"

Everyone nodded before Bo said, "I still want you to have your rifles ready but don't let the Pawnee see them. I want all the womenfolk and kids in the wagons if they show up. Now fill your bellies so we can get movin' again."

The men dispersed and Bo angrily turned away to talk to Mort and Chuck. He had explained what was likely to happen when they crossed many of the Indian lands before they left, and this was only their first and probably one of the less hostile tribes. He hoped the settlers would be more understanding when they met the Sioux, Cheyenne and Arapahoe. But even those tribes preferred trading, at least on his last two trips. He was still worried about the impact of the army stripping the western forts and the rumors of the transcontinental railroad.

UNWANTED

Joe had expected the wagons to begin moving by now and thought that one must have had a mechanical problem that delayed their departure. He hadn't been able to see the scouts' hasty return. He was impatient and decided to get out in front but headed south first to avoid being seen.

After losing sight of the wagons, he turned northwest to parallel the Trail as best he could. He'd keep an eye out for the tops of the wagons but if he didn't pick them up again, he'd shift more to the north. He didn't think he'd be spotted by the scouts, at least not today. He'd figure out what he'd do tomorrow when he set up camp.

But the sun soon announced the unconditional surrender of the weaker clouds and the plains burst into bright sunlight. Joe removed his slicker and waited for Bernie to pull his cart past before folding it and tossing it onto the row of backpacks. The cart was now almost completely full, but most of the volume was taken by branches. Joe would manage his supply of wood, but knew that even if he minimized its use, the cart would be free of wood to burn before he left Nebraska Territory.

It was mid-afternoon when Joe first observed specks on the western horizon. He initially thought that it might be a herd of buffalo that were so dominant in the Great Plains, but soon recognized men atop horses and knew they were Indians. He kept watching and counted sixteen riders. They were about a mile out now and still riding north. He pulled Bernie to a stop, then walked to the back of the cart where he exchanged his walking stick for a Mississippi and the Henry.

He carried the rifle and the carbine back to the front and let Bernie stay put before he called Newt back. He was surprised that the Indians kept riding northward and wondered if they had even seen him. From all the tales he'd heard about the Plains tribes, he couldn't imagine that he had remained undetected.

He was still watching when they began to swing more to the east and realized that they were heading for the wagon train. They had been too far away for Joe to see how they were armed but decided that he couldn't just let them attack the wagons if that was their plan. Faith was there.

He hurried back to his cart, returned the Mississippi to the bedroll before he walked to the front and took Bernie's harness and pulled him northeast. He had no idea how far away the wagons were, but judging by the direction the Indians had taken, he figured that he'd soon see the tops of the lead wagons.

He spotted the first canvas roof before he picked up the band of Indians who were slowly approaching but were still a mile or so northwest of the lead wagon. He let go of Bernie's reins, said, "Stay, Newt," then returned and pulled his

Mississippi free again before trotting through the tall grass. He noticed that the wagons weren't moving, and he hoped that he wouldn't have to use his weapons.

———

Bo was flanked by Mort on his left and Chuck on his right as they waited for the Pawnee to arrive. Unlike Joe, Bo was able to evaluate their weapons and found six to be armed with single-shot muzzle loaders, but two others had pistols, which surprised him. The other eight were carrying bows but didn't have any arrows nocked. He and his scouts weren't carrying their rifles as they were unnecessary, but each had a Colt at his hip with all six chambers filled.

It was another twenty minutes before War Chief Tall Antelope pulled his band in front of the three white men and in surprisingly good English, he said, "You must pay to cross Pawnee land."

Bo stepped closer and looked up at the chief before he asked, "What do you want?"

Tall Antelope looked at the distant herd, held up four fingers and said, "Four cattle, four sheep and four goats."

Bo was surprised that they hadn't even mentioned rifles or ammunition before he said, "You ask too much. We have many days journey ahead of us and other tribes will demand more. I will give you one cow and one sheep."

Tall Antelope snorted then said, "It is not enough. We will accept three of each, but no less."

Bo shook his head as he replied, "I can only offer you two cows and two sheep, but no more."

"It is still not enough. I have fifteen warriors behind me and more waiting if you do not pay what I ask."

"And I have many men with rifles ready behind me. Do you wish to bury so many warriors just to have one more cow and woolie?"

"We are warriors and are not afraid to die. Can you say the same for those men who have wives and children?"

Bo was about to add a goat to the deal when Mort snapped, "I'm a good shot with my Colt, Injun!"

Tall Antelope glanced at Mort before he asked, "Who is this stupid man who speaks?"

Bo glared at Mort before he replied, "He is stupid and should not have spoken. I will add a billy goat to my offer because of his poor manners."

Tall Antelope nodded as he said, "We will accept the payment."

Bo turned to Chuck and said, "You and Mort take them to the herds and let the owners give you the two cattle, two sheep and one goat."

UNWANTED

Chuck replied, "Okay, boss," then waited for Mort to turn before they headed to the back of the wagons leading half of the Pawnee.

Bo waited with Tall Antelope and seven of his warriors for them to return and hoped that Mort didn't do something stupid. He was depending on Chuck to keep him in line. When the Pawnee were gone, he'd have a few words with Mort.

Despite having already walked for more than two hundred miles since leaving his shelter, Joe was getting winded after jogging through the grass for more than a mile. He was still moving, but the Mississippi felt as if it weighed a hundred pounds, and the Henry wasn't far behind. He was sweating under his jacket as he watched the two scouts lead eight Indians to the back of the train while eight others sat on their horses in front of Mister Ferguson. He assumed that there would be no confrontation and guessed that the eight Indians were being taken to the herds to collect some sort of ransom.

He was still breathing heavily when he changed direction to the back of the wagon train in the hope of seeing Faith before he had to return. He was about three hundred yards out and noticed that many of the men were standing next to their wagons and some were following the Indians. His curiosity was piqued, so he continued wading through the tall grass as the scouts reached the herd. He didn't see Faith but had noticed Mister Moore sitting in his driver's seat.

As he passed the wagons, he wondered if he had somehow been rendered invisible. None of the men on the wagons or those walking to the herds had seen him either. Maybe they all just thought he was dead or just didn't bother looking in his direction. He guessed that they were just more interested in their first encounter with Indians.

He passed the Moore wagon and saw some of the white man leading cows, sheep and a goat from the large mixed herd. As the Indians began inspecting the animals, Joe stopped and watched the two scouts rather than the Pawnee. The nice one was just watching, but Mort was glaring and had his hands clenched into fists. He wasn't happy about something, but Joe knew that it wouldn't take much to make Mort mad anyway.

He figured out that they were giving the critters to the Pawnee as a toll to cross their land. But despite the successful negotiations, Joe felt his heightened sense of calm and awareness arrive. He kept his eyes focused on Mort as he lowered his Henry's butt to the ground and clamped it between his knees then cocked his Mississippi. It was awkward but he wasn't about to let his precious repeater fall then have to clean the magazine tube.

Mort was growing more furious as he watched the damned Indians examining the cows as if they were being cheated. His anger was fueled by hearing that English-speaking Indian calling him stupid. Then it was exacerbated when Bo agreed with him. As he glared at those Pawnee laughing and chatting in their Indian-talk, Mort's fury was reaching volcanic levels and was about to erupt.

Joe didn't have his Mississippi in a firing position as he closely watched Mort. He could almost feel his seething rage from two hundred yards and knew that if Mort lost his temper, he could start a full-blown skirmish. If that happened, Faith could be hurt, and he had promised to protect her.

Once he added Faith into the equation, he brought his rifle's sights to his eyes and set them on Mort. He had a good line of fire as Mort was standing at a forty-five-degree angle. Joe knew he could put his .54 caliber slug into a four-inch circle on Mort's chest but didn't want to kill him. He aimed for the ugly sagging hat atop Mort's head. He couldn't hold the sights in place for very long because of the rifle's weight but thought Mort would soon either calm down or pull his pistol. The problem was that Mort's Colt was on his right side and Joe couldn't see it. He'd have to wait until Mort pulled it from his holster but hoped that he would let it stay where it belonged.

Joe calmed his breathing as he held the long barrel still and studied the angry scout.

Amazingly, none of the Pawnee noticed Joe as they looked over the animals and joked about the angry white man. Mort was too focused, and Chuck was making sure that the Indians didn't try to take another critter. The owners of the animals were sadly watching the Pawnee and the others who were nearby were all observing the trade. All of the women and children were hiding in the wagons as the wagon master had ordered.

Joe had been about to lower his Mississippi when one of the Pawnee made the mistake of pointing at Mort then saying something to his fellow warriors that made them all laugh. It was a stupid and unnecessary thing to do, but it lit Mort's fuse.

Mort unwittingly gave Joe a warning when he shouted, "You damned Indian bastards!" then reached for his Colt.

He quickly pulled it from his holster and cocked the hammer as he was bringing it level when his hat flew away, and he collapsed to the ground in a heap as the Mississippi's thunderous echo reached their ears. Blood was pouring from the top of Mort's head as his cocked pistol dropped into the dirt and everyone's heads whipped to the south where they saw Joe lowering his smoking rifle.

Joe hadn't missed, but the long delay and the weight of the rifle had dropped his muzzle just a fraction of an inch, so the Minie ball had grazed the top of Mort's skull. Joe was surprised and thought he might have killed Mort, so he grabbed his Henry then began trotting to the herds.

Chuck quickly identified the shooter before he dropped to his heels and checked on Mort. He felt a strong heartbeat and then looked at his wound. It wasn't that bad but at least Mort hadn't shot one of the Pawnee.

UNWANTED

The Pawnee realized what had almost happened and would have gone on a rampage, but the stupid scout had been shot by another white man, so they just watched as the incredibly tall young white man headed their way.

Chuck had ripped part of Mort's shirt to make a temporary bandage before picking up his pistol and releasing the hammer. He looked down the line of wagons and spotted Bo and the other Pawnees rapidly approaching.

Bo saw Joe as he trotted toward the herds and wondered why he had opened fire but knew he hadn't shot one of the Pawnee because they were all just standing there with their arms folded. He soon spotted Mort on the ground and noticed that Chuck had Mort's pistol tucked under his waist. It didn't take long for him to realize that the kid had shot Mort but didn't know why.

Joe arrived first and breathlessly asked, "Is he still alive?"

Chuck nodded and replied, "Yup. You only grazed the top of his noggin. He was pretty lucky that you missed."

Joe stopped and looked down at Mort as he said, "I missed a bit low. I was just trying to shoot the hat off his head when I saw him pulling his pistol."

Chuck quickly asked, "You were tryin' to shoot off his hat? You've got to be kiddin' me! How far out were you?"

"A couple of hundred yards or so. It wasn't that bad, but my arm must have been getting tired after holding the rifle for so long."

"How long were there watchin' all this?"

"Not long. I reckon it was a minute or so."

Joe was looking at the Pawnee who were studying him when Bo and Tall Antelope arrived with the other seven Pawnee warriors.

Bo glanced at Joe before he turned to his scout and asked, "What happened, Chuck?"

"The Pawnee were checkin' out the critters and seemed to be havin' a good time. After the chief there called Mort stupid, I reckon he got kinda mad. Then one of 'em who were takin' the critters pointed at Mort and said somethin' that made the others laugh. Mort blew his stack, then yelled and went for his Colt. He had it cocked and was about to shoot the one who pointed at him when the kid unloaded from two hundred yards. He said he only wanted to shoot his hat off to make him stop, but the bullet creased the top of his skull. He'll be okay when he wakes up, though."

Bo turned to Joe and asked, "Is that right, kid? You really wanted to just shoot his hat off at two hundred yards? That sounds like a tall tale to me."

UNWANTED

Joe shrugged but didn't answer before Bo looked down at Mort and said, "Take him to our wagon and don't let him go anywhere even if he wakes up."

Chuck replied, "Okay, boss," then waited for the wagon master to help lift Mort from the ground then draped him over his shoulder.

As Chuck walked away with this unconscious burden, Bo looked at the still stunned white men and said, "You men can go back to your wagons now and tell your womenfolk to stay put until I tell you we're ready to move."

They murmured their consent before they began wandering away from the herd.

Bo then turned to Tall Antelope and said, "My scout's stupidity and temper almost caused great harm."

"Yes. But my men should not have laughed at your scout, and I will punish them for their foolishness."

Then the war chief pointed to Joe and said, "The young one is much wiser. You should have hired him as scout."

"He's just a kid and only showed up when we were gettin' ready to roll, and I already had two scouts."

"He is much older than the one who was about to shoot."

Bo replied, "The stupid one is almost twice as old as he is."

"I do not speak of years. The tall one is older in his heart and mind."

Bo then asked, "Can we cross Pawnee land now?"

"Yes, you will be safe until you reach the land of the Ogallala which is ten days' journey."

Bo nodded then looked at Joe before he pointed to the southeast and said, "Let's talk over there."

"Alright."

Joe followed the wagon master and wondered what he would say. He hoped that he'd be grateful enough to allow him to trail more closely now so he could talk to Faith again.

Harry Moore had been stunned by the unexpected shot then quickly turned to find the shooter and was startled to see Joe Beck lowering his rifle before hurrying out of sight. He leaned around the wagon then watched him as he trotted to the herds before sitting upright and wondered what had happened. He almost thought about leaving the wagon to find out but expected Bo Ferguson would send the kid away then he'd be able to ask the wagon master about the incident.

Inside the Moore wagon, Faith was holding onto John and Alfred while Mrs. Moore held William in her arms. It was a tight squeeze, but she'd been able to watch the Indians as they accepted their payment. She was looking at John to answer a question when Mort shouted, and Joe made his shot. When they heard the nearby gunshot, each of them believed that it was fired by one of the Indians at the front of the train and expected that the air would soon be shattered by a flurry of gunfire.

But after almost a minute of silence, Faith asked, "What do you think happened, Mrs. Moore?"

She glanced at her husband who didn't seem excited at all before she replied, "I don't know. But as long as we're all safe, it doesn't matter."

Faith nodded but turned her eyes back to the herd and was confused. She noticed that the Indians and the men from the wagons were all standing and looking south. The nice scout was crouched on his heels, but she couldn't see what attracted his attention.

As she studied the scene, Faith was shaken when she saw the scout stand and she spotted the body of the other scout on the ground. She knew she should have been horrified but felt guilty for hoping that he was dead. Marigold told her that it had been Mort who had told Joe to leave.

But just as Joe's name appeared in her mind, the real Joe appeared in view and her heart nearly exploded. She'd been right! He hadn't gone back to Kansas City! *But what was he doing here?*

Then she noticed him talking to Chuck and that he was holding two rifles. She knew then that Joe had shot Mort and hoped that they weren't going to hang him. But she immediately realized that it made no sense at all. *Why would Joe shoot him with all those others around, especially the Indians?* Besides, despite the story he'd told her about shooting the eight soldiers, she didn't believe that Joe would murder anyone. But just seeing him as he talked to the scout filled her with joy.

She was still focused on the scene and ignored John's barrage of questions when she saw Mister Ferguson arrive with the rest of the Indians. She wished she was close enough to hear but noticed that the wagon master didn't seem angry at Joe, which gave her hope that Joe might not even be sent away again. When Mister Ferguson helped lift Mort's body onto Chuck's shoulder, she was convinced that he was dead.

When Joe walked off with Mister Ferguson, Faith could no longer see him, so she finally turned and looked at Mrs. Moore, who had probably been watching as well.

She asked, "Did you see all that, Mrs. Moore?"

"Not all of it. Was that the boy who talked to you?"

"Yes, ma'am. It seems that Joe shot one of the scouts."

Mary quickly said, "You should be grateful that we had him sent away, Faith."

Faith was startled and exclaimed, "*Why did you do that?* He would never hurt me or anyone else!"

UNWANTED

"He just shot a man in cold blood! He's an animal and would probably rape you if he had the opportunity!"

Harry turned around and shouted, "Quiet! I'll talk to Bo Ferguson about this after those Indians are gone."

Faith was close to bolting out of the back of the wagon but was locked in place by the two boys and didn't want to hurt either of them. They were just innocent children, even if they were Moores.

John looked up at Faith and asked, "Was that the tall man with the dog who found Buster when he ran away?"

Faith smiled as she replied, "Yes, he is. He's a very nice man; isn't he?"

Faith could almost feel Mrs. Moore's icy stare as John giggled and replied, "Yes, Miss Faith. He's really brave, too!"

Then almost as a warning, Faith said, "He is very brave. Almost a year ago when he was only fifteen, he shot eight soldiers who were trying to kill a Union officer."

John's eyes grew wide as he exclaimed, *"He did? Really?"*

"He did. And he has all eight of their bayonets and two of their rifles, too. The captain he saved sent him all sorts of gifts even though he didn't ask for anything."

"Wow! Did any of those soldiers shoot him?"

"Before he started shooting, one of them shot his hat right off his head, but he didn't flinch."

Mary quickly snapped, "That's all a lie, Faith! You are just a foolish young girl. He was just trying to impress you. How could he possibly shoot eight soldiers without being shot himself?"

Faith smiled as she replied, "It's all true, Mrs. Moore. He didn't brag to impress me. I asked him, and he just told the story. The captain had a Henry repeater, so Joe picked it up and began firing. He'd never even fired one before. The captain gave it to him as one of the gifts along with a pistol. He even showed it to me. He used a lot of what he scavenged from the dead soldiers to trade for his cart and even his dog."

John looked at his mother and said, "His name is Newt, and I like him."

Mary stared at Faith and realized she had made several blunders. First, she had admitted that she and her husband had told Bo Ferguson to send the boy away. Then she'd compounded the mistake by insulting him despite knowing that Faith was smitten with Joe Beck. She looked at her husband who was no longer paying attention to whatever was happening inside the wagon and hoped that he'd be able to convince the wagon master to send him away again. But even if he did, she suspected that Faith may try to run away just to find him. Their plan and her hidden agenda were both unraveling.

UNWANTED

Harry had those same concerns as he waited to get the word to start rolling again. He didn't know why the kid had shot Mort but doubted that the wagon master would punish him. It might have been different if he'd shot Chuck Lynch.

Joe and Bo Ferguson had stopped about fifty yards from the herds and Bo felt a bit odd as he looked up at the teenager. He'd rarely had men even reach his own eye level.

Before the wagon master could say anything, Joe asked, "Did you really send Mort to tell me to stay out of sight, or was that his idea?"

"Yeah, I told him to let you know. It was because Harry Moore said that you were hangin' around his nanny and Marigold Smith. He made it sound as if you were plannin' on takin' one of 'em away."

"I would never hurt anyone, Mister Ferguson."

"You can tell that to Mort when he wakes up. But what were you even doin' here in the first place? You were supposed to be outta sight."

"I was until the rains came, then I was moving faster than your train, so I stayed out of sight as I passed to the south. I was about a mile or so ahead of the front wagon when I spotted the Indians. I didn't know what was going to happen, so I grabbed one of my rifles and my Henry and tried to get here before they did in case I could help."

"I noticed the Henry. Where'd you get it? I ain't seen one up close before."

"It was a gift from a Yankee captain."

Bo knew there was a story behind the gift, but that would have to wait. He needed to figure out what to do with the kid first.

He looked up at Joe and said, "I don't blame you for shootin' Mort. If I'd seen him pullin' his pistol, I woulda killed him. But you only wounded him and that gives me my own headache. I'm short a scout and when Mort is able to ride, he'll be lookin' to pay you back."

"I think he wanted to shoot me before if he could. When he told me that you wanted me to stay out of sight, he warned me that you said I'd be shot if I was seen again."

Bo let out a breath before he replied, "I didn't tell him that, but I'm sure he said it."

Joe quickly said, "Until you get your scout back, I can stay a few miles ahead of the wagons to act like a scout, but I'll want to camp closer each night. After he's better, I'll just follow behind again, but I won't stay out of sight. I have my dog to warn me if he tries anything."

Bo's eyebrows rose slightly before he asked, "Are you sure that you don't want to ride? I have two spare horses and an extra saddle."

"No, sir. I don't want to leave my cart. I'm used to walking anyway."

"Well, I appreciate the offer and I'll take you up on it. I hope you don't take offense, but I don't remember your name."

"It's Joe Beck and I'm not offended. I only spoke to you for a minute or so and that was more than a week ago."

Bo offered his hand and as he and Joe shook, he said, "I'm glad to meet ya, Joe."

Joe grinned before he said, "I'm going to get my cart and my dog, then I'll catch up to you."

"That's fine. Chuck will be handling the scouting duties for the rest of the day. We won't have any trouble with the Pawnee, thanks to you."

Joe nodded then turned and started walking toward his distant cart. He glanced at the back of the Moore wagon and wondered if Faith was able to see him. Even though he knew it was unlikely because of the sharp angle, he lifted his Henry over his head and smiled before he lowered the carbine and entered the tall grass.

Faith hadn't been able to see him, but when she saw the Indians leave with their critters then spotted a smiling Bo Ferguson, she suspected that it wouldn't be long before she saw him again.

———

In the front wagon, Chuck grinned down at Mort as he moaned and touched his head wound.

Mort focused on Chuck and asked, "What the hell happened? Did one of them Injuns shoot me?"

"Nope. That tall kid you pissed off did. He said he just wanted to shoot your hat off your head but was a bit low."

Mort exclaimed, "*That bastard shot me?* Where's my hat?"

"I imagine the boss is gonna bring it back when he shows up. He wasn't very happy when I told him that you were gonna shoot that Pawnee."

"That damned redskin laughed at me! He deserved a bullet, and I was gonna shoot every one of those bastards for laughin', too!"

"Really, Mort? Let me see. There were eight Pawnee, and I don't think your Colt is an eight-shooter. Maybe you figgered that the other two would wait for you to reload."

Mort snapped, "Shut up!"

UNWANTED

Then he made the mistake of suddenly trying to sit up. A wave of nauseating dizziness overcame him, and he collapsed back onto the wagon's floor.

Chuck snickered but before he could poke Mort with another witty rejoinder, he felt the wagon shake and waited for Bo to step onto the driver's seat. He wondered what he had decided to do with the kid. He thought he might even go as far as sending Mort back to Kansas City on his lonesome and offer the scouting job to the tall boy. After talking to him, Chuck found that he liked the kid and if he'd really tried to shoot the hat off of Mort's head, then Chuck would feel a lot safer having him covering his back. He'd also noticed Joe's unfired Henry which made him even more valuable.

Bo clambered onto the driver's seat and stared down at Mort who was already defiantly glaring back at him.

He tossed Mort's abused hat onto his chest then said, "You're really lucky, Mort. If I'd seen you pullin' that Colt, I woulda put a .44 up your nose."

Mort glanced at the big hole in his hat before he sharply snapped, "You're too nice to them Indians, Bo! Somebody's gotta show 'em who's boss."

"If you had shot that Pawnee, they woulda let loose and a lotta folks woulda died. Then anyone still livin' would have to head back to Kansas City before the entire tribe came lookin' for blood. I gotta side with that Pawnee chief. You're just plain stupid, Mort."

Mort paused long enough to control his anger before he asked, "Are you gonna send me away and try to make it all the way to Oregon with one scout? Or are you gonna hire that skinny kid?"

"I actually thought about it, but I'll give you one more chance to do what you're bein' paid to do. Joe Beck will be on point with his cart until you can ride. Then he'll follow a hundred yards back. You won't bother him at all, and I'll give him permission to shoot you if you do. You've got a couple of days to come around, Mort. I ain't gonna give you another chance."

Mort thought about just leaving anyway but didn't like the idea of riding all the way to Kansas City on his own, especially after angering the Pawnee.

He managed to hide his growing rage as he almost meekly replied, "Okay, boss."

Bo wasn't sure that Mort would really mend his ways, but he needed a second scout and Joe Beck seemed adamant about staying with that odd tent-cart of his.

He said, "Chuck, I'll go talk to the men and get these wagons rolling. You can ride point on your own until Mort can ride again. You shouldn't have any problems while we're in

UNWANTED

Pawnee territory and we should spot the Platte late tomorrow or the next day."

Chuck nodded then waited for the wagon master to leave the driver's seat before he clambered down behind him to mount his gray gelding.

Bo watched the Pawnee drive their bounty away before he started back to talk to the group of men waiting to learn what he had happened and what he would do. He glanced to the south and saw Joe Beck in the distance and smiled. He no longer doubted that he really had tried to shoot Mort's hat from his head.

As he approached the large group, Bo knew that some of the men had witnessed what had happened, so he couldn't gloss over Mort's poor judgement.

After he stopped, Bo said, "We almost had a small war with the Pawnee when Mort Jones got mad 'cause the Indians laughed at him. That tall young feller heading south to get his cart is named Joe Beck. He saw Mort goin' for his gun and shot his hat off to stop him. He was a little low and his bullet creased the top of Mort's head. He'll be alright, but we all owe Mister Beck. If he hadn't taken that shot, there woulda been hell to pay."

Harry quickly asked, "What are you going to do with him?"

"I was close to sendin' him back to Kansas City, but I figured I'd give him one more chance."

Harry exclaimed, *"He almost killed your scout and you're letting him stay nearby? That's crazy talk!"*

Bo grinned as he replied, "I was talkin' about Mort, but Joe Beck is gonna act as a scout out front until Mort can ride. Then I told him he could go wherever he wanted."

"But I already told you about the danger he poses to my nanny and Miss Smith."

"I don't reckon he's a danger to any woman, Harry. But if Miss Goodchild wants to talk or even dally with Joe Beck, that's up to her. Just because you paid her pa to be your nanny doesn't mean she's gotta do what you tell her. You don't own her, Harry."

Harry was mortified when the wagon master mentioned that he had paid Faith's father but shouldn't have been. Most of them had seen her standing with the sign around her neck before they left Kansas City.

While Harry stood in silence, Ben Smith said, "I met him when he gave us a large sack of venison and I thought he was very polite."

Bo nodded then said, "Alright. We're wastin' time just talkin'. Let's get ready to start movin' again and we can talk when we set up camp."

As the men quickly hurried back to their wagons, Bo focused on Harry Moore and wondered why he seemed to almost hate Joe Beck. If he didn't know better, he'd swear that Moore was jealous. Bo then turned and headed back to the lead wagon where he'd check on Mort.

By the time Joe reached Newt, Bernie and his cart, the wagon train had been rolling for twenty minutes. He slid his dirty Mississippi and his clean Henry into their bedroll scabbards then pulled out his oak walking stick. He tapped Bernie's haunch and the donkey began pulling the tent-cart in the direction of the wagon train.

Newt was out front already, so Joe looked at the jack and said, "I think I made a bigger enemy out of Mort even if he didn't hate me already, Bernie. If those Indians made him that mad just by laughing at him, I reckon that I made him close to crazy. What makes it kinda scary is that he was going to shoot that Indian with seven more of them right there. That means either he's not very smart or he doesn't care if he dies. Either way, he's a lot more dangerous than those Indians."

Joe wasn't about to change his plans for staying close to the Moore wagon so he could talk to Faith, but he'd have to stay aware of Mort's location until he set up camp. Then he'd have to depend on Newt's nose.

They were gaining on the wagons when Joe said, "Maybe I should set up some booby traps each night. Nothing fancy, just a few holes covered with branches from the cart. Then I'll put them back in the morning. I don't think I'll run out of wood before he tries to kill me, either. I figure Mort's the kind of man who doesn't have a lot of patience, so I probably won't need the booby traps for more than a week."

Then he looked at the donkey and laughed before saying, "You sure are a good listener, Bernie."

———

Harry was sitting on the driver's seat holding the reins as his oxen plodded behind the Smith's wagon. As the wagon trundled along, he had been watching Joe Beck drawing closer. He hadn't spoken to Mary since he returned because Faith was nearby. He could have told her to mind the goats but knew that she'd probably see Joe Beck and that might create a bigger problem.

He had to figure out how to get the kid out of the picture but realized that Bo Ferguson seemed to trust him and so did his other scout. What made it worse was hearing the other men talking about the kid as if he was a damned hero.

Harry finally realized that he couldn't prevent Faith from talking to Joe Beck, so he had to come up with some other way end their relationship. He was still thinking when he let his eyes wander to Marigold Smith who was walking beside their wagon with her twelve-year-old brother Jimmy and her seven-year-old sister Libby.

UNWANTED

Marigold was much a more physically developed and livelier girl than Faith and he knew that she was probably just as smitten with Beck as Faith was. Harry saw her as the perfect weapon to drive Faith away from Joe Beck without realizing that his wife was already working on how to inspire Marigold.

———

Faith had been watching out the back of the wagon at the herds and was hoping to see Joe again. She normally would have been out with the goats at this time of day but was pretty sure why Mister Moore hadn't told her to leave. After learning that he had been the one who had complained about Joe, she realized that he didn't want her talking to Joe anymore.

But she didn't understand his motive for making the complaint. She would still be herding the goats while she talked to Joe and even if she visited him in his camp, it was only after the boys were asleep. Mrs. Moore wasn't due for another two weeks and seemed to be doing better than she'd been when they started out, so that wasn't the reason. Whatever it was no longer mattered now that Joe was back. When she saw him again, she'd just leave the wagon because Mister Moore didn't own her.

———

It was an hour later when Joe reached the herds and was able to look inside the Moores' wagon. He couldn't see inside the shadows but waved, hoping that Faith was watching.

Faith saw him even before he waved and had already been shifting the boys out of the way. She was crawling over their belongings before she snatched her walking stick near the back then sat on the tailgate momentarily before she dropped onto the ground. She expected to hear loud protests from Mrs. Moore but didn't care as she hurriedly walked towards Joe.

Mary hadn't said a word because she had expected Faith to leave and needed to talk to her husband alone anyway.

Joe was already smiling before Faith's feet touched the ground and it continued to grow as he watched her walk quickly towards him. She was carrying her walking stick but wasn't using it for its primary purpose. Faith was grasping the center of the rod almost as if she was going to use it as a spear.

Faith wasn't about to spear Joe but was walking too fast and thought the walking stick would slow her down. When she finally reached Joe as he walked beside his donkey, she turned and matched his speed before finally dropping the point of the walking stick to the ground.

"What happened, Joe?"

Joe grinned as he replied, "It's nice to see you too, Faith. What happening are you asking about? My vanishing act or my missed shot at Mort's hat?"

Faith stopped abruptly before hurrying to catch up again then asked, "Did you kill him?"

Joe was a bit surprised when he looked down at Faith then said, "No, but I thought you would have heard the story by now."

She shook her head before saying, "I watched some of what happened from inside the wagon, but Mister Moore didn't tell me what happened when he returned. I saw Chuck Lynch carrying Mort away and thought you'd killed him but didn't know why."

"I already had his hat in my rifle's sights when I saw him pulling his pistol to shoot one of the Indians. I guess my tired arms let my rifle drop a little bit when I fired, and my bullet grazed the top of his head. Mister Ferguson said he'd be alright after a few days."

"Are you going to have to disappear again?"

"No, ma'am. I'll be out front with the other scout until Mort can ride again, but I'll set up my camp about a hundred yards behind your wagon each night. Mister Ferguson told me that I could go wherever I wanted, so I guess I'll be annoying you a lot more now."

Faith laughed then said, "You're not annoying at all, Joe. At least not to me. I think Mister Moore doesn't want you around, though."

"Neither does Mort, but I'll be alright. I just heard that it was Mister Moore who complained to Mister Ferguson in the first place. Does Mrs. Moore need a nanny that badly?"

"She's going to have another baby soon and I guess he's worried about her. But I need to tell you something that I should have mentioned already when you said something about them not paying me enough."

"Do they pay you more than ten dollars a month?"

Faith sighed then answered, "No. They don't pay me at all. I was kind of sold to Mister Moore in Kansas City. The day before you arrived, I was standing with my father in front of the supply store with a sign around my neck. If someone paid my father sixty dollars, they could take me along as a nanny or anything else they wanted me to do."

It was Joe's turn to momentarily freeze then take two long strides to catch up before he quietly exclaimed, "*Your father sold you?*"

Faith nodded then replied, "We had a large family, and I was the oldest and a girl. I guess my parents thought that I soon would be leaving home anyway, so they may as well profit when I did. It was humiliating enough standing there with that sign dangling in front of me as if I was a tired mule, but what made it much worse was when my father bargained my sales price with Mister Moore."

Joe asked, "How much did he pay your father?"

"Twenty-five dollars."

Joe felt a surge of anger but didn't let Faith see it before he said, "You don't owe the Moores anything, Faith. You're free to do as you choose just as much as I am. Why didn't you tell me before?"

"I thought you might think that I was, I don't know, a kept woman."

"I wouldn't think that of you, Faith. Besides, you're Faith Hope Charity Virtue Goodchild. How could you possibly be a kept woman?"

Faith was immensely relieved as she laughed then said, "Thank you, Joe. Now can you tell me about everything I missed earlier today?"

Joe nodded then began his story by saying, "After the rains, I decided to stay out of sight, but ahead of the wagons. I was walking about a mile ahead when I saw a band of Indians…"

As he spoke, Faith listened intently but focused on the Moores' wagon. She knew that Mrs. Moore was watching but it no longer mattered.

Joe was also watching the wagon but was expecting to see Mister Moore's head pop around the front to glare at him. He continued to explain the events and by the time he was almost finished, he still hadn't seen Mister Moore and that actually concerned him. It wasn't consistent with his earlier behavior and what Faith had just told him.

Joe finished his story when he said, "…and he even offered me the use of one of his horses, but I told him that I'd rather walk."

Faith smiled as she said, "I'm happy that you're walking now, Joe."

Joe nodded then quickly said, "Keep walking. I'll be right back. I have a present for you."

Faith's eyebrows rose slightly, but she just replied, "Okay."

Joe turned and waited for Bernie to pull the cart past him before walking behind the tent-cart and pulling out his folded slicker.

He quickly returned to Faith and held it out to her as he said, "I have two more that I haven't cut up yet, so I thought you'd like to have one to keep you dry when the spring rains return."

She accepted the rubberized cloth and said, "Thank you, Joe. Did you scavenge this one from those Confederate soldiers?"

"Yes, ma'am. If that bothers you, then I'll take it back."

"No, no. It doesn't bother me at all. I was just asking because Mrs. Moore called me foolish for believing you when you told me that you'd shot eight soldiers without being shot yourself."

"It is kind of unbelievable, but if you look inside, you'll find the CSA stamp to prove your point."

"I believed you, Joe. But it will be nice to show Mrs. Moore those letters. She and her husband both seem to think poorly of you without cause, Joe. I first thought it was because they were worried about me, but that didn't last long. Then I figured it was because they didn't want to lose my services, but now I'm not so sure."

"I noticed that Mister Moore wasn't fond of me when I offered him the venison. There was no real reason to decline the offer and Mister Smith was very happy to have the meat. I think Marigold was just happy to see me, too. Do you talk to her at all?"

"I do, and you're right that she was happy to see you."

After a short pause, Faith quietly asked, "Are you interested in Marigold? She is your age and more, um, developed than me."

Joe smiled as he replied, "I noticed, but to be honest, she actually scares me. I don't know why, either."

Faith laughed before saying, "I find it hard to believe that anyone or anything could scare you, Joe. But I'm not ashamed to admit that I'm pleased to know that you aren't interested in her."

Joe was growing uncomfortable with the direction of the conversation, so he said, "I find it hard to believe that your father would sell you like that. How could he stand next to you like a snake oil salesman trying to convince strangers to buy what he was selling?"

"I was surprised myself. I didn't see it coming until he told me to pack my things. My mother didn't say anything, and I wasn't even allowed to say a proper goodbye to my brothers and sisters. I guess they just didn't want me anymore."

They walked in silence for a minute or so before Joe said, "I know what it's like to be unwanted, Faith. I knew the moment that I set foot on my uncle's farm that I was unwelcome. The only reason they kept me there was because of the promise my aunt had made to my mother before she died. My uncle and my cousins stripped our farm of anything they wanted and sold it, but I all I had was my father's Mississippi rifle and my clothes.

"I lived in the barn and worked on their farm more as a hired hand than a relative. They grudgingly fed me and gave me hand-me-downs as I grew, but I used my father's rifle to hunt so I could eat better. I knew that I'd be banned from the farm when my uncle died, and I really didn't care.

UNWANTED

"All that mattered to me was my father's rifle. I had hidden it in the barn's loft and after my uncle's burial, I tried to get there before my cousin. But I was too late. I left with only my clothing and a remembrance of my parents that I had hidden, and they didn't even know existed. Losing the rifle really hurt and it wasn't just because I couldn't hunt."

Faith softly asked, "Is that why you kept those two rifles and traded the others?"

"Yes. They're the same model but they still don't replace my father's. For a while I even thought about taking them to the Quimby farm and trading them both for my father's gun but figured my cousin Jeremy would ask for a lot more. The other reason I didn't go was because I thought that Jeremy hadn't taken good care of the rifle and it would anger me to see it corroded or broken."

"Can I visit you in your camp tonight, Joe?"

"I'd be disappointed if you didn't, Faith."

Faith hesitatingly asked, "Joe, if I had to leave the Moores, could I, um, stay with you?"

Joe should have expected the question, but he hadn't and was stunned into an awkward silence.

Faith quickly said, "I'm sorry, Joe. I shouldn't have asked you that question."

Joe had recovered sufficiently to say, "No, it's okay. You just took me by surprise, that's all. I hadn't thought about it because until a few minutes ago, I thought the Moores were paying you to be their nanny."

"I'm still sorry for shocking you that way. Can you forget that I asked?"

"No, I can't, and I don't want to forget. But if you feel afraid for any reason, find me and tell me what happened. If you need to stay with me, you can. I'll always protect you, Faith. Okay?"

Faith nodded then replied, "Alright. I promise that I'll only ask if things get out of hand."

"But that doesn't mean you can't talk to me or visit my camp, Faith."

"I wasn't about to stop seeing you, Joe. I just wanted to warn you ahead of time. If I do have to leave the Moores, I think it might cause trouble for you, too."

"I'm not worried about anything that might happen. I already have Mort to worry about, anyway. Don't let your concerns about possible trouble keep you from leaving. Okay?"

Faith was relieved as she said, "Okay."

Joe grinned as he looked down at her and said, "Good."

UNWANTED

After Faith left the wagon, Mary turned to her husband and asked, "What did Ferguson tell you, Harry?"

Harry kept his eyes on the Smith wagon as he relayed Bo's version of events. He then told her about the problems that Joe Beck now posed and his plan to inject Marigold Smith into the picture. Mary was surprised that Harry had come up with the idea because he was a man but didn't tell him that she had already thought of it. She let him have his pride of discovery and agreed that it was perfect. She told him that she'd start nudging Marigold in Joe Beck's direction when they stopped for the night.

Neither believed it would be difficult to convince Marigold to visit Joe Beck but needed to pick the right time and ensure that Faith remained in the wagon. What they hadn't understood was the growing friendship between the two young women.

Totally unaware of the plot being devised a hundred yards ahead of them, Joe and Faith continued their conversation after crossing the Monumental Divide that had been created when Faith had asked if she could stay with him.

The sun was low in the sky when Joe said, "I'm surprised that Mrs. Moore hasn't called you back yet. I would have thought that the small boy would have required your attention by now."

"You're right that William probably needs a new diaper by now, but I have no idea why Mrs. Moore hasn't asked me to return."

"Their oldest boy seems to be pretty adventurous. His name is John; isn't it?"

"I'm impressed that you remembered his name. And yes, he is very much a little boy. After I saw you with your two rifles as you talked to Chuck Lynch, I asked Mrs. Moore if she'd seen it. She came close to accusing you of being a rabid murderer and said I should have been grateful that her husband had you sent away. After I argued with her, John asked me if you were brave, and I told him you were very brave and then just to annoy Mrs. Moore, I told John about how you'd faced eight Confederate soldiers and shot all of them."

Joe interrupted her as he said, "That might not have been very wise, Faith."

"I know, but she really irritated me. Then she accused me of being a foolish young girl for believing you as it was impossible to shoot that many times without being shot. Even after I told her that you'd used a repeater, she still seemed to believe you to be one step away from being Satan himself."

Joe nodded as he looked at the back of the Moore wagon with a different perspective. After learning of Faith's true status, he suspected that there might be an ulterior motive for parting with the twenty-five dollars. As he stared at the rolling wagon, he was trying to imagine what it could be. If Mister Moore had been a widower, then there would be no question of his motive. But Mrs. Moore was about to deliver their fourth child, so that couldn't be the reason.

Then, just an instant later, Joe had a stunning and almost despicable epiphany. He quickly turned to look down at Faith and asked, "How is Mrs. Moore doing?"

Faith was curious why Joe had asked the question but replied, "Just as I already mentioned, she was almost sickly when we started, but she's doing much better now."

"I'm sorry that I forgot about that. When is she going to have her baby?"

"I think it's two weeks or so. Is it important?"

"I'm not sure. I was trying to think of an excuse for their somewhat strange behavior. First, they refused my offer of the fresh venison, then Mister Moore complained to Mister Ferguson and had him banish me from sight. I thought it was just odd until you said that Mister Moore had paid your father rather than hiring you as a nanny."

"Why would that make a difference?"

"I think they believe that they own you and you have to do whatever they say."

"They know different now, Joe. But even so, what do you think they expected of me?"

"If Mister Moore had been a widower, it would have been obvious that he would have wanted to have you for a wife and mother to his boys. But he's married and his wife is about to deliver another child, so I discarded that as the motive. But then I had a startling thought. What if they're preparing for the possibility that she doesn't survive the childbirth?"

Faith's mouth dropped open before she exclaimed, "*What?*"

"I know it sounds bizarre, but childbirth is very dangerous for women. I'm sure you know that. Mrs. Moore isn't even five feet tall, and she'll be giving birth in a wagon rolling across the plains. I imagine she and her husband both recognize the very real possibility that he may become a widower with at least three children to raise. You live with them and know them much better than I do, so does that seem possible?"

Faith was about to quickly deny the likelihood but before she answered, she thought about it. As they continued to walk beside Bernie, Faith began to look at the Moores differently. She had always seen them as a family but now separated the three boys from their parents before she examined Mister and Mrs. Moore as individuals.

As Joe watched Faith, he was growing more convinced that he was right but wondered if she would accept it as at least a possibility. When he saw her eyes begin to widen, he knew that he had his answer before she spoke.

Faith turned her big blue eyes to look at him as she said, "I think you're right. Now that you asked about it, I recalled the first time I saw the Moores. I was standing there with that sign hanging from my neck when they passed slowly by, and Mrs. Moore looked at her husband and said something. At the time, I thought she was just saying how sad it was, but now I realize that she had almost studied me before she said it. What can I do about it?"

Joe stared at the Moores' wagon as he said, "I could be wrong, Faith. But there's no reason to panic. I'll be close now. What you have to do is to pretend that I never mentioned it. Just go about your days as you have been."

"How can I do that? I already feel sick just thinking about it."

"I'm sorry that I told you, but you can't change your behavior. What you can do is to pretend that you aren't you."

"What?"

"Make believe that you aren't involved at all. Pretend that you're like a sheriff investigating a crime. Observe what they do and say and look for clues to their intentions. Make it a mental game."

Faith sighed then said, "I'll try."

"For the next two or three days, I'll be way out front but before the sun goes down, I'll set up my camp nearby. After that, I'll always be visible. Okay?"

Faith smiled as she nodded and replied, "Alright. Thank you for making me feel safe, Joe."

"I promised that I would, Faith."

Joe then changed the topic to Newt who had returned from smelling the herd. Faith scratched his head and laughed when his tail began frenetically wagging.

She was still laughing when Joe spotted Marigold heading towards them and said, "I wouldn't tell Marigold about it, Faith."

Faith looked up from Newt, saw Marigold and replied, "I won't tell a soul."

Marigold was smiling broadly before she reached them then turned and matched their pace on Joe's left side. He felt somewhat awkward being framed by the two young women but couldn't help noticing how unalike they were. Even though he knew that they couldn't be more than a year apart in age, their physical differences were immense.

Marigold was probably four inches shorter than Faith's five feet and five inches. She dark brown hair and deep brown eyes as opposed to Faith's blonde hair and light blue eyes. But just as noticeable was Marigold's more mature figure. She appeared to be a woman while Faith looked like a girl. But physical characteristics isn't what made a girl a woman or a boy a man. Faith was much more mature in her character, and even with their limited conversation, Joe thought Marigold seemed much younger.

Marigold looked at Joe and said, "Everyone is talking about what you did, Joe. My father said that you saved everybody by stopping Mort from shooting the Indian. He even believes that you tried to shoot off his hat even though some think you just missed."

"I did miss. I hit the top of his head, but I guess it was better than just knocking off his hat. I should have thought of that. If I had been accurate, he'd still have his cocked pistol in his hand and would probably have shot one of the Indians anyway."

She then looked at Faith and said, "You must have seen it all from your wagon; didn't you, Faith?"

"Some of it, but not after Joe and Mister Ferguson walked away. I thought Mort was dead."

"I wish he was."

Then Marigold looked up at Joe and said, "He's going to want to kill you, Joe."

"I know. But I have Newt to warn me if he tries to sneak into my camp at night."

Marigold looked down at the hound and patted his head before saying, "He's a nice dog."

"He's a good friend, too."

As Faith watched Marigold rub Newt's head, she was surprised when she felt almost offended as if Marigold was taking over. What made it almost ridiculous was that she didn't feel that way when Marigold was smiling at Joe.

———

In the darkness of their crowded wagon, Mrs. Moore had seen Marigold arrive. Then she noticed how Marigold was smiling and chatting with Joe and realized that maybe she wouldn't have to nudge Marigold much at all.

She still focused on Joe and the two girls as she loudly said, "Marigold is already moving in, Harry. I'll still have a chat with her after supper, but I think it won't be too long before Joe Beck concentrates on Marigold and forgets about Faith. Then she'll have to stay with us."

Harry turned, smiled at his wife then said, "Let's hope that happens soon, Mary."

Mary then waddled to the back of the wagon and shouted, "Faith, I need your help!"

Harry grinned knowing that Mary wanted to give Marigold some private time with Joe Beck.

UNWANTED

While both Moores were happy with the improving situation, neither had paid any attention to four-year-old John who didn't understand why his mama wanted Joe Beck to not like Faith. He liked Faith, and Joe Beck was really brave and had a dog, too.

———

Faith heard Mrs. Moore's shout, looked at Joe and said, "I've got to go."

"I'm not surprised. I'll talk to you later, Sheriff Faith."

Faith laughed before she began trotting away.

Marigold was pleased to be able to talk to Joe alone and asked, "Why did you call her Sheriff Faith?"

"She asked me if I had been a deputy, which is kind of silly because I'm only sixteen. So, I asked her if she had been a sheriff."

Marigold giggled then said, "That is pretty silly. How did you learn to shoot like that?"

"I was hunting since I was eight or nine. When you're shooting a jackrabbit with a muzzle loader, you have to be accurate."

"I'm glad that you're a good shot. I like your walking stick, too. It's different; isn't it?"

"Yes, ma'am. This one is oak and has a knot for a knob."

"I wish I had one sometimes."

"Hold on. Just wait here."

Marigold stopped and was surprised when Joe stayed beside her as Bernie continued plodding along. A few seconds later, Joe sidestepped then reached into his cart and pulled out his old walking stick. Then he handed it to Marigold before they began to walk again.

Despite his advanced level of mental maturity, Joe was still deficient in the subject of women. By giving the walking stick to Marigold, he had unwittingly indicated an interest.

As she walked with her new walking stick, she smiled and said, "Thank you, Joe. This is much better. My father said that you'd be staying close again. Will you be walking behind the wagons now?"

Joe suddenly realized his innocent blunder but didn't want to be rude, so he replied, "Yes, ma'am."

"Call me Mary, Joe."

"Alright."

After Faith had climbed into the Moore's wagon, she asked, "What do you need, Mrs. Moore?"

"I'm getting very tired, so I need to rest before we pull up for the night."

"Yes, ma'am."

Mary smiled as she closed her eyes and Faith squeezed in between John and Alfred then put William on her lap. She was able to watch Joe and Marigold through the back of the wagon and noticed that Marigold was using a walking stick. She knew Joe had given it to her and it stung. She saw Marigold laughing and chatting with Joe and was more hurt than jealous. She was suddenly painfully aware of her thin figure and knew there was nothing she could do about it.

It was torture to watch Marigold taking her place with Joe, but she still focused on them. She even forgot about her recent revelation about the Moores' motive for buying her.

Joe may have been smiling as he listened to Marigold chatter about subjects that held no interest for him, but he wished that Faith was still there. Marigold had included praise and compliments as she talked, but to Joe, they meant nothing. It was as if she was trying to force him to compliment her. After he realized his mistake for giving her the walking stick, he wasn't about to compound it by telling her that she was pretty, even though she was.

It was late afternoon, and he was wishing that the sun would hurry to bed when Marigold said, "I suppose my parents are wondering where I am, so I'd better get back. Thank you for my walking stick, Joe."

Joe was relieved as he replied, "You're welcome, Mary."

She smiled at him before hurrying away leaving Joe with just Newt and Bernie, which he felt was an improvement.

After she'd passed the Moore wagon, Joe said, "Newt, I think I just created a whole new problem. At least she won't try to shoot me."

―――

About twenty minutes later, Chuck Lynch returned from his scouting duties and then after rolling for another mile, the wagons began pulling up for the night.

Joe was about to turn Bernie to the south when he spotted Mister Ferguson striding towards him and hoped it wasn't to deliver any bad news.

He held up and as he waited for the wagon master to reach him, he wondered if Mister Moore had made another complaint after seeing him walking with Faith. Maybe Marigold's father had registered his objections. It was only when he saw Mister Ferguson's face that he realized he wasn't in trouble.

UNWANTED

When Bo reached Joe, he said, "I wanted to talk to you while they're setting up camp. Mind if I come along while you make yours?"

"No, sir."

Joe turned Bernie and then started him south before Bo asked, "What made you decide to follow my wagon train in the first place?"

"I had no place to stay and no one to talk to anyway, so I figured I may as well head west just to see what's out there."

"There ain't much out there except Indians and buffalo, at least until you cross the mountains."

"I've never seen any buffalo or mountains and only saw my first Indians today."

"Those were Pawnee and they're more reasonable than the Arapahoe or the Ogallala Sioux. The Cheyenne and the Crow are even worse. And now that those forts have been stripped, it could be real dangerous."

"Then why didn't you hire more scouts?"

"A lot of those settlers asked me the same thing and I told them I'd hire a couple more, but it would cost them another four hundred dollars and they changed their mind. That's one of the reasons I wanted to talk to you."

After Joe realized that he wasn't in trouble, he suspected that having only one useful scout might be the real reason for the wagon master's visit.

Bo continued, saying, "Now you're comin' along anyway, and I can't pay you, but I'll give you a horse and saddle if you'll agree to act as a scout."

"I don't think Mort would like that, Mister Ferguson. He'd probably shoot me as soon as look at me."

"You're right about that. I spent a while tryin' to tell him he was lucky you were such a good shot, but I don't reckon that he agreed with me. He didn't argue, but he's convinced that you meant to kill him. I can't afford to let him go, especially this far from Kansas City. I need his gun out front, but if you take my offer, you can ride on the south point with Chuck in between you and Mort. That'll put about a mile of space between you and Mort. What do you say?"

Joe scratched his stubbly cheek as he said, "I can't just leave my cart and hope my donkey follows the wagons on his own."

"I know that, but I already asked Ben Smith if he could have one of his boys lead your cart near the herds. They have to watch their critters anyway."

They were walking through the tall grass as Joe thought about it. His only concern now was his possessions. *Could he trust a boy he never met not to rummage through his supplies?*

He was still thinking when he pulled Bernie to a stop then said, "I don't know Mister Smith or his boys. Do you think that my supplies would be safe?"

"Yup. I trust Ben Smith and his boys seemed kinda honored just to be asked. I reckon that you're like a hero to 'em after hearin' about that shot."

"Alright. I'll see how it works."

Bo grinned before he slapped Joe on the right shoulder and said, "I'll bring the horse and saddle in a little while. I'll adjust the stirrups, too. You gotta be a couple of inches over six feet and I reckon you might have more growin' to do."

"I hope not. I already outgrew my boots, and they still have a lot of leather on the soles."

"Do you have another pair?"

"Yes, sir. Two more pairs."

"Good thinkin'. I'll see you again shortly."

Bo waved then trotted away making a path through the tall grass. Joe smiled knowing that it hadn't been good planning on his part that had provided the extra pairs of boots.

Joe looked at Bernie and said, "I'll be riding now, Bernie. But that doesn't mean I'll abandon you. You'll just have new company."

Then he looked down at Newt and wondered if he should have the hound come with him, but decided he'd be more useful if he stayed with the cart. He wouldn't have to walk so far or at such a fast pace, either. It was just a question of making him understand his new assignment.

He unharnessed Bernie and led him to a small pond that would be dry in another month then walked back to the cart as the donkey drank his fill.

When Joe reached the back of the cart, he removed the shovel and began digging his fire pit. After days of trying to stay out of sight, he was looking forward to having a hot meal.

After returning the spade, he pulled out some of the branches and began breaking them into smaller pieces as he looked at the wagon train. He hoped that Faith was able to avoid blurting out an accusation when she was with the Moores. If that happened, she might not be allowed to leave the wagon. He debated about visiting the wagons if she hadn't arrived in a couple of hours. He could use the excuse of wanting to talk to the Smith boys who would be watching his cart, but that would probably give Marigold the idea that he really wanted to see her.

UNWANTED

Joe selected his supper ingredients then tossed a large piece of jerky to Newt before he began to prepare his dinner. He needed to do some more hunting and now that he'd be on horseback, he'd have a much better view and be able to spot larger game.

He was stirring the odd mix in his frypan when he spotted Bo Ferguson leading a horse his way. Joe had only ridden a mule and that was years ago. He hoped he didn't make a fool of himself when he mounted the horse in the morning.

As the wagon master drew closer, Bernie trotted towards the horse and Joe suddenly realized he had an unexpected problem. The horse was a mare and Bernie obviously was planning on doing his part in creating a mule.

Joe pulled the frypan from the grid then trotted to catch Bernie before he introduced himself to the mare.

He'd just grabbed hold of Bernie's halter when Bo laughed and said, "I woulda brought you the gelding, but the mare is younger and she's prettier, too."

Joe said, "Let me tie off Bernie so they don't get busy."

After he yanked the love-stricken jack back to the cart and tied him to the right wheel, he returned to the wagon master.

Joe rubbed the mare's nose as he said, "She's a pretty horse. What's her name?"

"I call her Bessie, but I don't think she cares much. Her shoes are in pretty good shape, so you won't need to change 'em for a while."

"Does she even need shoes? The Indians don't shoe their horses and Bernie is doing fine without them, too."

"I reckon you're right. I lowered the stirrups for ya, so do you need anythin' else?"

Joe looked at the setup and asked, "Do you have an extra scabbard? If you don't, I can tie on a bedroll and slide my Henry inside."

"Sorry, I only have that one and mine. I don't figure Mort would be willin' to give you his."

Joe grinned as he replied, "I reckon not."

Bo then asked, "Mind if I look at your Henry? I've never seen one before."

Joe nodded, said, "Sure," then walked to his cart and slid the Henry from its bedroll and took the mare's reins before handing it to the wagon master.

Bo grinned as he looked at the carbine then asked, "Mind if I take a shot or two?"

"Go ahead. I have four boxes of cartridges for it. There are fifteen in the magazine tube, and one is already in the chamber."

UNWANTED

Bo cocked the hammer and aimed the carbine to the south but in the fading light, he wasn't able to pick out a specific target. He squeezed the trigger then rapidly cycled in a second round and fired again.

Joe watched the second muzzle flare and hoped that Bo didn't take a third shot. He may have four boxes of .44 cartridges but didn't want to use his supply so frivolously.

Bo lowered the repeater and handed it back to Joe as he said, "It shoots real nice, Joe. There ain't much kick, either. I just wanted to see how fast I could get off a second shot. I appreciate you lettin' me try it out."

"You're welcome, Mister Ferguson."

"Call me Bo. You may only be sixteen, but you sure behave a lot older. Mort acts more like a teenager than you do."

"I guess that's because I've been on my own for so long. It kind of drove the boy out of me."

"I'm glad it did, Joe. I'll bring the two Smith boys over before we start rollin' in the mornin'."

Joe asked, "What did Mort say when you told him?"

"I figured that I'd tell him and Chuck about it in the mornin'."

"I reckon Mort isn't going to be very pleased."

"That's his problem…and yours, I guess. I'll see you tomorrow, Joe. I really appreciate you helpin' me."

Joe nodded as Bo turned to leave, but then stopped and looked back at Joe and said, "I reckon that you're kinda smitten with Faith Goodchild, but do you know her situation?"

"That they paid her father twenty-five dollars for her?"

"Yeah. That and Harry Moore seems to be kinda jealous about you talkin' to her."

"I know," Joe replied then asked, "Bo, do you think that Mister Moore brought her along in case his wife died when she had their baby? You know, to take her place?"

Bo's eyebrows shot up before he answered, "Now that you mentioned it, I reckon that could be the reason he's tryin' to keep her away from you. But there's nothin' I can do about it."

"I know. I just asked because you know them better than I do."

"You just keep talkin' to Faith and I figure she'll be okay. Oh, and I reckon that Marigold Smith has her cap set for you, too."

"It took me a while to figure that out, so that's a much different problem for me to handle than Mort."

Bo smacked him on the shoulder then said, "Take care of Bessie. She's yours now."

UNWANTED

"I will."

Bo strode through the grass leaving Joe holding Bessie's reins and his dirty Henry. He led her to the back of the cart, set his carbine down then pulled her away from Bernie before he began examining the mare.

She wasn't a powerfully built animal, but she was handsome. She was a chestnut brown with a black tail and mane. Her face sported a large, white, four-pointed star whose tips just kissed her large brown eyes.

Bessie stared back at Joe as he said, "After I introduce you to Newt, I'll take off your saddle and tie you off on the other side of the cart. I hope you and Bernie don't rip it apart."

Joe snickered then began unsaddling Bessie and squeezing the tack into his cart as Bernie watched closely and Newt sniffed in the air near the mare at a safe distance.

After tying her reins to the cart's other wheel, Joe walked to the other side, stroked the donkey's nose and said, "Relax, Bernie. Pretty soon you and Bessie can go about creating a jack or jenny. Did you notice that your names are spelled the same except for the two middle letters? I reckon you were meant to be together."

Joe laughed then walked to his smoldering fire and quickly devoured his cooling supper before returning to the cart and pulling out a length of thick cord. He soon created a halter and after removing Bessie's bridle, he attached the halter and led her to the pond.

As the mare drank, Joe knew he'd have to figure a permanent way of taking care of the horse. With the paucity of trees, he figured he'd use his trusty collection of bayonets to create a portable hitching post.

―――

Faith was helping Mrs. Moore prepare dinner when Mary rested her hand onto her bulge and said, "My legs are beginning to cramp, so I need to take a short walk. I should be back shortly."

Faith nodded as she replied, "Yes, ma'am," before Mrs. Moore slowly walked away.

Faith continued preparing the family's supper and didn't pay attention to where Mrs. Moore was going. She was relieved that she'd been able to follow Joe's advice but appreciated each minute she wasn't around either Mister or Mrs. Moore. William was already asleep in the wagon and Mister Moore was checking on the goats, so she had John and Alfred both sitting on the ground watching her.

Faith was chopping an onion when John stood and asked, "Why don't you like Joe Beck anymore, Miss Faith?"

Faith stopped chopping before she looked down at John and said, "I still like Joe Beck very much. I even talked to him a long time this afternoon. Why did you think I didn't like him anymore?"

"'Cause mama told papa that Joe Beck would like Mary gold then you would stay with us. Were you gonna leave, Miss Faith?"

Faith glanced to her right and spotted Mrs. Moore with the Smiths before she looked back down at John and said, "No, John. I wasn't going to leave you."

John grinned then plopped back down before he said, "That's good."

Faith didn't know what to make of what John had just said. He was only four, so he could have totally misunderstood what his mother had said. But the fact that she had even mentioned Marigold set off warning bells. When she'd her and Joe walking together, Faith had been close to abandoning her planned visit to Joe's camp. Now it had become imperative. She had to know what was going on with Marigold.

After she'd reached the Smith's wagon, Mary had planned to engage Ben and Beatrice in a brief, mundane conversation before having a private chat with Marigold. That changed when Ben mentioned that Bo Ferguson had asked if Russell and Jimmy could walk with Joe Beck's cart while he rode out front as a scout. Mary had been more than mildly surprised by the news but hadn't pressed the issue for a very simple reason. While her legs weren't cramping, they were getting tired after carrying the extra weight around. She ended the conversation then drifted closer to Marigold who was talking to Russell about Joe Beck.

Mary was tired of hearing that boy's name but still managed a smile as she quietly asked, "Mary, may I speak to you for a minute, please?"

Marigold was surprised because Mrs. Moore had never asked to speak to her before but replied, "Yes, ma'am."

Mary then stepped a few feet away and Marigold followed, growing more curious with each step.

After they had a measure of privacy, Mary leaned closer and whispered, "Are you interested in Joe Beck, Mary?"

Marigold blushed and hesitated before softly replying, "Yes. But why did you ask?"

"I was just curious because I saw you walking with him this afternoon and he seemed to like you very much."

"Faith likes him, too."

"But she's just a thin girl and you already have a fine figure. I think you're prettier, too. I also know how much value boys and men place on a well-figured girl like you, Marigold."

Marigold smiled as she asked, "Do you think he likes me that way, Mrs. Moore?"

"Yes, I do. I'd better get back to help Faith feed the boys. Don't tell her I said anything. Okay?"

"I won't."

Mary smiled then headed back to her wagon thinking that she'd played Marigold like a fiddle. She might even sneak into Joe Beck's camp tonight.

As Marigold watched Mrs. Moore leave, she looked past her and saw Faith preparing the family's supper. She knew that Faith didn't have a good figure but believed that Mrs. Moore had been wrong when she said that she was prettier than Faith.

But what really bothered her about the unexpected visit was her transparent attempt at matchmaking. She returned to her family and would talk to Faith about it tomorrow. She may have liked Joe Beck, but she knew that Faith probably loved him, and she suspected that Joe felt the same way about Faith. The more she thought about it, the more determined she became to thwart whatever plans Mrs. Moore had. If Faith had confided in Marigold what she now believed was the Moores' motive, Marigold wouldn't have waited until the morning to talk to Faith.

Faith hadn't noticed Mrs. Moore's conversation with Marigold. If she had, she might have decided to grab her bag and leave. But after Mrs. Moore returned, Faith was just planning to have a long talk with Joe after supper.

Joe had washed his frypan and then cleaned and reloaded his Henry. After setting out his bedroll, Joe finally took out the smaller pair of boots that Captain Chalmers had sent to him. He smiled as he searched his clothes and found one of the unworn pair of socks and carried them back to the bedroll.

Newt watched as he slowly pulled off his work boots then after splashing some water from a canteen onto his feet, Joe began massaging them and noted the thick callouses.

He pulled on the thick socks then tugged on the tall, black leather boots. He was relieved to be able to wiggle his toes before he stood and carried his old boots to the cart and stored them near the front. He didn't know what he'd do with them but wasn't about to throw them out.

For the next few minutes, Joe paraded around his campsite getting used to the new boots. They were surprisingly comfortable, probably because of the high-quality leather. His old boots were thick, unfinished leather that had taken a beating over the past two years.

As he made his circuits, Newt trotted behind him as if it was a game while Joe kept looking toward the wagons hoping to see Faith heading his way. He had a lot to tell her now and wanted to know if she'd heard anything.

UNWANTED

Faith had finished cleaning up and was about to leave when Mary grimaced then put both hands over her swollen belly as she bent over.

"Faith, can you help me into the wagon?"

"Yes, ma'am."

As she helped Mrs. Moore up the side, she looked for Mister Moore, but he wasn't in sight.

Once Mrs. Moore was lying on her back on the narrow space, Faith asked, "Do you want me to get Mrs. Smith?"

Mary shook her head and replied, "Not yet. This could be false labor. I had them with Albert. I don't want to worry my husband, so could you just stay with me until the contractions get worse or go away?"

Faith nodded then said, "Yes, ma'am."

Mary smiled then grunted slightly before replying, "Thank you, Faith. You're a good girl."

Faith felt trapped. She wasn't sure if Mrs. Moore was really about to have her baby but couldn't assume that she was just faking it to keep her from seeing Joe. If she went into labor, then she'd have to find Mrs. Smith quickly then help with the delivery.

So, as Joe waited expectantly for her arrival, Faith sat in the dark wagon with a satisfied Mary Moore who wasn't having labor pains, real or otherwise. She was giving Marigold an open field. She also knew her husband wouldn't be back until it was too late for Faith to go anywhere.

Joe finally realized that Faith wouldn't be showing up and hoped that it wasn't because the Moores had learned of her suspicions. The suspicions he had planted.

He finally laid on top of his bedroll still wearing his gunbelt, coat and new boots. To take his mind off Faith, he looked at his tent-cart and revisited the issue of getting things wet when he crossed deep creeks or rivers. He stared at the odd tent for almost ten minutes before he suddenly grinned.

He said, "I'm not very smart. All this time, I was thinking of all sorts of ways to keep everything dry by covering it or coating it with grease and it was staring me in the face all this time."

He closed his eyes and began designing his new supports for his cart. He'd simply tie off one Mississippi rifle between the tent supports then run two lengths of cord between each set of heavy supports like double clothes lines. He'd hang his backpacks with his clothes and other necessities from the top ones and use the bottom ones to hold them in place. It would make the cart more top heavy, but not much. He'd worry about that issue when the wood was gone.

UNWANTED

With that issue finally settled, Joe closed his eyes and waited for sleep to take him, still wondering why Faith hadn't arrived.

CHAPTER 7

The sun hadn't risen, and Bo Ferguson hadn't rung his bell by the time Joe had saddled Bessie and harnessed Bernie before he washed and shaved at the tiny pond.

He had only grabbed a few pieces of jerky for breakfast and added some to his new saddlebags along with some crackers and one of the jars of pickles. He tied down a bedroll behind the saddle seat and slid the Henry inside before slipping one of the Mississippi rifles into the scabbard. He didn't bring any spare ammunition for the big muzzle loader but dropped the partially used box of Henry cartridges into the other saddlebag.

The sun had just sent its first rays of bright light across the plains when he led Bernie and Bessie away from his campsite toward the wagons. He hoped to see Faith outside milking a Moore cow. Her bright blonde hair made her easy to spot, but she wasn't there.

But he did see Bo walking towards him flanked by the two Smith brothers. He couldn't recall how many Smith youngsters there were, but guessed the older brother was a couple of years younger than he was and the other one was about eleven or twelve years old.

UNWANTED

He pulled Bernie and Bessie to a stop, but Newt continued to trot towards the wagon master and the boys to give them a sniff of approval.

Russ and Jimmy both grinned when Newt arrived, and Jimmy began patting his head as they approached Joe.

Bo said, "Joe, this is Russell Smith and his brother Jimmy. They'll keep an eye on your cart while you're out front."

Joe shook Russell's hand then Jimmy's before Jimmy asked, "Are you taking your dog with you, Mister Beck?"

Joe grinned as he replied, "Nope. I was going to leave him with you, so he doesn't get tired chasing me around. And call me Joe. I'm not that much older than Russell."

Russ looked up at him and said, "You sure are tall, though."

"I just hope I'm finished growing up and start growing out."

The boys laughed before Bo said, "I told Chuck and Mort about you actin' as a scout and Chuck was real happy about it and Mort just kinda sulked. After the boys take the cart, we'll head over there, and I'll introduce you to Chuck."

"We already met, but I didn't recall hearing his name."

Joe then looked down at Newt and said, "Stay with Bernie."

He didn't know if it meant anything to the hound but began walking away from the cart holding Bessie's reins. Bo stepped beside him and after they were a good twenty yards away, Joe looked back and was pleased to see that Newt wasn't following. He figured he was too busy being rubbed and scratched by the two Smith boys to even notice that he'd gone.

As they walked to the front of the line of wagons that were being harnessed for the day's journey, he still didn't see Faith and almost turned to the Moores' wagon to make sure she was alright. But it was a passing thought because he suspected that it might be the worst thing he could do.

He did notice Marigold talking to her mother but even though she looked his way, he didn't dare wave. Luckily, he passed by before she could wave. He would have waved if he understood Marigold's new perspective.

As they continued walking, Joe asked, "Bo, after I'm gone, can you check on Faith for me? I expected her to visit last night, but she didn't. I didn't see her this morning either and I hope I didn't get her in trouble by talking to her for so long yesterday."

"I'll check at the noon break."

"Thanks."

Chuck was waiting outside the wagon holding his horse's reins as he watched them approach and could still hear Mort's loud muttering. He hadn't been surprised when Bo had told him that he'd asked the kid to scout, but he was when the boss had told him that he'd be giving him the mare. She was Bo's horse, so it didn't affect him at all. But Mort hadn't heard about the horse yet and Chuck suspected that it would only make him even angrier. He hoped that Joe Beck was as good as he appeared to be.

When they reached Chuck, Bo said, "Joe, this is Chuck Lynch. He'll tell you what to do on the way out front."

"Okay."

Chuck smiled at Joe and said, "Let's get movin', Joe."

Joe nodded, said, "Yes, sir," then placed his new left boot into the stirrup and swung his long right leg over his Henry before taking the reins.

Chuck winked at Bo before he quickly mounted then set his gray gelding into a medium trot and Joe followed.

Joe was surprised that he didn't have any difficulties after having been afoot for so long. The mare responded well to his slight tugs on the reins and taps with his boots.

He soon caught up to Chuck and after pulling alongside, Chuck asked, "I heard a couple of shots last night and Bo told me that you let him try your Henry. Can I try it later?"

"Sure. If we're lucky, we'll spot some game, so when you try it, you can make good use of the bullets."

Chuck grinned and said, "I'm lookin' forward to it. Is that the rifle you used to shoot Mort's hat off his noggin?"

"Nope. I have two and this is the other one."

"If you got a pistol, you're better armed than I am."

"I have a Colt New Army under my coat."

Chuck laughed then said, "I'm not surprised. You may need all of 'em when Mort can ride again. The boss didn't tell him that he gave you his mare, so I reckon he'll be mighty pissed when he sees you ridin' her."

"I figured he was ready to shoot me the first time he saw me."

"You're probably right. Now, we'll ride ahead but we need to spread apart about a thousand yards or so. You take the south side and I'll ride on the north. We'll keep the ruts in the middle. We look for anything that could slow down the wagons. Now that we have clear passage through Pawnee lands, that means changes in the ground or swollen creeks. Okay?"

"Yes, sir."

"And quit callin' me sir. I'm not that old. I'm Chuck. Okay?"

"Yes, sir...I mean Chuck."

Chuck grinned as he said, "Just before noon, we'll meet at the ruts, and you can let me try out the Henry."

UNWANTED

"Okay...Chuck."

Chuck snickered before he shifted his gelding to the right and Joe angled the mare to the left. He was surprised that Chuck hadn't asked more questions. He needed to learn more about what to expect as well.

He glanced back at the wagon train and hoped that Faith wasn't in trouble before he began studying the terrain. It wasn't a difficult task in the plains, but it wasn't exactly flat, either. There were low hills, creeks, and the slow unnoticeable incline could be the top of a plateau that would suddenly end in a dangerous cliff. It may not be more than twenty feet high, but it would be impassable for a horse, much less a wagon.

He continued for a few minutes on that heading until he estimated that he and Chuck were more than a half a mile apart then shifted Bessie back to a parallel course with the ruts. They were so deep that they were easily seen, and he could follow their path until they disappeared over the horizon. He knew that they should soon reach the Platte River then they'd turn west. In another four or five days, they'd reach Fort Kearny.

He wondered how many soldiers still manned the post now that the western forts had all been stripped to bare bones or simply abandoned. The whole purpose of building those forts was to protect the wagon trains of settlers heading west, but the war shifted the army's priorities. The wagon trains were left to defend themselves and Joe remembered Bo saying that the

Pawnee were relatively pleasant compared to many of the tribes further west.

He was enormously grateful for Captain Chalmers' gift of the Henry and wished he had even more boxes of cartridges. Maybe he could buy some at Fort Kearny but would be surprised if they had any available. It was still a rare weapon for civilians to have. Almost all of them were being bought by soldiers or relatives of soldiers. A couple of Union colonels had actually bought enough to outfit a whole company with the repeaters because the army wasn't interested in buying them.

―――

Harry Moore had seen Joe ride away before he nodded to his wife to let her know it was safe to let Faith leave the wagon. He then gathered their oxen to harness them while Mary took care of the boys and had Faith prepare their morning meal.

As she fixed breakfast for the family, Faith was sure that Mrs. Moore had lied about having her false labor pains. But it wasn't her anger than dominated her mind. She had been very confused when she'd seen Russell and Jimmy Smith walking beside Joe's cart. They even had Newt with them which made her afraid that something horrible had happened to Joe. That intense concern was amplified after recalling those two gunshots around sunset.

UNWANTED

By the time she finished making the family breakfast, Faith was convinced that Mort Jones had snuck out of their wagon and shot Joe with his pistol. She didn't dare ask Mister or Mrs. Moore about it but as soon as she could, she'd hurry to the cart and talk to the Smith boys.

After cleaning up, she had to milk one of the cows before the wagons started moving. She trotted away from the wagon carrying her bucket but stopped before reaching Joe's cart.

She looked at Russell as she quickly asked, "Where's Joe?"

Russell grinned and replied, "Mister Ferguson gave him a horse and saddle, so he went out with Mister Lynch to scout 'til the bad one's head is better."

"He's alright then?"

"Yup. He rode right past your wagon a little while ago. He'll be back later. Mister Ferguson asked us to take care of his cart while he was gone. Jimmy is gonna head back to our wagon in a minute. Newt is gonna stay with us, too."

Faith was immensely relieved and not surprised that Mister Moore hadn't mentioned it. She was sure that he knew and had probably seen Joe ride past.

She smiled, said, "Thank you, Russ," then hurried away.

Russell looked at Jimmy and said, "I think she likes Joe Beck."

Jimmy snickered before he rubbed Newt's head then began jogging back to their wagon.

They were only about four miles ahead of the wagons and Joe had lost sight of Chuck a couple of times due to the terrain but didn't mark any obstructions. Chuck was out of his view when he spotted distant movement at his ten o'clock position. It was too far away to identify, so he continued to stare in that direction as Bessie drew him closer.

After another minute or so, he realized what it was. He had never seen them before but identified them as buffalo. It wasn't a giant herd like those he'd read about, but more like a family of about a dozen animals. He glanced north in the hope of spotting Chuck and when he saw him, Joe took off his hat and waved it over his head. When Chuck waved back, Joe pointed at the buffalo.

Chuck spotted the animals then turned his gelding to the southwest and set him to a fast trot.

Joe kept Bessie moving and pulled his Mississippi. He doubted that the Henry had enough power to kill one of the big, hairy beasts, even with five or six shots. By the time Chuck reached him, they were about a mile from the small herd of bison.

Chuck said, "We could take at least two of 'em before they scatter. When we get close, we'll pick out a couple of cows that don't have young'uns."

"Okay. We're upwind of them right now, so won't they run when they pick up our scent?"

"Nope. They may look at us, but they won't spook. They won't even run off after we fire."

Joe nodded and wondered why the buffalo wouldn't run. Maybe they were just too confident that their size and massive horns would keep them safe.

He and Chuck continued to approach and soon slowed their horses to a walk when they were just two hundred yards away.

Chuck said, "Cock your hammer. I'll take that cow up front and on the right side. You can shoot the one at the far left. Okay?"

"Okay."

They continued walking their horses closer and when Chuck raised his rifle, Joe did the same. He aimed at the big cow and waited for Chuck to fire first. He expected Chuck to stop to make sure he had a good shot, but he kept his gelding moving.

The buffalo were just fifty yards away and were all looking at them, but Chuck hadn't pulled up. So, Joe took his reins in his left hand and gave them a short tug. After Bessie stopped moving, Joe settled his sights on the enormous cow but had a much smaller target now that she had turned her head.

He was almost startled when Chuck fired, but quickly pulled his trigger. He watched his cow drop to the ground before he looked to his right and saw Chuck sliding his rifle into his scabbard. Chuck was just twenty yards away from the small herd and the cow he'd shot was still standing but swaying as blood poured down her right shoulder.

Joe didn't know what Chuck was doing, but slipped his Mississippi into his scabbard, slid the Henry from the bedroll and nudged Bessie into a trot to catch up. Just as Chuck had told him, the buffalo hadn't scattered but simply moved a few yards away.

Before he reached Chuck, the second cow rolled onto her side, but Joe could see that she was still breathing. Chuck had dismounted and was pulling his pistol as he approached the wounded cow when Joe noticed a large bull about ten yards away from Chuck begin to snort and paw the ground.

He shouted, "Chuck, watch out!"

Chuck turned to look at Joe before the bull bellowed. Chuck's head whipped around, saw the bull then pointed his Colt at the bull's massive head and fired.

Joe didn't have time to see if Chuck's bullet had any effect but quickly leveled his Henry and fired. Chuck fired his second shot before Joe fired his second and then his third before the bull crumpled to the ground just a few feet in front of Chuck.

Joe kept his Henry level as he scanned the rest of the small herd as Chuck turned away from the bull and put two more .44s into the cow's head before holstering his pistol.

Joe finally dismounted then led Bessie to Chuck's gray gelding, took his reins and waited for Chuck.

As he stepped closer, Chuck grinned and said, "I didn't expect that bull to get so damned mad. I was almost a goner, Joe."

"I reckon you must have shot his favorite girl."

Chuck snickered then said, "I woulda thought he'd prefer one of the younger ones. Thanks for warnin' me and then helpin' me to put him down."

"It took a few slugs to do it, but I still think we were lucky."

"Let's go see where those bullets hit."

Joe nodded then handed Chuck his gelding's reins before they walked back to the dead bull. The other buffalo had wandered away but still didn't seem to be frightened.

Chuck whistled as he looked down at the giant, hairy head then said, "One of those bullets went right though his left eye. I reckon it was the only way to kill the big boy with a .44."

Joe asked, "What do we do with them?"

"One of us can start harvesting the meat and hide while the other goes back to get the flatbed wagon."

"I'll take care of the dirty job, Chuck. How long will you be gone?"

"We're not that far ahead, so I reckon it'll be a couple of hours or so."

"Okay."

Chuck looked at the two dead cows and said, "You dropped yours right off. That's some good shootin', Joe."

Joe just shrugged before Chuck smacked him on his left shoulder then mounted his gelding and rode away.

Joe returned to Bessie, slid his Henry back into the bedroll, then tied her reins to the bull's big horns before taking out his big knife and walking to his cow.

———

After milking the cow and giving the milk to the boys and drinking the rest, Faith washed out the bucket using water from the wagon's barrel. She hung the bucket on its hook then walked to the tailgate.

UNWANTED

She slid her walking stick from the wagon and said, "I'm going to walk with the goats," then stepped away without waiting for permission.

She didn't walk all the way to the goats but when she reached Joe's cart, she got in stride with Russell.

"How much did Mister Ferguson tell you, Russ?"

Russell quickly began telling her all that the wagon master had told him, but nothing that he said gave Faith any valuable insight.

He had almost finished when she saw Marigold walking towards them using Joe's walking stick. Faith knew that she wasn't looking for Joe because she would know that he was out scouting. She figured that Marigold must be coming to relieve Russell.

Russ didn't know why his older sister was paying a visit but suspected that he may soon witness a girl fight.

He was disappointed when Marigold reached them and said, "I'll take over while you get some lunch, Russ."

"Okay."

He delayed his departure for a few seconds to see if anything happened, but when Marigold just stared at him, Russ knew that it was safer just to leave.

After her brother was far enough away, Marigold said, "I needed to talk to you, Faith, but you weren't around this morning."

"Not by choice. I think Mrs. Moore pretended to be going into labor just to keep me in the wagon last night and then used all sorts of excuses to keep me from seeing Joe before he left. I didn't know where Joe was until I asked Russell. Before I did, I even thought that Mort Jones had shot him last night. Did you hear those gunshots?"

"I did. But my father told me that Mister Ferguson had tried out Joe's repeating rifle after he brought him a horse and saddle. You didn't hear about that?"

"Not a whisper. What did you need to talk to me about?"

"It's about a visit I had from Mrs. Moore around suppertime. She called me over and asked me if I was interested in Joe. Then she told me that I was prettier than you and I had a full figure that interested boys like Joe. It was like she was trying to marry me off to him. Then before she left, she told me not to tell you that she'd spoken to me. It's really kind of scary."

Faith asked, "Are you interested in Joe?"

Marigold didn't hesitate before she answered, "Yes. I'm not ashamed to admit it, but I know you like him more than I do and I think that he likes you just as much. Do you know why Mrs. Moore would do such a thing?"

"I think so, but you can't tell anyone. Okay?"

Marigold nodded before Faith said, "After I told Joe that Mister Moore paid my father twenty-five dollars for me, he suggested that he wanted me for kind of insurance if Mrs. Moore died when she had her baby. I didn't believe it at first, but now it seems very reasonable."

Marigold stared at Faith for a few seconds before she exclaimed, "My goodness! That's disgusting! But it does make sense of what she was trying to do."

Then after a brief pause, Marigold snapped, "That witch! She was trying to use me as a tart to keep Joe away from you."

"What are you going to do, Mary?"

"Not what she wants me to do. This makes me want to go to that wagon and scream at her!"

Faith quickly said, "No, you can't do that. The last thing I want is for Mister and Mrs. Moore to realize that I know about their plan. I thought I'd say something stupid by mistake after Joe told me his theory. But Joe told me to pretend to be a sheriff and act as if I was investigating a crime. That way I could be objective."

Marigold laughed and said, "So, that's why he called you Sheriff Faith."

"Yes. It worked too. I didn't give them a hint of my suspicions. They didn't reveal their intentions, but little John asked me why I didn't like Joe anymore. I guess when Mrs. Moore saw you walking alone with Joe, she said something to Mister Moore and John overheard what she said but didn't understand it."

"I guess I'll have to be your deputy now and keep the secret. What happens when she really does go into labor?"

"I don't know. We never had a chance to discuss it. Joe told me his suspicions just before you arrived yesterday, and Mrs. Moore called me in. At the time, he believed he'd always be close. Now he's way out front, but at least he's on a horse, so he can move faster. I'll ask him when he returns."

"You've talked to him a lot; haven't you?"

"I've spent hours with him and learned a lot about him."

"Has he kissed you yet?"

Faith blushed before replying, "No. He's never even held my hand. We just talk."

Marigold smiled as she said, "If I was as lucky as you, I wouldn't let him just sit and talk, but that's the way I am. I think I scare him a little."

Faith laughed lightly before she said, "He actually told me that you did. I guess your nice figure was intimidating."

"I don't think it was my impressive bosom that spooked him. I think it was my intense nature. I might have seemed too obvious in my intentions, but you don't have to worry about me anymore."

"I'm not very intense or impressive. I guess that's why we get along because I don't make him uncomfortable."

Marigold looked at Faith as she asked, "Have you ever had a boyfriend?"

"Heavens, no! My father would never let me speak to a boy who wasn't my brother. When Joe first returned the Moore's lost kid goat, he was the first boy I'd spoken to in my entire life other than just a few hellos at church."

"Really? Was your father a preacher or something?"

Faith laughed again before she replied, "Joe asked me the same question. No, he wasn't a preacher, but he was very strict. To give you an idea of what my parents expected of me, my full name is Faith Hope Charity Virtue Goodchild."

It was Marigold's turn to laugh before she said, "I'm just Marigold Joanne Smith."

"Did you know that Joe doesn't even have a middle name? And Joe isn't short for Joseph, either. His entire name is only seven letters long."

"That's odd. But I can't believe that you didn't at least meet any boys in school."

Faith hesitated before saying, "I didn't go to school. My mother taught me all that my parents believed a girl would need to know to keep house and raise children. They only taught my brothers how to read."

Marigold didn't comment and was about to ask more about Joe when Faith noticed a rider in the distance and asked, "Is that Joe?"

Marigold focused on the distant rider then replied, "I don't think so. Chuck Lynch rides a gray gelding, so it's probably him."

"Oh. I wonder where Joe is."

"I'll go up front and find out. I'll send Russ or Jimmy back to take over. Okay?"

"Alright."

Faith watched Marigold jog away and was jealous that she bounced when she trotted knowing that she could run full tilt without anything bouncing. But she was happy that she'd talked to Marigold and now counted her as a true friend. Marigold could have just done as Mrs. Moore intended and snuck into Joe's camp last night, but she hadn't. Instead, Marigold had told her what had happened and didn't even hide her own interest in Joe. But despite that confession, Marigold had told her that she would no longer need to worry about her acting on that interest.

As she walked beside Bernie with Newt trotting in front of her, Faith watched the other scout drawing closer to the wagon train and hoped that nothing bad had happened to Joe.

―――

Joe had begun to appreciate just how big buffalo were as he still worked on the first cow. He'd stripped off most of the wooly coat and spread it on the ground before he began to carve off big pieces of meat. There was more meat in one massive haunch than there was in that entire deer. He had finished removing all he could before he folded the skin over the pile and moved onto the second cow.

When he reached Chuck's kill, he noticed that his bullet had struck the cow in her shoulder joint which was why she hadn't fallen right away. He attributed it to the motion of Chuck's gelding when he took his shot before he began harvesting the second cow.

As he worked, he occasionally scanned the horizons for any large scavengers. He didn't care about the ones overhead but didn't want to be surprised by a wolf or a coyote. He didn't think he had to worry about bears. He also looked to the east in the hope of seeing the roofs of the wagons but would be almost as happy to see Chuck driving the flatbed wagon.

He finished with the cow but before he started on the bigger bull, he walked to Bessie and removed his canteen. He swallowed half of its contents before returning to his saddle then reminded himself to bring two canteens tomorrow.

It was almost noon and Joe was about halfway finished with the bull when he spotted Chuck in the distance driving the flatbed wagon. He didn't stop working as he wanted to finish before Chuck arrived.

He had just folded over the hide onto the large pile of meat and was washing the blood from his hands when Chuck pulled up then clambered down from the more than half-full wagon.

"You got that done pretty fast, Joe. I figured you'd have two done at most by the time I got back."

"I had a lot of practice. I guess we need to get them loaded before all the sharp-toothed critters start showing up."

Chuck glance at the cloud of buzzards circling overhead before he stepped to the bull's hide and said, "I'll get this end."

Joe took one stride to the opposite corner then they took hold of the hide, lifted the load of buffalo meat and lugged it to the back of the wagon.

After they slid it onto the bed, Chuck said, "I didn't think we'd get it on there. I reckon that must be almost three hundred pounds of meat. You're stronger than you look, Joe."

Joe grinned then said, "We have two more, Chuck. At least the cows weren't as big as the bull."

As they walked to the next hide-covered wealth of meat, Chuck said, "The one who was close to showin' me who was boss."

After the last of the meat was stored in the bed of the wagon and lashed down to keep it from falling off the back, Joe mounted Bessie and walked her to the driver's seat.

He pulled his Henry and handed it to Chuck as he said, "You can only take two shots, or I'll have to give Bo another one."

Chuck grinned as he accepted the repeater then aimed it in the air at the circling buzzards and fired his two shots in rapid succession. The big birds didn't notice and continued to fly in their circular patterns waiting for the humans to leave.

He handed the Henry back to Joe and said, "That sure shoots nice, Joe. Thanks for rememberin' to let me try it. I didn't wanna ask again."

Joe slid the carbine back into his bedroll then said, "You're welcome, Chuck."

After Chuck snapped the reins and the wagon lurched forward, he looked up at Joe and said, "Oh, and I'm supposed to tell you that Faith is okay and was worried about you."

"I'm relieved to hear that she's alright. I asked Bo to check on her because I hadn't seen her since afternoon. I'm surprised that she was worried about me, though."

"Bo was the one who told me you wanted to know she was okay, but Marigold Smith was the one who told me about Faith bein' worried. She is one fine-lookin' girl."

Joe felt a slight swell of jealousy before he replied, "I think so, but she thinks she's too skinny."

Chuck snickered then said, "I wasn't talkin' about Faith, Joe. Don't get me wrong. I think Faith is a pretty girl too, but Marigold is kinda special."

Joe looked down at Chuck as the wagon rolled southeast along the Trail and asked, "Are you gonna do anything about it?"

Chuck grinned as he replied, "Maybe. So, how close are you and Faith?"

"We talk a lot and I think I really understand her. Marigold scares me a bit."

Chuck snorted then said, "Well, she don't scare me at all. How did you get here, anyway?"

Joe knew they had at least another hour of travel but began telling Chuck the story from when he left Missouri. He felt that only Faith needed to know about his earlier life.

UNWANTED

Mary Moore had watched Faith and Marigold talking as they walked near Joe Beck's cart. She had hoped to see the conversation burst into a shouting match, but that hadn't happened. She still watched but when they began laughing, she knew they might have to come up with a new plan.

When Marigold finally trotted away just before the noon break, she turned and asked, "Where is Marigold going, Harry?"

"She went up front somewhere. I lost sight of her. Did Faith get mad at her?"

"No, and that has me concerned. I told Marigold not to tell Faith what I said last night, but I'm not sure she kept that secret. I'll try to learn what they talked about when Faith returns."

"Don't be too obvious, Mary."

Mary snapped, "I'm not a fool, Harry!"

"No, dear."

Marigold was walking with Faith again after she'd talked to Chuck. On the way back, she had told Russell and Jimmy that they could take over their cart-watching duties when they stopped for the noon break in a little while.

Faith had been relieved to hear that Joe was alright and was pleased to hear about the successful buffalo hunt, even though she'd never seen one of the large beasts before.

Marigold said, "Chuck said that Joe warned him about a giant angry bull who was about to charge, and he had to use his pistol and Joe fired his repeater to stop him. He fell just a few feet in front of him. He said that one of their shots had gone through his eye or he would have been gored to death."

"Oh, my God! That must have been terrifying!"

"Chuck said that it happened so fast that there wasn't time to be afraid. He even said that it was Joe's last shot that put the bull down because he had seen his bullets bounce off the bull's thick skull."

"Why am I not surprised?"

Faith glanced at the Moores' wagon then said, "I bet that Mrs. Moore is watching us right now. I wonder what she's thinking."

Marigold hadn't even thought about Mrs. Moore after telling Faith about their secret conversation, but after hearing her name again, she had a good idea what Mrs. Moore was thinking.

Marigold said, "I think she's wondering if I spilled the beans about what she told me last night. I'll bet she expected us to start slapping each other. Maybe we should put on a show for her."

Faith shook her head as she said, "I think it's too late for that. I think we should act as we have been, but if she asks, I'll tell her that you asked me a few questions about Joe. I'll pretend that I was a little jealous but only enough to make her believe that her plans are still working. Okay?"

Marigold giggled then said, "Alright, but it'll be a hard thing to do, Faith. Even for a sheriff."

"I'll try. I guess we'll be pulling up for the noon break pretty soon. Joe should be back sometime later this afternoon if they had to harvest the meat from the buffaloes."

"Chuck and Mister Ferguson had to move things around on their flatbed wagon before he drove it back to Joe, but they weren't that far out front, so we should see them soon. We'll probably have a community feast with all that meat tonight, too."

"I'd rather spend some time with Joe."

Marigold smiled as she said, "You are more than just smitten; aren't you, Faith?"

"Yes. I just wish I wasn't so skinny."

"I told you that you're not as thin as you believe. Besides, I get the impression that Joe doesn't mind as much as you do."

Even though Marigold had said that she shouldn't worry about her, Faith still wanted confirmation, so she asked, "Does that mean that you're not interested anymore?"

"I was interested, but not like you. I guess it was more like an infatuation. Chuck Lynch seemed to be interested when I talked to him, so I think I'll spend some time with him during the feast."

"I think Mister Lynch would be a fool not to start visiting you, Marigold."

"So, do I."

Faith laughed as they continued to lead Bernie and follow Newt. It was just a couple of minutes later when she spotted the wagon and a rider appear on the distant horizon.

She exclaimed, "There's Joe!"

Marigold smiled and said, "And Chuck Lynch is with him."

Faith smiled but knew it would be at least another hour before the heavily loaded wagon arrived. But just seeing Joe and knowing that Marigold was now interested in Chuck lifted her spirit.

―――

Bo still hadn't told Mort about giving Joe Bessie, but Mort had learned how much he was on the outs when Chuck returned to pick up the flatbed. He'd been driving the lead wagon when Chuck rode back and told the boss that he needed the flatbed wagon to load the meat from three buffalo.

While Chuck and Bo moved the barrels to the front of the uncovered wagon to make room for the meat, he listened as Chuck loudly spoke of Joe Beck's value as a scout. As much as he hated Joe before, Mort Jones now despised the tall kid with every fiber of his being. He would have gone ballistic if he'd known that Bo had given him Bessie and a saddle.

Chuck's gushing praise of that damned kid also made Mort add him to his hate ladder, but one or two rungs below Joe Beck's position at the top.

But even as Mort fumed, he saw Marigold Smith approach Chuck then spoke to him for a few minutes. He noticed now Chuck admired the girl as she walked away, too. He knew that Beck was fond of that blonde girl that the Moores had bought in Kansas City, but Chuck's obvious interest in Marigold Smith might prove useful.

Mort's earlier plans to simply shoot Beck had been thwarted by that damned dog of his and now it seemed that everybody liked the tall bastard.

By the time he spotted Chuck and Beck heading back with the buffalo meat, he decided to hide his hatred and wait for the right opportunity to make them both pay.

———

As soon as he'd seen the canvas roofs of the first wagons, Joe had been searching for Faith. As they drew closer, he kept staring at the line of folks walking beside their wagons until he spotted his tent-cart. He smiled when he spotted a blonde head just in front of the cart. He wanted to set Bessie to a canter to get there quicker but managed to contain his impatience.

Chuck loudly asked, "How much of this meat do you want, Joe? You're entitled to half of it."

"I only want about thirty pounds or so, and I'll probably scrape off some of the fat. I would appreciate the use of a good-sized pot for the night, too."

"I can let you have one from the trade goods. But that's all you want?"

"It's enough to last me and Newt for a week. I reckon we'll run across more of those big beasts in a few days."

"We will, but not for a while. You'll probably get to see one of those massive herds when we're out of Pawnee lands. I've seen 'em so big that they ran from horizon to horizon."

Joe was still staring at a distant Faith as he said, "I'd like to see that. I'm still surprised that they let us shoot them without running off. That bull was the only one who even seemed to notice that we were there."

"It's really odd; ain't it?"

Joe nodded but was itching to leave as the wagons were now less than a mile away. Then he noticed that they had pulled to a stop and the drivers were getting down to join the walkers. He began to shift in his saddle without realizing it until Chuck brought it to his attention.

Chuck was grinning as he looked up at Joe and yelled, "*Will you just get goin'?* You're makin' me nervous just lookin' at ya!"

Joe laughed then saluted Chuck and tapped Bessie's flanks. She accelerated to a fast trot leaving the slower moving wagon behind.

Joe soon noticed that Faith was walking with Marigold but just after he saw them together, Marigold walked away from Faith and headed for her family's wagon.

Faith then waved at him as she walked next to his cart and Joe waved back. He was just a hundred yards from the first wagon when he noticed that Mort driving. While Mort had made a serious effort to hide his hatred, it wasn't good enough.

Joe saw his glare then shifted Bessie a few yards to the right just in case he tried to pull his pistol. He knew it was highly unlikely but suspected that when Mort had learned that Bo had given him a job as a scout and then his horse, it wasn't out of the realm of possibility.

He waved to Bo before passing the lead wagon without incident and slowed Bessie to a walk as he began riding alongside the row of stopped wagons. He was surprised when some of the other folks waved at him, so he returned their waves. He wasn't surprised that the Moores ignored him as he rode past.

He soon reached Faith and his cart, then hurriedly dismounted, took Bessie's reins and led her closer to Faith.

"I'm surprised to see you guarding my cart, Faith. I thought the Smith brothers were going to do that."

Faith couldn't contain her joy as she smiled and said, "I talked to them for a while then Marigold joined me. We chatted until just a few minutes ago."

"I noticed. How are you? Is everything okay?"

Faith glanced at the back of the Moores' wagon before replying, "I'm alright, but I have a lot to tell you later."

"Why didn't you show up last night?"

"Mrs. Moore said she was having labor pains, but I think it was just an excuse to keep me there. I'll explain later. Are you going back out front again after the break?"

"I think so. I'll take the cart up front to gather some of the buffalo meat and Chuck is going to give me a big pot."

UNWANTED

Faith was about to tell Joe about her conversation with Marigold when Mrs. Moore shouted, "Faith, I need you!"

Faith smiled at Joe before saying, "Now there's a surprise. I'll talk to you tonight."

"Okay."

Faith hurried away with her walking stick as Joe watched. He paid more attention to Mrs. Moore and wondered if he had been right about their intentions. He may have been right about Harry Moore's plans but couldn't have imagined Mrs. Moore's hidden agenda.

He looked down at Newt, then extended his hand in front of his curious nose and said, "Guess what you're having for lunch, Newt."

Even though he'd washed his hands, he watched as Newt's nose rushed across his hand as his tail beat furiously,

He laughed before tying off Bessie to the back of his cart then leading Bernie to the front of the line of wagons.

———

As Faith prepared their lunch, Mrs. Moore didn't bother using any subtlety when she asked, "What were you and Miss Smith talking about for so long?"

Faith didn't even look at her as she replied, "Mostly we talked about Joe Beck. She seems to be very interested in him."

Mary smiled inside as she asked, "Does that bother you, Faith?"

"Yes, but I like Marigold and understand that she has more of the, um, womanly features that men like. All I can do is talk to him because I know I'll never impress him as she can. I guess if Joe prefers her to me, there's nothing I can do about it."

Faith thought she was laying it on a bit thick but was pleased as Mrs. Moore seemed to sympathize when she said, "Don't worry, dear. I'm sure that soon, other men will want you just as much."

"I hope so."

Faith expected Mrs. Moore to go rushing to tell her husband the good news but was almost disappointed when she stayed to help prepare their lunch.

―――

Joe had pulled his cart close to the flatbed wagon then he selected some good cuts from his cow and set them aside before he, Chuck and Bo Ferguson moved the rest of the cow's meat to the other buffalo hide's stack.

Joe then tossed a large piece to Newt before wrapping his selections in the heavy buffalo hide and put it onto his stack of wood.

Chuck gave him the large, black iron pot and he squeezed it into his cart before Joe asked, "Do you need any more help, Bo?"

"Not here. After you finish havin' lunch, you and Chuck can go back to the front. You should see the Platte River pretty soon, but maybe not 'til tomorrow mornin'."

"Okay."

Joe led his cart away then to the back of the long line. Newt had remained behind as he was busy ripping his lunch apart.

He stopped at the Smith wagon then left his cart and walked to the other side where he found the family sitting on a blanket having their lunch.

Marigold spotted him then quickly popped to her feet and said, "I heard you and Chuck shot three buffalo and one almost gored him."

Joe smiled as he replied, "Yes, ma'am. I think there's about five or six hundred pounds of meat in the wagon. Chuck said that there would be big feast tonight."

"Did you talk to Faith yet?"

"For just a few seconds before Mrs. Moore called her in. I just stopped by to tell Russ and Jimmy that they're back on duty. I'll take my cart to the back right now. I have to clean and reload my Henry, too."

"Okay. But be sure you talk to Faith as soon as you can."

Joe's eyebrows rose slightly as he nodded then looked at Russell who waved and said, "I'll be there in a few minutes, Joe."

Joe waved back then turned on his heels and walked to his cart. Newt had finished his enormous chunk of buffalo meat and was sitting by Bernie with a satisfied look on his doggie face.

Joe took Bernie's halter then began turning him around to head back as he grinned at the hound and said, "You may think you want more meat right now, Newt. But if I gave you another bite, you'd look like you were about to have a litter of puppies. Then folks would think you're a bitch."

As he started back, he wondered what was different about Marigold. He didn't notice any changes, but she wasn't as scary as she'd been before. He had been astonished when Marigold had seemed to accept that he was only interested in Faith but didn't know why. He shrugged and continued leading Bernie past the Smith's wagon.

UNWANTED

He glanced at the Moores' wagon as he passed and spotted Mister Moore on the other side but couldn't see anyone else.

When he was about fifty yards behind the last wagon, he walked to Bessie and pulled his Mississippi and Henry free and set them in his cart.

Russell arrived as he was beginning to clean the muzzle loader but didn't say anything and just quietly watched which surprised Joe.

Ten minutes later, after quickly cleaning both weapons, he had reloaded the Mississippi then returned it to its scabbard before reloading the Henry with five cartridges from the open box in his saddlebag.

After sliding it into his bedroll, he turned to Russell and said, "What kind of guns do you have, Russ?"

"We've got a shotgun and a Springfield that looks a lot like yours."

"Are you a good shot?"

"Fair to middlin'. My father doesn't like to waste ammunition."

Joe nodded then reached into his cart and pulled out one of the ammunition pouches.

He handed it to Chuck and said, "The balls will probably have to be melted down and reformed to fit but there are twenty-four percussion caps and a lot of powder you can use. Keep the ammunition pouch, too."

"Gee, thanks, Joe. Pa has a crucible and press so we can use all the lead."

"Thanks for keeping an eye on my stuff. And watch out for Newt. He may have stuffed his stomach, but he knows that there's a lot of fresh meat in the cart now. Okay?"

Russell rubbed Newt's head as he replied, "Okay."

Joe then took a few minutes to salt the meat then pushed it as far to the front as possible then moved the big pot behind it. It wasn't that he didn't trust Russell; it was that he suspected Newt might find a way to steal another large piece.

He glanced at the Moore wagon, couldn't see Faith, then said, "If Faith returns, tell her that if she can't talk to me later, I'll stop by the Moores' wagon."

"Okay, Joe."

Joe untied Bessie, mounted then waved to Russell before trotting past the long line of wagons. He had never counted them before, but if he skipped the uncovered wagon and Bo Ferguson's lead wagon, there were twenty-two families making the long journey.

UNWANTED

He suspected that they'd lose as many as one in four to diseases and accidents. He guessed after a few weeks, there would be quarrels and fights and some would even result in shootings. He didn't know the rules but assumed that Bo Ferguson or Mister Carlisle would enforce them.

For all the talk about the hostile Indians, he'd learned that most tribes just traded with the wagon trains. He had been surprised that the Pawnee had traded for livestock and not guns or iron cookware. He knew he was woefully ignorant, but he'd been out of sight for much of the journey. Now that he could mingle, he'd learn more. So, after he and Chuck rode away from the wagons, he began his education.

"Chuck, why did the Indians trade for critters instead of guns and other things they can't get?"

"I was kinda surprised myself, but Bo said that the buffalo herds are gettin' thinned out by settlers and the army. We were lucky to see that small herd and I reckon if the Pawnee had seen 'em, they woulda asked for a couple of rifles instead."

"Do you bring rifles and other things to trade?"

"Yup. We don't have any Henrys, though. We keep the rifles, ammunition and a lot of cookware and other stuff just for tradin' in the lead wagon along with the folks' money. That way nobody has to worry about anybody stealin'."

"I guess there are still fights among the families sooner or later."

"There are, but they don't usually show up this early. After a couple of months, it can get pretty wild. Most of those families have a couple of jugs of moonshine and that makes it worse."

"Why do most of them come? I noticed some of the wagons are almost fancy compared to others. Some look like they won't last another hundred miles."

"You got that right. Wait 'til we cross a good-sized river, and you'll see how many don't make it. They come for all sorts of reasons. I reckon that most of 'em have problems back East. You know, they lost their farm, or their business failed. A few are tryin' to escape the law."

"Do you know why the Moores joined the train? I would think that Mister Moore would have waited until his wife had her baby."

"I figured that you'd ask me about 'em, but I don't know much about the Moores. They tend to keep to themselves. They even asked to be at the back of the line which struck me and Bo as bein' kinda queer. That's usually the worst place to be. Catchin' all that dust is just one of the reasons."

"I figure there are rules to follow, so if somebody breaks the rules, who decides on the punishment?"

Chuck looked across at Joe and asked, "You aren't plannin' on breakin' any; are you?"

"Nope. I just want to know how everything works."

Chuck nodded then said, "Mister Carlisle is their leader, but there's a council of six other fellers. They're the ones who will decide what to do with anyone who breaks the rules. Nobody has yet, but that'll change."

"Those rules don't apply to you, Mort and Bo; do they?"

"Nope. But Bo has his own rules and is a stickler for me and Mort to keep in line. He won't even let us drink."

"Why do I figure that you don't give Bo any problems, but Mort is constantly testing the boss?"

"Mort was okay on our first trip, then a bit of trouble on our last one. He almost missed this one and Bo was close to leavin' him in Kansas City. I reckon if he'd known you a bit longer, he woulda, too."

Joe nodded as he let his eyes follow the ruts that disappeared over a rise ahead.

Then he looked at Chuck and asked, "Who does the preaching?"

Chuck laughed then replied, "That's Mister Newbury. He's a Methodist deacon and does the Sunday services. He'll baptize the babies that'll be born on the way and marry a few couples. I reckon that's why you asked."

"It was, but it's not just a matter of being smitten, Chuck. I want to protect Faith and I'm beginning to think that the only way I can do that is to marry her."

Chuck looked at him curiously as he asked, "Why do you have to marry her to protect her?"

Joe replied, "I'll tell you, but it's just a theory. But Faith agreed with me when I told her. There were just too many oddities that didn't make any sense otherwise."

"What is this theory of yours?"

Joe explained his suspicions and why he and Faith believed they were correct. He expected Chuck to start laughing, but he didn't. He listened intently and nodded a few times before Joe finished.

Then he said, "It's not that strange, Joe. I've seen it before."

Joe exclaimed, "*You have?*"

"It wasn't exactly the same, but close. On our first train, there was a family named Pritchard. They had three young'uns, but Mrs. Pritchard was kinda sickly. Just before we rolled, Mister Pritchard went into town and returned with a young girl named Molly Cooper. She looked like she was twelve or thirteen and nobody thought much about it.

UNWANTED

"Whispers started makin' the rounds that Mister Pritchard was diddlin' Molly, but Mrs. Pritchard was still alive, so nobody gave 'em much weight. Then about two months along, Mrs. Pritchard died and after they buried her, her widowed husband married Molly. It was only when she started showin' two months later that we knew those rumors were right. I found out that Mister Pritchard had found Molly in an orphanage. I reckon the folks who ran the place were happy to get rid of her and she seemed to like bein' the new Mrs. Pritchard."

Joe took a deep breath then said, "You can't tell anybody, Chuck."

"I wasn't about to. Have you told Faith about your plans to marry her?"

"Not yet. I'll tell her tonight if the Moores let her leave."

"They can't keep her just 'cause Harry Moore paid her pa twenty-five dollars for her."

"I know. I just don't want to cause trouble unless it becomes necessary."

"I don't reckon you need to worry about it, Joe. You're mighty popular with the folks since you stopped Mort from shootin' that Pawnee."

"Maybe so, but I still don't want to start trouble."

Then Joe asked, "What day is it, anyway? I've lost track."

"It's Thursday, so in three days, Mister Newbury will hold services in the mornin'. We'll be late startin', but some of the trains don't even move on Sundays. I reckon it's time to split up. See all of them buzzards ahead?"

"I imagine there are a few coyotes on the ground, too."

"Maybe some gray wolves, too."

Joe said, "I reckon I'll be close enough to find out," then waved to Chuck and turned Bessie to the left.

Chuck turned his gelding to the right and they began separating.

As Joe scanned the landscape ahead, he thought about what he'd already learned in just a few minutes. Life on the wagon trains wasn't that much different than it was in a small settlement except it was always moving and much more dangerous.

Chuck's story about Molly and the Pritchards added even more substance to his theory. He'd tell Faith the story tonight and decided that if she hadn't shown up by sunset, he'd pay a visit to the Moores' wagon. He didn't know that Faith had already ensured that it wasn't going to be necessary.

―――

UNWANTED

Faith was walking beside Marigold again but not near Joe's cart. They were walking near the herds and each young woman had her walking stick.

Marigold was grinning as she asked, "And do you think she believed you?"

Faith nodded then replied, "I could hear the satisfaction in her voice when she told me that pretty soon, other men will want me just as much as they want you."

Marigold giggled then asked, "Are you going to the big buffalo feast tonight?"

"No. I need to talk to Joe."

"I'm going to spend some time with Chuck Lynch."

"Just don't make it so obvious that Mrs. Moore will think you've lost interest in Joe."

"I'll try."

Faith then sighed and said, "I don't know how much longer I can keep up this act. Mrs. Moore is due in a couple of weeks, and I hope Joe can come up with an idea before then."

"Why does Joe have to figure out something? Why don't you just ask him tonight if you can stay with him?"

Faith was about to argue that it wasn't a moral thing for her to even contemplate but suddenly realized that she was thinking like her father.

So, she smiled at Marigold and said, "Maybe I will."

Marigold laughed before she swatted one of the Moores' cows on her butt with her walking stick.

―――

After another twenty minutes of riding, Joe spotted the Platte River in the distance. He looked to Chuck as he rode about a thousand yards away then turned Bessie to his right to join him. He assumed that they'd be heading back soon anyway.

By the time he was close, Chuck had pulled his gelding to a stop.

"There's the North Platte, Joe."

"The North Platte? You mean there's a South Platte River?"

"It's still the Platte right now, but in about another week or so, it'll split. The South Platte heads down into Colorado and the North Platte heads northwest up to Idaho Territory."

"Are we going to cross it?"

UNWANTED

"Not yet. We'll ride on the south side for a while then cross where it splits. The trains that leave from Omaha pass along the northern side until the Trail joins up at that crossin'."

"Where to the trains from St. Joseph go?"

"Didn't you see the ruts a few days ago? We follow the Independence, Kansas City path then the St. Joseph trains follow the ruts we're on now."

"I must have missed it when I was told to stay out of sight."

"Well, I'm sure glad that you're around now, Joe. Let's head back. The wagons should be passin' the buffalo carcasses by now. Did you see any four-legged scavengers?"

"Yup. There were a bunch of them, but I wasn't close enough to see if they were all coyotes or there were some wolves mixed in."

"They were probably just coyotes. They don't get along with wolves, but I reckon the wolves will take their place at the supper table tonight. Let's get movin'."

Joe nodded then wheeled Bessie around and set her to a medium trot. As they headed back to the wagons, Joe wondered if Faith knew why the Moores had chosen to make the hazardous journey, especially with Mrs. Moore about to give birth.

Faith and Marigold spotted the two riders as soon as they crossed the horizon because they'd both been focused on that direction for at least an hour.

Faith asked, "I wonder how much longer before Mrs. Moore calls me back in?"

"Mister Ferguson will be ringing the bell to have us pull over for the night pretty soon, so I'd better head back. Are you going to take over for Russell?"

"That's a good idea, he's far enough on the other side of the ruts that Mrs. Moore won't be able to see me."

Marigold smiled as she said, "That's a good idea, Faith."

After Marigold practically ordered her younger brother to give up his post to Faith, she and Russell headed back to their wagon. Russell showed Marigold the ammunition pouch and explained that Joe gave it to him, so she didn't think that he'd stolen it.

Faith scratched Newt's head but didn't bother taking hold of Bernie's halter or the odd harness. The donkey simply continued pulling the cart because it was his job.

She continued watching Joe approach but glanced at the Moores' wagon to remain in the narrow blind spot so neither adult Moore could see her.

UNWANTED

Joe had picked Faith out of the long line of walkers shortly after seeing the wagons. He smiled knowing that she'd taken over Russell's duty and wished that she didn't have to rejoin the Moores after he returned.

He and Chuck were around a mile from the lead wagon when they heard the loud clang of Bo Ferguson's bell. Within seconds, the wagons began stopping and the walkers began blending into the gaps between them.

Soon, Faith was one of the few still visible, but Joe expected she'd be summoned before he arrived.

When they were close, Chuck loudly said, "I'll see you in the mornin', Joe."

"Okay. Mort is sitting on the driver's seat, so when do you think he'll join us?"

"I wish it wasn't hell freezes over, but I reckon he'll be comin' along tomorrow."

"That'll be interesting. Thanks for the lessons, Chuck."

Chuck waved and angled his gelding to the left and Joe kept Bessie trotting in straight line. As he began passing the wagons, he saw Faith wave and expected that she'd soon start walking to the Moores' wagon. But after he returned her wave, he was surprised and enormously pleased that she remained standing beside Bernie.

He slowed Bessie to a walk and greeted a few of the families as he passed yet still thought that Faith wouldn't be there when he arrived.

But when he pulled up and dismounted, Faith smiled and said, "Welcome back, Joe."

"I'm surprised that you're still here. Not that I'm complaining."

"I'll probably have to leave soon anyway. At least I don't have to help with supper tonight. But I think Mrs. Moore may tell me to help with the big feast. Are you going to be there?"

Joe hadn't even thought about it because he was so accustomed to being on his own. But maybe it wasn't a bad idea. He'd still have to cook and smoke his buffalo meat, but that could wait.

"I'll be there if it won't cause you any trouble with the Moores."

Faith was about to answer when Harry Moore shouted, "Faith, you need to help Mrs. Moore."

She smiled at Joe then said, "I'll see you later, Joe."

He nodded before she hurried away then shifted his eyes to Mister Moore who was unharnessing his oxen. He waited until Faith disappeared from view before he turned Bernie and the cart to the south and led him and Bessie away.

UNWANTED

Newt was bouncing alongside, obviously anticipating more meat and the sight of the hound's excitement made Joe smile. He wished his life was that simple.

After stopping the cart near the small stream that crossed the Trail, he unsaddled Bessie then put on her halter before unharnessing Bernie. He led them both to the stream then after they'd quenched their thirst, he walked them back to the cart.

He didn't tie them down but used a length of rope to tie their halters together before saying, "Now you two can do whatever you want."

He was grinning as he returned to the cart and figured he may as well start cooking now because the communal feast wouldn't start for at least two hours.

He pulled out the heavy pot then set it on the ground before sliding out the heavy buffalo hide. He wasn't about to throw it away after the meat was gone.

He cut a reasonably sized piece and tossed it to Newt before he took out his spade and dug two firepits. One would be for the pot and the other for the cooking grid and skillet. After adding the small branches for kindling and breaking some of the thicker ones and setting them on top, Joe returned to the cart. He took out the board from the burnt-out barn that he used for a cutting board and began to slice off some steaks before chopping an entire roast into chunks. He put some lard in the frypan then laid the steaks on top and sprinkling on some salt before temporarily piling all of the cubed buffalo meat onto the fresh cuts.

He glanced down at Newt to make sure he was still busy before taking out a canteen and emptying it into his new pot. He had to dig out the big bag of dry beans before pulling out the rice. He opened both then used his tin cup to dump two of each into the pot of water. He let it sit as he tied off the open burlap sacks with some cord then returned them to the front of the cart.

He took out the jug of molasses and poured some into the pot then after closing it, he removed one of the jars of pickles. He pulled one out, put it in his mouth then poured some of the vinegary juice into the pot leaving just enough to cover the remaining pickles. After sealing and returning the pickle jar to the cart, he quickly ate the one he'd taken then started the fires.

He put the pot onto the first then dumped in the cubes of buffalo meat. He was frying the two steaks when Newt sidled close and sat down next to him.

"I'll let you have a piece of one of the steaks, but no more, Newt."

Newt's tail was wagging, but Joe knew it was because he was expecting a lot more than just a piece.

UNWANTED

He finished cooking both steaks and then after giving Newt a piece of one of them, Joe gave into temptation and ate the second. He hurried back to the cart and cut two more and soon added them to the skillet to make use of the dying fire. He'd have to smoke the rest soon. He began stirring the stew and knew it would take hours to cook, but once it began bubbling, he wouldn't have to add more wood to the fire.

He had just flipped the steaks when music began floating across the ground from the wagons. He smiled and wondered if Faith would ask him to dance. He hoped she didn't because he'd probably just step on her toes with his big feet.

He began humming as he mixed his bubbling stew and was startled when Newt suddenly popped to his feet and trotted away. He turned to see what could be more important to Newt than frying meat and was pleasantly surprised to see Faith approaching with a big smile lighting up her face.

"I thought you were going to the feast?"

As she sat beside him, she said, "I did, but when you didn't show up, I slipped away. What are you making?"

"A stew of beans, rice and buffalo meat with some molasses and pickle juice."

Faith laughed then said, "Pickle juice and no pickles?"

Joe grinned, then stood and walked to the cart, removed the recently opened jar of pickles and unscrewed the lid. He slipped one out, handed it to her then grabbed another one with his teeth before sitting down again.

As Faith began eating her pickle, Joe dumped the rest of the contents of the jar into the mix without bothering to chop the pickles into smaller pieces.

Faith started laughing again and Joe grinned at her as he began taking big bites of his own pickle.

When he swallowed his last bite of the sour vegetable, Joe asked, "Did you eat anything?"

"No. I was waiting for you."

"You can have one of these steaks. I already had one and Newt can have the other half of his."

"Thank you, sir."

Joe slid one of the steaks onto a tin plate with the fork he'd been using to flip them then handed Faith his big knife before he set the plate onto her lap.

When she began cutting her steak, Joe tossed the other half steak to Newt who caught it in mid-air.

"Do you think the Moores will be angry when they figure out that you're gone, Faith?"

She swallowed then replied, "I don't know, but I wanted to talk to you about this whole situation."

"Okay, but before you do, I have to ask you something that might change everything. You might even decide that you never to talk to me again."

"I doubt if that's even possible, but I'll let you ask your question first."

Joe took a deep breath then said, "After you didn't show up last night, I was worried about you all morning. I thought that the Moores had done something that made you too ashamed to see me. You can't imagine how relieved I was when Chuck told me that you were fine. This afternoon, I realized that I'd have those same worries every time I didn't see you and that was a horrible thought."

Faith stopped eating and stared at Joe. *Was he about to ask her what she was preparing to ask him?*

Joe was incredibly uncomfortable as he looked at Faith. He was going to take the biggest risk of his life. It was much worse than facing eight Confederates who were trying to shoot him. So, he quickly began a flanking maneuver rather than using a direct assault.

"Faith, you and I get along really well. I don't know if it's because we think the same way or because we're here because of somewhat similar circumstances."

Faith was marginally disappointed when she asked, "What do you mean?"

"You're here because your parents didn't want you and I'm here because the Quimbys didn't want me. But when I'm with you, I don't feel that way."

Joe paused to see Faith's reaction but in the low light of his dying fires, it was difficult to see her eyes. But he soon had his answer, and it wasn't by trying to read her expression.

Faith ended the brief pause when she said, "I don't feel unwanted either, Joe. And it's not because I live with the Moores."

Joe smiled as he said, "That's because I want you to stay with me, Faith. I don't want you to have to worry about what the Moores might do or anything else ever again. But the only way I can think of doing that is if, um, is if I marry you."

Faith may have been hoping to hear Joe to ask her to stay with him, but proposing marriage was totally unexpected. Her mouth dropped open and her eyes grew so wide that even in the dim light, Joe could see her stunned expression.

He quickly exclaimed, "I'm sorry, Faith! Please don't get mad! Can't we pretend that I didn't tell you?"

Faith closed her mouth before replying, "There isn't any reason to do that, Joe. I was just surprised. I was hoping that you'd ask me to stay with you, but it was beyond my imagination that you would ask to marry me."

"You wanted to stay with me, even if we weren't married?"

UNWANTED

"Yes, and I don't care what anyone thought of me except you. I was worried about asking because I didn't want you to think less of me."

"I wouldn't have, but I figured that if I didn't marry you, then Mister Moore would be able to cause trouble. He still might, but I don't think he'll have much support."

Faith began poking at her cooling steak with her fork as she asked, "Is that your only reason wanting us to get married, Joe?"

If Joe was uncomfortable before, he was approaching panic now.

After a delay of three heartbeats, he replied, "No. I, well, I've never felt this way before, but I think I love you, Faith."

"I haven't felt this way before either, Joe. But there's no doubt in my mind or heart that I love you, too."

Joe relaxed then smiled and asked, "Then you'll marry me?"

"Of course. How do we do that?"

"I was talking to Chuck today and he told me that Mister Newbury, who does the prayer services on Sunday, is a deacon and can baptize babies and marry people. We can talk to him tomorrow. Do you want to get married on Saturday?"

"That would be wonderful!"

Joe exhaled then smiled at Faith and said, "Your steak is cold."

Faith looked down at the plate on her lap and said, "Oh. I'll finish this while you stir your pot."

Joe didn't have to do anything else with his stew except let it simmer but still began pushing the heavy wooden spoon through the thickening mix as he watched Faith eat.

While Faith cut and ate her steak and Joe stirred his stew and looked at her, Newt took advantage of their distraction and snatched the last steak from the frypan.

Joe saw the hound flash in front of him then laughed before saying, "You're lucky that the pan is cold, Newt."

Faith laughed but had to put her hand over her mouth to prevent expelling the meat she'd been chewing.

She soon set her plate down and left Joe's big knife on the plate assuming correctly that Joe would want to clean it.

Joe pulled the wooden spoon from the pot and set it on the plate before looking back at the wagons and hearing the sounds of celebration coming from the other side.

"It sounds like they're having a party over there."

"I just hope that Mister and Mrs. Moore don't notice I'm gone."

UNWANTED

"Soon, you won't have to worry anymore."

Faith nodded then after a long, equally shared awkward pause, she asked, "Joe, when you said that you love me, do you mean like a man loves a woman? Or do you mean like a friend you want to protect?"

For just a moment, Joe considered giving her the safer answer but quickly decided that he needed her to know that he truly wanted her to be his wife.

"You are the best friend I've ever had, Faith. But I want you to be my wife because I love you as a woman."

Faith exhaled sharply before she smiled and said, "I was afraid that you only saw me as a girl because I'm so skinny."

"I'm not exactly fat, Faith. And even though I don't think that you're as thin as you seem to believe, I still have, um, well, um, desires for you."

Faith almost laughed at Joe's awkwardness but was able to hold it to a big smile knowing he'd be hurt if she did.

After a few seconds, she asked, "I've been having dreams about you too, Joe. They aren't exactly the kinds of dreams that a good girl is supposed to have, either."

Joe grinned as he said, "I'll bet that they aren't close to being as lascivious as mine."

"Lascivious? I've never heard that word used before, but I can imagine what it means."

"You'd be right, too. But you shouldn't feel bad about having those thoughts or dreams, Faith. They don't make you bad or immoral. On my tenth birthday, just a month before I lost my entire family, my mother sat me down and explained all of the changes in my body and my life that would soon be coming. I was horrified, but she spoke to me for an hour or so over each of the next few nights until I changed my mind.

"She said that many preachers condemned sex as something shameful, but that wasn't true at all. By the time she and the rest of the family got sick, I was actually looking forward to those talks. I'm glad that she told me before I had to move to live with the Quimbys. I got the impression that my uncle saw marital relations as only necessary for procreation."

Faith quietly said, "I found out about it much differently. I was seven when our neighbor brought his bull over to mate with our cows. I hadn't seen it before, so I watched from the porch and when my mother stepped out of the house, I asked her why the bull was trying to hurt our cow and my father didn't try to stop him. She ordered me back into the house and told me in a very harsh way that the bull was mating with the cow so it would have a calf and then produce milk. I thought that was the end of the lecture, but it wasn't.

"She then explained that it was necessary for God's creatures to have children but that it was just a duty and nothing more. I should have let it go, but I asked her if she and my father had done that to make me and my brothers and sisters and she reacted as if I'd slapped her. She wagged her finger at me and said that I was to never say a word about it again. So, I didn't."

Joe's eyebrows rose as he asked, "You never learned about, um, what men and women do after they get married?"

Faith replied, "My mother sat down with me the night before I left and explained it as if she was teaching me how to knit. I didn't know why she had finally explained it to me until my father took me away the next day. You probably know a lot more about it than I do."

"I reckon so. But I've never even kissed a girl before."

"Really? Never?"

"Not unless you count my sister, and she was seven when she died."

"Are you going to kiss me now that we're almost married?"

Joe nodded, said, "Okay," then stood and took Faith's hand before she rose to her feet.

Joe removed his hat and tossed it to the ground as he put his arms around Faith, and she wrapped her arms around him. They were both wearing their heavy coats but just holding each other was a new and exciting experience for each of them.

Joe quietly said, "I hope you're not disappointed when we're finished."

"I won't be, unless you bite my lips."

"I'll taste like pickles."

Faith smiled but didn't reply as she looked up into his dark brown eyes.

Joe slowly lowered his lips to hers and was surprised how wet it was but soon bypassed the initial sensation and felt a flood of warmth rush through him.

Faith never even noticed the moistness but was so overwhelmed that she felt her knees weaken and squeezed him even tighter.

When their lips parted a few seconds later, Joe whispered, "I love you, Faith Hope Charity Virtue Goodchild. I want to marry you and make love to you."

Faith smiled as she softly replied, "I love you Joe 'no middle name' Beck. Can you kiss me again?"

Joe didn't need the invitation and quickly answered her question without speaking.

UNWANTED

When their second kiss ended, Joe glanced over the top of her blonde head at the distant wagons and saw shadows heading towards them and said, "Somebody's coming."

He grabbed his hat and pulled it on as he and Faith turned to stare at the two figures, unable to identify them in the shadows.

Joe looked at Newt who didn't seem to be annoyed at all, so Joe knew that Mort wasn't one of the two, but they may be the Moores.

He had just noticed one was wearing a dress when he heard Chuck loudly ask, "Mind if we come into your camp, Joe?"

"Come on in, Chuck."

Faith smiled as she asked, "Is that you, Mary?"

They were close when Marigold replied, "Yes. We wanted to stop by to warn you."

Joe glanced at Faith then looked at Marigold and asked, "Does it have to do with the Moores?"

"Yes. They're looking all over for you, Faith. They don't seem to be very happy, either."

Faith replied, "I think they're probably worried because they saw you talking to Chuck, but you were supposed to be interested in Joe."

Then she turned to Joe and said, "I'd better get back."

"I suppose so. I'll see you tomorrow when I get back. Okay?"

"Alright."

Joe was thinking of kissing her when Chuck said, "Oh, by the way, there'll be three of us tomorrow. Mort said he's feelin' okay."

"That could be interesting."

Marigold hooked her arm through Faith's before the three of them headed back to the wagons as the sounds of the buffalo feast still echoed through the darkness.

Joe turned back to his smoldering campfires and scratched Newt behind the ears. While he was disappointed that Faith had to return, he was very pleased that she'd been so happy about his proposal. Soon, she would always be with him.

CHAPTER 8

Before Bo even rang his wakeup bell, Joe had heated a large portion of his stew for breakfast then stored the rest in the empty pickle jar and one of his empty clay pots then covered it with gutta-percha. He knew he wouldn't be able to smoke any meat for a while, so he gave a two-pound piece to Newt then salted the rest and stored it in a leather pouch. He had scraped the inside of the buffalo skin after Faith left, then draped it over his cart's canvas roof with the fur side down before saddling Bessie.

He led his tent-cart and Bessie to the Smith's wagon and left it with Russ and Jimmy but didn't see either Faith or Marigold. He figured he'd ask Chuck about it when he had the chance. Despite not seeing Faith, Joe's biggest concern was now Mort. He hoped to get an idea of just how big of a problem he might have when he saw Mort in a few minutes.

He walked Bessie to the front of the line as the folks began moving their oxen and mules to their harnesses in the predawn light. He saw Bo harnessing his oxen with Mort's help but didn't see Chuck. What caused him concern was when he saw Chuck's gray gelding still tied to the back of the wagon without a saddle.

He pulled up, dismounted, then led Bessie to front of the wagon.

Before he could ask, Bo looked at him and said, "Chuck's havin' stomach problems. I reckon he ate somethin' bad last night. He's over in the Carlisle's wagon."

Joe nodded, then after glancing at Mort, he asked, "Is he going to be alright?"

"I reckon. He'll probably be fit as fiddle by this afternoon."

"Did anybody else get sick?"

"Not that I heard."

Mort then said, "I'll be ready to go after we get these critters harnessed."

"Okay."

Joe was surprised at Mort's almost congenial tone and didn't see any animosity. While he should have been pleased, he was actually more suspicious. He'd have to keep a close eye on Mort. When Bo said that only Chuck was sick, Joe wondered if Mort hadn't slipped some poison into his food.

―――――

Ten minutes later, as the predawn gave way to the morning sun, Joe and Mort rode away from the wagons. Joe wasn't worried about Mort while they were so close to the wagons but soon, they'd be out of sight and that's when things might get dicey.

Neither spoke for almost a half an hour before Mort said, "Let's split up. You can take the south side of the Trail and I'll ride along the Platte."

Joe replied, "Alright," then angled Bessie to the left as Mort turned his dark brown mare to the right.

Joe felt better after he had a good four-hundred-yard gap between him and Mort but still glanced to the north every few seconds to make sure Mort was aiming his rifle at him. But Mort wasn't even looking at him as he rode parallel on the north side of the Trail. If Mort tried to shoot him, it would be an almost impossible shot.

They were probably about seven or eight miles from the wagon train, and nothing had happened. The trail ahead was clear and devoid of danger. They were still on Pawnee land, so Joe began to relax.

He had been surprised when he first saw the Platte River. He'd expected it to look like the Missouri, but while it was as wide as the Mighty Mo, it was probably only six or seven feet deep. He imagined that by late summer, it would be even shallower.

He'd crossed two narrow feeder creeks when he spotted a much bigger one ahead. He figured that he'd dismount and refill his canteen.

Before he reached the fast-flowing creek he noticed something odd about it. The water was heading south when it should have been flowing north to the Platte River. He pulled up and dismounted before leading Bessie to the water. As he unscrewed his canteen's cap, he studied the terrain.

There was a low, broad hill to his right that blocked the water's path. He figured that it had probably caused the creek to make a long bend before it eventually turned back to empty into the Platte. He removed the canteen and screwed the cap back on before setting it on the ground. Then he sat on his heels he began thinking about Faith and let his imagination take hold. As he fantasized, he had totally forgotten about Mort, so he didn't know that Mort already had him in his sights.

While he had nothing to do with Chuck getting sick, Mort had viewed it as almost providential. He knew the terrain ahead and had already climbed the hill with his rifle and expected Beck to stop to water Bessie. So, when Joe Beck had pulled up, Mort wasn't surprised. But when he saw the kid dismount and drop to his heels, he was enormously pleased. He thought it was almost as if God Himself had ordered the obnoxious kid's assassination.

He was lying prone on the hill and knew he'd never have a better opportunity. He thought he'd have to fire quickly and had almost fired twice already but wanted to be absolutely sure that he wouldn't miss. He was around two hundred and fifty yards out and it would be the longest shot he'd ever made.

UNWANTED

Joe was still deep in his dreamland when his world exploded. He felt as if someone had kicked him in his left side before he fell face down into the creek. As the rushing water floated him downstream, Joe rolled onto his back so he could breathe then felt his chest. He knew he must be bleeding but wasn't able to determine how badly he'd been hurt because his coat was already soaked. He needed to get out of the water quickly but struggled to reach the bank. His waterlogged heavy coat was dragging him underwater, and the rushing creek kept pulling him downstream.

Mort was elated as he scrambled to his feet. He knew he hadn't missed but could no longer see the kid's body after he hit the water. He hurried back down the hill to his horse, slid his rifle into its scabbard, then mounted and rode back to where he'd seen Joe fall into the creek.

Joe had finally managed to crawl onto the muddy bank then rolled onto his back and opened his coat. He ripped open his shirt and looked at the wound. The bullet had ripped a small piece of muscle off his left side, but it wasn't deep or long. He had to get out of his coat and then try to stop the bleeding.

Mort reached Bessie, dismounted then took both horses' reins and walked to the creek's edge. He looked downstream and couldn't see Beck's body. He knew he should check to make sure he was dead, but time was growing short, so he decided to return to the wagon train to report the bad news. He tied Bessie's reins to his saddle then mounted and after a few more seconds in the saddle looking downstream, he turned his mare around and headed back to the Trail. He needed to concoct a story to explain what had happened. He knew that Bo and Chuck would both suspect that he'd murdered the kid, so he needed to clean and reload his rifle before he got back.

Joe had wiggled out of his soaked coat and pulled his knife. He still had his pistol and amazingly, his hat was still on his head, but he knew that he was in trouble. As he sliced off his shirt sleeves, he kept looking north for Mort. He knew that if Mort found him, he wouldn't stand a chance. Mort would be able to stand a hundred yards away and take his time to shoot him again.

After he'd removed his shirtsleeves, Joe tied them together, then gritted his teeth and sat up. He wrapped it around his chest and tied it off before dropping back down onto his coat.

He finally removed his hat and looked up at the blue sky overhead. It was such a pleasant spring day and unless his luck changed, Mort would soon spot him, and he'd never see another one. What was even worse, he knew that he would no longer be able to protect Faith. But beyond the serious concerns, he was surprisingly irritated when he thought that Mort might decide to finish him off with his Henry.

He kept his eyes focused on the north as he listened for hoofbeats over the sound of the rushing water. After almost twenty minutes, Joe began to believe that Mort wasn't going to show up which surprised and confused him.

UNWANTED

Joe checked on his wound again and found the blood had soaked through his shirtsleeve bandage, but there was nothing he could do unless he cut his shirt into new bandages. So, he pulled his Colt New Army, set it on his stomach, then just continued to watch for Mort. He was fighting to stay awake as his blood continued to add red stains to his already wet coat.

———

Faith had been relieved when the Moores didn't even chastise her for visiting Joe and this morning, they seemed to be almost pleasant. She was walking with Russell as he led Bernie and had her walking stick which she was using it as a weapon to keep the yellow-kerchiefed goats in line.

Russell had explained Joe's reason for putting the buffalo skin upside down on the tent but had mostly chatted about the feast.

Then Russell said, "Marigold said that you and Joe Beck are gonna get married."

Faith glanced at the Moore wagon out of habit before she replied, "When he comes back today, we'll visit Mister Newbury, and we'll get married on Saturday."

"What did Mister and Mrs. Moore say about it?"

"I don't want them to find out yet. Joe can tell them when he thinks it's okay."

Russell grinned then said, "That oughta be funny."

"I wish it would be. Where's Marigold?"

"She's up front in the Carlisle wagon. She's nursing Mister Lynch."

Faith quickly asked, "What happened to Chuck?"

Russell shrugged then replied, "I ain't sure. I think he just ate something bad."

"So, Joe is out there alone with Mort Jones?"

"Yup."

Faith began chewing her lower lip as they walked. She wondered if Mort had poisoned Chuck so he could try to kill Joe. She didn't think that Joe would let Mort have a chance to even pull his gun, but it was still unnerving. She kept her eyes focused ahead waiting to spot Joe when he returned for the noon break. She would be very anxious until she saw two riders come over the horizon.

―――

Mort had stopped to clean his rifle before reloading it. He stopped short of oiling it because it hadn't been oiled when he left. As he rode back, he had decided that his best story would have to be vague. He'd say that he'd headed south to tell Beck that it was time to head back and found his horse standing near the creek. He had ridden alongside the creek for thirty minutes but hadn't seen him. His disappearance would just be a mystery.

He knew that the wagon train wouldn't even reach the creek until tomorrow morning, so by then his body should have been washed into the Platte or dragged away by coyotes or wolves. As he rode, he glanced back at the kid's Henry and wished there was some way he could take it, but that would be too obvious.

It was almost noon when he spotted the lead wagon in the distance and prepared to be grilled by Bo Ferguson. He'd have to give the best acting performance of his life.

The wagons had begun to stop for the noon break when Faith spotted the two horses but only one rider and her stomach twisted into a giant knot. As the rider drew closer, she soon realized that Mort Jones was leading Bessie. Joe was gone.

Russell had also noticed and asked, "How come Joe's not riding his horse?"

Faith quickly replied, "I don't know, but let's get Bernie moving faster. I want to be up front when that bastard arrives."

She began to jog as Russell grabbed Bernie's halter and tugged him into a faster pace. Newt trotted beside Faith as she began passing the wagons.

Bo hadn't seen Faith or Mort yet as he was busy talking to Mister Carlisle.

But before Faith reached his wagon, Ed Carlisle looked past the wagon master and said, "You only have one scout coming back, Bo."

Bo whipped around, spotted Mort leading Bessie and exclaimed, "Son of a bitch!"

He forgot about whatever he and Ed Carlisle had been discussing and began walking towards Mort. He was furious knowing what Mort had probably done but felt sickened knowing that he'd even allowed Mort to ride off with Joe.

Mort had modified his story when he was halfway back. He'd say that Beck was riding near the Platte, and he was riding south of the Trail. So, if they searched, they'd never find his body. Even if there were vultures circling overhead it would be miles away from the river and was a common enough sight anyway.

He could already see the anger in Mo's face as he drew close and had to avoid overplaying his hand. If he acted sorrowful over the kid's death it would make him appear even guiltier.

Then he noticed that blonde girl almost running toward the lead wagon and had to avoid smiling. He'd get a little extra pleasure watching her burst into tears. Maybe he'd even offer to comfort her.

UNWANTED

Bo didn't see Faith yet as he stared at Mort and as his scout began to dismount, he shouted, *"What the hell happened, Mort?"*

Mort led his brown mare closer to the wagon master then replied, "I don't really know, boss. I was ridin' south of the Trail about a mile or so when I figured it was time to head back. So, I turned to the north to find Beck, but he wasn't where I figgered he'd be. Then I spotted Bessie grazin' near the river and headed over there. I didn't see the kid anywhere, so I tied off Bessie to my saddle and rode west along the bank for a few minutes before turnin' around and searching downriver. I never saw a lick of him, Bo."

Bo didn't reply but walked to Bessie and inspected the saddle. He didn't find any blood but pulled Joe's Mississippi rifle from its scabbard and found that it hadn't been fired. After checking his Henry, Bo walked to Mort's horse, pulled his rifle and found that it hadn't been fired either. After sliding it back into its scabbard, he turned and walked back to Mort.

He was about to say something when Faith arrived looked at Bo and between her deep breaths, she asked, "Where's Joe?"

Bo replied, "Mort says he just disappeared. I checked both of Joe's rifles and Mort's, too. None of 'em have been fired. The only reason for him disappearin' like that is if Joe fell into the Platte. Even if he knew how to swim, his heavy coat woulda dragged him down. With the snow melt and the spring rains, even the Platte can be nasty."

Faith stared at Bo for a few seconds before she turned her blue eyes onto Mort. She hoped to see a sign of glee in his eyes but found nothing that indicated that he'd killed Joe.

She looked back at Bo and asked, "Mister Ferguson, are you going to send out a search party?"

"No, ma'am. We'll be headin' that way soon enough. We should get there before we break for the night."

Faith exclaimed, "*You aren't doing anything?*"

Bo felt bad enough, but he was just doing his job. He wasn't about to send Mort out to search for Joe's body. Even if he found it, Bo thought it was best that Faith didn't see it.

"We don't know where he is, Miss Goodchild. I'm sorry."

Faith was furious as she sharply asked, "*Do you want your horse back now?*"

"No. I gave her to Joe, so you can have her."

Faith glared at Mort as Bo walked to Bessie, untied her reins from Mort's saddle then led her back to Faith.

He handed her the reins and said, "I'm real sorry, Faith."

She replied, "It's not your fault, Mister Ferguson," then she pointed at Mort and said, "It's his."

She turned around just as Russell arrived with Bernie and the cart then said, "Let's go back to your wagon, Russ."

Russell had heard much of the conversation but didn't know what Faith was going to do now.

Faith had made up her mind what she would do as soon as Mister Ferguson had said that they wouldn't search for Joe. She wouldn't ride Bessie, but she'd tie her to Joe's cart. Then she'd go to the Moores' wagon, take the bag with all of her possessions and just leave. She didn't care if she had to walk all the way to Oregon by herself. If Joe was dead, then she didn't care what happened to her.

But even as she led Bessie back to the Smith wagon, she realized that she had one significant advantage when she searched for Joe. She would trust Newt's incredible nose to find his friend.

―――

Joe had drifted off then suddenly awakened when he felt something squawk nearby. He thought it might be a vulture, but when he found the squawker, he smiled. It was a racoon, and it was staring at him as it stood on its hind legs.

"Sorry, mister. I don't have any food."

The racoon lost interest and trotted away before Joe decided to move. He holstered his Colt then tightened his jaws before he began to sit up. He felt a sharp pain on his left side but still managed to sit upright. He looked at his bandage and while it was still soaked with blood, he didn't see any fresh blood leaking out. So, he untied the knot then carefully removed it from the wound. He knew it would start bleeding again but didn't want it to turn into a gusher.

He was relieved when the wound only oozed some blood, so he decided to stand. He rolled onto his right side before he used his arms to push him from the muddy bank. He got to his knees then rocked back and stood. He wasn't dizzy, which surprised him, but was grateful. He carried his bloody bandage to the creek and washed it as best he could before he hung it over his shoulder.

Now that he was on his feet, he began to scan the area expecting to see Mort or Bessie. But the horizons were clear and while not seeing Mort was a good thing, not spotting Bessie left him in a tough situation. He didn't know how far he'd drifted south but doubted if Bessie was still waiting for him where he'd left her. But even as he realized his difficulties, he wondered how Mort would be able to convince Bo Ferguson that he hadn't tried to kill him.

But if he had managed to make up a believable story, then Joe couldn't afford to let Mort return to find him. He had to hide until he spotted the wagons. But even then, he had to avoid letting Mort see him first.

He returned to his coat and pulled it from the mud then had to soak it in the creek again. After it was reasonably clean, he draped it over his right arm and began walking south to make it more difficult for Mort to find him.

———

Marigold was still in the Carlisle wagon with Chuck, so after Faith told an astonished Russell what she was going to do, she led Bernie and the tent-cart to the Moores' wagon. She stepped to the back of the wagon and climbed onto the tailgate.

The Moores were all on the other side of the wagon and Mary was waiting for Faith to return to admonish her for failing to help her prepare the family's lunch. So, neither she nor her husband spotted Faith as she tossed her bag into Joe's cart then led the cart and Bessie south until she was a couple of hundred yards away and then turned right to parallel the wagons. She knew that she'd probably be spotted by a few people, but she didn't want to waste time.

She led Bernie past the wagons with Newt trotting in front of her and she wondered how she could ask Joe's hound to find him. She knew she probably wouldn't find him today but not for one moment did she believe that Joe was dead. She refused to even allow the thought to enter her mind. She simply couldn't.

She hadn't eaten much yet but knew that Joe had stored some of his stew and could have that for supper if she hadn't found Joe by then. She kept her eyes on the wagons as they passed by and only saw a few people looking back at her, but when she reached the front of the line, she was relieved that Mort Jones wasn't one of them.

She continued following her path until she was well ahead of the wagons and knew that they'd be rolling soon. So, she began angling toward the ruts, just to make the going easier.

After Faith was close to the Trail, she turned Bernie to stay outside of the deep ruts. Then she spotted the hoofprints that could only have been left by Joe and Mort Jones.

She was only a thousand yards or so ahead of Mister Ferguson's wagon, and she knew that he could see her. She hoped that he didn't sent Mort after her, but as she looked back to make sure he didn't, she let her eyes rest on Bessie. She thought about riding, but she had never ridden a horse before and couldn't depend on Bernie to keep walking if she was just sitting in the saddle.

So, Faith continued leading Bernie and noticed that she was outpacing the wagons. While she wouldn't be able to get that far ahead of them, she wasn't planning on stopping when Mister Ferguson rang his bell to end the day's travel.

―――

UNWANTED

Mary Moore hadn't seen Faith since they had stopped for the noon break and after they'd started rolling again, she couldn't see her with the cows and goats either.

She spent a few minutes wondering where she was before she realized that Joe Beck's odd cart wasn't behind them.

She turned to the front of the wagon and loudly asked, "Harry, where is Faith?"

"How should I know? Isn't she back with the cows?"

"No. And that Joe Beck's cart isn't there either."

Harry swore under his breath, and if Mary wasn't so encumbered by their unborn child, he would have had her take the reins so he could leave to find out what had become of her.

Mary then asked, "Do you think that boy came back here and took her away?"

"If he did, he'll be sorry. We paid good money for her."

Mary didn't think it was much of an argument, but it was all they had. She had been close to believing that Marigold Smith was now blocking Faith from any relationship with Beck. But after seeing Chuck Lynch spending all that time with Marigold, she suspected that Marigold had shifted her attention. If that had happened, it would explain Faith's absence from the feast last night and now her disappearance.

She finally boosted herself out of the wagon and onto the driver's seat.

"I'll drive while you find out what happened to Faith."

Harry was surprised, but replied, "Alright," before scrambling down from the wagon and trotting to the front of the line to ask Bo Ferguson about Beck.

―――

Joe had been walking for almost an hour when he became too tired to continue. He dropped his mostly dry coat to the ground then checked his wound before wrapping his completely dry sleeve bandage around his chest and slowly sat down beside the creek. His stomach was growling; but going without a few meals wasn't unusual for him. It was one of the reasons he was so thin.

Joe spotted a jackrabbit nearby and would have shot him with his Colt but didn't want the pistol's report to alert Mort. He assumed that Mort was out scouting for him again, even if he had returned to the wagon train.

He scanned the horizons again before he stretched out his coat and laid down. He pulled his blue hat over his eyes just to cut down on the sun's glare but soon drifted to sleep.

―――

Mort had been pestering Bo to let him go out front again, but the wagon master told him that there was no use to search for Joe's body. His real reason was that he thought that Mort wanted to make sure that Joe's body was well hidden. While all of the guns had been clean and loaded, Bo hoped to find Joe's body. If he found a bullet hole, he's shoot Mort without waiting for an explanation.

He was sitting on his driver's seat when Harry Moore trotted alongside and loudly asked, "Bo, where is Joe Beck?"

Bo looked down at him and said, "He went out scoutin' this mornin' and Mort found his horse near the Platte but didn't find him anywhere. He's probably dead."

Harry was startled then asked, "Have you seen Faith Goodchild?"

Bo pointed ahead and said, "She's about a mile up front. She's got Joe's cart and horse and figures that she can find him."

Harry stopped and stared at the western horizon and soon spotted the distant cart-tent. He then identified Faith as she walked alongside.

He began jogging again then when he was even with the driver's seat, he shouted, "Why didn't you send Mort to bring her back?"

Bo replied, "I can see her and she's not in any danger."

Harry took one last look at the distant tent-cart before he turned and headed back to his wagon to tell Mary. Just as Bo had believed, he expected that Faith would return to the wagons when they stopped for the night. He couldn't wait to give Mary the news that Joe Beck was dead. It was better than trying to get Marigold to push her aside.

———

Faith let Bernie keep walking, but she stopped and waited until the back of the cart passed. Then she stepped beside Bessie and rummaged through Joe's things to find something to eat. She found his used pickle jar of stew and then had to hunt for a spoon. After she trotted to get ahead of Bernie again, she unscrewed the top, slipped it into her dress pocket, then dug the spoon into the stew. She took big bite and was astonished how good it was. The mix of sweet molasses, sour pickle juice and the meaty flavor from the buffalo meat blended into a very tasty meal.

She only ate half of the jar before screwing the top back on then heading to the back of the cart and setting it inside. She took out a canteen of Joe's water and after drinking almost half, she used some to wash the spoon. After returning the spoon and the canteen to the cart, she hurried to the front with her walking stick. She guessed she had another two hours of daylight and looked back to see how far she was away from the wagons.

UNWANTED

They were more than a mile away now and she still hadn't seen Mort ride out. She guessed it was because Mister Ferguson suspected that he had shot Joe. She didn't doubt that he had but still believed that Joe was only wounded. Faith was determined to find him and do what she could to help him. What they did after that was up to Joe.

―――

Joe had awakened from his nap and quickly checked for unwanted visitors, specifically Mort Jones. He didn't see anyone, so he slowly stood and pulled on his hat then his coat before he walked to the creek and began scooping and slurping the cold water.

He checked his bandage and found that it was still dry. He could probably discard it but would need it if the wound's scab broke open. After buttoning his sleeveless shirt, he wondered if he should follow his backtrail. He was too far south to even spot the wagon train as it passed, so he decided to head north along the creek. He kept a slow pace but with his long strides, he expected to reach where he'd been shot before sundown. The wagon train would probably camp about two or three miles east of the creek, and he would still be about a mile from the Trail. He was tired and would be exhausted when he found those ruts, but he wasn't about to let Mort escape punishment for what he had done.

―――

Mary had been pleased to learn of Joe Beck's death, but annoyed that Bo Ferguson had allowed Faith to lead that boy's cart so far ahead.

She asked, "Harry, what do you think Beck has in that cart?"

Harry looked back and replied, "We know he's got another rifle and supposedly a lot of ammunition. He even gave Russell Smith a full ammunition pouch. I'll bet he's got money, too. He bought a lot of supplies at the store in Kansas City."

"Do we have any claim on it? After all, Faith belongs to us."

"I don't know. Let's wait for Faith to return and we'll ask her."

As he drove, Harry was uncomfortable with Mary's comment about Faith. While he may have agreed with her decision to have Faith become his wife if she died, even he didn't think that Faith belonged to them.

———

Chuck was sipping some hot tea when Marigold climbed back into the Carlisle wagon.

He smiled and said, "I'm doin' a lot better, Mary. You're a good nurse."

Marigold sat close in the cramped space before saying, "I just heard that Joe Beck is dead. Mort rode back at the noon break with his horse and told Mister Ferguson that he'd found the horse near the Platte River but couldn't find Joe anywhere."

Chuck was startled and quickly set the tea down before he asked, "Did Bo believe him?"

"I don't know. Russell just told me."

"I hope he didn't let Mort go out searchin' for him."

"No, he's still with Mister Ferguson. But after she heard the news, Faith took his cart and horse then left. She's out front and almost out of sight now."

Chuck's eyebrows rose before he asked, "Bo let her go out there alone?"

"I guess so."

"I'll go up front and talk to him. Maybe I'll go join her."

"I don't think you should, Chuck. I'm sure Faith will be back soon."

Chuck nodded then replied, "I reckon you're right. But I'll still talk to Bo. Do you wanna come along?"

Marigold smiled as she exclaimed, "Of course!"

Chuck slowly stood and crawled out of the wagon with Marigold following. He helped her down from the tailgate before they started toward the first wagon, which wasn't a long walk as the Carlisle's wagon was the second in line.

He thanked Flora Carlisle for the use of their wagon before they passed the driver's seat and thanked her husband.

Before they arrived at the lead wagon, he spotted Bo walking alongside, so Mort must be driving. He called out to Bo, who turned around and headed back. He didn't want Mort to overhear their conversation.

Before Chuck could say a word, Bo said, "I checked all of the rifles and none had been fired, Chuck. I'm just not convinced that it didn't happen like Mort said."

Chuck asked, "Did you check his pistol?"

"Nope. I reckon if he got that close to Joe and pulled his Colt, it woulda been Joe who rode back alone. I wish it had happened that way, too."

"So, do I. But why did you let Faith start searchin' for him?"

"I didn't even see her until she was out front, and she'll be okay while she's still in sight. She'll be back before sunset."

"What happened to Bessie?"

"I gave her to Faith. I figured if she needed to get back here fast, she'd be able to ride. Besides, she was gonna marry Joe pretty soon anyway."

Marigold asked, "How did you know about that?"

Chuck answered, "I kinda mentioned it to him last night."

"Oh."

"How are you doin', Chuck?"

"I'll be able to go out tomorrow. Do you think we'll find Joe's body?"

"Maybe. But you keep Mort in sight. He might try to hide it, so we can't see a bullet hole."

"Okay."

Marigold then said, "I've got to get back to my family. I don't want them to think that I've been doing anything immoral."

Chuck grinned as he said, "I don't reckon it's immoral, Mary."

She smiled then turned and hurried away before Chuck looked at Bo and asked, "How long before we pull up for the night?"

"Not long."

Chuck nodded before he and the wagon master hurried to catch up to their wagon.

———

Joe had reached the spot where he'd been shot and slowly sat down. He was too tired to walk all the way to the Trail tonight, but figured he'd be able to get there before the wagon train arrived in the morning. He was still undecided about what he would do when he saw Mort again.

He checked his wound once more before laying on the ground and was pleased that the clotted blood was already forming a thick scab. He left his coat on for warmth because it was going to be a cold night.

―――

Faith looked behind her and noticed that the distant wagons had stopped for the night. She was sure that they all expected her to return because she was just a skinny girl, but while she was still skinny, Faith no longer considered herself a girl. She was a young woman who had been kissed and was soon going to be Mrs. Beck. Now she needed to find her future husband.

The sun was setting, and Faith knew that she would soon lose sight of the hoofprints. She pulled Bernie to a stop and called Newt. The floppy-eared hound trotted back and sat in front of her obviously expecting food.

Faith turned and walked to the back of the cart as Newt trailed behind. She found Joe's leather bag and dug out the smallest piece of meat she could find, but it was still pretty large. She tossed it to Newt then began going through Joe's clothes, hoping to find something he'd recently worn, but was surprised to find everything washed and folded. She was about to just ask Newt to find Joe when she remembered that he had told her how he wished his feet weren't growing so quickly. It took her almost three minutes before she discovered his old boots near the very front of the stack of wood.

She stepped back and wasn't surprised to find that Newt had already consumed the salted buffalo meat.

Faith dropped to her heels and held out the boots to Newt. As Newt sniffed the work boots, she said, "Joe. Joe. Joe."

She stood straight then tossed the boots back into the cart and walked to the front again. She took hold of Bernie's harness then pointed ahead and exclaimed, "Joe! Joe! Joe!"

Newt looked up at her and she thought the hound didn't understand what she wanted him to do, but after just a few seconds, he turned and began trotting ahead. Faith tugged Bernie's harness and followed the white tip on Newt's tail hoping he wasn't just going that way because she'd pointed.

She watched as he snaked his way to the west. She expected him to shift toward the Platte River soon, but if anything, the dog began angling to the south. She wasn't sure what was pulling Newt in that direction, but she had more trust in the dog's nose than in Mort's honesty.

———

Faith's absence was raising concerns in the lead wagon and in the trailing wagon.

Bo had lost sight of the cart before sunset but had expected to see it again when the sun touched the horizon. But the sun was gone, and the sky was growing darker, yet Faith hadn't returned.

He and Chuck were staring west while Mort fixed supper.

Chuck asked, "Do you want me to go look for her, boss?"

"No. I reckon we'll find her in the mornin'. She's probably just camped for the night. She had enough supplies in Joe's cart and she had his dog with her, too."

"Okay. I'm gonna head back and tell Marigold. I figure if the Moores want to know where she is, they can pay you a visit."

Bo nodded as Chuck left to tell Marigold while he continued to look for any sign of Faith.

———

The Moores were more angry than worried. After a long discussion, they decided that Bo Ferguson and the rest were part of a conspiracy to steal Faith from them. Mary had even suggested that Joe Beck already had relations with Faith and was now carrying his child. How she would have even detected her pregnancy after a few days didn't change her accusation. Her husband didn't argue the point.

UNWANTED

With the sun down and the stars providing her only illumination until the moon rose, Faith was growing more concerned about where Newt was leading her. She could see Newt's tail and the outline of the landscape surrounding her but little else. If she wasn't so worried about Joe, she would have at least stopped until the sun rose. But Newt was still busy following his meandering path with his nose either near the ground or stuck into the air above the prairie grass. If she hadn't been so worried, Faith would have thought it was funny.

What she didn't appreciate was the breeze coming from the west that carried Joe's scent. If Joe hadn't dismounted at one of the narrow creeks to fill his canteens, Newt probably wouldn't have picked up the scent earlier. But now it was getting stronger, and the coon hound's path was growing straighter. He also picked up the pace knowing his friend was close.

The moon had finally made its appearance, but Faith still didn't notice Newt's faster speed or the straighter course because they were gradual. But she did notice that Newt stopped sniffing the air nearly as much. She may not know where she was, but she began to hope that Newt had done his job.

She was startled when he suddenly barked and began to run.

Joe was sleeping when the bark awakened him. He didn't move but simply listened. He slowly pulled his Colt from his holster and waited. He thought it was a coyote or a wolf but waited for the critter to make another cry to discover its location.

Faith spotted the big creek and believed that Newt had probably just smelled a nearby rabbit or beaver. Then she saw a dark object on the ground near the bank and realized it was a human body. She almost broke down in tears when Newt barked again then approached the black shape.

When Joe heard the nearby recognizable bark, he smiled. He had no idea how Newt had found him, but it didn't matter.

He holstered his pistol then loudly said, "Newt," and soon felt the hound's sloppy tongue cleaning his face.

He started to laugh as he rubbed the dog but was unable to sit up because Newt's head was hanging over his nose.

When Faith heard his voice then saw his hand leave the ground to pet Newt, she shouted, "Joe!" then raced through the prairie grass.

Joe was stunned when he heard Faith shout his name and quickly pushed Newt away to sit up. When he did, he felt a sharp stab of pain from his left side to remind him of his condition.

Faith slowed just before reaching him then stopped and asked, "Are you hurt, Joe?"

Joe slowly rose to his feet, smiled and said, "I have a bullet wound on the left side of my chest, but unless it gets infected, I'll be alright. What in tarnation are you even doing here?"

"I had to find you, Joe. Mort said you fell into the Platte River and drowned. But I didn't believe him, so I took your cart and had Newt find you."

Joe glanced behind her and spotted his tent-cart and was surprised to find Bessie tied to the back.

Then he said, "We'll talk but I have to treat my wound first."

"Okay. How bad is it?"

"Not too bad."

"I'll help as much as I can."

"I know you will. Let's go to the back of the cart."

He took her hand before they headed back to the cart and after passing Bessie, Joe pulled off the buffalo hide and stretched it on the ground.

He then walked to the back of the cart and rummaged around until he found his cache of bayonets. He pulled one out, set it on the buffalo blanket, then began taking branches from the cart and tossing them to the ground. When he had enough, he pulled out one of his boxes of matches, a canteen, and returned to the buffalo hide.

Faith watched him and didn't know what he was planning to do. She thought he was going to make a clean bandage, but he hadn't removed any cloth.

Joe tossed his hat onto the ground, then carefully removed his coat and let it drop. After he unbuckled his gunbelt and set it on the coat, he began unbuttoning his shirt and hoped that Faith wouldn't be too horrified by what he needed to do.

He slipped his sleeveless shirt off then lowered it to the ground before untying his bandage and setting near the branches. It would end its life as kindling.

Joe sat down and Faith soon joined him and stared at his ugly wound.

"That looks a lot worse than I expected, Joe."

"I reckon so. That big bullet took out a chunk of flesh near my ribs and the scab is all that's holding the blood back. I have to wash the scab off before I fix it. I'll need you to do that when I tell you. Okay?"

"Alright. What are you going to do, Joe?"

"I'm going to cauterize the wound with the bayonet."

"What does cauterize mean?"

"I guess the closest word is to burn it closed."

Faith was shocked into silence as she watched Joe break a few branches and set them on top of his bandage. He struck a match, set the cloth ablaze then immediately picked up his shirt and ripped it in half. He unscrewed the canteen's cap and soaked both halves in water.

He handed one half to Faith and said, "Use this to clean the scab when I tell you."

"Okay."

Joe nodded then wrapped the other wet cloth around his hand and grabbed the bayonet. The dry branches were fueling the fire as Joe slid the bayonet's tip into the flames.

Faith watched in a mixture of fascination and terror as the steel began to slowly change color.

Joe could feel the heat through the damp cloth and knew it had to get even hotter. He watched the bayonet until it began to glow orange then lifted his left arm and grasped the side of his neck with his left hand.

"Okay, Faith. Begin to clean off the scab."

She replied, "Alright," then began to wipe away the blood from the side of his chest.

When she saw blood start to ooze from the wound, she said, "It's bleeding again, Joe. Do I keep going?"

"Just a few more seconds. Don't be gentle, Faith."

"Okay."

Faith closed her eyes before she began rubbing much harder and almost started to cry when Joe said, "Okay, Faith. You can stop."

She quickly pulled her hand away but didn't open her eyes.

Joe didn't have time to look at her before he pulled the bayonet from the fire and looked down at his bleeding wound. He aligned the flat edge of the bayonet to the wound at an angle that would minimize the damage to the rest of his chest and quickly pressed the glowing metal to his ribs.

The pain was excruciating as he heard the sizzle of frying flesh and almost yanked it away. But he managed to hold it in place for five seconds before hurling it aside and dropping onto his back with his eyes closed and sweat poured from his forehead. He didn't pass out but began pawing the ground for the canteen.

Faith opened her eyes, saw Joe obviously trying to find the canteen then grabbed it and began pouring cooling water onto his cauterized wound. She thought it looked even worse now because it was bigger and almost bubbling. The burn extended a good inch on either side of his wound and knew it must be horribly painful. But Joe hadn't even cried out in pain which she found remarkable.

Joe felt the water slide across his burned flesh then sighed in relief, opened his eyes, smiled and said, "Thank you, Faith."

"What else can I do to help?"

"Right now, just tell me how you got here."

"Can you tell me what really happened first?"

"Yes, ma'am. It's your fault that I'm in this fix; you know."

Faith exclaimed, "*It's my fault?*"

"Only because I was thinking about you and didn't see Mort on that hill to the north. I was on my heels near the creek bank and letting my mind fill with thoughts of you when I was slammed into the creek. I immediately realized that Mort had shot me but had to avoid being pulled beneath the water by my heavy coat. I thought he'd follow, but…"

Faith was filled with hate for Mort Jones as she listened to Joe tell the story. She knew that Joe had been very fortunate that Mort's shot hadn't hit him just two more inches to the right. But he could have been luckier if it had been just a fraction of an inch further left and just ripped off part of his coat.

When he finished, Faith said, "They should hang that bastard when we get back. He said that you drowned in the Platte River and couldn't find your body."

"I guess that he really believes that I'm dead, but he'll want to make sure. I think Mort will ride out looking for me really early tomorrow morning. He'll find the ruts left by the cart and know that you came here. He'll probably follow them and think you're alone and helpless, so that puts you in danger, too."

"But I'm not alone and have you to protect me now, Joe."

He smiled then said, "No, you're not alone, but I'm concerned that the damage to my left side might cause my shots to be off target. I need to let it heal for a while if I can."

"Where will we go?"

"I think we should rest and talk for an hour or so, then we head south. Mort will probably follow, but I'll leave something behind, so he'll know that you found me and I'm not dead. That will spook him. He may still follow, but he'll go slower. From his saddle, he would be able to spot the tent-cart and Bessie from three miles and get here before anyone else even knew where we were."

"How long will it be before we can return to the wagons?"

"I really don't know. I'll need to be able to hold my rifle steady, so it could only be a day or two. But it could be a week or more. I wish I could give you a better answer, Faith."

"I'm not anxious to return to the wagons, Joe. I just want to see Mort punished for what he did."

"I know. So, tell me what happened when he got back and how you got here."

Faith began explaining what she'd heard Mort tell Mister Ferguson before he gave her Bessie. Then she told him how she'd taken her things from the Moores' wagon and just led Bernie away from the train then followed Newt after sunset.

Joe watched her as she spoke and used his concentration to diminish the constant, throbbing agony he had created with his cauterization.

He still kept his eyes focused on Faith as his fingertips found the wet cloth that she'd used to clean the wound. He laid it across the burn and felt a surge of relief. He knew it was temporary but knew that it would last longer than just pouring water over the damaged skin.

Faith saw him lay the wet cloth over his chest before she finished but continued until she reached the end of her explanation. Then, without asking, she picked up the canteen and poured more water over the cloth.

Joe smiled and said, "Thank you again, Faith."

"I'll fill all the canteens in a few minutes. I imagine that you must be hungry."

"I am. I saved some of my stew in a jar and a pot. I'd love to have some of it right now."

Faith smiled and said, "I already found it and had some for lunch. It was very good, too. I'll be right back."

Joe nodded and watched as Faith hopped to her feet and took two long steps to reach the back of the cart. He would have gotten it himself but didn't want to let the wet cloth drop off. He'd have to figure out how to keep it in place without exerting too much pressure. He did manage to sit up without losing the cloth.

Faith soon returned with another canteen, the half-full jar of stew and a spoon. She set the canteen on the buffalo hide then handed the jar and spoon to Joe and sat next to him.

Before he took his first bite, Joe said, "The large pot was next to the jar. It has a gutta-percha cover that's held in place with a cord. You can bring it out and have some for supper, too."

"I'll wait until you're finished."

Joe nodded then began to spoon out the stew. He had to admit that it did taste even better than he expected. But he knew how filling it was and that was more important. He needed to heal quickly. Being only sixteen was another, even more important factor to aid the process.

When he finished, he set down the empty jar then picked up the canteen and after unscrewing the cap, drank almost half of its contents.

Faith then asked, "Aren't you cold. Joe?"

"Kinda, but I'm not about to put on my coat again. I'll go get a shirt from my cart and then we can start walking south. Okay?"

"Can I have something to eat first?"

"Yes, ma'am. I'll bring the pot of stew back with me and you can use the spoon in the empty jar."

"I'll come with you."

Faith quickly popped to her feet before Joe slowly rose and let the damp cloth fall to the ground before they stepped to the back of the cart. Joe slid the gutta-percha covered pot from the side and handed it to Faith before he reached deeper into the cart to grab another shirt. He grunted as he did, and Faith grimaced but knew that there was nothing she could do to help him now.

Joe followed Faith back to the buffalo skin and after she sat down, he slipped his right arm through the sleeve then realized that he should have modified his normal dressing routine when he automatically reached behind his back to grab the left sleeve. He grunted then slipped the shirt from his right arm before he slid his left hand through the sleeve.

He noticed that Faith was staring up at him, so he smiled and said, "I should have thought of that before I tried to put it on."

"It really hurts; doesn't it?"

"I'd be lying if I said it wasn't excruciating. But I'll soak the left side of the shirt to help with the pain, then after sunrise, I'll cover it with lard and use a pair of my new socks as a bandage. Now you go ahead and eat while I finish dressing."

"Yes, sir."

Faith then began spooning Joe's delicious concoction into her mouth as she watched him button his shirt. It was only then that she realized that she'd seen his naked chest. Despite his claims of being thin, she was stunned when she recalled seeing his muscled torso. He wasn't bulky but his svelte, smooth body excited her. She was relieved that she hadn't noticed it while she had stared at his wound.

Joe snatched his hat from the ground, pulled it on, then picked up his gunbelt and buckled it on his waist as he stared at his coat. It knew it would soon be getting colder, so he regretfully leaned down and picked up the coat.

He remembered to insert his left arm first before pulling on the coat. He didn't button it but left it open before he slowly sat beside Faith.

She had just put another spoonful of the stew into her mouth when she looked at him and smiled as she chewed.

Joe asked, "Do you want to ride on Bessie when we leave? You must be exhausted after walking for that long."

Faith swallowed then asked, "Aren't you tired?"

"Not anymore. I slept a few hours, so I think I could manage a nice stroll. We can still talk while you're up there."

"Then I'll ride. I thought about it earlier, but I didn't know if Bernie would keep following Newt."

"Bernie would follow Bessie to the ends of the earth if you had decided to ride."

"But I've never ridden a horse before."

"Then it's time to learn. Bessie is a very gentle soul and it'll only take you a little time to learn how to guide her."

"I'd like that."

"Good. Now finish eating, drink some water, then we'll fill the canteens and be on our way."

"I'm finished already."

Joe nodded then replaced the gutta-percha cover and tied the cord in place. Before he could pick it up, Faith stood, grabbed the pot and carried it to the cart.

Joe looked at Newt and said, "You're a good dog, Newt. Thanks for leading Faith to me. She never would have found me if you hadn't shown her the way."

He scratched behind Newt's ear before he slowly stood then grabbed the buffalo skin and grunted when he tossed it onto the tent. He had to walk in front of Bernie to pull it down on the other side, but he wasn't about to abandon it. It still needed to dry and lose more of the gamey smell.

Faith was waiting beside Bessie when Joe arrived and asked, "What are you going to leave to let Mort know that you're alive?"

"I already did. *See my scrap of shirt over by the glowing ashes?* I don't want it to be too obvious or he'll think I'm setting a trap for him. I just want him to realize that I'm alive and we're together. It's also possible that Chuck may find the ashes and the scrap of cloth, but it's more likely that Chuck will be searching for my body near the Platte. Mort will know where my carcass should be and will head here."

"Oh. Can you take your rifle out of the bedroll so I can get in the saddle?"

"Yes, ma'am."

Joe stepped past Faith, slid his Henry out of the bedroll then watched as she lifted her left foot and placed it in the stirrup. As she swung her leg over the saddle, Joe witnessed more womanly leg than he'd ever seen before. He tried not to stare but after Faith settled into the saddle, she looked down then laughed.

Joe suddenly ripped his eyes from her bare left leg and sheepishly looked up at her as she asked, "They're pretty skinny; aren't they?"

"Um, no. I think your legs are very nice. Are you comfortable up there, or do you want me to adjust the stirrups? It'll only take me a couple of minutes."

Faith was still smiling as she replied, "Alright."

Joe slid the Henry back into the bedroll, but it did take longer than he expected to adjust the stirrups as he was distracted by Faith's bare legs.

Faith could have pulled her dress down more but had been pleased when Joe had complimented her on her legs. She wished that he'd be just as pleased with her upper half.

Joe untied Bessie's reins then looked up and said, "Are you ready, Faith?"

"Yes, sir."

Joe smiled then led Bessie past Bernie and said, "Let's go, boys."

Bernie started pulling the cart and Newt ran ahead as they followed the creek heading south. Joe knew it would probably make a curve to the east before heading north again, but he'd be looking for a reasonable ford to get to the other side. He planned to stay out of sight for as long as possible.

———

They successfully forded the creek less than an hour later and Joe led Bessie and her precious cargo west for another hour or so before he felt they were out of sight.

The moon was directly overhead when Joe helped Faith down from Bessie then led the mare to a smaller creek as Bernie followed.

As the donkey and horse dipped their muzzles into the water, Joe said, "I think we both need some sleep now. Newt will warn us if anyone or any critter comes close."

"I could use some sleep."

Joe nodded, then after putting on Bessie and Bernie's halters and tying them to the cart's long pulling poles, he yanked the buffalo skin onto the ground.

He smiled as he looked at Faith and said, "I just made our bed."

Faith laughed then said, "And we aren't even married."

She laid down on her left side leaving room for Joe. Joe knelt on the buffalo mattress, took off his hat, and slowly rolled onto his right side until he was just inches from Faith.

Then he lifted his left arm and wiggled a little closer before he pulled her against him and slid his right arm under her head to act as a pillow.

Faith slipped her left arm under his neck and draped her right arm over his shoulder before she quietly asked, "Does that hurt?"

"No. It's fine."

Joe knew that she desperately needed sleep. So, he just leaned forward, kissed her softly on her forehead and said, "Goodnight, Faith."

Faith whispered, "Goodnight, Joe."

Joe watched her close her eyes before he shut his own. He didn't fall asleep as he thought about how to deal with Mort Jones. He needed to test his ability to handle the heavy Mississippi, too. The Henry was lighter and with its rapid-fire ability, he could afford to miss. But he knew that if Mort found them, he'd need the Mississippi's range.

He finally drifted to sleep twenty minutes after Faith had entered the dreamworld.

CHAPTER 9

Joe and Faith were still sleeping when Bo rang his loud bell to wake up the folks. While the sound had died long before it reached them, Joe opened his eyes just a few minutes later as the predawn broke. It wasn't an external alert that brought him into the real world but an extremely full bladder.

When he opened his eyes, he was deluged with other information flooding into his mind. Faith's face was still just inches from his, his right arm was almost numb, and his cauterized wound hurt like hell.

He knew he couldn't pull his arm away without waking Faith, so he quietly said, "Faith? I need to get up."

Faith's eyelids fluttered and her blue eyes emerged from hiding before she blinked then smiled and said, "Good morning, Joe."

"Good morning to you too, Faith. But I really need to get up."

"Oh! I'm sorry."

Faith quickly sat up freeing Joe's right arm before he stood and almost ran to the other side of the cart. Faith needed relief herself and was immensely pleased when Joe reappeared less than a minute later.

He was buttoning his britches when he said, "You can use our open privy now, ma'am."

"Thank you, sir."

As Faith disappeared behind the cart, Joe scanned the dimly lit landscape. He didn't think that he'd see Mort for at least another two hours but was already modifying his earlier decision about the direction of their day's travel.

When Faith returned, he said, "I need to put some lard and another bandage on my wound."

"Do you want to make a fire? It's pretty chilly."

"I think it's safe. The wagon train must be about six or seven miles from here."

"I'll cook breakfast."

"Thank you, Miss Goodchild. We'll fry most of the remaining salted buffalo meat and give the rest to Newt. I was going to smoke it, but we don't have the time. Before I build the fire, I need to check on my wound."

"Do you want me to get the lard?"

"If you don't mind. And I'll need a pair of my socks, too."

Faith nodded then said, "I'll be right back," before she trotted to the back of the cart.

Joe slipped off his coat then unbuttoned his shirt. He was surprised that the shirt was still damp where he'd soaked it. He thought it might be blood until he pulled it off and the shirt didn't stick to the wound.

He tilted his head to look at the angry wound and had to admit that even as badly as it hurt, it looked much worse. He knew he'd have that nasty scar for the rest of his days.

Faith had found his socks easily but had to hunt for the lard. When she picked up the socks, she found two hats close by. One was a knitted wool cap that she pulled onto her head and the other was a sorry excuse for a hat with a pair of large, ragged holes in the crown. She stuffed the socks into her dress pocket then carried the lard and the hat back to Joe.

Joe was touching the perimeter of the damaged skin as Faith approached. When he looked up and saw her wearing his wool cap, he grinned.

She smiled then held up the damaged hat and asked, "Is this the one you were wearing when you stopped those rebels from killing the Union captain?"

"Yes, ma'am. I don't know why I kept the old thing, but you can keep the wool hat. It'll keep your head warm."

Faith stepped closer, said, "Thank you," then handed him the lard then touched his chest near his wound.

"Does it hurt as badly as it looks?"

"No. I'd be crying like a baby if it hurt that much."

"I don't think so."

As Joe opened the crock of lard, Faith said, "I wonder what Mrs. Moore is going to do after she has the baby. That's assuming that she survives."

Joe had scooped out some lard and as he slathered it over the wound, he replied, "She'll be a mother again and feed the baby until it's weaned."

Faith laughed then said, "If I had a baby, it would constantly cry out of hunger."

Joe looked at Faith and said, "No, she wouldn't. By the time you have our baby, Mother Nature would ensure that you could keep our little girl well fed."

Faith was startled by Joe's reply. She was flushed when she heard him say that she would have larger breasts, but almost stunned when he so casually said that they'd have a baby. She was also confused and curious why he seemed to believe that it would be a girl.

Joe hadn't realized the impact he'd just had on Faith as he pulled the socks out of her pocket, then pushed one into his pants' pocket before holding the other against his chest. The thick coat of lard held it in place well enough for him to pick up his shirt.

As he pulled it on, left sleeve first, he looked at Faith and saw her still staring at him.

He smiled and asked. "Did you think that we were going to get married and just shake hands, Faith?"

As he buttoned his shirt, Faith slowly shook her head as she replied, "No, but until you mentioned it, it was always just in the back of my mind."

Joe was tucking in the shirt when he said, "That's alright. We have other things to worry about first. I'll start the fire and we need to talk about where we'll go from here."

"I thought we were just going southwest to keep from being found."

"We're already far enough. I'll explain when we're having our buffalo breakfast."

"Okay."

Joe and Faith walked to the back of the cart and Newt trotted behind expecting that they'd soon be giving him something tasty.

UNWANTED

Twenty minutes later, as they sat eating their meat with a side dish of reheated stew, Joe began describing their day's journey and the reason for his decision.

"I figure that the wagon train is about six or seven miles northeast of us but mostly north. After Chuck and Mort ride off, they'll split up and I'm pretty sure that Mort will take the south side. He'll reach the place where he shot me within an hour or so then probably follow your tracks once he figures out that I'm still alive.

"But he can't follow us all the way here, so he'll have to go back. We already crossed the creek, so we'll head west for an hour or so then swing northwest. The wagon train should be a couple of miles ahead of us by then and when we reach the Platte River, we'll be behind them. They won't even know we're back there."

"What about Mort?"

"We'll figure out the best way to deal with him while we're moving. Okay?"

"Alright."

Even as Joe told Faith that Mort wouldn't follow them, he didn't realize that Mort wouldn't even visit where he believed he'd killed Joe.

———

Bo Ferguson had both of his scouts before him as he said, "I want you both to ride along the Platte. You should spot his cart and Faith pretty soon. After you send her back, I want you both to search for Joe's body."

Chuck asked, "How far out do you want us to look, boss?"

"Just ride along the Platte until the noon break."

Mort quickly asked, "Both of us?"

Bo didn't quite reach the hostility of a glare as he looked at Mort and replied, "Yeah. Both of ya."

Chuck avoided snickering as Bo had already told him that he needed to keep a close eye on Mort all day.

A few minutes later, as Mort and Chuck rode away, Bo wasn't surprised to see Harry Moore striding towards him with an angry expression. Bo was already in a foul mood and thought that Moore had no reason to complain that Faith hadn't returned.

Even though Chuck hadn't mentioned Joe's suspicions about why Faith was with the Moores, he had already formed that opinion after learning that Harry had paid twenty-five dollars for the pretty girl. What he couldn't have imagined was Harry's wife-inspired belief that Bo and Chuck had conspired to let Faith run off with Joe Beck.

UNWANTED

Harry stopped before the wagon master and angrily asked, "Where is our nanny, Ferguson?"

Bo noticed the accusatory tone but calmly replied, "I just sent Chuck and Mort out to look for her. I reckon we'll see Joe's cart in an hour or so."

Harry's eyes narrowed as he asked, "Did you and Chuck Lynch fix it so Beck could steal our nanny?"

Bo's eyebrows shot up as he sharply asked, "What did you say?"

"You heard me. You like that tall kid and he probably asked you to fix it so he could steal Faith."

Bo snapped, "You're nuts, Moore! Mort went out with Joe yesterday and came back alone. I figure that he probably shot Joe Beck and dumped him into the Platte River. Then he cleaned his rifle and invented that story about Joe just fallin' into the river. I can't prove it, but that's what I'm thinkin'. If you wanna believe somethin' as stupid as what you just said, then you go right ahead. But don't come here and accuse me of doin' somethin' like that again!"

Harry was suddenly embarrassed by his accusation but rather than apologize, he simply wheeled around and trotted away. He'd tell Mary that Ferguson had sent out the scouts to find Faith but denied conspiring with Beck. He was sure that when he passed along the wagon master's suspicions that Mort had murdered Beck, it would put her in a good mood.

Joe and Faith were both walking through the tall grass as Newt trotted ahead. Bernie was pulling the tent-wagon with Bessie lashed to the back.

Faith had declined Joe's offer to ride, not because she would show so much leg, but because conversation would be easier if they both walked.

He was carrying one of his Mississippi rifles on his right shoulder while Faith used her walking stick. She was still wearing the knitted cap because of the morning chill but had left her mittens in her bag of clothes.

Joe was looking over Faith's head as he scanned the northeast in case Mort had left early. He didn't see anything except a few deer and a large hawk circling overhead looking for his breakfast.

She waited until he looked down at her before she asked, "How does your wound feel now, Joe?"

"It's okay all things considered. It was worse when I tried to aim my rifle. I couldn't keep my sights from moving no matter how hard I tried. I'll try again in a little while, and I don't want to see those wagons until I can hold it steady."

"What if Mort shows up?"

"I don't think he will, but if he does, then I'll have to do as best I can. We'll have a long time to get ready after we spot him."

"What can I do? I've never fired a gun."

"If he shows up today, just hide behind the cart, and I'll deal with him. I'll show you how to shoot the Henry later. It's lighter and you don't have to worry about missing because you can fire sixteen times without reloading."

Faith didn't know the repeater's capacity and quickly asked, "That many?"

"Yes, ma'am. That's only if there's a cartridge in the chamber. The magazine tube holds fifteen. But after about five shots, the barrel gets hot and if you're not wearing gloves, you might want to wait before firing again."

"Did you have gloves on when you shot those eight rebel soldiers?"

"Nope. That's how I learned how hot it could get but didn't notice it until I put it down to help the captain. It has a couple of other problems, but it's still a nice weapon."

"And you think I can shoot it?"

"I'm sure you can. You're a tall woman and I know you're strong enough to work the lever."

Faith smiled and asked, "Do you think I'm a woman, Joe?"

Joe grinned as he replied, "I think you're the most woman I've ever met, Faith."

Faith hadn't expected him to answer her almost rhetorical question as he had, so she said, "Joe, I'm only fifteen and maybe I'm not as skinny as I believed, but I'm not nearly as well-formed as Marigold is."

"That has nothing to do with it, Faith. When I meet folks, they almost always tell me that I'm just a tall, skinny boy. But the ones who mattered, like Captain Chalmers, Bo Ferguson and Chuck Lynch, all told me that I seemed much older. You're the same way, Faith. Marigold may have bigger, um, may be larger, um…well, she's heavier than you. But she's still much more of a girl than you are. I noticed that the first time I met her, when I dropped off the venison that Mister Moore didn't want."

"Do you really think so?"

"I asked you to marry me; didn't I?"

Faith smiled as she nodded then Joe asked, "Speaking of the Moores; do you know why they're heading to Oregon?"

Faith shook her head as she replied, "No. I never asked, and they didn't tell me. I never even heard them mention where they'd come from. Why do you want to know?"

"Chuck was telling me that most folks leave because they have troubles, either money or with the law. I also learned that the Moores actually asked to be the last in line, which he thought was odd because it gets all the dust."

"I didn't even know that. But does it matter?"

"I suppose not, but I'll bet that they're really mad that you're gone."

Faith grinned then said, "I wonder if they'll try to hire Marigold now."

"I don't think her parents would let that happen. Besides, I reckon Chuck is going to marry her before we get to see Mister Newbury."

"I think you're right."

Joe grinned then they continued to chat as they walked northwest.

―――

Chuck and Mort were following an almost parallel course four miles north of Joe and Faith as they rode between the ruts and the Platte River.

Neither had spotted Faith and the tent-cart which had surprised them. Chuck was scanning for a body that he knew wasn't there and Mort was looking south wishing he could check for a body he knew was there. But he had to stick to his story and stay near the Platte where he claimed Beck had drowned.

By the time they returned for the noon break, the wagons would be past the creek where he'd shot Beck. His worries would be over, but he was curious where that blonde-headed girl had taken Beck's tent-cart. He figured that Beck's dog might have led her to the killing spot, but there was nothing there now. He thought she probably retraced her path and was probably far behind the wagons by now. She'd be so far back that she wouldn't be able to catch up until tomorrow. Then she'd be back under the Moores control again.

Chuck may have been searching in the waters and on the banks of the river for any signs of Joe, but he still kept an eye on Mort. He noticed that Mort focused on the south and would mention it to Bo. But if he'd shot Joe south of the Trail, there was nothing they could do. Their job was to get the wagonloads of settlers to Oregon safely. He just wished that he could prove his and Bo's suspicions.

―――――

The unmurdered Joe Beck and Faith had stopped for a short break to let the critters drink in a fairly wide creek. Faith was filling their canteens while Joe tried to control the pain that affected his shooting accuracy.

He leveled his Mississippi at an oddly shaped bump in the ground about two hundred yards out and let his sights settle on the target. He cocked the rifle's hammer, blew out his breath and then just held his firing position. He tried to ignore the throbbing pain in his side but wasn't able to keep it from screaming at him. The sights refused to stay in the same place and after twenty seconds, he exhaled and lowered his muzzle. He released the hammer and shook his head before turning around and finding Faith looking at him.

"Still bad?" she asked as she stepped closer with the four full canteens.

"I'd be able to fire without a problem, but I wouldn't trust any shots past two hundred yards unless the target was a buffalo the size of an elephant."

"Is that important?"

"Only if Mort sees us and opens fire at long range. But I think he fired from about two to three hundred yards when he shot me. If I was healthy and taken that shot at that range, I wouldn't have missed so badly. So, maybe it's not so critical."

"If we approach the wagons from behind during the morning, he won't even be there. We'd be able to tell Mister Ferguson what happened while he was gone."

Joe smiled then surprised her when he kissed her and said, "You're a smart lady. I may not even have to fire this thing."

Faith was all smiles as she walked with Joe back to the cart. After he slid the Mississippi into a bedroll then took out his oak walking stick, she laid the full canteens inside.

After crossing the creek, they continued walking northwest as the day warmed.

———

While the Moores discussed the likelihood of Faith's return, the rest of the families were abuzz with the unusual rumors. Joe's death, while somewhat confusing, wasn't unusual. But when Faith disappeared with this donkey-drawn cart, horse and dog, it added a lot of spice to their daily chatter.

Marigold was walking with Russell, Jimmy and eight-year-old Libby as they talked about Faith's disappearance.

Russell sharply asked, "*Chuck figures that the other scout shot Joe?*"

Marigold nodded then replied, "So does Mister Ferguson, but they can't prove it."

Jimmy asked, "Is that why Faith ran away?"

"She didn't run away, Jimmy. She went to find Joe. She's convinced that he's still alive."

"What if she finds him dead?" asked Russell.

"I think she'd come back with proof so Mister Ferguson could shoot Mort Jones."

Jimmy then asked, "But shouldn't she be back already if she did?"

Marigold had already prepared her answer, so she quickly replied, "She probably found him alive and is helping him to get better. I'll bet that she and Joe will show up soon and then they'll get Mister Newbury to marry them."

Russell grinned as he said, "Then you and Chuck can get married, too."

Marigold blushed but didn't reply, so Jimmy laughed then asked, "Are you really gonna marry Mister Lynch?"

She looked at her brother as she replied, "Maybe. It's up to him to ask me."

Libby giggled then said, "Mister Lynch is really old, Mary."

"No, he's not. He's only twenty-two."

Libby smiled and said, "That's still old, Mary."

Marigold shook her head before she looked back at the Moore wagon. She was surprised to see Mrs. Moore in the driver's seat talking to her husband. She'd been lying down for most of the past three days as her time approached. Marigold guessed that the only subject that was important enough to make her sit in the sun was Faith, or rather the lack of Faith.

———

Chuck and Mort had turned around and headed back to the wagons after having found no sign of Joe's body. But it was the lack of any clues to where Faith had gone that created a much bigger mystery, at least for Chuck.

If they hadn't ridden on the north side of the Trail, they might have spotted those narrow tracks left by Joe's cart before Faith followed Newt into the open prairie. Now that short trail was behind the wagon train and soon would return to its unaltered state.

Bo spotted his two scouts as soon as they crossed the horizon and knew that they hadn't found Faith. He really hadn't expected them to see her or the cart because she would have returned if she wanted to be found. But he mistakenly believed that after she learned of Joe's death, she'd taken his cart and horse and after making a wide loop, had headed back to Kansas City. It might be a dangerous thing to do, but she was a love-struck teenaged girl who didn't possess much common sense. He hoped that Joe's dog would keep her safe.

―――

As they neared yet another creek, Joe said, "Let's take a long break for lunch."

Faith replied, "Okay. I think I'll take off my coat and hat now, too. It's getting pretty warm."

"I'll leave my coat in the cart as well."

After letting Bessie, Bernie and Newt drink their fill, Joe joined a coat and hatless Faith at the back of the cart. He carefully removed his coat and as he laid it on the stack of branches, his gutta-percha enshrouded pouch fell to the ground. He'd forgotten that he even had it in his pocket but as he quickly bent over to pick it up, a sharp stab of pain reminded him of his infirmity.

He grunted as Faith smiled and picked up the small odd-looking item, handed it to him and asked, "What's that?"

He replied, "It's all I have to remind me of my family after my cousin stole my father's rifle. It's a pocket watch made my great-grandfather in Switzerland. It stopped working when my father lost the windup key, but he still kept it. I wasn't going to get the watch because I wasn't the oldest son, but after everyone died, I figured I was the last of his line. One of these days, I'll try to have a watchmaker make a key for it."

Faith quietly asked, "May I see it, Joe?"

"I was going to show you, Faith, but we had a few interruptions."

Joe slowly removed the gutta-percha protection then slid the watch from the leather pouch. He was relieved that it hadn't been damaged or even soaked after his time under the water.

He turned it over and showed Faith the script. He was about to translate the German when she quickly said, "I can't read, Joe."

Joe was surprised, but didn't show it as he said, "My great-grandfather's name was Johann Beck and the inscription reads, 'Go with God, Johann'. It's in German, so I can't read it either. My father told us what it meant."

"Oh. So, I didn't have to confess my ignorance after all."

"You're smart, Faith. You can learn to read after we're married. Okay?"

"Then you're not disappointed?"

Joe smiled before he kissed her then said, "No. I'm not disappointed in you and never will be."

Then he sheltered the watch from the northwestern breeze and opened the lid as Faith looked on.

"This is a lock of my mother's hair. I cut it just before they took her away because I knew it was all I would ever have to remind me of her other than my memories."

Faith looked at the small snippet of hair and said, "It looks reddish."

Joe closed the lid to keep it safe then said, "My mother didn't have bright red hair, but it was a dark reddish blonde. She was Irish and would sing Irish songs to us each night. I still sing one of my favorites."

"Will you sing it for me?"

"Tonight, when we're ready for sleep. That's when I remember her the best."

"What was her name?"

"Maureen Ann."

Faith then surprised him when she asked, "Why did you tell me that we were going to have a baby girl?"

"Um, I don't know. It just popped into my head."

"Oh. I thought it had something to do with your mother."

"Maybe it did, but I didn't make the connection on my own."

Faith smiled then said, "Let's get something to eat. Bessie and Bernie are already clearing some of the grass."

Joe nodded before they started removing ingredients for their lunch.

Bo asked, "You didn't see a sign of her?"

Chuck shook his head as he took a big bite of crusty bread then after he chewed and swallowed, he replied, "Nope. Nothin'. I wonder where the hell she went."

Mort was out of hearing range as he shoveled beans into his mouth, so Bo said, "I reckon she mighta been upset after hearin' about Joe's death and took his cart and headed back to Kansas City."

Chuck was about to take another bite when he said, "I don't think so, Bo. I figure it's more likely that she went lookin' for him. She's a smart gal and probably used Joe's hound to find his body. Neither one of us expected that we'd spot it in or near the Platte."

"I hope you're right."

"I'm gonna talk to Marigold for a bit to see what she thinks."

Bo smiled as he said, "I'm sure that's the only reason."

Chuck laughed then waved and trotted away as Mort followed him with his eyes. It was bad enough that the Goodchild girl ran off, but now Chuck was movin' in on the Smith girl, and she was really impressive.

But as much as he wished to push Chuck out of the way, Mort knew that he'd have to bide his time. Bo wouldn't believe any cover story this time, no matter how good it was. He wasn't a patient man by nature, but they still had months to go on the long journey and danger was everywhere.

―――

Joe and Faith had been walking for almost an hour after the break when Faith pointed to the southwest and asked, "What's that?"

UNWANTED

Joe looked then replied, "I think it's a prairie dog village, but I've never seen one before."

"Look how big it is! Can we take a look?"

"Anything to make you happy, Faith."

She smiled as Joe turned Bernie toward the expansive collection of small volcanic burrows. He suspected that Newt would have gone that way even if Faith hadn't asked.

Just a couple of seconds later, his suspicions were confirmed when Newt suddenly shot straight at the prairie dog settlement creating a path through the tall grass.

Faith laughed as she watched Newt race ahead and Joe said, "This ought to be fun when he gets there."

They were still more than a hundred feet from the edge of the rodent-filled area when Newt exploded out of the grass.

Faith pointed and shouted, "Look at them scatter!"

Joe grinned as they continued to walk and had to admit it was a very entertaining sight watching the prairie dogs make their life-saving dashes to the nearest hole. Newt would chase one, then after it disappeared, he'd jerk away to pursue another one with his floppy ears flying with each sudden turn.

They were almost out of the grass when the only critter left standing was Newt and he was trotting from one burrow hole to the next with his nose buried near the ground inhaling the new scents.

Faith and Joe were still smiling when the hound stopped near one of the holes that seemed to be more interesting. He slowly approached the tiny volcano and stuck his nose into the hole.

Faith said, "I guess one of them is looking back out at him."

Joe replied, "I reckon he found something diff…"

He suddenly shouted, "Newt!" then dropped his walking stick and raced into the prairie village.

Faith was startled but before she could ask Joe what was wrong, she heard Newt bark, then almost an instant later, saw his head jerk back and a thick shaft flashed out of the burrow.

Joe was reaching for his pistol as Newt whelped and fell back awkwardly. He knew he was too late as he watched the three-foot-long prairie rattlesnake quickly slither away.

By the time he reached Newt, he knew there was nothing he could do but hope that the snake had just used some of its venom to kill a prairie dog. If Newt was a large dog, he'd have a better chance, too.

He dropped to his heels and looked down at his whimpering friend. He examined his face and didn't see any blood. For a few seconds, he had hope that the snake hadn't been able to extend its fangs. Then he looked at his neck and almost vomited. There was blood already flowing from the puncture wounds that weren't hidden by his thin coat of fur.

Faith had watched the large reptile make his escape and hurried to where Joe sat next to Newt.

Joe didn't hear her approach as he was concentrating on Newt and felt useless as he watched his friend suffer.

Faith didn't say anything as she knelt beside Joe and watched Newt as he began to shake. She could see the blood and his neck which was already beginning to swell.

Joe thought about shooting Newt to end his suffering but knew he couldn't do it. Besides, there was a chance that Newt might survive, but Joe didn't know if there was any way to improve his chances.

He laid his hand on Newt's head as he shook and said, "I'm sorry, Newt. I wish I could help."

Newt's eyes were open but didn't seem to be seeing as he whined. Suddenly he vomited explosively, and Joe's hand flew away, but as soon as Newt's head flopped back down, Joe placed his hand back on his canine companion's head.

For almost ten minutes, the poison made its way through Newt's veins and his symptoms became magnified. Neither Joe nor Faith moved as Newt suffered. Suddenly he suffered a massive spasm from his nose to the tip of his tail before he mercifully stopped breathing.

Joe kept his right hand on Newt's head for almost another minute before he slowly stood, removed his hat and began whispering a prayer for Newt.

Faith rose and took his hand but waited for him to speak.

Joe finally blew out his breath, yanked his hat back on and said, "I'm going to bury him. And I'm going to bury him deep, so no scavengers will find him."

Faith then quietly asked, "Won't that hurt?"

Joe turned his head and snapped, "Of course, it will hurt!"

Faith was startled by his angry response and quickly said, "I'm sorry, Joe. It was a stupid thing to say."

Joe had instantly regretted his retort and wrapped his arms around her, ignoring the stab of pain from his side when she hugged him.

He softly said, "No, Faith. It was a concerned and compassionate thing to say. I'm the one who needs to apologize."

"I understand, Joe. Newt was your friend."

"He was the first friend I had since losing my family over six years ago. He was my only friend until I met you. It was only the two of us who set out from Missouri, and I talked to him all the time. Even after we found Bernie...well, it was actually Newt who found him, I thought of Newt as my only friend."

Before he released her, he kissed her softly then said, "But then I found you and you became my best friend and always will be. I love you, Faith."

Faith already had tears in her eyes as she said, "I love you, Joe."

Joe stepped back and Faith asked, "Do you need me to help?"

"No. This won't take long."

Faith turned to retrieve their walking sticks as Joe dropped to his heels and scooped Newt's body from the ground. He'd held Newt before but now he seemed much heavier as he drooped over his arms.

Joe carried the hound's body far enough from the prairie dog village to keep them from burrowing into his grave then laid him down in the grass.

He stepped to the back of the cart and retrieved his pickaxe and spade then left his hat and took off his shirt. He had to peel the sock from his lard-covered skin before he carried both tools back to Newt's body.

Faith stood near Bessie and watched as Joe began swinging the pickaxe to break up the top layer of soil. She couldn't help but notice the large raw red patch where he'd cauterized his wound and wanted to learn how to fire a gun so she could shoot Mort Jones herself.

Joe was soon scooping out dirt with his spade as he dug the small hole. When the edge of the grave reached his hip, he tossed the spade aside and was able to reach Newt's body with his long arms. He slid Newt into his arms and lowered it to the bottom of the hole before he scrambled out. He couldn't look at his friend before he grabbed the shovel and started refilling the hole.

When it was slightly higher than the surrounding soil, he picked up his pickaxe and carried it and the spade back to the cart.

After he laid them inside, Faith handed him an open canteen.

Joe smiled before he said, "Thank you, Faith," then upended the canteen and began drinking the lukewarm water.

He emptied the canteen, tightened the cap, set it in the cart then said, "I'm going to let the sweat dry off before I put more lard and the sock back on, but let's start moving again. Okay?"

"Alright."

UNWANTED

As soon as they left the site of Newt's stunning death, Faith said, "I'm sorry that I wanted to see that prairie dog village. Newt would still be alive if I hadn't asked you to go that way."

"Don't blame yourself because it's not true at all. Newt was already going there before we changed direction. It's what he did all his life, Faith."

"I guess he did seem excited."

Joe smiled at Faith and took her hand before saying, "He had a lot of fun for those last few minutes, so I guess he's in doggy heaven right now bragging to all those other hounds about how he terrified a whole town full of vicious critters."

Faith laughed and squeezed Joe's hand as they led Bernie and Bessie northwest through the grassland. Joe's side had been in agony before the pickaxe's point punched into the prairie, and he counted himself fortunate that he had caused more damage.

Joe returned to scanning the north for any signs of the wagons or Mort. There was also a chance that he might spot Chuck. He'd be able to identify them easily by their horses. Mort rode that light gray gelding and Chuck rode a dark brown mare, much like Bessie. If he spotted Chuck, he'd fire a round to get his attention in case he hadn't seen the cart. Then he looked at his tent-cart and realized that the buffalo hide covering its canvas roof made it less visible.

He looked at Faith and said, "I just realized that I camouflaged the cart with the buffalo hide."

Faith turned and looked back before she said, "That's a good thing; isn't it?"

"Yes, ma'am."

―――

The camouflage didn't matter as neither of the scouts were close enough to see the cart even if it had been flying a white flag. They were still riding on the north side of the ruts with the Platte River on their right.

Chuck had noticed that Mort's behavior was different somehow but couldn't figure out why. He hadn't even seemed annoyed when Bo had told them to continue searching for Faith near the river.

With each passing minute, Mort became more convinced that Joe Beck was dead, and Faith Goodchild would soon join him if she hadn't already. Women didn't last long out here, and she was just a girl.

His thoughts had now shifted away from Joe Beck to Chuck Lynch. While he knew that they still had a long way to go before reaching Oregon, Mort also realized that if Chuck suddenly disappeared, it would make him the only scout and he would be able to demand more from Bo Ferguson.

UNWANTED

He still planned to wait a few days to let things calm down but was already beginning to make a list of what Bo would have to give him to keep him from riding back to Kansas City. The only chink in his plan was if they met up with another wagon train.

It had happened on their last trip when they spotted a line of wagons on the other side of the Platte just before they reached Fort Kearny. The two trains had linked to form a larger and safer group by the time they'd left the fort. But that was two years ago, and since then, a lot had changed and there weren't many wagon trains leaving out of Omaha any longer.

Omaha was just a normal town a couple of years ago and not even as big as Nebraska City a few miles south along the Missouri River. Then they decided to use the northern route for the new transcontinental railroad and President Lincoln had chosen Council Bluffs in Iowa to be the eastern starting point. But Thomas Durant ignored Lincoln and decided to use Omaha, just on the other side of the river. Suddenly, the town became important and began attracting all sorts from around the country. Many were deserters and cheats, so it slid into a wild place bordering on lawless.

The chaotic conditions and the war had almost completely halted wagon trains from leaving Omaha. That gave Mort hope that he wouldn't see any wagons on the other side of the Platte before he assumed his critical role as their lone scout.

In the last wagon, Mary Moore hadn't been able to sit on the driver's seat but was able to talk to her husband as she lay on the narrow mattress with only little William next to her. John and Albert were sitting next to Harry.

Over the squeaking and rattling, she loudly said, "Even if Joe Beck is dead, I don't think we'll see Faith again."

Harry kept his eyes ahead as he replied, "I don't think so, either. If she's not on her way back to Kansas City, then she'll get lost trying to find Beck's body."

"I'm going to need help, Harry."

"I know. I was going to talk to Ed Smith about having his boys keep an eye on the cows and goats and they can share the milk as payment. I don't want to have anything to do with Marigold, but I'll talk to Abe Witherspoon about having Becky help you personally."

After a short pause, Mary asked, "What about the rest of our plans for Faith?"

Harry scratched his bearded chin then said, "We'll have to wait to see what happens."

Mary exclaimed, "That's not good enough, Harry!"

Harry turned to look at his wife and snapped, "It's all we can do now!"

Mary wasn't pleased with their situation and blamed that damned Joe Beck and hoped he was burning in hell.

Harry almost dreaded talking to Abe Witherspoon after they stopped for the night, but his daughter was their best option. She wasn't nearly as pretty as Faith and bordered on homely. But she was already eighteen and had a much more impressive figure that some might call chubby. The good news was that she was their only surviving child, and he believed that the Witherspoons were desperately hoping to find a suitor who was willing to overlook her less than handsome face and advancing years.

———

Joe and Faith stopped to set up camp before sunset after they'd crossed a small stream. While Faith cooked their supper over the fire, Joe created improved sleeping arrangements. He had removed the rifles and the Henry from their bedrolls then used them and two more bedrolls to make a thick mattress. Then he laid the buffalo skin over the bedrolls before sliding his two woolen blankets over the top. He then folded his last surviving bedroll lengthwise to create a long pillow.

After he returned to the fire, Faith handed him his plate with the last of his stew with a pickle on the side and said, "That's a very nice bed, Joe. It looks really comfortable."

"It should be warm, too. It'll be nice to sleep with bare feet for a change. Most of the smell is gone from the buffalo hide, too."

Faith nodded then began eating when Joe said, "I'll miss having Newt as an alarm. I think Bessie and Bernie can warn us if anyone or any critters show up while we're sleeping, though."

"He was a good dog, Joe. If it hadn't been for him, I never would have found you."

Joe exhaled, then quietly said, "I know. It's funny. I haven't felt this sad since I lost my family. I stood at my Aunt Mary's gravesite as they buried her and didn't feel any sense of loss, even though she was my mother's sister. When I watched them bury my Uncle William, I wasn't even thinking about him. I was worried about getting back to the barn before my cousin could steal my father's rifle. But I feel terrible about losing a dog. Is there something wrong with me?"

"Not at all. I feel sad myself, and I only knew Newt for a little while. I guess it only matters if someone means something to us."

"I guess so. Newt did mean a lot to me."

Then he turned and smiled at her as he said, "But not nearly as much as you do, Faith."

Faith grinned then said, "I wonder if I should be flattered for being more important than a coon hound."

Joe laughed then leaned over and kissed her before he began to eat.

Faith watched as Joe pulled off his boots and socks then slid beneath the blankets to join her. She felt his right arm slide beneath her neck before she slid closer and carefully placed her right arm over his chest to avoid his wound.

Joe smiled as he said, "This is much nicer; isn't it?"

Faith whispered, "Yes."

There was a long pause before she quietly asked, "Um, how far away is the wagon train?"

"If I had to guess, I'd say about five miles due north. If we followed that small stream right now, we'd probably reach them in three hours."

"I'd rather take our time. I don't know if I ever want to see the Moores again."

"You know, it might be kind of interesting when they do see us together. They might believe that you were so sad when you found my dead body that you leapt into the Platte River in dismay. But what they think doesn't matter and whatever plans they may have had no longer exist."

"You're right, but I just don't like them very much."

After another long, awkward pause, Faith was about to ask a very intimate question when her right hand moved slightly, and Joe grunted in pain.

She quickly pulled her hand away and said, "I'm sorry, Joe. It really hurts; doesn't it?"

Joe rolled onto his back then replied, "It's alright. It's my fault for lying on my right side just to get so close to you. It didn't give you anyplace else to put your hand."

Faith turned onto her back and Joe held her hand as they stared at the Milky Way.

Instead of posing her original question, she asked, "Joe, will you sing the song your mother used to sing to you?"

"I will if you promise not to laugh at my horrible singing voice."

"I won't laugh."

Joe wasn't sure she'd be able to at least hold back a giggle but began softly singing the opening words to Kathleen Mavourneen.

Faith listened as he sang the Irish ballad and was surprised by his voice. It wasn't nearly as bad as he seemed to believe, but powerful emotion was woven into each word.

She closed her eyes and tried to picture a young Joe Beck sitting with his brothers and sister as their mother sang to them.

Joe hadn't been watching Faith as he sang because he didn't want to see her trying to keep from laughing, so he didn't know that she'd closed her eyes.

When he finished, he finally turned to look at her and found her already peacefully sleeping.

He smiled and was going to kiss her goodnight but expected that it would probably just wake her.

He just whispered, "Goodnight, Faith," then closed his eyes and added, "Goodbye, Newt."

CHAPTER 10

Faith was startled when she awakened and didn't find Joe lying beside her. She quickly sat up then turned and looked to the cart where she saw him saddling Bessie.

Joe had caught her movement out of the corner of his eye then turned and said, "Good morning, Faith."

"Why didn't you wake me? It's almost sunrise."

"You seemed so peaceful and warm that I didn't have the heart to disturb you."

Faith tossed aside the blankets then stood up and began pulling on her shoes as she asked, "How long have you been up?"

"About an hour or so. I got Bernie in harness and almost finished saddling Bessie."

As she stood, she straightened out her dress and said, "You must have done something else if you've been up for an hour."

"If you must know, I grabbed a bar of soap and a towel and took a bath in the stream. I only cleaned off the dirt and sweat from digging that hole yesterday but figured it was time to get rid of the rest of it."

"How much did that hurt?"

"Actually, it made the wound feel much better and when I dressed, I soaked the sock in water and used my shirt to hold it in place. It'll dry out soon, but I'll soak it again when we find another creek."

Faith glanced at the flowing water and asked, "Can I use your soap and towel?"

"Yes, ma'am. I figured you might ask, so if you look at the bottom of the blankets, you'll find them waiting for you."

Faith looked towards her feet and only saw the tip of the towel sticking out from where she'd flipped the blankets.

"Oh. I'll change my dress and wash this one, too."

"I was thinking that you might want to wear one of my spare britches under your dress so you can ride more comfortably."

"I'll keep that in mind, but today I'll just walk."

"I'll build a fire after I finish saddling Bessie."

Faith nodded then left the towel and soap and hurried to the cart where she opened her cloth bag, pulled out her only spare dress, bloomers and camisole.

As she passed Joe to pick up the soap and towel, she smiled but didn't say anything.

Joe was surprised as he expected her to ask him to respect her privacy. But he didn't spend any time dwelling on her reason for not asking as he finished saddling Bessie. He would have been very surprised if Faith hadn't moved her hand making him grunt in pain. She would have asked her very quiet, yet intense question, then he would have realized that Faith now wanted him as much as he wanted her. But that small shift in her hand's location had at least postponed the inevitable. So, an ignorant Joe Beck began adding kindling to the firepit and breaking some of his thicker branches.

Faith didn't even look back at the cart as she quickly stripped her clothes and stepped into the frigid water. She erupted in goosebumps before she slowly sat in the stream then splashed water over her shoulders and began to scrub.

After the initial shock from the icy water, she quickly adjusted to the temperature and began to hum Joe's song because she couldn't remember the words. But the melody and the emotion of his voice would never leave her memory. She finally dipped her dark blonde hair into the water and worked in a heavy lather.

Joe had set up the cooking grate when he stood to select their breakfast. Even though she hadn't asked him not to look while she bathed, Joe still felt as if he was cheating when he took one step to his left and peeked around the side of the cart.

Faith was scrubbing her hair as she sat in the stream, so all he could see was her upper half. She constantly claimed that she was skinny, but in the gentle light of the predawn, Joe thought Faith was perfect. He gawked until she dipped her hair into the stream then quickly jerked it out sending water flying into the air over her head. He knew he was getting too distracted and reluctantly stepped behind the cart.

Faith had no idea that he'd been watching and actually hoped that he was. When Joe had passed along his mother's beliefs about men and women, she'd found it to be much more appealing and reasonable. She quickly rejected all the prudish notions that her mother had instilled in her and wholeheartedly embraced the idea that sex didn't need to be considered a chore.

She stepped out of the stream then quickly snatched the towel and began to dry herself as she looked at the cart. She didn't see Joe and was disappointed, but the cool morning air demanded that she dress quickly. After she was dressed and reasonably warm, she used the same bar of soap and washed her dirty clothes.

Joe had the fire going and breakfast cooking when Faith stepped around the corner, held out her newly washed clothing and asked, "Where can I hang these?"

Joe smiled when he saw her straggly wet hair and replied, "Just pull out one of the branches and hang them there until we're ready to leave. Do you want to use my hairbrush?"

Faith was already pulling out a branch when she quickly turned and asked, "You have a hairbrush?"

"Yes, ma'am. I bought it about an hour after meeting you, but I never would have dreamt that you'd be using it."

"I'll take over cooking if you'll find your hairbrush."

Joe stood and said, "It's a deal."

Faith hung her wet clothes on the branch then passed Joe and sat on her heels near the warming fire.

As she took over the cooking chores, Joe had to rummage through his backpacks to find the hairbrush. He hadn't used it since leaving Kansas City for one reason or another. But before he found it, he discovered his scissors and took them and the hairbrush from their CSA backpack and stepped to the fire. He sat beside Faith and handed her the hairbrush.

Faith smiled as she accepted it then asked, "Can you take over again?"

"I can, but after you brush your hair, I need you to use these scissors to trim my hair. I don't want anyone to confuse me with an Indian."

Faith laughed as she began to brush out her kinks then said, "It is getting a bit long, but I don't think anyone would confuse you with an Indian. You can trim mine, too."

"Okay, but not too much. I like it when you wear it long instead of all bundled up like most ladies."

"That's because I'm not sixteen yet. My father said that girls had to wear their hair long until they married or turned sixteen."

"Now that's a silly notion. I hope you're not planning to wrap it up into a big bun after we get married."

She continued to fight her hair war as she replied, "Not if you like it this way."

"Then I reckon you'll be wearing your hair long until it turns gray."

Faith smiled and began to win her ongoing battle as the brush began sliding more easily through her blonde strands.

―――

The wagons had begun rolling and Bo Ferguson was sitting on his driver's seat as he watched Mort and Chuck disappear over the horizon. He was still uneasy about what had happened to Joe Beck and disturbed by Faith's failure to reappear. The folks had been constantly barraging him with questions about the two odd disappearances.

The exception was the Moores. He had expected Harry to badger him about Faith but after his short visit yesterday, Bo hadn't heard a peep from him. It was odd, but Bo didn't know the reason. It wasn't his problem anyway. If it became a problem, it would belong to Ed Carlisle and his committee.

Bo's big problem had just crossed the horizon with Chuck. What made him more anxious was that Mort seemed to be almost pleasant, which wasn't his normal behavior. He hadn't even been sneaking nips from the folks' stashes of corn liquor. Mort was up to something, but Bo had no idea what it might be.

———

The Moores hadn't bothered asking about Faith because Harry had already found her replacement. After a productive chat with Abe Witherspoon, Harry had arranged for Becky to start helping Mary with the boys and other chores. Abe seemed almost relieved and was grateful for the offer of the buttermilk as their cow had stopped producing.

Becky was very happy when she'd been told about her new duties because more than anything, she wanted to have her own baby. While the child wouldn't be hers, she couldn't wait to hold the Moores' newborn.

Mary was very pleased and completely forgot about that blonde-headed witch and her string bean boyfriend.

———

UNWANTED

As they walked with the sun behind them, Faith's drying clothes were stretched out on top of the buffalo hide which was covering the tent part of the cart.

They were carrying their walking sticks as they pushed through the tall grass when Joe asked, "Are you sure that you don't want to wear one of my spare shirts over your dress? It's still a bit chilly."

"No, I'm alright. Besides, I still have the rain slicker you gave me to keep off the breeze."

"Okay. We've been lucky so far about the rain. We've only had one good soaking since we left Kansas City, so we're overdue."

"I know. When it does rain, what will we do?"

"We'll put on our slickers and keep going. When we stop for the night, I'll make a covering with my spare tarp, and we can use the buffalo hide for the floor."

Faith smiled as she said, "That sounds cozy."

"Not if it the wind kicks up at the same time. I use some of the bayonets to anchor the tarp, but if the wind shifts, it could yank that tarp away and send it all the way back to Missouri."

Then as he looked ahead, he said, "It's kind of strange not seeing Newt's tail weaving through the prairie grass. I just hope we don't run into any more prairie rattlers. If we do, then maybe we can have him for supper."

"You'd eat a rattlesnake?"

"It's just meat and from what I've heard, it's really pretty tasty. But even if we don't see a snake, I need to replenish our meat supply. I have plenty of beans, rice and corn flour, but we can't go without meat. My only concern is that Mort might hear my gunfire and show up to investigate. He's probably about six or seven miles to the northwest about now, and sound can travel pretty far over open country."

"Wouldn't that be to our advantage if he headed this way?"

"Not necessarily. If he spotted us first, he'd be able to find an ambush site and wait for us to get within range. He'd shoot me first then I imagine that he'd figure you weren't dangerous and ride down here. That's why I've got to show you how to shoot the Henry and maybe my Colt."

"I hope you're wrong about him trying to shoot you again, but I do want to be able shoot him if I see him again."

Joe grinned and said, "We'll keep walking for a while then when we stop for a break, I'll take out the Henry and give you a quick lesson. You won't be firing any live rounds, so it won't warn Mort if he's close."

"Okay."

UNWANTED

While Joe may have been right to be concerned about Mort hearing any gunfire, he was woefully wrong about his location. He wasn't six or seven miles to the northwest, but five miles almost due north as he rode between Chuck and the Platte River.

Joe didn't realize just how much faster he and Faith had been moving since they crossed that first wide creek. Nor did he notice that they hadn't been traveling northwest, but only a few degrees north of due west, which was entirely different. He and Faith had passed the slow-moving wagons long ago, and even their extended sleep didn't affect the growing gap.

If they had been moving northwest from the start, then he and Faith would have seen the tops of the wagons as soon as they broke camp that morning. And more critically, they would have been spotted by Mort who still scanned south of the Trail.

Before the noon break, when Mort and Chuck turned around to report back to Bo Ferguson, Joe and Faith continued walking. They finally stopped at a grassy pond and let Bernie and Bessie drink while they had a quick, early lunch.

After they finished and refilled the canteens, Faith removed her dry clothes from the buffalo skin and Joe walked behind the cart. He leaned his walking stick on the side then pulled out one of the wool blankets.

Faith was folding her dress when she saw Joe remove and then spread the blanket on the ground.

She stared at the wool blanket and asked, "Are we going to stay here?"

Joe grinned and said, "No, ma'am. I need it there for a much different reason," then walked close to Bessie and slid his Henry from the bedroll.

He stepped into the center of the blanket and began working the lever. Faith was putting her clothes away as she watched and immediately understood why he needed the blanket on the ground.

After the repeater stopped spewing .44 caliber brass and lead cylinders, Joe stepped off the blanket and approached Faith.

He said, "You saw how I worked the lever. When I do that, the mechanism inside pushes a cartridge into the chamber so it can be fired then pulls a fresh cartridge from the magazine tube and ejects the spent cartridge. At the same time, the hammer comes back. So, when the lever is finished moving, the gun is ready to fire."

"Do I have to know all that?"

Joe grinned and replied, "Not really. I was just showing off. It's very easy to use. The hammer is still back but the chamber is empty. I'll give it to you, so you can hold it and then aim it south before you squeeze the trigger. Then, if you want to take a second imaginary shot, just cycle the lever as I did. Okay?"

She replied, "Alright," and Joe handed her the Henry.

Faith took what she believed was a shooting stance, put the carbine's butt against her shoulder and set the sights on a bush before she pulled the trigger. The hammer snapped down and she quickly cycled the lever and fired her second invisible bullet.

She turned and smiled at Joe as she handed him the Henry.

"It was pretty easy, Joe."

"You did very well, Faith. Even if you don't have to shoot Mort, I'll let you use it when we do some hunting."

"I'd like that."

Joe smiled then stepped back onto the blanket and sat down among his scattered cartridges.

Faith sat close to Joe and watched as he slid a tab under the magazine tube then twisted it around until it was hanging sideways beneath the barrel.

As Joe began picking up cartridges and sliding them butt first into the tube, Faith started gathering some of the ones further away from Joe.

After she had six in her palm, she asked, "Can't those bullets go off when you're putting them in?"

Joe didn't look up as he replied, "They make the cartridges to minimize that risk, but it can still be a problem if you stand it straight up when you reload. You have to keep it at a low angle like this. I was lucky that I talked to Mister Plummer, the gunsmith in Pleasant Hill about them before Captain Chalmers sent me this one.

"I told you about the other problem with the design that I discovered when I was shooting at those rebels. Because that tab on the bottom has to keep pushing the cartridges down the magazine tube, they can't put a forearm under the barrel. So, after a few shots, it gets almost too hot to hold. I reckon they'll have to figure out how to fix it when they come out with a new model."

After the Henry had been safely reloaded, Joe returned it to the bedroll then folded the blanket, took out his walking stick and he and Faith resumed their journey.

As they led Bernie, the cart and Bessie across the plains, Joe let Faith hold his Colt and had her aim it to see if she could hold it steady. Although she said it was heavy, she said that she could fire it if necessary. He explained that she should use her left hand to cock the hammer before returning it to his holster which was the sum of her pistol lesson.

UNWANTED

But before the short lesson even began, Joe had unknowingly corrected his earlier navigational error. There was a long bulge in the terrain that steered them to the north. By the time he had returned the Colt New Army to its modified holster, they were walking north-northwest and began to quickly close the gap to the Oregon Trail.

―――

During their lunch break, Chuck had paid a visit to Marigold just to chat as he had no news to give her.

She had been anxiously waiting for him and the moment she spotted him walking towards her family, she hurried in his direction.

When they met, Chuck said, "No news, Mary. I just wanted to see you."

"I'm glad that you do, Chuck. What do you think happened to Faith?"

"I reckon that she went huntin' for Joe and the only direction she coulda gone without us seein' her or Joe's cart would be south. I hope she didn't find Joe's body and fall apart."

"She was really in love with him, but I can't imagine her just falling apart. Maybe she found him after Mort shot him, and now she's nursing him back to health."

While he believed his theory was much more realistic, Chuck still replied, "It could be that way. If she found him down there, then Joe would want to wait until he was strong enough before they started back. But that could be a while and then the wagon train would be miles further west. If I was Joe, I'd take Faith back to Kansas City."

Marigold chewed her lower lip for a few seconds then said, "I guess you're right. But I was just talking to Becky Witherspoon, and she was excited because Mister Moore asked her to help take care of the boys and do some other chores."

Chuck's eyebrows rose as he asked, "She was happy about that?"

Marigold nodded as she replied, "Very. She gushed about how she couldn't wait to help with their new baby. She even said," then after looking around for potential eavesdroppers, she leaned forward and whispered, "She said that she wished she could nurse the baby herself."

Chuck snickered then said, "I reckon they shoulda asked her before payin' Faith's pa the twenty-five dollars."

Marigold giggled then asked, "Has Mort given you any problems?"

"Nope, and that has me a bit confused. He's actin' almost like a real partner now. He's not chatty or nothin', but he doesn't argue like he used to. He even smiled a few times."

"Why has he changed?"

"I reckon he figures he got away with murderin' Joe."

"Well, don't let him even get close to shooting you."

"Trust me. I'm still keepin' a close eye on that bastard."

Marigold smiled then hooked her arm through his so he could escort her back to the first wagon.

Chuck wished he could spend more time with Marigold, but he had to get out front again. He knew that he wouldn't have to search for her when he returned.

Mort wasn't surprised when Chuck returned with Marigold attached to his arm. He had to look away to hide his growing hate for his fellow scout. Now that Beck was out of the way, Chuck Lynch had become the focus of his rage since Bo Ferguson had called him stupid. He was growing tired of keeping up appearances, especially when he was alone on the trail with Chuck.

After they mounted and rode away from the wagons, Mort glanced at Chuck and saw him wave to Marigold. He jerked his eyes away and gritted his teeth. He had to maintain his façade for a few more hours at least.

Chuck may have been suspicious of Mort's apparent transformation, but he was unaware that Mort was already thinking about shooting him as his mind was occupied with Marigold.

As they trotted away, Joe and Faith were only three miles south of the Trail and four miles ahead. If it had been flat ground, the two converging parties would soon spot each other, but it wasn't totally flat. The Trail paralleled the Platte River as it meandered east to its Missouri River destination. The deep ruts were about a mile apart on both sides of the shallow, wide river. But rivers usually found the easiest path across the landscape, and the Platte was no different.

The terrain on both sides were higher, but not noticeably so. But it wasn't just the change in the ground's altitude that hid Joe and Faith from the scouts. There was a long line of low bumps that could barely be classified as hills that stretched for miles. It was a lone copy further east that had provided Mort with his opportunity to shoot Joe. This time, if they hadn't been there, he would have soon realized that he had failed.

Joe still believed that they had been walking northwest all along, so when he spotted the hills, he looked at Faith and said, "I think we're getting close to the Trail. If those hills weren't there, we might even see the wagons."

Faith examined the low mounds and asked, "They could be on the other side?"

"Maybe. They might be ahead of us, too. I'd sure like to sneak up on top of one of them to take a good look. I should at least be able to see the river to get an idea where they might be."

"Why don't you take Bessie for a ride? I'll follow you with Bernie."

Joe looked at her and asked, "Are you sure? You won't have any protection while I'm gone."

"You can leave me your pistol if you're worried."

Joe grinned and unbuckled his gunbelt. He stepped in front of Faith as she smiled back at him then swung the belt around her back and caught the buckle. He was able to avoid grunting at the stab of pain which he accepted as an indication that he was healing.

She asked, "Are you sure it won't fall to the ground?"

"I'm sure. There are soldiers who have smaller hips than you do, ma'am."

He slid the end of the belt through the US buckle and tightened it. He wasn't surprised that there were still two holes left available.

After he snugged it down, he took her face in his big hands and kissed her softly before saying, "I'll be back soon. I'll stay in view, too."

"I'll be alright."

Joe smiled then walked to where Bessie waited. He untied her reins, then mounted and turned her to the north. The closest hill was about a mile away, so he set the mare to a slow trot then waved to Faith as he rode away.

Faith turned Bernie and began following Joe's path. Having the heavy pistol at her waist gave her an unexpected sensation of power and safety. She hadn't even fired the thing but knowing that she could was good enough.

Joe was about halfway to the hill when he pulled the Mississippi. He wasn't concerned about being spotted but hoped to find some game near the river.

———

Since they'd passed the first of the line of hills, Mort began to estimate how far they'd gone and how far the sound of a gunshot would travel. This situation was much different than when he'd shot Beck. The kid didn't even know he was there. Chuck was not only close, but Mort knew that he wouldn't be able to pull his rifle or his pistol without being seen. So, they continued to ride just north of the ruts looking for any unexpected obstacles or trouble.

———

Joe pulled up behind the hill, dismounted, then tied Bessie's reins to a young cottonwood that would probably be eaten by the next prairie wildfire. It was the reason that there were so few trees on the Great Plains.

He looked back at Faith and waved his hat over his head before pulling it back on and beginning the short climb to see how close they were to the Platte River.

———

Mort was still thinking how to get a free shot when Chuck provided the golden opportunity.

He pulled his horse to a stop then loudly said, "You can keep ridin', Mort. I gotta pee."

"Go ahead, I'm just gonna wait."

Chuck's overfilled bladder didn't even let him reply before he stepped down. He walked a few more yards closer to the river before he began unbuttoning his britches.

Joe had reached the top of the hill and was pleased to see the river so close, then looked west and didn't see the expected wagons, so he swung his eyes to the east and was stunned when he spotted Mort and Chuck just three hundred yards away. He almost turned and hurried down the hill when he saw Chuck dismount and then as he began working his britches, Joe saw Mort slowly slide his rifle from his scabbard.

He didn't have time to worry about his wound as he cocked his Mississippi and brought it level. He was setting his sights on his target just as Mort swung his rifle toward Chuck.

Joe yelled, "Hey, Mort!" then squeezed his trigger.

Mort's ears had just registered Joe's shout when they received the much louder echo from Joe's rifle. He had his finger on his trigger when just a few milliseconds after the sound waves arrived, a .54 caliber slug of lead plunged into the left side of his neck where it connected to the shoulders.

He screamed as the bullet drilled through muscle, smaller blood vessels and then ripped through his common carotid artery before lodging in his right lung's upper lobe.

Chuck was in mid-stream when the shout, shot and scream all made him whip around just as Mort tumbled awkwardly to the ground. He landed on the right side of his head and his neck almost bent at a right angle when he hit. It probably saved Mort a few seconds of pain before he died on the ground near the ruts of the Oregon Trail in Nebraska Territory.

Chuck was still exposed as he automatically pulled his steel pistol to look for the shooter. He expected to see deserters or Indians but was shocked when he saw a supposedly dead Joe Beck standing on the top of one of the low hills with his rifle surrounded by a cloud of gunsmoke.

Joe had seen Mort fall and was relieved as he lowered his Mississippi. If he'd missed, Chuck would be lying on the ground then he'd have to run back down the hill to retrieve his Henry.

He lifted his rifle over his head then pointed it to the south before stepping back down the hill to mount Bessie so he could tell Faith what had happened.

Faith had watched him as he stood on the hill and wondered what he was seeing when she saw him suddenly fire his rifle. Then he held up the rifle as in a victory salute before he started back down. She thought that he must have shot a deer or maybe another buffalo, so she just waited for him to return.

Chuck was buttoning his britches as he stared down at Mort's dead eyes then kicked his lifeless body and growled, "You, bastard! You're not only a cheatin' coward; you really are stupid. Did you think that Bo would believe that I fell into the river, too? And why the hell did you need a rifle at thirty feet?"

He spit on Mort's body before he took his rifle from the ground, released the hammer and slid it back into Mort's scabbard. Then he unbuckled Mort's gunbelt and put it in Mort's saddlebag before he tied the mare to his saddle, mounted, and turned his gray gelding south to find Joe.

His fury about Mort's assassination attempt had finally diminished enough for him to return to the stunning realization that Joe Beck had shot Mort. *How the hell did he get here?* As he headed for the gap between the hills, he wondered if Marigold's hopeful theory hadn't been right after all.

Faith waited for Joe to dismount before she quickly asked, "What happened? Did you shoot another buffalo?"

Joe shook his head as he tied off Bessie and replied, "No. I found the Platte just on the other side of those hills and could see the ruts, too. I didn't see any wagons, but I spotted Mort and Chuck a couple of hundred yards east. Chuck was standing on the ground looking at the river when Mort pulled his rifle. So, I cocked my Mississippi and as soon as Mort aimed it at Chuck, I fired. I think he's dead, but we have to wait for Chuck to show up. He should be here soon."

Faith looked at Joe with wide eyes as she quietly asked, "Why would he want to shoot Chuck? Are you sure he wasn't just shooting at a beaver or something?"

"No, I'm not sure. I couldn't take that chance, Faith. I won't go into the morality issue because there's no point. That bastard tried to kill me, and I don't feel bad for shooting him even if he was trying to put some meat on the table."

"I'm sorry, Joe. That came out all wrong. I was just surprised that he would have tried to kill Chuck. It doesn't make any sense. If he convinced them that you had just drowned, surely he couldn't tell that lie again."

"I wouldn't think so, either. But I'm sure he was going to shoot Chuck. Speaking of the devil, here he comes."

UNWANTED

As Joe leaned his Mississippi against the cart, Faith shifted her eyes to the north and spotted Chuck coming towards them leading Mort's horse. She wondered if Chuck realized that Mort was going to kill him or if he believed that Joe was just seeking revenge. She'd soon have her answer.

As soon as he cleared the hills, Chuck spotted Joe's odd tent-cart and started laughing. Then he found Faith talking to Joe and was tickled even more. It was turning into one hell of a day. He felt like a fool for not watching Mort but hadn't expected him to do anything that rash and stupid. Regardless of his almost fatal mistake, he was incredibly happy to see Joe and Faith again.

Faith had her answer about Chuck's reaction before he pulled up when she saw the big smile on his face.

He was still grinning when he hurriedly dismounted then before he said a word, he threw his arms around Joe and embraced him like a long-lost brother.

Joe grunted loudly and jerked before Chuck stepped back and exclaimed, "Sorry, Joe! Are you hurt?"

"Mort didn't miss by much when he tried to shoot me, but his ball did nick the side of my chest."

"Why did he think that he killed you?"

"I was woolgathering near a strong creek that ran south for a while. When I was hit, I fell face first into the water and the current dragged me downstream. I guess he didn't bother looking after that. I'll just thank my lucky stars that he missed."

"He was only about thirty feet away and woulda killed me for sure if you missed. I don't know why he used his rifle at that range, but you saved my life, Joe."

Joe shrugged then asked, "Why was he trying to kill you anyway?"

"I have no idea. He was actin' out of character for the past couple of days, so I guess whatever set him off had been buildin' inside. It's not important."

Then Chuck looked at Faith and smiled before saying, "Mary said that you went off lookin' for Joe and then found him shot and needed to nurse him for a while. I thought she was just hopin', but I reckon she had the right of it; didn't she?"

Faith smiled as she replied, "She did, but I didn't have to do any nursing. Joe cauterized his wound with a bayonet."

Chuck grimaced as he looked back at Joe and said, "That must have felt like the gates of hell."

"It wasn't any fun and it sure looks ugly. It's still pretty intense but I'm almost used to it."

Chuck grinned then said, "Except when some idiot gives you a hug for savin' his life. You'll have to show it to me and

Bo later. I've got to head back now. Do you want to ride Bessie and Faith can ride Mort's mare?"

"No. We'll walk to the Trail. How far back are the wagons?"

"About an hour or so. I'll head back and get rid of Mort's body then ride back to tell Bo. I'll leave his horse with you. Even if you don't want her, you should take his gunbelt that's in his saddlebag seein' as how you gave yours to Faith."

Joe laughed then said, "I only let her borrow it while I went to take a look at the top of the hill."

"Well, he had a nice Colt Navy if you want it. It's not as nice as that New Army Faith's wearin', though."

As Chuck untied Mort's horse from his own and tied her to the cart beside Bessie, Joe didn't ask what he was going to do with Mort's body. He suspected that he might drag it to the Platte River and let it float to the Missouri River. Then maybe it would travel with the currents all the way to New Orleans.

Mort mounted and said, "So, we'll see you in an hour or so."

Joe looked up as he replied, "I reckon so. We'll need to talk to Mister Newbury right away, too."

Chuck grinned then waved and turned his horse to the north before riding off at a rapid pace.

Faith smiled at Joe and asked, "Are you going to ask Mister Newbury to marry us today?"

"Is that alright? I don't want the Moores to even think that you should return to their wagon."

"Of course, it's alright. If you must know, Mister Beck, I had hoped that we would have consummated our marriage last night. But I was worried about your wound."

"Then I guess you won't mind if I tell you that I was thinking the same thing. I also have to confess that I peeked when you were taking your bath."

Faith laughed before saying, "I was actually disappointed when I didn't see you looking."

Joe's eyebrows peaked as he exclaimed, "*You were?*"

"It's not what you would have expected from a girl who had been lectured on the evil of lewd behavior for her entire life; is it?"

"No, I guess not. Especially a woman named Faith Hope Charity Virtue Goodchild."

Faith laughed then said, "I suppose we have to start moving to those hills."

"Let's pass between the two to the west of the one I used. I don't want to know what Chuck did with Mort's body."

As they began leading Bernie towards the hills, Faith asked, "Do you think he just threw it in the river?"

"Maybe. He could have just pulled it close to the bank so folks couldn't see it. If they don't bury him, then the scavengers will find him."

"He deserves to be found by the most hideous scavengers God ever put on the earth."

"I'm not going to argue with you, ma'am."

Faith smiled as she took his hand and said, "You can't argue, sir. I have your pistol."

Joe laughed as he looked at her but hoped that the Moores didn't cause any ruckus. If Chuck had been able to stay a little longer, Joe would have learned that Becky Witherspoon had already taken Faith's place.

———

It was just a few minutes after reaching the Trail that Chuck spotted the lead wagon. He had just remounted after dragging Mort's body past the ruts and almost fifty yards closer to the river where he left it behind a short row of juniper bushes.

After riding for another ten minutes, he was able to make out Bo sitting on his driver's seat, so he took off his hat and waved it over his head. He was sure that Bo had already seen him but wanted the boss to understand that he had important news to report.

Bo had been watching Chuck's approach long before he waved his hat and noticed that Mort wasn't anywhere to be seen. When Chuck waved his hat, Bo suspected that Mort must have tried to drygulch Chuck but had failed in the attempt. He may have been relieved that the troublesome scout was gone, but that did put him into a quandary. He could function with one scout, but that would put Chuck at a greater risk. He may have to hire one of the older boys to drive the lead wagon while he took Mort's place.

It was already late afternoon, so before Chuck arrived, Bo reached over and began ringing his bell. After the last peal echoed down the line, he leaned back on the reins and the oxen stopped walking.

He quickly bounded down from the wagon and walked to the front of the team where he waited to hear Chuck's news. He had his arms folded as he stood out front when he noticed the big grin on Chuck's face.

He mumbled, "What are you smilin' about?"

Ed Carlisle and Wilmot Drummond approached Bo and noticed the lone scout returning.

Ed asked, "Where's Mort?"

Bo kept his eyes on Chuck as he replied, "That's what I'm about to find out."

Chuck pulled up twenty feet in front of the three men, dismounted and took his horse's reins as he walked closer.

"What happened, Chuck?"

Chuck glanced at Ed and Wilmot before replying, "I left Mort's body about four miles back down the trail. The bastard tried to shoot me in the back when I was takin' a pee. He was just thirty feet away and I didn't even know that he'd pulled his rifle."

Bo quickly exclaimed, "*He missed from thirty feet with a rifle?*"

"Nope. I was doin' my business when I heard a rifle shot and by the time I turned around, Mort was leavin' his saddle. I was hellish mad when I figured out that Mort was gonna shoot me, but then I looked at the shooter and couldn't believe my eyes. It was Joe Beck. He was about three hundred yards out and when he saw Mort pointing his rifle at me, he fired. If he hadn't been such a good shot, I'd be dead."

Bo's eyes were wide as he loudly asked, "*Joe is alive?*"

"Yup. After he waved to me, he went down the other side of the hill. By the time I got around the hill, I found him next to that odd cart of his talkin' to Faith Goodchild."

Bo shook his head, then grinned and asked, "Where are they?"

"Joe said that they'd be waitin' on the Trail. It looks like you stopped for the night a bit early. Do you want me to go tell 'em?"

Bo looked at the sun before he turned to Ed Carlisle and said, "We'll stay here, Ed. I'd appreciate it if you and Wilmot kept this news quiet until I can talk to the folks."

Ed nodded then said, "I'll try, but some folks probably already noticed that Chuck rode in alone."

"If they ask, don't lie to 'em."

"Okay."

After Ed and Wilmot walked away, Bo turned to Chuck and asked, "What did Joe tell you?"

"Not much 'cause I had to move Mort's body out of the way and get back here to tell you what happened. He did tell me that Mort tried to drygulch him, but his shot just hit the side of his chest. It knocked him into a creek, and Mort musta figured he was dead."

"I don't care if Mort was trying to clean his rifle when Joe shot him. Losin' Mort created a problem but findin' Joe gave me the answer right off. Go back and tell them to come in, or they can camp out there if they want."

"Okay. Oh, and Joe seemed real anxious to talk to Mister Newbury. I figure he and Faith wanna get hitched."

Bo snickered then said, "Go see Fester Newbury and ask him to come along. You can borrow Ranger if he does. We owe it to Joe. And tell him he can have Mort's horse and tack for Faith as a wedding present."

Chuck grinned then mounted and trotted to the Newbury wagon to convince him to take a short ride.

―――

Joe and Faith had unharnessed Bernie and were leading him and the two horses to the Platte River. Neither had seen Mort's body, so they didn't know if it was in the water or just hidden. It didn't matter as long as they didn't see it.

As the animals drank, Joe said, "I thought we'd see the wagons by now."

"So, did I. It's almost sunset, so they probably already pulled up. Are we going to go back there if we don't see them soon?"

"No. We'll set up camp further west. I don't want to be this close to where Mort fell."

Faith was staring to the east as she nodded and asked, "What will we do after we rejoin the wagon train?"

"Do you mean after we get married?"

Faith turned to look at him, smiled and replied, "Yes, sir. I mean after that."

"I don't know. I imagine that Mister Ferguson will expect me to scout with Chuck, but I don't want to leave you alone, either."

"I wouldn't be alone, Joe. I'd be walking with Bernie and I'm pretty sure that Marigold will be there as well. We don't have to stay near the Moores' wagon, either."

"I guess that would be okay, but when we stop for the night, I'd prefer that we camp away from the wagons like I used to before I was banished."

Faith grinned as she asked, "Are you worried that Mister Moore might steal me away during the night?"

"Not a bit. It's just that, well, I want a little privacy after we're married."

Faith looked east again and was about to request a vivid explanation of the need for privacy when she spotted riders in the distance.

"There are two riders coming."

Joe turned and looked before saying, "That's Chuck and I guess that Bo Ferguson must have wanted to talk to me."

"You can identify him from this far?"

"Not him. It's his horse. Let's get Bernie, Bessie and the other mare back to the cart before they arrive."

"Alright."

They both watched the approaching riders as they led the three animals back to the Trail and after just a few steps, Joe said, "That's not Bo Ferguson with him, but he's riding Bo's horse. I don't recognize him; do you?"

As they continued to walk, Faith squinted as she stared at them for a few more steps before smiling and looking back at Joe.

"That's Mister Newbury."

Joe smiled as he said, "I guess Chuck figured out why I wanted to talk to him."

"Does he just want to talk to us, or can he marry us out here?"

"I don't know, but let's get the horses and Bernie tied off first."

She nodded as they picked up their pace to reach the tent-cart. They had just finished knotting Bessie's reins when Chuck and Mister Fester Horatio Newbury arrived and dismounted.

Joe and Faith stepped away from the cart as Chuck said, "I told Bo that you really wanted to talk to Mister Newbury, so he said to ask Fester if he'd be willing to come along."

Joe looked at the wagon train's spiritual leader and said, "Thanks for coming, Mister Newbury. Faith and I want to get married as soon as possible. It's not because we, um, have to, you understand. It's because I love her and don't want her to return to the Moores."

Mister Newbury smiled as he replied, "I understand why that is so, Joe. There have been rumors about their motives for paying her father for her services. Those whispers just grew louder when Harry Moore hired Becky Witherspoon after he believed Faith had gone back to Kansas City or died."

Faith quickly asked, "*They hired Becky Witherspoon?*"

It was Chuck who replied, "They sure did. Marigold said that she was happy about it, too."

Faith was astonished but it no longer mattered as Joe asked, "Mister Newbury, can you marry us right now?"

"Chuck told me that was what you would probably ask, so I brought my prayer book. I'll get it out of the saddlebags then we can start. It won't take long."

As Mister Newbury turned around, Joe smiled down at Faith and took her hand.

Chuck took hold of both horses' reins and stood in front of the couple. He'd witnessed six marriages on his two previous trips across the western half of the country, but none had been as unusual or as significant at this one.

UNWANTED

Mister Newbury stopped before Joe and Faith and opened his prayerbook. In the dim light, he seemed to be reading the marriage passages but didn't need to see the words as he knew them by heart.

The sun was setting behind Joe and Faith creating a spectacular backdrop as the deacon pronounced them man and wife.

There had been no rings exchanged nor did Mister Newbury end the ceremony by telling Joe that he could kiss his wife. But Joe didn't need to be told as he wrapped his arms around Faith and kissed her softly and didn't even feel any objection from his chest.

Chuck glanced at Fester Newbury, winked then waited for Mister and Mrs. Beck to end their kiss before he said, "We've gotta get back, Joe. Congratulations to you and Faith."

Joe grinned as he shook Chuck's hand, then Mister Newbury's before he said, "Thank you both."

Chuck said, "I'll see you folks in the morning. I'll get here before you see the wagons and you can tell me the rest of the story. Oh, and Bo said to keep Mort's horse and gear as a wedding present. I owe you a lot more, Joe."

"I was just glad to be able to help, Chuck."

Mister Newbury then said, "Your marriage is real in the eyes of God, but not in the laws of man until we write it down on paper. So, come to my wagon tomorrow where both of you need to fill out some papers then I'll enter your marriage in the record book."

Joe nodded as he said, "Yes, sir."

As Mister Newbury returned his prayer book to the saddlebags and mounted, Chuck stepped closer and in a low voice, he said, "I didn't want to say this in front of the deacon, but Marigold told me that Becky Witherspoon actually said that she wished she could suckle the Moores' baby."

Faith's eyes popped wide as Chuck slapped Joe on his left shoulder then turned and mounted. He waved, then he and Mister Newbury set off at a fast trot to return to the wagons.

Joe and Faith were still holding hands as they watched them fade into the distance before Faith looked up at Joe and asked, "Where will we camp?"

Joe turned and pointed south as he said, "Right between those low hills."

She nodded then quietly asked, "Are we really married, Joe? I don't feel any different."

"Neither do I. I think it was because we already felt as if we were married."

They turned and walked back to the cart and Joe had to release Faith's hand as he moved Bernie back between the cart's long poles then began to put him back into his harness.

Faith was close as he worked and thought about their imminent wedding night. Since Joe had first kissed her, she fantasized about what it might be like but didn't really know what to expect. She knew that she loved Joe and had almost desperately wanted him to touch her, but those were nothing more than thoughts and desires. She would soon experience what her mother had described as duty, yet Joe had portrayed as nothing less than ecstasy. She prayed that Joe was right.

―――

After leading the cart and horses into the shallow valley between the two almost-hills, Joe took the rope hanging on their new mare's saddle, tied one end to the cart's right wheel then stretched it across the ground and anchored it to a lonely juniper bush. He unharnessed Bernie and loosely knotted his halter to the rope before walking back to the horses.

Faith had already removed two bedrolls from the cart and unraveled them next to each other when he returned, so he said, "Let me get the buffalo skin down before I unsaddle the horses."

"I can do it, Joe."

He smiled then said, "I put it up there, so it's not a problem."

He grabbed hold of the heavy skin with both hands and because he was anxious, he made the mistake of pulling with his arms instead of just stepping back and letting his legs do the work. As his arms flexed, a sharp pain shot up his left side making him grunt and drop his hands.

Faith exclaimed, "Joe! *Are you alright?*"

Joe smiled as he replied, "I should have just stepped away."

He then took hold of the skin and began stepping back but his chest protested so much that he thought he might have to ask Faith to get it down. But the heavy robe fell to the ground and Joe was able to drag it over the bedrolls before letting it go.

Faith again asked, "Are you alright? What happened?"

"I'm okay. My wound just reminded me it was there."

"When we finish setting up, we need to check it."

"Yes, ma'am."

Joe let Faith continue making the bed as he walked to the horses. His chest suddenly hurt when he breathed but he didn't think his wound had been reopened. He glanced back at Faith to make sure she wasn't looking and pressed on the left side of his chest. He winced when he pressed near the scar, so he figured that he'd probably just torn a muscle. He cursed himself for doing something that stupid at the worst possible time.

He still had to unsaddle the horses and hoped that his chest would feel better by the time he had to saddle them again. He soon had Bessie's saddle on the ground and then the one belonging to the other mare. He led both horses to the long line and just tied their reins to the rope rather than removing their bridles. He quietly apologized to both ladies before he headed back to the cart.

After painfully lugging both saddles to the cart, he took Mort's saddlebags and carried them to the finished bed where he found Faith staring back at him.

He smiled and said, "Do you want your smaller wedding gift now, Mrs. Beck?"

Despite her concerns about his wound, Faith smiled and asked, "It's not a foal; is it, Mister Beck?"

"No, ma'am. But I reckon we'll have a couple of baby mules by next year."

He sat down beside her then pulled the saddlebags closer before he opened a flap and pulled out Mort's gunbelt.

Joe slipped the Colt Navy from its holster and did a quick examination before looking at Faith and saying, "This is a Colt Navy. It's a little smaller and lighter than my Colt and it shoots a smaller bullet. It's in good condition and I think you'd be able to fire it easier."

Faith smiled and said, "You really just want your own gun back; don't you?"

Joe grinned as he replied, "Kind of. But my pistol has a stronger kick and you'd be able to control this one better. I'll let you keep my gunbelt, though."

"Okay. I suppose I should take it off now, anyway."

Faith unbuckled the gunbelt and handed it to Joe. He put both gunbelts in the saddlebags and set them nearby as Faith watched. She wanted to see if he was gritting his teeth to keep from showing pain. It may be their wedding night, but she wasn't about to let him hurt himself.

Joe was already worrying about his increased level of pain as he began unbuttoning his shirt. While the new injury probably wouldn't prevent him from consummating their marriage, it would be a noticeable distraction and possibly an untimely interruption.

After just lifting the left side of his shirt away, he looked at the scar in the dim light of the rising half-moon.

As he gently touched the skin, Faith asked, "It doesn't look any different, but does it hurt more?"

Joe was about to at least minimize the amount of pain but immediately thought it would be not only dishonest but foolish, so he replied, "I'm afraid so. I think I tore a muscle in my chest when I pulled down the buffalo skin."

"I've done that myself and it can really hurt. And your chest was already painful from the gunshot wound and being cauterized."

"The muscle was already damaged by the bullet, but I didn't notice it as much until I cauterized it. I think that the cauterizing kind of attached the muscle to the skin or something. At least it won't get any worse, and there's no sign of infection, either."

"That's an optimistic way of looking at it. You rest and I'll cook supper."

"I can still build the fire, Faith."

She nodded then stood and said, "Just don't overdo it."

Joe smiled as he rose and replied, "Yes, Mama."

Faith laughed before she walked to the cart with Joe trailing. Neither had mentioned their wedding night but it was on their minds as Joe began to build the fire and Faith collected the ingredients and the cookware for their supper. They only had some of Joe's smoked venison and jerky for meat, so she would have to be creative.

Joe knew that he needed to replenish their supply of meat and his earlier concerns about not being able to shoot accurately were now magnified.

―――

The story of Mister Newbury marrying Joe and Faith had ripped through the settlers like a prairie grassfire. It helped that they were all together around the large fire having supper when Chuck and Fester Newbury returned.

The Moores heard the news but despite their surprise, neither cared any longer. They were very pleased with Becky Witherspoon's eagerness and Mary was even happier when Becky had confided in her that she wished she could suckle their baby. She hadn't told Harry about it but there was no reason to let him know.

The folks were abuzz with the news of Mort's demise as well which made for a lively meal and for a couple of hours after the plates were cleaned and put away.

Chuck and Marigold had snuck away as the others continued to chat and soon found a private place near the Platte River.

After Chuck laid his slicker on the damp ground, they sat down and he said, "I can't tell you how touching it was watching Joe and Faith get married with the sun setting behind them."

Marigold sighed then took his hand and said, "I wish I could get married."

Chuck swallowed before he asked, "Would you marry me, Mary?"

Marigold smiled as she replied, "Not until you kiss me."

Chuck smiled then put his free hand behind her neck and kissed her.

Marigold surprised Chuck with her passionate reaction and before the kiss ended, she pulled him back until they were laying on the slicker.

Forty minutes later, after hurriedly dressing, Chuck and Marigold walked away from the river to visit her parents.

———

While the premarital consummation was taking place four miles away, Joe finally brought up the subject.

"Faith, in a little while, we'll be close together under the blankets as husband and wife. Almost since I met you, I've fantasized about being with you. Even as I was lying by the creek with that bullet hole in my side and no way of returning to the wagon train, I dreamt of you. I want you so badly that it hurts, but I don't want to disappoint you, Faith. Not tonight and not for the rest of our lives."

Faith sighed then said, "You won't disappoint me even if we can just hug and kiss tonight. I was already worried that you might rip another muscle if we became too enthusiastic."

"I know that we could consummate our marriage, but that's not good enough. I want you to realize as much pleasure as possible and I don't think I can with the pain in my chest inhibiting me."

Faith smiled and placed her hand on Joe's forearm before saying, "We have a long journey ahead of us and plenty of time to let your injuries heal. Just don't get any new ones."

Joe laughed then set his plate down before he leaned over and kissed her then said, "I'll make it up to you, Faith."

"I hope so."

As he picked up his plate again, Joe asked, "Were you as excited as I was about tonight?"

"Honestly? I was very excited until we started back and then I began to get a little nervous. I suppose all new brides feel that way, but this is my first time."

Joe chuckled then said, "I wonder if Marigold is going to be nervous on her wedding night with Chuck."

Faith laughed then replied, "I think Chuck will be the more nervous of the two because he'll be worried that he might not be able to satisfy Marigold's lust."

"Did she talk to you about those kinds of things?"

"More than you'd expect. It may have been just talk, but I got the impression that Marigold would be more than willing to consummate their marriage before they stood before Mister Newbury. I was a bit surprised how quickly she shifted her attention to Chuck, too. I guess that once we became friends, she didn't want to hurt my feelings."

"Maybe she realized that I loved you, Mrs. Beck."

Joe smiled and thought about asking Chuck about Marigold when they went scouting. He just hoped he'd be useful on the Trail with his added chest injury.

―――

Chuck had already returned to the front wagon after receiving her parents' permission to marry Marigold when Faith and Joe slid beneath the blankets.

They were both still dressed but were barefoot as they lay on their backs side by side on the buffalo skin. It was a unique and unusual situation that neither could have imagined.

As they both looked at the moon suspended in the sky over their heads, Joe said, "I'm really sorry, Faith. I feel like an idiot for causing this delay."

Faith didn't reply because she was torn between agreeing with him and making him angry or lying.

After a few seconds of silence, Joe smiled and said, "Thank you for not disagreeing with me."

"You should have known that you were doing too much. You could barely hold a rifle level yesterday."

"I know. I guess I should have been smarter. Does this mean that now that we're married, you're going to turn into a nag?"

Faith rolled onto her left side and smiled as she said, "Maybe. You just have to keep that from happening by thinking before you do something that might seem stupid after you do it."

Joe then rolled onto his right side before he replied, "I can't make that promise, Mrs. Beck. All the time I was growing up, I've watched my brothers, cousins and other boys and men do stupid things, but not my mother or other women or girls. What I thought was even funnier was that some of us would be watching, and we all knew it was stupid, but no one said anything."

Faith asked, "Really? Like what?"

"When I was seven, my oldest brother Billy was making his own firecracker for the Fourth of July. My other brother, Hal and I watched and as Billy poured the gunpowder, he giggled and said, 'I bet Billy's gonna blow his finger off!'. I didn't say anything but just watched wondering if Hal was right. But after he said it, I began to see how dangerous it was.

"Billy already had a small fire going just a couple of feet away from the pile of gunpowder. It wasn't a big mound, about eight shots worth of powder. But to make a firecracker, it has to be contained. So, Billy was scooping it into a hollowed out stick of wood. He had even made a fuse of cloth and powder.

"Anyway, Hal and I were about ten feet away when Billy was pushing his fuse into that stick of powder. Then a squirrel dropped down from nearby tree and Billy turned to see what it was. When he did, the tip of his fuse touched the fire and before either Hal or I could say anything, that piece of cloth almost exploded in flame. It set off Billy's homemade firecracker and the gunsmoke filled the air."

Faith quickly asked, "Did your brother lose his hand?"

"Nope. As soon as the flame licked his fingers, he let it go and then, when it went off, it just burned ferociously. That stick didn't even break open."

"Why didn't it explode?"

"My father said that it was because Billy hadn't packed it tightly and both ends of the stick were left open."

"I imagine your father was really mad when he heard about it."

Joe grinned as he said, "No, he wasn't mad at all. He must have known what Billy was going to do after he took the powder but let us go into the woods. He might even have been nearby watching but never admitted to it. After the gunsmoke cleared, he walked up to Billy, picked up the failed firecracker and told him what he'd done wrong."

Faith was wide-eyed as she asked, "Your father let him do it even though your brother could have blown off his hand?"

"My father said that we needed to learn from our mistakes, but he did make us promise not to tell our mother. Libby had just turned four, so she wasn't a problem."

"Obviously, you didn't learn from your mistakes, Mister Beck."

"Actually, I did learn a lot from that lesson. I never took those kinds of risks unless it was necessary, like when I had to shoot those rebels. I really didn't think pulling down that buffalo hide would cause any damage, but I was too anxious to make the bed."

"Then I guess I'll forgive you this time."

"Then you won't mind if I take the risk of kissing you?"

She smiled and asked, "Why is it a risk?"

"Because I want you so badly that I might not be able to stop."

Faith whispered, "As much as I don't want you to stop, I'll keep you from releasing the first button on my dress."

UNWANTED

Joe smiled then carefully leaned forward and kissed her with as much passion as he dared. But even then, the sharp pain from his chest warned him of the consequences of strenuous exercise.

After the kiss ended, Faith sighed and rolled onto her back, so Joe did as well.

Faith said, "I know it's our wedding night and I should be terribly disappointed, but I'm not. I feel so content just having you lying beside me. I guess I'm not the hussy I was beginning to believe that I was."

Joe chuckled then said, "You were never a hussy, Faith, and I'm only disappointed in myself. But I know why you feel so content because I feel the same way. When we met just a couple of weeks ago, each of us was alone and unwanted. Now we have each other, and we know that we'll never feel that way again."

Faith stared at the moon and softly said, "I hope we're never apart again, Joe."

"We just vowed to stay together until death we do part, Faith. We have decades ahead of us, and wherever it may be, I want to fill our new home with children, grandchildren and great-grandchildren."

Faith turned her head to look at Joe as she asked, "How long before we begin the process of filling our home?"

Joe laughed then replied, "As soon as I can shoot on of my Mississippi rifles to get us some meat."

Faith laughed and wished Joe's injuries healed as fast as possible but was a bit relieved that she didn't have to learn if her mother or Joe was right about the experience.

CHAPTER 11

Because they didn't have to travel that morning, Joe thought that they'd be able to stay snug under their warm blankets until sunrise. But as soon as the sky began to lighten, Joe's eyes popped open almost in panic.

He was breathing rapidly and almost sat up before he realized where he was. He calmed down and looked at Faith's peaceful face and wondered what had spooked him awake. He scanned the immediate surroundings and found Bernie and the two mares still sleeping and nothing else seemed amiss. There weren't even any small critters scurrying through the grass.

Joe managed to slide out from under the blankets without disturbing Faith then carefully stood and stepped barefoot to his boots and socks at the foot of their bed. He bent at his knees to pick them up before walking to the cart where he slowly sat on his saddle.

As he pulled on his socks, he thought about what had disturbed his sleep. If he'd awakened as he normally did, he'd just attribute it to habit. He was tugging his left boot on when he figured out the reason. It was Newt, or rather his absence. Each morning since they'd been together, Newt had usually started hounding him for breakfast as soon as the sky began to shed the night. He smiled as he stuck his right foot in his boot and visualized those predictable and sometimes unwanted wakeup calls.

He soon walked behind the cart where he emptied his bladder before taking one of the full canteens to wash and shave.

Joe was watching Faith as he scraped off his stubble and hoped she slept a little longer. He needed to test his ability to function with that nasty muscle pull. He hadn't challenged it yet but could feel the constant throb.

After putting his razor and the canteen away, Joe finally pulled Mort's rifle from his scabbard; the one he'd used to shoot him and was going to use to kill Chuck. He was surprised to find that it was a Sharps carbine and wondered how Mort had been able to get one.

While it had a shorter barrel than the rifle, Joe knew it was still a very accurate weapon and should have killed him. But what made it even more valuable to him was that it was a breech loader and could be reloaded in less than half the time as a muzzle loader. He knew it used a smaller ball than his Mississippi rifles but expected to find ammunition in Mort's saddlebags.

He did a quick examination then slid it back into its scabbard before he stepped over to his saddle then bent at his knees and grasped it with his right hand before standing up again. He carried it to Bessie without any problems before returning to the cart to retrieve the two horse blankets.

He began saddling Bessie but kept glancing at Faith almost as if he didn't want to be caught. He was able to get the saddle onto her back without too much difficulty and soon had her ready to ride. He was almost giddy when he returned for Mort's saddle and followed his new routine for lifting it then carried it to the brown mare.

As he saddled what used to be Mort's horse which included adding the Sharps carbine, he finally took time to examine the mare in the dim predawn light. Her coat was a bit lighter shade of brown than Bessie's, and she didn't have any markings at all. She was around two years older than Bessie, so he figured that would make her seven years old, which was still young enough to foal.

He was able to get her saddled before he saw Faith move. He didn't jog back but took long strides to return to the cart before she opened her eyes. But even after he reached the tent-cart, she remained sleeping. She had just rolled over in her sleep and taken his spot under the blankets.

Joe snickered before he slid one of his Mississippi muskets from the cart. He wondered if Faith would count this as one of those stupid things if he tried to test his ability to hold the heavy rifle. Even if she did, he knew that it was necessary.

He turned sideways and slowly raised the rifle with his left elbow tucked in close to his chest. He could have put on his heavy coat as a cushion, but Joe wanted it to be more realistic. He soon had the Mississippi level and was able to ignore the pulses of pain from his chest as he looked down the iron sights. He held them fairly steady for twenty seconds before he lowered the muzzle and then returned the rifle to the cart.

Joe smiled in satisfaction then looked at Faith expecting her to be watching. But her eyes were still closed, and Joe was relieved. He was surprised that he'd been able to hold the heavy rifle steady at all, much less for that long. He'd had much more trouble after he'd cauterized the open wound.

Despite his success, Joe was determined not to stretch his luck, so he took his time removing ingredients and cookware to cook their breakfast.

Faith finally opened her eyes as the sun popped over the horizon. She immediately noticed that Joe was gone and quickly sat up then spotted him at the fire.

She threw back the blankets and loudly asked, "Joe, how long have you been up?"

Joe turned to look back at her then replied, "About an hour or so. I'll have breakfast ready in about ten minutes."

Faith didn't have time to ask any more questions as she stood, grabbed her socks and shoes, then hurried to the other side of the cart.

As she disappeared from view, Joe wondered why people, including himself, were so concerned about being seen performing normal bodily functions. It was just an abstract thought and quickly faded away as he continued to stir their bean and beef jerky breakfast. Now that he knew he could hold his rifle, he was confident that they'd soon have a new supply of fresh meat.

When Faith reappeared a few minutes later, she said, "I noticed that you already saddled both horses. How bad was it?"

"Not bad at all. I was very careful."

"Then maybe we could have consummated our marriage last night after all."

As she sat down beside him, Joe said, "I still think it could have been a disaster, but I was surprised that I was able to get the horses saddled without even having to grunt."

"Maybe it's not so bad."

"Either that or I'm just used to the pain now. I even tried aiming my rifle a few minutes ago and was able to hold it steady for twenty seconds."

"That's surprising. You said you were having trouble doing that a couple of days ago."

"I know. I thought it would be a lot worse, but it wasn't."

As Joe began scooping the bean mix onto their plates, Faith asked, "How long before the wagons show up?"

"I'd guess in about another hour or so. We'll be able to see them pretty soon."

"Then we need to see Mister Newbury and fill out those papers."

Joe handed her a plate and said, "Maybe I'll go ask Marigold if she's still interested before I sign anything."

Faith laughed before she said, "Go ahead. If Chuck doesn't shoot you, then I will."

Joe snickered before he began to eat.

―――

The sun was up, the teams were all in harness, but the wagons hadn't begun rolling. Mister Newbury was performing his second marriage ceremony less than a sixteen hours after having married Joe and Faith.

There was a large gathering of settlers to witness the unexpected marriage of Chuck Lynch and Marigold Smith.

UNWANTED

Even the Moores were in attendance and Becky Witherspoon was standing beside them rather than with her parents.

After the short ceremony, Chuck and Marigold accepted the polite applause from the crowd before they began dispersing. The newlyweds walked with Mister and Mrs. Newbury to their wagon to do the paperwork, and Bo Ferguson headed back to the front wagon.

Bo had been stunned when Chuck returned last night and told him that he and Marigold were going to be married the next morning. It was more than a shock as it meant that he now had two married scouts and while Joe could take care of his and Faith's living arrangements, Bo wasn't sure what to do with Mr. and Mrs. Lynch.

After overcoming his initial shock, Bo and Chuck worked out a basic restructuring of the wagon and the flatbed wagon. The wagon was more or less towed behind their covered wagon by having a long rope attached to the four-mule team's harness. Sometimes boys would volunteer to drive just for practice. It contained barrels of extra supplies but there was enough free space to take a little more. They'd moved the barrels into a tighter arrangement to make room for the buffalo meat and now that empty area could be filled with some of the trade goods from the wagon so Chuck and his new bride could have some semblance of privacy each night.

So, while Joe and Faith waited a few miles away, Chuck and Bo began removing some of the bulkier items from the lead wagon and putting them on the flatbed until it was so full that they had to stretch a rope around the back to keep things from falling out. How the wagon would survive a river crossing was a problem they'd worry about when it arrived.

When the wagon train finally got underway, the sun had been up for over an hour. Bo had allowed Chuck to remain with the wagons as they knew that Joe was a few miles ahead, and he'd be able to warn them of any danger, if not eliminate it.

Bo was riding Ranger just fifty yards in front of the wagon while Chuck drove the wagon with Marigold sitting close beside him. Bo wasn't about to look back to see what they might be doing.

Marigold had her hand on Chuck's thigh as she said, "I wonder if Faith had as much fun as we did last night."

Chuck grinned as he replied, "I doubt it. But when I get a chance to talk to Joe, I'll ask."

"I'll ask Faith, too. But I'm not sure that she'll even admit that they did anything. She's a bit of a prude because of her parents."

Chuck asked, "Really?"

"She told me that she wasn't going to be that way after she and Joe got married, but I didn't believe her."

Chuck laughed then said, "I guess we'll find out soon enough."

Faith smiled as she began to rub Chuck's thigh.

―――

Faith was looking to the east with her hand pressed to her forehead to block out the morning sun as she said, "I don't see them yet. Shouldn't they be here by now?"

Joe used his cavalry hat's brim to serve the same purpose and couldn't see the top of the lead wagon yet either, which surprised him.

"I thought so. I'll climb the hill and get a better look. Do you want to come along?"

"Alright."

He took her hand, and they began to walk up the low hill. Each was wearing a gunbelt and Joe had his New Army in Mort's holster. He was carrying one of his Mississippi rifles just as a precaution.

As they neared the top, they stopped when they spotted the wagons about two miles away.

Faith said, "I guess they were further away than we thought."

Chuck shook his head as he said, "I don't think so just by how long it took Chuck to return with Mister Newbury. I guess they got a late start this morning for some reason. It's not Sunday, so maybe someone discovered a broken axle after they began rolling."

Then Faith asked, "Why didn't Chuck show up yet?"

Joe was surprised that Faith noticed the aberration before he did but replied, "I don't know. This is getting stranger. Let's get to the top and watch them get closer."

Faith nodded then just a few steps later, they stood on the top of the hill to watch the slowly approaching wagons.

After a few more minutes, Joe said, "I think that's Bo Ferguson riding out front and unless I'm wrong, Chuck is driving the wagon with Marigold sitting next to him on the driver's seat."

Faith squinted then said, "You're right. I wonder why she's with Chuck and not her family."

Joe grinned as he said, "Maybe we inspired them to get married."

Faith stared at the front wagon as she said, "I was just joking about Marigold seducing Chuck, but maybe I was wrong. Then he would have asked her to marry him in case she had conceived."

UNWANTED

Joe didn't comment as it reminded him of their inconclusive wedding night. But as he watched the wagons, he hoped that his ability to handle the pain would allow them to end their platonic marriage.

Joe saw Bo wave his hat over his head then lifted cavalry hat high and after one swing, he said, "Let's get back to the cart and wait for them."

"Okay."

Joe expected Bo might ride out ahead, so they hurried down from the hill and soon reached the cart. Joe slid his rifle into the bedroll then he and Faith walked to the front of the cart and Joe took Bernie's halter.

As they headed for the ruts, Joe spotted Bo Ferguson riding at a fast pace.

"I guess Bo will explain all of those oddities."

"We need to see Mister Newbury, too."

"I wasn't going to forget, ma'am. I don't want some other beau to tempt you away before you finished with the paperwork."

Faith didn't smile as she asked, "Do I have to fill out anything; or can I just sign my name?"

"I'll write all the information and you can just sign. You can write your name, but you can't read?"

"My mother had me practice writing my name so when I married, I wouldn't embarrass the family."

"That's a terrible reason. But in a few months, you'll be able to write whatever you want, Mrs. Beck."

Faith did smile as she said, "I want that almost as much as I want to consummate our marriage."

"I'll see what I can do about that, too."

"Please make it soon."

Joe smiled at her as he said, "Okay. The first letter is A."

Faith laughed before she turned her eyes back to the east and noticed that Bo Ferguson was just a few hundred yards away. She was beginning to feel a bit hypocritical by acting more like Marigold while trying to ignore her straitlaced upbringing. It was an odd sensation to be anxious to take that final step yet feel relieved for the delay.

Bo pulled up, quickly dismounted then led Ranger closer to Joe and Faith.

Joe said, "It looks like you got a late start and didn't send Chuck out ahead. What's going on?"

Bo grinned as he said, "You can blame Chuck. After he came back with Mister Newbury and told me the news about you and Faith gettin' hitched, he went off with Marigold Smith and a couple of hours later, he tells me that he was gonna marry her this mornin'."

Faith looked at Joe and winked as she smiled then let Joe reply, "I guess Faith was right. Is that going to change anything?"

"Not much. Me and Chuck moved some supplies out of the covered wagon onto the flatbed to give him and Marigold someplace to do their shenanigans. How are you doin', Joe? I haven't talked to you since you disappeared."

"I had to cauterize the gunshot wound that Mort gave me but it's not infected. My chest is pretty sore, but I can ride and shoot."

"I really appreciate you stoppin' Mort from shootin' Chuck, maybe not as much as he does, but it's a lot."

Joe nodded as he asked, "Did you find Mort's body?"

"I didn't see it, but Chuck told me where he left it. It's behind a stand of juniper bushes about fifty yards north of the ruts. The wagons will be well past it by the noon break and I'm not about to dig a hole just to keep the critters away."

"I don't blame you."

Bo smiled at Faith and asked, "How does it feel bein' a married woman, Faith?"

"Not much different than I did before and that surprised me."

"I reckon so. I didn't make any accommodations for you and Joe, but I figured you'd just use that cart now. If you want to move some of the wood onto the flatbed, that'll give you more room, Joe."

"We'll see. Is Chuck going to ride out with me after the noon break?"

"He'd better. Faith can ride with Marigold or just sit on the driver's seat of the flatbed if she wants."

Faith said, "I'll sit with Marigold some of the time and let Russ or Jimmy Smith walk with Bernie when I do. I wanted to talk to her anyway."

Bo snickered then said, "I reckon you two young ladies need to discuss your new husbands."

Faith blushed, but not for the reason that Bo suspected. When Bo had passed his suggestive comment, she'd immediately visualized Marigold engaged in passionate lovemaking with Chuck, and it had sent a rush of blood to her face.

Bo then said, "I'm going to head back now before Chuck and Marigold let the oxen decide which direction to go."

He snickered then mounted Ranger, waved and wheeled him around before riding away.

Faith looked at Joe and said, "I can't believe that Marigold and Chuck are already married. I wonder if she really seduced him after hearing that Mister Newbury had married us."

"I'm not going to ask her, and I doubt if Chuck will admit that it had been Marigold's idea. So, if anyone can find out, it'll be you."

Faith smiled as she said, "I don't believe that I'll even have to ask. Marigold is probably bursting to whisper all the sordid details as soon as we're alone."

Joe nodded as he said, "We need to move soon. We'll travel in front until the noon break then we'll go visit Mister Newbury. Okay?"

"Yes, sir."

It wasn't long before they were walking west again with the lead wagon just four hundred yards behind. Bo was riding in the middle as he studied the sun. They could travel another four miles before the noon break.

As they walked, Faith asked, "How is your chest?"

"It still hurts a lot, but I'm getting used to it again. I just have to avoid doing anything sudden like laughing."

"Do you think it'll get worse if we, um, you know?"

Joe looked down at her as he smiled and replied, "No, ma'am. I don't think I can make it any worse. It's just a matter of ignoring the pain and expecting the sudden jerks if I move too fast. I don't want either to interfere with us, Faith. I want to give you as much attention as possible."

"I don't need a lot of attention, Joe."

"It's not what you need, Faith. It's what you deserve."

Faith knew that there was nothing she could say to affect Joe's decision and tried to ignore the sense of relief she felt when she heard his answer. She knew that when she talked to Marigold, she would have to confess about their quiet night. It might prove embarrassing, but she hoped Marigold would understand. She was also pleased that Marigold was on the first wagon now so she wouldn't have to see the Moores. But she did wonder if there had been any more developments in the Becky Witherspoon situation.

Faith hadn't been wrong about Marigold's powerful need to gush about her all-too-short time with Chuck near the Platte River. As Marigold sat close to her new husband, she watched Faith and Joe walking a few hundred yards ahead and couldn't wait to tell Faith and to hear her own story of their wedding night.

―――

Faith and Joe remained a couple of hundred yards ahead as they stepped along with their walking sticks. Faith had been surprised that they actually had to slow down slightly to avoid pulling away.

For the next two hours, they talked about many different subjects but avoided any topic that might include their second night as a married couple.

Bo finally figured that he had to ring the bell for the noon break and glanced behind him to make sure that Chuck and Marigold weren't engaged in any shenanigans before he turned Ranger around and walked him back to the lead wagon.

When Chuck saw him turn his horse, he automatically reached over and began ringing the bell. He waited for a few seconds then pulled the team to a halt and set the handbrake before he clambered down. He turned and gratefully assisted Marigold to the ground then took her hand and walked to the front of the wagon to meet Bo.

As soon as he heard the bell, Joe had Bernie make a wide U-turn before he and Faith headed back to the wagons to find Mister Newbury.

"I don't even know which wagon is his," Joe said as he looked at Bo talking to Chuck.

"I do, but I'm sure he'll be expecting us anyway."

As they drew closer, Faith's assumption proved correct when she spotted the deacon as he approached the wagon master.

Faith waved to Marigold who waved back then said, "I can see Mister Newbury."

"So, can I. In a few more minutes, we'll be legally married. You aren't going to change your mind; are you?"

She smiled and said, "As if I had a line of suitors waiting to marry a skinny fifteen-year-old girl."

"Do you really still believe that you're skinny after all those times I've told you that you weren't?"

"I've been hearing how skinny I was a lot longer than you've been trying to convince me that I'm not."

"I guess you'll only believe me when you're waddling around like Mrs. Moore."

Faith laughed but didn't reply because it was getting too close to her anxious hope and hidden concern that they'd soon take the first step to make her that way.

Bo dismounted and waited with Chuck, Marigold and now Fester Newbury as Joe and Faith drew closer.

Chuck asked, "How's Joe doin'?"

Bo replied, "He said he can go out with you this afternoon."

"I woulda thought he'd be laid up a lot longer after bein' shot and then cauterizin' that wound. I know I would."

"Hell, I'd still be lyin' down in the wagon. After I drilled Mort, of course. I guess it helps bein' sixteen."

"I still can't believe he's so young. I thought I was young, but he seems older than me."

Marigold laughed then said, "When Russ asked if you were going to marry me, Jimmy said you were old. When I told them you were twenty-two, Jimmy still thought it was old."

Chuck smiled at Marigold but soon looked back down the trail as Joe and Faith drew nearer.

They soon stopped about a hundred feet front of Bo's oxen team and left Bernie in charge as they walked to the four members of their welcoming committee.

When they were close, Bo said, "I reckon you two need to see Mister Newbury first."

Fester Newbury said, "This won't take long."

As he turned to go back to his wagon, Joe and Faith followed the deacon to take care of the necessary paperwork.

―――――

They soon stopped behind the Newbury wagon where the deacon had already lowered their folding side table and had set out the papers and his log book. There was a pen and a bottle of ink alongside.

He picked up the pen, dipped it in the bottle of ink, then looked at Joe and asked, "What's your full name, date and location of birth, and the names of your parents."

"Joe Beck, not Joseph and no middle name. I was born on February the eighth in 1847 in our farmhouse near Warrensburg, Missouri. My father's name was James John Beck and my mother's maiden name was Maureen Ann O'Dowd."

Then Mister Newbury looked at Faith who said, "My full name is Faith Hope Charity Virtue Goodchild."

Before she could continue, Fester Newbury snickered then said, "I may not be able to put them all on one line. I'll do the best I can."

After he'd managed to squeeze her long name onto the line, she continued saying, "I was born on the fourth of October in 1847 in my parents' farmhouse south of Kansas City, Kansas. My father's name is Basil Edward Goodchild and my mother's maiden name was Elizabeth Ann Fitch."

Mister Newbury finished scratching Faith's information then handed the pen to Joe. Joe signed his name then gave it to Faith and watched her carefully pen her name below his.

UNWANTED

When she finished, she exhaled and gave the pen back to Mister Newbury who said, "I'll make a copy for you after I enter your information in the record book below Chuck and Marigold Lynch."

Joe shook the deacon's hand, said, "Thank you, Mister Newbury," before he and Faith turned and headed back to the first wagon.

As they walked, Faith said, "I'm glad that's over. I was worried that he might ask me to write something."

"You shouldn't be embarrassed, Faith. A lot of folks can't read or write and it's not your fault anyway. Blame your narrow-minded parents for thinking that girls shouldn't be taught to read and write. My sister Libby was only seven, and she was already reading and writing. My mother started teaching us when we were five."

"Really? How hard was it for you?"

"I was kind of the family oddity when it came to reading. I had watched her teaching my older brothers, so by the time I was five, I could already read. She said I could read better than either of my older brothers, too. I had to work on my penmanship because I was clumsy. Arithmetic was pretty easy, though."

They were almost to the front wagon when Faith asked, "How long will it take to teach me to read?"

"Not long. You're a very smart lady. I noticed that right away."

"How?"

"It's because of how quickly you figure things out. I think you're smarter than I am."

Faith laughed as she shook her head and said, "I think you're just saying that to make me feel better. I'd be happy just being nearly as smart as you."

Joe didn't have a chance to reply as Bo, Chuck and Marigold were waiting just ten feet away.

Bo said, "Let's get somethin' in our bellies before we start this mess rollin' again."

Joe nodded then he took Faith's hand before they walked to the other side of the wagon where Marigold had lunch waiting.

———

Twenty minutes later, Bo rang his bell again as he watched Joe and Chuck ride away. Russell had taken over Bernie duties while Faith and Marigold were sitting on the driver's seat of the overloaded flatbed wagon. Marigold had their marriage certificate in her dress pocket.

After the wagons were moving again, Marigold grinned and excitedly asked, "*Can you believe this, Faith?* Here we are old married women already!"

Faith smiled but was already embarrassed as she replied, "I know. Two old, married teenaged girls."

Marigold laughed then said, "I don't feel like a teenaged girl anymore after Chuck made love to me last night."

Faith's eyebrows popped up as she exclaimed, "You didn't!"

Marigold giggled as she nodded then said, "We did and it wasn't difficult to convince Chuck to make it happen, either. I wonder if we did it before you and Joe did, and we hadn't even been married yet."

Faith quietly replied, "I'm sure you did because, well, we haven't consummated our marriage yet."

Marigold's jaw dropped as she stared at Faith in disbelief.

After almost ten seconds of stunned silence, Marigold asked, "Why not? I thought he really loved you. Is it because you're thin?"

Faith shook her head as she replied, "No. He told me that he wants to make love to me very much, but after he cauterized his wound, he hurt it again."

"He just rode off with Chuck, so it can't be that bad."

"I think he's trying to hide it as much as he can. He grimaces a lot, especially if he has to bend over or lift something. He said it hurts most if he laughs or moves too quickly. But he told me that the reason we haven't been together is that he wants to be able to give me all the attention I deserve."

Marigold smiled and said, "Chuck gave me a lot of attention, but it was over too quickly. I was incredibly excited and wanted him to keep going, but I think he was worried that my father might show up with a shotgun."

Faith then asked, "I know that you were anxious to have the experience. So, was it all that you hoped it would be?"

Marigold sighed then answered, "It was at the start, but after we had finished, I felt a little empty. I think it will be better when Chuck doesn't have to worry about being caught."

Then after a short pause, Marigold smiled and said, "But the danger of being found while in the throes of passion only added to my excitement."

Faith smiled but decided not to ask Marigold any more marital questions as her first replies made her wonder if her mother hadn't been right after all. If a lusty young woman like Marigold felt empty, then how could she expect to feel the joy that Joe seemed to believe.

So, Faith shifted the subject when she said, "Tell me about the Moores and Becky Witherspoon."

Marigold giggled again then began passing all the rumors that had made their way among the community's womenfolk.

UNWANTED

After leaving the wagons behind, Chuck's first comment wasn't about marriage or sex, when he said, "I see you've got Mort's gunbelt and your Henry in his scabbard."

"I gave my gunbelt and Mort's Colt to Faith, but this holster suits me better than mine. It has a hammer loop and looks better, too. Did you know he had a Sharps carbine?"

"Yup, but I'm glad you got it now. How are you really doin', Joe? I don't reckon you're healed."

"No, it's not. Then I made it worse when I ripped a muscle in my chest. I just have to watch what I do. I can't laugh or do anything abruptly or fast. As long as I take it a bit slower, I'm okay."

Chuck grinned then said, "I'll bet Faith appreciated you goin' slow last night."

"She probably would if we'd done anything."

Chuck's eyes popped wide as he exclaimed, "You and Faith didn't…"

Joe interrupted him when he quickly said, "No, we didn't. I didn't want to suddenly jerk away when a spasm of pain hit. It takes a lot of concentration to keep it at bay and I want to give her all of my attention."

Chuck still stared at Joe as he said, "I gave Marigold all of my attention last night. She kinda caught me by surprise, though. I thought we'd just do a little sparkin', but before I knew it, well, we had to get married pretty soon."

Joe smiled when he recalled what Faith had suggested then said, "So, while Faith and I lay beside each other just talking, you and Marigold were doing what we should have been doing."

Chuck grinned and said, "Yup."

Joe looked ahead and saw nothing interesting before he asked, "How far is it to Fort Kearny?"

"About four more days if we don't have any problems. We have one wide creek to cross in a day or two. We haven't lost any wagons yet, so that's a good sign."

Joe asked, "It's only been two weeks and you're surprised we haven't lost any wagons?"

"In my other trips and from what Bo told me about his, there are usually some that turn around after a week or so when they figure it ain't what they expected. Some have other problems and the folks who have bad wagons don't get very far."

"What happens when a wagon breaks down?"

"It depends on where we are and who they know. Some of 'em just set up a farm where their wagon breaks and others manage to move some of their stuff into another family's wagon."

"I imagine that the broken wagons become a good source of firewood after the trees disappear."

"You got that right. But mostly, folks use buffalo chips as fuel when we lose the trees. They burn a lot faster, so they need a lot of 'em. We're lucky those big herds of buffalo further west are still out there makin' those chips. As the settlers move west, they're pushing them out. We were lucky to see that small herd you found."

"I reckon that'll make the Indians even madder once they start building that transcontinental railroad. I can't say I blame them, either."

"I just hope they ain't mad already. I'd rather trade with 'em than shoot 'em. But some men, like Mort, don't think that way."

"I'm with you, Chuck. I still hope I don't have to shoot anyone again, at least until my wound feels better. We do need to find some game, though."

"We will, but until we see those big herds, we'll likely only find beavers, raccoons and possums."

Chuck then quickly said, "Say, I just noticed. Where's your dog?"

Joe took a breath before replying, "He was sniffing in a prairie dog hole when a rattler shot out and bit him in the neck. I buried him an hour later."

"Sorry to hear that."

Joe nodded then began scanning the banks of the Platte River for signs of smaller critters that could provide some meat for a day or two. He had almost gotten over losing Newt when Chuck asked and wondered how long the emotional ache would linger this time.

They were about four miles in front of the wagons when Joe spotted a shadow scurrying along the riverbank then a second followed.

He pointed and said, "Chuck, there are at least a couple of large raccoons near the river bed."

Chuck turned to look where Joe was pointing and asked, "Why don't you use your Henry? Maybe you'll get more than one."

Joe nodded then slowly dismounted and pulled his Henry from its scabbard as Chuck took Bessie's reins. He cocked the hammer as he began walking toward the river. Raccoons were smart but curious critters, so he wasn't concerned about the wind. He was only worried about his ability to hold his Henry's sights steady. He had to avoid rushing the shot to keep the pain at bay, too.

As he stepped closer to where he'd spotted the raccoons, he decided that even if he missed, he'd work the lever and take another, just to test his ability to take that second shot.

He soon spotted not two, but four raccoons gathered about twenty feet from the edge of the river. They hadn't even noticed him yet, which surprised him because he was only about a hundred feet away.

He stopped and before he raised his Henry, he picked out two targets. They were all large raccoons, but he chose the two biggest.

He took a breath, then raised his repeater and placed the sights on the one farthest to the right. He let his sights settle before he squeezed his trigger. The Henry's butt popped against his shoulder and Joe quickly cycled the lever. The brass shell of the expended cartridge flew away as he shifted his sights to his second target. He found the raccoon looking back at him with his mask-like face but didn't hesitate once his sights were aligned. He squeezed his trigger a second time then automatically worked the lever and brought a fresh cartridge into the chamber. He shot a third racoon and was about to fire again when the last one dashed away and disappeared into the nearby grass.

Joe lowered his carbine and released the Henry's hammer before he turned to Chuck and smiled as he held up three fingers.

Chuck grinned before he started his gray gelding forward to rejoin Joe.

Joe was surprised and pleased with the results but admitted that the raccoons were easy targets and hadn't even moved until the survivor ran off. Still, he was relieved that he hadn't had as much difficulty as he'd anticipated.

He walked to the three raccoons to see how far off he'd been with his shots. If he'd shot a racoon this size when he was ten, his father would be disappointed if he returned with the carcass and the bullet hadn't taken off his head. A large slug would spoil a lot of meat if he had missed.

When he reached the racoons, he dropped to his heels and inspected each hit before he smiled and said, "You'd be impressed, Papa."

He stood and turned as Chuck arrived and dismounted.

He led the horses to Joe, looked down and said, "Those are some mighty fat raccoons, Joe. I reckon those two big ones must weigh over forty pounds. Even the smallest one is over thirty. And that was some fine shootin', even if you weren't hurtin'."

Joe just asked, "Did you want to harvest them here or just bring them back?"

"That's up to you."

"I didn't bring my meat bag along, so I guess we can hang them over our saddles. I'll take the small one and the one on the right. You can have the other one."

"I appreciate it, Joe. Let's get them tied on."

After the raccoons were lashed behind their saddles, Joe and Chuck returned to the trail and continued west. They'd turn back in another hour or so.

As they rode, Joe was more pleased that he was able to accurately fire the Henry than he was about adding the meat to their diet. It gave him a glimmer of hope that he'd be able to give Faith the attention she deserved. The biggest difference was that firing the repeater was a predictable series of practiced motions. He may not have any experience in what he and Faith would do to consummate their marriage, but he was certain that it would be much more energetic and unpredictable. It was that concern that weighed heavily in his mind as they rode west.

Faith and Marigold were now walking next to Bernie after relieving Russ. Faith had to explain to Russell what had happened to Newt before he left, and she wasn't surprised to see the effect it had on him.

Despite her efforts to avoid the subject, Faith found it impossible as Marigold continued to revisit the topic of her night with Chuck. Fortunately for Faith, Marigold seemed content to talk about her own experience rather than Faith's continued virginity.

The other primary subject of their conversation was Becky Witherspoon. While Marigold hadn't been able to provide any more information, the two young women spent much of their time inventing different scenarios. Some were quite bizarre, but almost all of them were salacious in nature.

As they laughed and chatted about Becky, even the titillating conversation about Becky seemed to mock her situation. As Marigold talked of Becky's large bosom, she couldn't help but feel almost inadequate and began to wonder if that was another reason for their delay.

She was beginning to slip into a mild funk when her right hand brushed against her pistol. Then she smiled when she remembered how Joe told her that it wasn't how she looked that made a girl a woman. Then she made the short leap and knew that she was his woman, regardless of whether she was a virgin or not.

The sun was low in the western sky when Faith spotted Joe and Chuck returning.

Marigold said, "There are our husbands, Faith. Good luck with Joe tonight."

Faith smiled as she asked, "You don't need any luck; do you?"

Marigold giggled then said, "No, I don't. I just hope we don't break Bo's wagon apart tonight."

Faith didn't reply as she picked up Bernie's pace a bit to get in front of the lead wagon's team.

Marigold had to trot to keep up as she was almost five inches shorter than Faith and most of Faith's added height was in her long legs. Bernie had no problem matching Faith's increased pace as he was used to Joe's long strides.

———

Joe spotted Faith and waved his hat over his head before Chuck laughed and said, "I reckon Faith is kinda anxious to see you, Joe. I know Marigold is already excited about tonight, too."

"I reckon so."

Just as Faith had tried to avoid the topic, Joe didn't want to return to their earlier conversations either. At least Chuck hadn't rambled on about Marigold's womanly features or her lusty nature. He was sure that Faith would ask him what Chuck said, but he wasn't about to ask her what Marigold told her and hoped she didn't plan to use Marigold's tactics. He believed that he might be able to successfully consummate their marriage but hated the idea of thinking of it as a duty.

They were still a few hundred yards away when Bo rang his bell then a few seconds later, the wagons stopped rolling.

While Marigold stopped at the lead wagon, Faith waved and continued leading Bernie and Mort's mare further west along the ruts.

Joe was surprised when he saw them separate, but soon pulled up. Chuck continued riding and said something to Faith as he passed that Joe couldn't hear before he dismounted.

Faith was smiling as she led Bernie close to Bessie then released her grip and stepped closer to Joe.

He smiled and asked, "What did Chuck say?"

"He just said, 'good luck' and kept going. That was what Marigold told me when she first saw you and Chuck."

Joe nodded then said, "Let's head south into the grass to let the horses and Bernie graze."

"Alright."

She took hold of Bernie's halter and Joe took Bessie's reins before they started walking southwest to create space between their campsite and the wagon train.

Faith said, "I noticed you have two racoons behind your saddle. Are they going to be our supper?"

"Yes, ma'am. They're pretty fat, so we'll get plenty of meat. I gave one to Chuck, too."

"He didn't shoot one?"

"Nope. I used my Henry to take them all. I wanted to see if I could fire more than one shot. I was very pleased with the results, too."

"It looks as if you did well. Did it hurt?"

"Not so much. I took my time, so I didn't yank that damaged muscle."

Faith nodded but didn't say anything as they pushed aside the tall prairie grass.

After Joe pulled Bernie to a stop about four hundred yards southwest of Bo Ferguson's wagon, he smiled at Faith and said, "I'll let you make the bed while I take care of the critters. Okay?"

"That's a wise thing for you to do, sir. Can you unsaddle the horses without too much pain?"

"Yes, ma'am. I kind of lock my left arm close to my chest and use my right arm for the hard work."

"Be careful, Joe."

"I promise."

Joe set up his rope line then unharnessed Bernie and tied his halter to the center. He removed the two heavy raccoons first then carefully unsaddled Bessie. He led her to the line and tied her to Bernie's left side, then after removing the other horse's tack, tied her to his right side.

Before he headed back to the cart, he patted his donkey's neck and said, "I hope you appreciate being the center of attention, Bernie."

He knew how painful it would be to laugh but still took the risk to snicker.

Faith already had made the bedroll and buffalo hide bed when Joe returned to the back of the cart.

He smiled at her as he asked, "Can you take out the big pot and my iron bowl?"

"Alright. What else do you need?"

"I'll just take my cutting board and spade for now. I'm going to skin and harvest the meat from the raccoons."

Faith nodded, then after retrieving the heavy iron pot and the iron bowl, she waited and watched Joe slide a wide, heavily scratched board from the cart then remove the spade. When she was satisfied that he hadn't tried to take the pickaxe, she turned and walked slowly to the other side of their bed.

Joe set the cutting board and spade down, then said, "I'll get the raccoons and you can grab a couple of canteens."

"They look pretty heavy, Joe."

Joe grinned and asked, "They are big boys; aren't they?"

UNWANTED

As they began walking back to the cart, Faith said, "I'm going to keep an eye on you, mister."

Joe shook his head rather than laugh as he reached the racoons. He knew this would be a serious challenge as they probably collectively weighed almost ninety pounds. He almost lifted the cord that connected both coons, but instead, he dropped to his heels, untied one end then used the cord to carry the first one back to where he'd build the fires.

Faith had watched and was pleased when he had separated the two carcasses. But Joe's surprising display of common sense also made her believe that his injury was much worse than she had believed. After removing the canteens, she kept her focus on Joe as he returned to retrieve the second raccoon.

Joe didn't want her to be too concerned, so he dropped to his heels, grabbed the raccoon by the scuff of his neck then stood and smiled at her before carrying it to join his brother.

Faith followed and after he dropped the second raccoon and picked up the spade, she sat down on the corner of the bed and watched. The sun hadn't set yet, so she had a good view of his face as he set the point of the spade into the ground and pushed it into the earth with his right foot.

Joe felt his chest begin to seriously protest as he lifted the first load of dirt from the ground and dumped it off to the side. He tightened the muscles in his jaw as he continued to dig, then after he'd created a teardrop-shaped hole, he moved a few feet away and began to dig again.

Faith had seen his jaw muscles bulge, so she knew he was in pain, but still just asked, "Why are you digging another hole?"

Joe continued to dig as he replied, "One is for the pot and the other is to roast our raccoons."

"You're building two fires?"

Joe had to pause before replying, "Yes, ma'am."

The second hole was a rectangular shape, and she thought he was finished digging when he stepped away. But he soon stepped closer and rammed the spade into the ground. He dug one small hole before bending at his knees and setting the spade on the ground.

"What's that one for?"

"To bury the parts of the raccoons we don't need."

"Oh."

Joe sat beside Faith and set his cutting board close before sliding the first raccoon onto the board. Faith stood and walked back to the cart rather than watch Joe harvest the meat. She wasn't usually squeamish but the closest thing she ever had to a pet was a raccoon. She had found him near the creek that ran across the back of their farm and began to sneak it food. She kept him well fed for almost six months until her father returned one afternoon carrying his rifle and the dead raccoon. She never said anything but found it difficult to eat supper that night.

Joe quickly skinned both raccoons and dumped all of the useless parts into the hole. He chopped up the hearts, livers and kidneys then dumped the pieces into the big pot. He left the cleaned bodies on their skins before standing and walking to the cart.

Faith was waiting when he arrived and asked, "What else do you need me to take from the cart?"

"I'll get the bayonets, but you can start taking out some of the branches. Okay?"

Faith nodded then waited for Joe to remove four bayonets and a box of matches before she began gathering some of the branches.

Joe skewered the raccoons on the bayonets then waited until Faith returned with the branches before he built a crude rotisserie. Even after removing more than half of the raccoons' weight, he wasn't sure if his arrangement would survive, but he didn't want to cook them in sequence and waste more wood.

Faith asked, "What else can I do?"

"Dump one canteen of water into the pot then get the salt and a couple of cups of rice."

She nodded then walked to the cart. She was grateful for the distraction provided by the long preparation as she dreaded discussing the conversation she had with Marigold. Thinking about what would happen when they slid beneath the blankets was even worse. She filled two cups with the rice then set them on a plate and poured about a handful of salt onto the plate.

As Joe built the fires, he was equally concerned about what would happen after the sun set. He was able to control the sudden flashes of intense pain by taking it slow and minimizing the use of his left arm. But digging the holes had been excruciating and he was certain that it would be much worse if he and Faith did what Chuck and Marigold had already done.

He soon had the fire going beneath the pot and would use the narrow opening of the teardrop hole to add more wood. He had just lit the wider rectangle fire when Faith returned and sat down beside him.

"Do I add the rice and salt to the pot?"

"Not yet. I'll use some of the salt on the meat when it starts roasting. When the water in the pot begins to boil, you can pull it off the fire and add the rice and salt. Okay?"

"Alright."

Joe had pulled his heavy glove onto his right hand and used it to turn the end of his bayonets.

He handed the left glove to Faith and said, "You can use this when you have to pull the pot from the fire."

She smiled and said, "I was going to use the hem of my dress."

Joe grinned as he said, "I'd warn you about getting it caught on fire, but women don't do stupid things like that."

"No. Our stupid things are mostly emotional."

Joe didn't ask what she meant as he turned the bayonets but said, "Chuck said Fort Kearny is another three or four days ahead. When we get there, we'll do some shopping. You can buy two or three more dresses, some underthings, socks and some good boots. I'd recommend you buy some britches that fit, too. That way we both could ride."

"Joe, that would cost a lot of money."

"I told you that Captain Chalmers gave me over two hundred dollars and most of it is in that small pot buried in my can of axle grease. I'll take out thirty dollars before we get there. You need the clothes, Faith."

"Are you sure?"

"Yes, ma'am. We can add some more food supplies, too."

She looked at her feet and said, "I do need new shoes, but boots would be better."

Joe smiled and continued to rotate the racoons as drops of fat melted and fell into the fire causing flares.

For the next twenty minutes, they talked about Fort Kearny before Faith asked, "Where will we settle, Joe?"

Joe looked at her and said, "I have no idea, but we have to stay with the wagon train because I accepted Bessie to be a scout."

"But what if you didn't have to be a scout?"

Joe paused rotating as he looked at Faith and after a brief pause, he replied, "I think I'd like to head to Colorado Territory."

"Why?"

"They found gold there, but I'm not interested in hunting for gold. What the gold did was to lure a lot of men there and then towns began springing up. Some were little more than lawless tent towns, but Denver City is already a real city. I heard there were almost five thousand people living there already."

"What would you do there?"

Joe resumed turning the roasting meat as he said, "Don't laugh, but I want to be a lawman. I know I'm only sixteen and have a lot to learn, but it's what I think I was born to do."

"Why would I laugh? I think you'd be a great lawman even now."

Joe smiled as he said, "I think the water's boiling."

Faith turned then pulled on his glove and slid the pot from the fire before dumping in the two cups of rice and the rest of the salt from the plate.

Faith stood then said, "I need the wooden spoon," before she walked to the cart.

Joe continued slowly turning the bayonet skewers as he thought about Faith's last question. He felt an obligation to Bo Ferguson and if he hadn't shot Mort, then maybe he and Faith could have just led Bernie to Colorado when the South Platte joined with the North Platte. Even if he returned both horses to Bo, Joe knew he'd still feel guilty for leaving them with only one scout when two was the bare minimum.

―――

As they put everything away after a very satisfying supper, Joe couldn't help but notice how quiet Faith had been since they set up camp. What bothered him was that he didn't know what was bothering her. He thought he'd already grown to understand Faith better than anyone he'd known since leaving his family farm.

When they sat on the bed and began removing their footwear, Joe finally asked, "What's wrong, Faith?"

Faith thought about giving him an honest answer but knew it would probably make him feel guilty.

So, she smiled and replied, "I never told you that I my only animal friend when I was a girl was a raccoon; did I?"

"No. You had a raccoon as a pet?"

As she pulled off her socks, Faith said, "Sort of."

As she slid beneath the blankets, she began to tell Joe the story of the lonely raccoon who eventually ended up in the family cooking pot.

Joe had managed to remove his boots without grunting before he carefully laid beside Faith and pulled the blanket over his chest.

Faith continued to tell her story as she looked at the stars and wished she could fall asleep before she finished.

Joe was staring at those same stars but even as he listened, he began to realize that the raccoons weren't the reason she had been so untalkative.

When she did finish, Joe turned his head and looked at her before saying, "That's a sad story, Faith. But I don't think it's the real reason you seem out of sorts. Do I have to apologize for something that I did?"

Faith turned her blue eyes to her left and replied, "No, you don't have to apologize for anything, Joe. I'm just worried about your wound."

Joe had a small epiphany then asked, "Are you worried about my wound or the limitations it puts on me?"

Faith sighed before she said, "I know how painful it is, and I don't want you to feel obligated. Do you understand?"

"Yes, I do. You know how much I want to make love to you; don't you?"

"Of course, I do. I feel the same way, and it makes me feel almost guilty for having those thoughts."

"You shouldn't feel guilty at all. I just don't want to you to think that I've lost interest just because we haven't, um, been together."

"I wouldn't have thought that you had for an instant. I'm still your wife even if we haven't consummated our marriage. When you believe your wound is healed enough, we can take that step. I can wait for as long as necessary. Okay?"

Joe nodded then slowly rolled onto his right side and kissed her softly before returning to his previous supine position.

Then he smiled and said, "I promise you that the moment I believe I can focus all my attention on you, I'll make you happier than you can imagine."

Faith smiled back as she said, "I know you will."

Joe searched for her left hand with his right and once he found it, he gently wrapped his long fingers through hers.

Faith did believe all she'd told Joe, but knew she wasn't being totally honest by failing to admit to her tiny but growing anxiety.

So, their second night as a married couple ended just as their first as they closed their eyes and slipped into sleep as virgins.

CHAPTER 12

The morning had been surprisingly normal and upbeat for Joe and Faith as they prepared for the day. The biggest question of the day was what to name Norm's mare. As she was going to be Faith's horse, Joe let her choose the name. It didn't take her long to christen her Betty which fitted well with Bernie and Bessie.

Less than an hour after Bo rung his bell, Joe and Chuck rode west, and Faith and Marigold watched as they walked with Bernie and the tent-cart.

Faith wasn't surprised when Marigold excitedly asked, "So, how was it for you, Faith?"

"I'm still a virgin, Mary. I'm not embarrassed about it either."

Marigold's eyebrows peaked as she exclaimed, "*Joe didn't make love to you last night?*"

"We're both very anxious to consummate our marriage, but Joe's wound is very painful."

Marigold giggled then said, "I don't think having an arm lopped off would stop Chuck."

Faith glanced at Marigold before saying, "You haven't seen his wound, Mary. If you had, you would understand. I was sitting next to him when he pressed that glowing steel bayonet against his open wound and heard the sizzle as his flesh burned. He was doing better until he tore a muscle. Now I just hope he doesn't make it worse."

"I'm sorry, Faith. I shouldn't have said that. How long will it be before he's better?"

"I don't know, and I don't really care if it's a week, a month or a year. We're married and that's all that matters now."

They took four more steps before Marigold said, "You must really love Joe a lot to be able to wait. I don't think I could hold back for three days."

"I do, and I know he loves me just as much. He's only waiting until he can give me all of his attention."

Marigold didn't reply for almost a minute before she finally said, "I wish…" then stopped in mid-sentence.

Faith looked at her friend but didn't ask what she was about to say before she said, "Joe let me name my horse. So, trailing the cart is my mare I named Betty."

Marigold was relieved that Faith hadn't asked what she was about to say and looked back at the brown mare before asking, "How can you ride with your dress?"

"Joe said I should buy some britches when we get to Fort Kearny in three days. He wants me to buy more dresses and a new pair of boots, too."

"Really? Joe can afford to buy you those things?"

Faith realized she might have divulged too much information, but decided to trust Marigold and replied, "I told you how he saved that Union captain. The captain sent him a lot of gifts as a reward and that included almost a hundred dollars in Yankee currency."

Marigold's eyes widened as she said, "A hundred dollars? I've never seen that much money."

"I haven't either. Joe didn't spend much because he traded much of what he'd scavenged from the rebel soldiers."

As Marigold began asking for more details, Faith felt a trifle guilty for only admitting to the hundred dollars. She'd still tell Joe about it when he returned as she began to fill in Joe's story for Marigold.

―――

Joe didn't have to explain anything, including last night's lack of passion as he and Chuck rode along the ruts. It wasn't because they had threats ahead of them, but because Chuck simply spoke endlessly about Marigold's insatiable lust. Joe didn't ask why Chuck thought she hadn't been satisfied as he scanned the landscape ahead.

Joe just rode quietly as Chuck continued to ramble on about Marigold.

After an hour or so, Chuck finally allowed Joe to ask, "What is Fort Kearny like?"

"It's almost a settlement, but that was before the army pulled most of the troops out to die on the other side of the Mississippi. I ain't sure how many of the regular folks stayed, but I reckon that most of 'em stuck around 'cause the Indians aren't going to attack the fort no matter how mad they get. It's probably the safest place for a thousand square miles."

"What's after Fort Kearny?"

"About four or five days after we get past the fort, there's a trading post and settlement called Cottonwood Springs. Then a few days later, we'll reach O'Fallon's Bluff."

"When do we cross the Platte?"

"Right before O'Fallon's Bluff. The South Platte breaks off just a mile or so east of there and they've got a ferry to cross the Platte before the fork."

Joe nodded and did a quick bit of addition to realize that the way to Colorado was only ten to twelve days' ride away. He suddenly felt an almost overpowering urge to head to Colorado Territory but knew his sense of obligation would keep him anchored to the wagon train.

UNWANTED

They rode for another hour without seeing any problems before they headed back to the wagons.

After sharing a very pleasant lunch with Faith, Joe mounted Bessie and joined Chuck before they headed west again. Joe was relieved and very pleased to find Faith in such a good mood and wondered if it had something to do with Marigold. Now that they'd overcome the consummation hurdle, he wouldn't have any reservations about asking her about their conversation.

Chuck didn't talk much as they rode between the ruts and the Platte River and Joe appreciated not having to listen to more Marigold gushing. Joe was riding on Chuck's right in case he saw any decent-sized critters near the river.

They'd ridden for almost an hour when they spotted a couple of specks appear on the horizon.

Chuck said, "I don't think those are critters, Joe. It looks like a couple of boys on horseback."

The afternoon sun was at their ten o'clock, so Joe tilted the brim of his blue hat down slightly before he said, "I think you're right, Chuck. Who would be riding out this way?"

"My best guess is that they're deserters. The replacements that the army sent to take the place of the regular soldiers were either conscripts or men who were paid to take the place of some rich man's kid. They shoulda been happy not bein' in the serious fightin' back east, but I reckon they didn't appreciate bein' stuck out in the middle of the prairie."

"If they're deserters, we can't let them reach the wagons."

"We won't. I'm sure that they can already see us, so let's see what they do."

"Okay."

———

Two and a half miles away, Private Wally Bedford loudly asked, "What do you make of 'em, Steve?"

Private Steve Clinton replied, "I don't reckon they're army, so maybe they're just headin' to Colorado to hunt for gold."

Wally said, "That don't make any sense. If they were goin' that way, they wouldn't be this far north."

"Sure, they would. They just follow the Platte after it splits, and they'd have water most of the way. What do we do about 'em?"

Wally was four years older and knew that Steve expected him to make all the decisions. So, he studied the two oncoming riders before he replied, "Let's get a better look first. We could use more supplies and they should have some."

Steve then asked, "Why don't they have a packhorse if they were gonna head to Colorado for gold."

Wally realized that Steve was right but didn't want to admit his mistake, so he ignored the question by saying, "Let's just let 'em get closer."

Then Steve asked, "You don't reckon that they're scoutin' for a wagon train; do ya?"

Wally could no longer avoid admitting to his error and said, "You could be right, Steve. What we gotta do now is to come up with a reason for bein' here."

Steve said, "We're wearin' uniforms, so maybe we should tell 'em we're scoutin' ourselves and the rest of the troop is a few miles back."

Wally grinned as he looked at Steve and said, "That's good thinkin', buddy. Okay, let's act real soldiery."

Steve snickered as he tugged down his cap and sat a bit straighter in the saddle.

Chuck said, "It looks like I was right, Joe. They're wearin' blue uniforms but haven't touched their rifles yet."

"What kind of rifles does the army issue to cavalry?"

"It's probably a carbine like your Henry but not a repeater. I'd guess they were issued either a Sharps carbine like Norm's or a Burnside."

"The Burnside uses a cartridge like the Henry, so it's faster to reload than the Sharps, but it's got a much shorter range. It still has twice the range of my Henry, though. Sharps carbines have the same range as my Mississippi, but I don't think it has the accuracy."

Chuck looked at Joe and asked, "Where did you learn all that?"

"From Mister Plummer. He was a gunsmith in Pleasant Hill back in Missouri. He loved guns and talked about them all the time because he knew I wanted to hear about them."

"I reckon so."

Chuck and Joe continued to stare at the two soldiers who were about a thousand yards away. As they continued to close the gap, Joe felt the same calm envelope his mind that he'd experienced when he faced the rebel soldiers. He began to focus more sharply on the two soldiers and could make out details he hadn't noticed before. Even at a half a mile, Joe was able to spot something that seemed out of place. He didn't even notice that in his elevated state, he no longer felt any chest pain.

He said, "Chuck, each of those boys has two pistols. I can't believe the army would issue two revolvers to privates."

"You can see that from here? I can barely make out their uniforms."

"I guess I've got a better angle. If they have two pistols, then I reckon you're right about them being deserters. They have pretty fat saddlebags, too."

Chuck squinted as he tried to confirm what Joe had told him, but still couldn't make out either detail.

The two pairs of riders continued drawing closer and Joe began estimating the decreasing range as he watched the two deserters. If they pulled their carbines while out of the range of his Henry, he'd have to use his Mississippi and hope that Chuck didn't miss.

As a precaution, Joe said, "If they go for their rifles, I'll take the one facing me, and you take the one on your side."

Chuck was startled as he'd been concentrating on the two soldiers, but quickly replied, "Okay, Joe. But don't get trigger happy on me. Let's see if we can talk to 'em."

"Yes, sir."

While he was far from being even trigger pleased, Joe figured he'd take the opportunity to use his right thumb to pull his hammer loop free. Each of the deserters may have a pair of Colts, but their holsters had flaps just like the one Captain Chalmers had given him. The one he'd cut off because it was in the way.

Wally said, "Ain't the tall one wearin' a cavalry officer's hat?"

"Looks like it. But I don't figure he's an officer or even in the army. The rest of his clothes ain't army. If they're scoutin' for a wagon train, maybe we can warn 'em about the Indian trouble ahead and make 'em head back."

Wally glanced at Steve then said, "Another good idea, Steve. You musta had some smart elixir or somethin' before we left."

Steve snickered then said, "I'll bet the captain is still fumin' 'cause you took his horse."

Wally grinned as he replied, "And he couldn't do anything about it, either. I told you the major wouldn't send anybody after us. Not with just one company and those Injun troubles brewin'."

Steve said, "They're gettin' close, time to be real soldiers again."

"I'll do most of the talkin', Steve."

Steve glanced at Wally before saying, "Okay."

———

The gap was down to two hundred yards and Joe knew that he'd be able to use his Henry before they could draw their carbines. He continued to study the two men who were chatting as if they were out for a Sunday ride. One was even laughing. He was sure that Chuck was right about their status as deserters but wondered why they were riding so easily. If they were just a couple of days away from Fort Kearny, he thought that they'd be worried about being captured.

He was still thinking about the minor mystery as the two pairs of riders pulled up just ten feet apart.

Wally grinned and loudly said, "Howdy. You boys scoutin' for a wagon train?"

Chuck replied, "Yup. It's a couple of hours back. What are you bluebellies doin' out this far?"

"We're scoutin' ourselves. We got a squad of troopers a few miles back. The Pawnee and the Arapahoe are havin' a tussle over a herd of buffalo out west and the captain wants to make sure it ain't spreadin' east."

"We met with some Pawnee a few days ago and they seemed peaceful."

"That may be so back thataway, but not a few days' ride west. You might wanna warn your folks. We'll head back and tell the troop that you didn't have any trouble."

Chuck nodded then said, "Okay," but waited until they turned around.

Wally and Steve were waiting for the two scouts to head back, so for almost twenty seconds the four men just sat in their saddles staring at each other.

Joe finally spoke when he looked at Wally and asked, "How come you're riding an officer's horse?"

Wally's eyes snapped to look at Joe wondering how he could have figured it out. As he tried to come up with an excuse, Steve believed they'd been found out and panicked.

Wally was about to lie when Steve ripped open his right holster's flap to pull his Colt New Army but wasn't able to get his fingers wrapped around the grip before he found Joe's Colt cocked and pointed at him. He quickly pulled his hand away from his pistol and automatically thrust both hands into the air.

Wally was stunned for a few seconds and Chuck wasn't far behind, but Wally slowly stuck his hands above his head as Chuck pulled his pistol.

Joe looked at Chuck to let him know he could take charge now.

Chuck then said, "I think you boys are deserters. Now maybe I'm wrong, but we can sit here and wait for your column to arrive. I reckon they should be here pretty soon."

Wally glared at Steve as he said, "Alright. There ain't no column. What are you gonna do about it?"

"We'll take you back to our boss and let him figure it out. I reckon he'll just tie you down then give you back to your commander."

Steve then said, "We weren't joshin' about the Pawnee and Arapahoe fightin'. You might need our guns in a few days."

Chuck replied, "I doubt it. Now we'll keep you under our pistols while we ride back and let our boss deal with ya."

Wally asked, "Can we put our hands down now?"

"Go ahead. Let's start ridin'."

Joe and Chuck waited until the two deserters had passed before they turned their horses and began trailing.

Joe said, "I'll keep them under my pistol for a few minutes then you can take over when my arm gets tired."

"Okay. How'd you know that he was riding an officer's horse, anyway?"

Joe shrugged then replied, "It was just a guess. He seemed to be a much better animal and the tack seemed almost new in comparison to the other one."

"Well, you sure spooked the other feller. I was wonderin' how long we were gonna sit there waitin' for someone to turn around."

"So, was I. That's why I asked."

Chuck snickered then said, "Wait 'til Marigold hears this story."

Joe shook his head and wondered how long it would be before Chuck stopped inserting Marigold into every conversation.

———

Marigold hadn't inserted Chuck's name very often into the long conversations she'd shared with Faith as they walked ahead of Bernie, the tent-cart, and Betty.

One of Marigold's favorite topics was the Moores and what they would ask of Becky Witherspoon as Marigold found it to be incredibly titillating. Faith just let her chatter as she watched the western horizon.

When she saw some dots appear in the distance, she interrupted Marigold by pointing and saying, "Here they come."

Marigold turned her eyes to the west then after a few seconds said, "It looks like there are four riders."

Faith used her left hand to shade her eyes as her right was gripping her walking stick before she replied, "You're right. There are four, but it looks like Joe and Chuck are in back of the other two."

"I wonder who they are?"

UNWANTED

Faith didn't answer as she continued to watch the distant riders.

Bo had also noticed the oddity but unlike Faith and Marigold, already had a good idea why Chuck and Joe were riding behind the other pair. There was only one reason, so it was just a question of who they were. They could be highwaymen, but out here that was unlikely. He put his money on deserters. It was a common occurrence and not just among the western forts. After the reality of war slammed into the face of those enthusiastic volunteers and less-enthusiastic conscripts, many of them decided that they'd rather be branded a live coward than praised as a dead hero.

It was too early to ring his bell, but knew he'd have to talk to Chuck when they returned. So, he shouted to Marigold to have her fetch Russell to take over driving the lead wagon.

After Russell arrived, Bo clambered down and let him take the reins as he walked out front to join Faith and Marigold, who had returned after fetching her brother.

When he reached them, Faith asked, "Who is riding with Joe and Chuck?"

"I reckon they're deserters. If they were just regular fellers, they'd be ridin' abreast."

Marigold asked, "What will you do with them?"

"Tie 'em up and drop 'em off at Fort Kearny when we get there."

Faith asked, "Where will you put them?"

"I ain't figured that out yet."

———

When they were about a half a mile out, Wally noted Joe's tent-cart and exclaimed, "What the hell is that?"

Steve snickered before he loudly said, "I don't care. Look at them two women walkin' in front of it."

Chuck growled, "Those are our wives, mister. If you want a bullet in your back, you'd better keep your trap shut!"

Joe was relieved that he had his pistol at their backs at the time because he thought that Chuck would have let his Colt do the talking. Joe may have been annoyed, but he knew that Chuck was much more affected by the deserter's comment.

While he may have had his pistol's sights on Wally Bedford's back, his eyes were focused on Faith. With the sun low behind him, the bright light illuminated her blonde hair making it seem brighter than usual. He wished that he could make her his wife in every sense of the word, but after the danger was over, his damaged chest resumed its constant, painful reminder. It was when that pain surged that he realized he hadn't even noticed it for more than five minutes as they approached the deserters. If he could figure out how to let his mind take control even when there weren't any threats, then he wouldn't have to wait.

They had been so close before he pulled down that damned buffalo hide. Of course, he could have ripped that muscle when he was engaged in a very different physically stressful situation. The past two nights lying beside her without doing anything was enough to drive him crazy. While he appreciated Faith's understanding and patience, he would much rather appreciate Faith.

―――

Bo stepped about twenty feet away from Faith and Marigold as they drew close. He pulled his Colt knowing that Chuck and Joe would have to dismount, and he'd be able to keep them from misbehaving.

Chuck loudly said, "You boys pull up and dismount when you're a hundred feet in front of my boss. He's that feller with the pistol in his hand."

Neither Wally nor Steve replied as they continued to ride. While Wally looked at the man with the gun, Steve studied the two young women. He'd noticed Faith's blonde hair first, but now he focused on Marigold. If he'd said anything, Chuck would have probably pulled his Colt again.

They soon pulled up and as the deserters dismounted, Chuck stepped down while Joe stayed in the saddle until

Chuck was able to pull his pistol before he holstered his Colt. Bo walked closer, so Joe dismounted and took Bessie's reins as he and Chuck waited for the wagon master.

Bo stopped a few strides away from the deserters and asked, "Are they deserters, Chuck?"

Chuck was leading his gelding closer when he replied, "Yup. What do you want to do with 'em, boss?"

"For now, let's get 'em disarmed then we'll tie 'em down on the flatbed's seat."

"Okay."

While Chuck kept his Colt pointed at their backs, Bo had them drop their four gunbelts. Once they hit the ground, Chuck holstered his pistol then took some pigging strings from his saddlebags and tied their wrists behind their backs.

Joe took the deserters' horses' reins as Chuck and Bo led them back to the lead wagon that was still rolling slowly towards them.

Joe still followed and Faith waited until he was close then got in step next to him.

"Are you alright, Joe?"

Joe smiled as he replied, "Yes, ma'am. It wasn't much of a problem. In a couple of days, we'll drop them at Fort Kearny, and you can buy those dresses."

Faith smiled back and watched as Chuck and Bo put the two deserters on the driver's seat of the slow-moving flatbed and managed to secure them with one long rope. Once they were tied down, Joe turned and walked with Faith to catch up to the cart as Bernie was still pulling it away. He was leading three horses, so he looked back for Chuck to give him the two spares.

Faith asked, "What happened?"

Joe began explaining the situation but hadn't even finished the first sentence when Bo trotted up and said, "I'll take the horses, Joe."

Joe nodded and handed Bo the reins. As the wagon master grabbed the leather lines, he said, "Good job with those two, Joe. Chuck said you were in a kinda standoff."

"It was a bit odd."

Bo snickered then led the two horses away before Joe tied Bessie's reins to the cart and let her walk with Betty.

Joe then resumed his story as they walked. He was sure that Chuck was already telling Marigold but wondered if he'd tell her about the deserter's comments.

When he finished his short narrative, Faith asked, "Do you really think that there are Indian wars west of here?"

"I don't know, but we'll find out when we get to Fort Kearny in a couple of days. I have no idea what Bo would do if it gets that bad, but I'm sure he already made plans before we left Kansas City."

"I hope so."

Joe then smiled and said, "When I saw you, the low sun was making you almost glow. You looked like an angel with your blonde hair."

Faith laughed before she said, "With a name like Faith Hope Charity Virtue, what else could I be?"

Joe started to laugh, then winced when a knifelike pain shot from his chest. He wished that Faith hadn't noticed, but he could already see the concern in her eyes.

He smiled and said, "Maybe your name should be Faith Hope Charity Virtue Patience. I'm really sorry for making us wait."

"It will make that night even more special."

Joe nodded but didn't reply as he thought it would sound disingenuous to agree. He thought it couldn't be any more special than it would have been on their first night as husband and wife.

Twenty minutes later, Bo rang his bell, and the wagons began their cascading stops. Joe pulled Bernie to a stop then he and Faith both looked back at the wagons and weren't surprised to see Chuck and Marigold walking towards them.

When they were close, Chuck said, "One of those fellers said that there was a new town about three miles east of Fort Kearny. It's called Dobytown."

"That's an interesting name. It sounds like it should be filled with magical elves or something. What about the Pawnee and Arapahoe issue? Is it real?"

"I don't know. We'll find out soon enough anyway. But that town was the big surprise. It wasn't there when we passed this way the last time. Oh, and we don't have to guard the deserters. The boss asked some of the men to do the job until we drop 'em off. Well, I guess we'll be headin' back."

Marigold put her hand around Chuck's waist then winked at Faith before they walked away.

Faith ignored the wink as she asked, "Where will we camp, Joe?"

"Over by the river. Okay?"

"That's fine."

Joe thought about taking Faith's hand, but didn't want to get her hopes up, so he just grabbed Bernie's halter and headed for the river. The cart bounced wildly as it crossed the deep sets of ruts before entering the thick grass. They walked northwest until they were about a quarter of a mile from the lead wagon before Joe pulled Bernie to a stop.

Faith looked back at the wagons and asked, "Do you feel as if we're almost outcasts because we don't camp near the others?"

"No, I don't. Do you?"

Faith hesitated before she answered, "Sometimes. I guess it's because I never lived alone like you did."

"Do you want to camp near Bo's wagon?"

"No, I was just passing a thought."

Joe nodded then walked to Betty and removed Mort's long coil of rope to build the attaching line. Faith's question had surprised and bothered him. He didn't know why she'd feel like an outcast as she spent her day with Marigold and other walkers. But she was right that Joe was more comfortable being on his own. He soon amended that idea to being content by having just one close companion. Newt had been that companion until he met Faith. He wondered if her feelings of loneliness weren't related to his inability to make love to her.

As he was unharnessing Bernie, he cursed his youth and inexperience with women. He had detected the two holsters on each deserter from a half a mile away yet couldn't understand Faith's concerns. Maybe if he was able to invoke his danger sense without the danger, he'd be able to figure it out.

He managed to unsaddle the horses and tie them off without any problems while Faith set up their buffalo bed. There was still plenty of cooked raccoon meat and the rice stew for supper, so they wouldn't have to build a fire.

As they sat in the fading light eating their cold supper, Faith asked, "Did Chuck talk about Marigold a lot?"

Joe grinned and replied, "He never stopped gushing about her."

"Did you talk about me?"

"Not nearly as much. I'm sorry."

"It's alright. I'm glad that you didn't."

Now that Faith had brought up the topic he had planned to avoid, he said, "But he did say something that made me a bit curious. More than once, he made it sound as if Marigold couldn't be, um, satisfied."

Faith held a forkful of meat in front of her mouth as she said, "That's funny. Marigold was talking about Chuck a lot. But after she asked about us, I told her that we had to wait until your wound was better. Then I said you wanted to be able to give me your undivided attention, and she said, 'I wish…' then stopped."

"What do you think she was going to say?"

"I'm not sure, and I didn't ask. But I wonder if it had something to do with what you just said. Maybe it wasn't what she hoped it would be."

Joe took a bite of the rice stew and began chewing which gave him time to decide whether to continue on the somewhat dangerous topic. Faith was relieved knowing that she had almost confessed her nagging concern about her first experience with Joe.

He swallowed then said, "Maybe they have a decent store in Dobytown, so you can do your shopping before we get to Fort Kearny."

Faith was chewing her meat, so she just nodded.

Joe quickly jabbed another piece of meat and shoved it into his mouth. For the remainder of the meal, neither spoke as the unfulfilled state of their short marriage now dominated their minds for different reasons.

―――

Joe and Faith were lying side-by-side as they looked at the Milky Way.

Joe quietly said, "I wonder how long it will be before we get that rain we've managed to avoid."

UNWANTED

Faith looked at him before saying, "I don't know, but when it arrives, I'll wear the slicker you gave me, Joe."

Joe turned his eyes to his right and said, "At least it's not snow or ice. We're not out of the woods yet."

"It's almost May, Mister Beck. I think we're safe."

Then after a short pause, Faith said, "I wonder if Marigold's pregnant yet."

"I imagine you'll be the first one she tells. Speaking of pregnant, what have you heard about Mrs. Moore?"

Faith had almost forgotten about the lengthy discussions she'd had with Marigold about the Moores and their new nanny. But once Joe asked his question, Faith began repeating all of the rumors that Marigold had told her.

While Joe still listened to what she said, he was more pleased just to hear her talk without worrying about what she was saying.

By the time she ran out of Becky Witherspoon gossip, Faith's eyes were closed, and she was losing her train of thought. Joe heard her voice fading as she said, "…and Becky is supposed to be…be wanting…"

He slowly rolled onto his right side, kissed her softly then whispered, "Goodnight, Faith," before flopping back down and closing his eyes.

CHAPTER 13

It was another uneventful morning as Joe and Chuck rode west as the sun rose behind them. Neither expected any problems even if the deserters were telling the truth about the Indian problems. Those problems, if they existed, would be waiting for them west of Fort Kearny.

As the wagons disappeared behind them, Joe waited for Chuck to start his morning's flood of Marigold stories. But when he did begin talking, it was about the time he and Bo spent talking to the deserters.

They passed another mound that was almost tall enough to be called a true hill when Joe noticed a lonely pine tree fighting to gain height about a thousand yards south.

Joe pointed and loudly said, "Hey, Chuck. Look at that tree sitting all by its lonesome."

Chuck turned to look then said, "It's gonna be lucky to last the summer."

"I've got my hatchet in my saddlebags, so I can cut it down on our way back. We sure can use the wood and a pine is a terrible thing to waste."

"I agree with ya. Are you gonna refill your stock in your cart?"

"Yup, but that'll still leave a lot for the folks."

Joe was already calculating how many of the trimmed branches he could fit into the cart as they left the hill and the lone pine behind.

After another twenty minutes, Chuck finally mentioned Marigold and it wasn't what Joe expected to hear.

Chuck sidled his gelding closer and said, "I got on Marigold's bad side last night 'cause I spent too much time talkin' to the deserters."

"What happened?"

"That's just it. Nothin' happened. By the time I crawled into the space Bo gave us in the wagon, she was already asleep. Even after I made a lotta noise, she never budged. I think she was only actin' like she was asleep."

"That doesn't make any sense to me, Chuck."

"I couldn't figure it out either. Then this mornin', she seemed okay but wasn't her usual happy self."

Joe shrugged before he said, "You know more about women than I do, Chuck."

"How are things with you and Faith? You still just sleepin' together?"

"I'm afraid so. I wish I didn't have to keep disappointing her, but this damned wound is really annoying."

Chuck nodded before he shifted his horse slightly to the right until he had created a twenty-foot gap.

Chuck's question reminded Joe to try to figure out how to trick his mind into believing that Faith was a threat. For the next twenty minutes, he began imagining all sorts of incredibly dangerous situations, but his chest still ached. He even took in a deep breath to see how bad it was and wasn't happy with his chest muscle's angry response.

They spotted some white-tailed deer in the distance but didn't change course as they were not only a good mile away, but they were also upwind.

Joe gave up trying to create a fantasy battle and let his mind generate a much more pleasant scene. He remembered seeing Faith as she sat in the stream taking her bath. It was such a powerful and exciting memory that he didn't notice the roofs of some buildings appear on the horizon.

He almost jumped out of his saddle when Chuck shouted, "There's that town, Joe!"

Joe blinked then looked at distant Dobytown before he turned to Chuck and said, "Let's check it out. I didn't think it was this close."

"It's almost time for us to turn back, so the wagons won't get here until tomorrow. Fort Kearny is only about a thirty-minute ride, so maybe we should bring those deserters with us tomorrow."

"That's a good idea."

As they picked up the pace, Joe suddenly realized that when Chuck had made him jump, his chest hadn't screamed at him. Dobytown began growing larger, but Joe was more interested in why he hadn't noticed the jolt of pain. He was sure that his damaged muscle hadn't miraculously healed.

They soon pulled up near the small town and after Joe saw the dry goods store, he looked west and said, "Do you want to press on to Fort Kearny? If we can get there in another thirty minutes, we can tell them about the deserters. Maybe they'll come back to take them off our hands."

Chuck laughed then pointed at the town before saying, "We don't have to go to the fort, Joe. Look yonder."

Joe turned and understood why Chuck had laughed. Four soldiers were leaving the dry goods store carrying crates and bags to a waiting wagon.

Chuck said, "Let's go talk to those boys."

Chuck nudged his gray gelding toward Dobytown, and Joe followed. He was still trying to understand why his chest wound hadn't protested when he'd jerked.

Two of the soldiers were mounting horses while the other two were climbing into the driver's seat when Joe and Chuck reached them.

When they pulled up on the street side of the wagon's four-mule team, Chuck said, "Howdy. My name's Chuck Lynch and we're scouts for a wagon train about four hours behind us."

The corporal in charge of the detail who was on horseback replied, "I'm Foster Venable. You got more scouts?"

"Nope. Just the two of us."

The corporal glanced at Joe before saying, "You might want a couple more. The Pawnee are kinda mad at the Arapahoe for takin' some buffalo from their land and there have been a few skirmishes."

"The Pawnee gave us safe passage through their territory."

"That was the eastern end and they're not havin' to deal with the Arapahoe. But that ain't the big problem. Our captain figures that all the tribes on the plains are unhappy about the railroad that's comin' and aim to get together."

"That's bad news. I'll pass that on with my boss."

"You ain't seen a couple of soldiers ridin' your way; did ya?"

UNWANTED

"You mean Privates Wally Bradford and Steve Clinton?"

Corporal Venable's eyebrows shot up as he exclaimed, "*You met 'em?*"

Chuck grinned as he replied, "Yup. Me and Joe bumped into your boys yesterday. We're holdin' 'em prisoner and were gonna deliver them to you at Fort Kearny when we got there."

The cavalry NCO slapped his thigh and laughed before looking at the two soldiers sitting in the driver's seat with big grins on their faces and saying, "Captain Gillespie is gonna be dancin' when we tell him."

Then he looked at Chuck and said, "Bradford stole the captain's horse and saddle which really pissed him off. We were too short-handed to send anyone after him, so he figured he'd never see Hooker again."

Chuck asked, "Hooker?"

Foster snickered then said, "He named him after General Joe Hooker 'cause he said that Hooker was a horse's ass. Anyway, I reckon he'll send some of us to pick them up in the mornin'."

"Me and Joe will bring them with us and meet you on the Trail."

"Good enough."

The corporal was about to tell the wagon driver to start rolling when Joe asked, "What is Captain Gillespie's first name?"

Foster looked at Joe and said, "Thomas. Why?"

Joe walked Bessie close to the corporal, removed his hat and handed it to him before he said, "I took that off a rebel soldier I shot near Lone Jack, Missouri. Look inside."

Corporal Venable stared at Joe for a few seconds before shifting his eyes to the hat and saw G. Gillespie scrawled on the sweat band.

"Well, I'll be damned! Captain Gillespie told us his brother got killed in Missouri last year. This must be his hat."

He handed it back to Joe as he asked, "You said you shot the rebel who was wearin' it?"

Joe tugged it back on and replied, "Yes, sir. I scavenged all of their gear before they sent a detail to recover their bodies. The hat was the only thing I took that touched skin because one of them had shot my hat off my head."

"I'd like to stay to hear more of that story but we gotta get back before sundown. I reckon the captain will want to hear about it, too. So, when your wagons get to the post, make sure you pay him a visit."

"I'll do that."

UNWANTED

The corporal tilted his head and asked, "How old are you, anyway?"

"I turned sixteen in February."

"And you shot that rebel last year?"

"In August of '62 during a battle."

Corporal Venable grinned, shook his head, then looked at the wagon-driving private and said, "Get that wagon rolling, Bishop."

Private Bishop snapped the reins, and the mules jerked the wagon away from the dry goods store. Once it started moving, Corporal Venable saluted Joe and Chuck then tapped his horse's flanks before he other mounted cavalryman trotted away.

Chuck looked at Joe and asked, "That hat is an odd coincidence; ain't it?"

"It's a little creepy if you ask me. Do you mind if we picked up a few things before we headed back?"

Chuck grinned as he replied, "I wanted to buy somethin' for Marigold anyway. I figure it'll make her happy again."

As they dismounted, Joe said, "I figure you know more about women than I do, but I have a suggestion that might help. I'll tell you on the ride back."

Chuck looked at Joe before they entered Todd's General Store. It wasn't a large establishment, but they had things that Joe hadn't seen in a long time.

He found a pair of boy's britches for Faith, but only had four dollars and eleven cents in his pocket, so he needed to limit his purchases until he could visit his grease can bank.

Other than the britches, all Joe bought were eighteen eggs and a small ham. The eggs were already in a small basket, so after he paid the bill of a dollar and forty-five cents, he carried the basket to Bessie and carefully stored it in his left saddlebag. He wrapped the ham in the britches and put it in is right saddlebag before he mounted Bessie and waited for Chuck. He was curious why he was taking so long but figured he wasn't sure what he'd be able to buy to make Marigold smile.

While he sat in his saddle, he revisited the mystery of his missing jolt of pain. He knew what he'd been doing when Chuck had startled him, but that didn't make much sense. When he and Chuck were approaching the deserters and he was in his 'danger mode', he hadn't felt any pain but that was understandable. Yet he wasn't in that state when Chuck made him flinch. He had been in a dreamworld filled with images of Faith as she bathed in the stream. That was as far from danger as imaginable.

Then he tried to recall if his freshly cauterized wound had hurt when he'd been spying on her. He couldn't remember if it hurt or not because she had his full attention. Suddenly, he wondered if that was the reason for not feeling the pain. It wasn't danger in itself, but his mind's intense focus on one thing. It didn't matter if it was someone trying to kill him or his powerful lust. His mind seemed to be able to shut out all the sensations that it didn't need, including pain. It also seemed to expand his awareness and slow time.

Chuck exited the store carrying a cloth bag and after stuffing into his saddlebag, he mounted his gray gelding and said, "Let's get back and tell Bo about meetin' the soldiers."

Joe nodded then wheeled Bessie to the south before he and Chuck rode out of Dobytown. He was still thinking about his theory as they turned east on the Trail.

His reverie was interrupted when Chuck loudly asked, "So, Mister Beck, what is your suggestion about makin' Marigold happy?"

He didn't flinch this time but answered, "Faith told me something that I didn't want to mention, but I figure it might help, so I'll tell you."

"What did she tell you?"

Joe felt a trifle uncomfortable as he replied, "Um, well, it was because Marigold asked Faith about our wedding night. After Faith admitted that we hadn't done anything but talk because of my injury, Marigold kind of confessed that she was, um, I guess, um, disappointed."

Chuck exclaimed, "*Disappointed?* She didn't seem disappointed to me!"

Joe quickly said, "Maybe that was a bad word to use. Faith said that Marigold had probably been fantasizing about that first time for so long, it would have been impossible for the reality to equal her imagination."

Chuck seemed somewhat mollified as he asked, "So, what is this suggestion of yours?"

Joe exhaled sharply before saying, "I probably could have consummated our marriage on the first night, but I told Faith that I wanted to give her my full attention because it's what she deserved. I know she was disappointed and so was I, but she agreed to wait. Um, if you don't mind my asking, how long do you and Marigold spend just sparking before you couple?"

Chuck stared at Joe as he thought about how he should answer the question. Their first time had been rushed for many reasons, but even their second night together after they'd been married hadn't taken very long. He had been so overwhelmed by Marigold's intensity and luscious body that he couldn't wait. Then last night, he'd spent all that time with Bo as they questioned the two deserters. By the time he'd entered the wagon, she was already asleep, or just pretending so she didn't have to talk to him.

He finally said, "I reckon it wasn't very long. You gotta understand just how excited Marigold gets and that gets me goin' even faster."

"I can understand, Chuck. But tonight, try focusing on Marigold. Ask her what she wants and then spend time making her happy. If you can do that, I reckon she'll never tell Faith she's disappointed again."

Chuck shook his head and asked, "Are you sure you've never been with a woman before, Joe? It sounds like you're almost one yourself."

Joe grinned as he replied, "Trust me, I'm not close to being a woman. I may not have ever been with a woman either, but my mother told me a lot of what makes women happy. And I intend to make Faith the happiest woman on the planet when I know I can give her my complete attention."

Chuck laughed but still decided to take Joe's advice when he and Marigold entered the wagon tonight. He almost forgot about the nice sweater he'd bought for her. It had cost him a dollar and ten cents, but it would keep her warm when he couldn't.

―――

Faith and Marigold were making good use of their walking sticks as they led Bernie and the tent-cart along the Trail about fifty yards in front of the lead wagon.

They had exhausted all the Moore and Becky Witherspoon rumors, so Faith said, "If he wasn't a scout, Joe said he wants to go south into Colorado when we reach where the Platte River splits."

Marigold looked up at Faith as she asked, "Really? Why would he want to go there?"

"He wants to be a lawman and said that Colorado Territory is really growing fast because of the gold strikes. He told me that Denver City already has more than five thousand people."

"He's not going to leave Chuck on his own; is he?"

"Oh, no. He said he has an obligation to Bo Ferguson and Chuck."

"I don't want Chuck to go out there by himself. It's bad enough that there are only two scouts, but my father told me that nobody wanted to pay for two more. They all have rifles and there are more in the first wagon, so they're not worried. But after listening to what those deserters said about the Indians, I don't feel safe at all."

"I'm not worried. Joe will keep me safe, and I have a pistol of my own now."

Marigold laughed then asked, "You haven't used it yet; have you?"

"Not yet, but Joe will teach me. He has plenty of ammunition and will let me use his Henry repeater, too. He let me dryfire the carbine already."

"What is dryfire? And I thought it was a rifle."

Faith smiled as she began explaining the term 'dryfire' and that the difference in barrel lengths determined what a gun was called. She even passed along Joe's explanation of the difference between smooth bores and those that are rifled. She knew she was just showing off, but it did offset her shame by being unable to read and write. But she was also relieved that Marigold hadn't returned to discussions about their nighttime activity, or the lack of it.

―――

As they approached the hill where Joe had spotted the single pine tree, Chuck asked, "Are you still gonna chop down that tree?"

"Nope, I figure we can do it tomorrow and I'll bring my saw. I want to surprise Faith with the eggs and ham."

Chuck grinned as he said, "That pine ain't goin' anywhere unless it grows legs and runs off. And when we get back, I'll try to pay more attention to Marigold."

Joe didn't reply as he stared east hoping to spot the wagons. He wasn't sure if his theory about being able to summon his elevated state was right but would experiment a few times over the next two days. And maybe after they left Fort Kearny, he'd be confident enough to put his theory to its most critical test.

———

Marigold was looking at Faith as she talked, but Faith was focused on the western horizon. The Platte was making a long bend to the south which made the Trail turn as well. The row of low hills was still on their left, so she was almost startled when Joe and Chuck popped into view less than a mile away.

She exclaimed, "They're back!"

Marigold stopped in mid-sentence and smiled as she said, "You seem pretty excited, Faith. Are you hoping that Joe's wound stopped hurting?"

"No. I'm just happy to see him again."

Marigold giggled as Faith watched Joe draw closer. She knew she been totally honest in her reply. While she was very happy to see Joe, she was far from giving up hope that he'd heal quickly. She wasn't surprised when he pulled off his blue hat and waved it over his head. She waved back and felt a flush of warmth flow through her.

She smiled and whispered, "Maybe I should be Patience Faith Hope Charity Virtue."

Marigold looked at her and asked, "What did you say?"

"Nothing."

Marigold then grinned as she said, "I'll head over to Bo's wagon to wait for Chuck so you and Joe can talk some more."

As Faith watched her leave, she wondered if Marigold had intended to add a jab about what she and Joe would be doing after sunset. She told herself that it didn't matter and let it go.

―――

After he pulled his hat back on, Chuck said, "I'll tell Bo all the news. I reckon you want to give those eggs to Faith before you break 'em."

"Thanks, Chuck."

As they made their ride back to the wagons, Joe had debated about telling Faith about his theory. He was torn between giving her hope and the very real possibility of disappointing her when he was unable to figure it out. He finally decided to keep his theory to himself. He couldn't face disappointing her again.

Faith didn't stop Bernie when Joe pulled up and dismounted and Chuck waved as he passed.

Joe took Bessie's reins and got in step with Faith before he said, "We found Dobytown and met some soldiers from Fort Kearny. They'll send a squad this way in the morning, and Chuck and I will take the deserters to them."

"What was the town like?"

"What you'd expect for a new settlement, I reckon. But they had a fairly nice dry goods store and I bought you a present."

Faith smiled as she said, "No one ever gave me a present before."

"Really? Not even for Christmas or your birthday?"

"No. My father believed it was a waste of money."

"But even so, your mother could have knitted you some socks or something and then given them to you on your birthday."

Faith shrugged as she said, "I don't know why they didn't do that, either. So, what did you buy for me?"

"It's not really anything special. I bought you a pair of boys britches so you could ride Betty without anyone else seeing your legs."

Faith laughed then said, "It's still a nice gift, Joe."

"But they might smell funny for a while. I bought eighteen eggs and a small ham, too. I wrapped the ham inside the pants before I stuffed them into my saddlebags."

Faith's eyes widened as she asked, "You bought eggs and ham?"

"Yes, ma'am. I figured that you'd enjoy a little variety in your meals."

"We still have the rice stew and raccoon meat. I guess we can make a big supper out of the leftovers and have eggs and ham for breakfast."

"That sounds fair. Before the wagon train reaches Dobytown, I'll dig out some more cash from our grease bank so you can buy more things. Okay?"

Faith nodded and didn't bother claiming that she didn't need anything because Joe was well aware of her limited wardrobe.

Joe then said, "When we talked to those soldiers, I learned something remarkable."

"What was that?"

He pulled off his hat and showed her the sweat band as he said, "That's the name of the Union lieutenant who owned the hat before a rebel killed him. His name was G. Gillespie."

Joe pulled his hat back on then continued, saying, "When we were talking to the soldiers, the corporal said that their captain would be pleased to get his horse back. He said his name was Thomas Gillespie. This hat belonged to his brother."

"That's an odd coincidence; isn't it?"

"Very. Oh, and we also learned that the problem between the Pawnees and Arapahoe is real and that their captain thinks all of the Plains tribes will be getting ornery because of the transcontinental railroad."

"What do you think Mister Ferguson will do about it?"

Joe shrugged as he replied, "I have no idea. The soldiers seemed surprised that there were only two scouts and I think my age made them believe that Bo was scraping the bottom of the barrel."

"He was scraping the bottom when he hired Mort Jones. You're better than Chuck already and you just started."

Joe was preparing to ask Faith about her afternoon when the bell clanged loudly behind them, and Joe flinched just a little. His damaged chest muscle stabbed him with pain, and he was able to avoid grunting, so he hoped that Faith didn't notice.

Faith noticed because she was walking on his left side and was already looking at him. But knowing that he was trying to hide his reaction, she didn't comment.

Instead, she asked, "Where will we set up camp?"

"Close to the river again. See that dune? We'll go to the other side. We can build a nice fire tonight because I spotted a single pine tree about four or five miles away. Tomorrow, I'll bring my saw with me and harvest some wood to fill the cart."

"There was just one tree?"

"Yes, ma'am. It's only about twenty feet tall, if that. I don't know how it got there, but I'm not going to feel that bad about cutting it down. I'm just surprised that none of the other wagon trains or the Indians didn't do it yet."

"Maybe it's a poison pine."

Joe grinned as he said, "Or maybe it's a predator pine preparing to pounce on potential poachers."

Faith laughed again as they continued to lead Bernie and Bessie towards the dune.

―――

Chuck and Bo were standing beside the flatbed wagon as Privates Clinton and Venable listened and learned their fate.

Chuck had just finished telling Bo about their informative afternoon when the wagon master asked, "So, you and Joe are gonna take those two with you in the mornin'?"

"Yup. We'll meet the soldiers then go with 'em to Fort Kearny. You should reach Dobytown tomorrow afternoon and I reckon the folks will want to do some shoppin'. We'll probably meet you there."

Bo nodded then asked, "How bad did that corporal make it sound?"

"Worse than we expected. What do you want to do about it?"

"I'm not sure yet. We'll figure somethin' out when we talk to that captain at Fort Kearny."

"The brother of the lieutenant that owned Joe's hat."

"That's one strange story. Well, you go see Marigold while I go talk to the folks."

Chuck turned and walked back to the lead wagon where he found Marigold waiting for him.

―――

After they were left alone, Wally asked, "We're gonna hang unless we can get out of these ropes, Steve."

"I know, but they did a pretty good job. They gotta let us loose again to get some chow, though. We gotta take the first chance we get. The only ones we gotta worry about are those scouts and the wagon boss. They're the only ones with pistols."

"But we ain't got our pistols either and don't even know where our horses are."

"We don't need either of 'em, Wally. We can grab somethin' that floats and make it to the Platte."

Wally thought about it for a few seconds before he said, "I reckon that it's better than hangin'."

Steve nodded and already began thinking about how they'd make their escape.

After jointly building their bed, Joe was impressed when he removed the basket of eggs and all of them were still intact. After handing it to Faith, she set them in the cart while he walked around Bessie and removed her new britches from his saddlebags.

He waited until she returned then unrolled the britches to expose the small ham. Faith laughed when the pork tumbled onto their blanketed buffalo bed. Joe was grinning as he gave her the britches then slowly bent over, picked up the ham and handed it to her.

"I'll unsaddle Bessie and take Bernie out of his harness. Then I'll start building the fire."

"I'll put the ham and my new leg-hiding britches in the cart then take out our supper. But I can't wait for breakfast now."

Joe smiled then turned to take care of Bessie, Bernie and Betty.

Supper was filling but even Joe was happy he'd bought the eggs and ham as he slid beneath the blankets.

The large sand dune just south of their camp blocked the view of the wagons and if they had been typical newlyweds, they would have appreciated the privacy.

But after Joe stretched out next to Faith, he just took her hand and said, "Chuck bought a sweater for Marigold because he thought she was mad at him. Do you think she was?"

"Not mad, just disappointed that he didn't visit her in the wagon until it was late. She could hear him and Mister Ferguson talking to the prisoners and felt, um, displaced."

"Displaced is a good word. Between what you told me and what he said about their private time together, I suggested that he needed to pay more attention to her."

Faith smiled as she replied, "For a young man who has never been with a woman, you're surprisingly wise to our feminine needs."

Joe smiled back as he said, "My mother taught me well. I imagine if my father had been the one to explain those things, the lesson would have been much shorter and less focused on the female half of the arrangement."

Faith rolled onto her left side and asked, "How is your wound doing?"

Joe was close to telling her his theory but believed that if he did, she might ask him to forgo his future tests.

So, he replied, "It's getting better. It's one of the advantages of being sixteen. If I was as old as Bo Ferguson, we'd probably be forty-year-old virgins."

Faith laughed nervously at the thought before she said, "Marigold reminds me of my status fairly often but not intentionally. She just constantly talks about Chuck. Even when we start gossiping about the Moores and Becky Witherspoon, she inserts his name a lot."

"How is that situation?"

"We really don't know. The Moores were always a bit standoffish, and now that Becky is staying with them most of the time, she's not around."

"I imagine you don't go looking for them anyway."

"I don't, and I'm not about to start, either. Mrs. Moore could have her baby any day now. Then things might get interesting."

"I hope that's all that gets interesting. We'll learn more about the Indian problems out west when we get to Fort Kearny."

Faith thought about asking Joe of his plans to go to Colorado but knew that even if he wanted to head south, his sense of obligation would keep that from happening.

She rolled onto her back again, closed her eyes and said, "Goodnight, Joe."

Joe released her hand and said, "Sweet dreams, Faith."

As he lay beside her, Joe kept his eyes open and stared at the three-quarter moon. He wasn't at all tired and began to think of how he could test his theory tomorrow. He recalled each of the three times he had felt the shift to the highly focused state and knew he wouldn't be able to create danger, but then he looked to his right and saw Faith's peaceful face and smiled. He'd use that erotic image of Faith taking her bath again and see if it worked. If it did, then seeing her in the flesh should have the same effect if not even more intensely.

He returned to staring at the moon as he started planning for tomorrow's ride to Fort Kearny with Chuck and the prisoners. He had to remember to bring his saw to cut down that tree, too.

―――

Wally Venable and Steve Clinton were lying on a single blanket on the north side of the flatbed wagon. While they were still bound, Steve had noticed that the scout who had tied them didn't do a very good job as he was anxious to get back to his woman. He hadn't even told Wally yet.

UNWANTED

They had only one guard, and he was just a farmer with a rifle. His replacement wasn't going to show up for another three hours. Steve was on the river side of the blanket and their guard was sitting on the flatbed wagon's driver's seat about twenty feet away. But it wasn't time to start working on the rope yet. He knew that their best path for escape would be to head northwest toward the Platte River. If they headed east, they'd have to pass all those wagons. It was now just a question of transportation and hopefully guns and some supplies.

As the moon passed slowly overhead, Steve suddenly remembered that tall, young scout who had noticed Wally's horse. He'd seen the kid talking to that blonde girl and heard the other scout talking to their boss about him. He had a cart that probably stored a lot of food and even trailed an extra horse. Steve suddenly modified their escape plan as Wally began to snore.

He closed his eyes and tried to think where the kid's cart would be. He hadn't been paying attention, but the kid and the blonde girl hadn't been with the others during supper. Then he smiled as he figured that they must be camped on their own somewhere west of the wagon train because they wanted to have some privacy.

Steve's only concern now, other than getting loose, was that they had to do it all before the next guard arrived. He opened his left eyelids just a crack to see the farmer. As he expected, their amateur guard already had his head down and might even be sleeping already. Life on a wagon train was hard and sleep was almost a luxury. Steve opened his eyes and began to work on the ropes binding his wrists as he focused on the guard.

Joe was still wide awake as he thought about the potential for a lot of danger if the tribes were as angry as the corporal believed. He knew that each settler had at least one rifle but had never asked about their shooting prowess. Having guns didn't matter unless you put the bullet where it needed to be. He assumed that most, if not all, were reasonably good shooters. They had to be if they were farmers. His father was a farmer and never wasted a shot.

Still, he knew that he had the only repeater, and he didn't know if anyone other than Chuck, Bo and himself had pistols. He then smiled and looked at Faith and added her to the list of pistol owners. He reminded himself that he had to let her fire a few rounds soon.

He returned his gaze to the man in the moon and started doing the arithmetic if it came to a shooting fight with the Indians.

Steve avoided grinning as his left hand slipped free from the rope. The guard was probably completely asleep by now, but Steve didn't take any chances. He was staring at the guard as he slowly sat upright and began untying the knots around his ankles. It only took a minute before he shifted his eyes to Wally and slowly placed the palm of his hand over his open, drooling mouth.

Wally's eyes popped open, but Steve muffled his startled exclamation before Wally realized that his partner had gotten loose. He nodded and Steve removed his hand then wiped it on his britches.

Wally sat up and as Steve began untying his ropes, he leaned forward and whispered, "When you're free, we're gonna sneak out headin' northwest. I reckon that kid scout is up that way with his cart and two horses. He's got guns, too."

Wally grinned as he nodded while Wally worked on his ropes. As soon as Steve told him of his modified escape plans, he realized how much better it was. He wasn't keen on floating down the Platte in the first place.

Steve was looking at the sleeping guard as he and Wally stood then slowly stepped away from the wagons and headed northwest to search for the kid's cart and his horses.

Once they were a hundred yards in front of the lead wagon, Wally asked, "Where do you reckon that he set up? I don't see a damned thing out there."

Steve didn't really know but quietly replied, "He's gotta be up ahead. He ain't back here with the others and he'll wanna be near the water."

"Okay. But what are we gonna do when we find 'em? We ain't got any guns."

Steve hadn't gotten that far in his planning, so he said, "Let's find 'em first. I reckon they'll be sleepin' after all that humpin'."

Wally snickered as they continued their slow walk along the moonlit river.

―――

Joe was still trying to envision what it would be like if they encountered a large war party. Yet without realizing the danger that was approaching less than a hundred yards away, he pulled his Colt New Army and began inspecting it in the moonlight. He added its six shots to the sixteen he'd have in the Henry and the two in his Mississippi rifles and one in the Sharps carbine, so he'd be able to provide twenty-five shots before having to reload. Then he looked at Faith and added six more from her Colt Navy.

It made him feel better and was about to return his pistol to its holster when he thought he heard something that seemed out of place. Normally, he would have just disregarded it, but that was when he had Newt to warn him of any danger.

He suspected that if it was a human noise, it would be Chuck or Bo, so he slowly slipped out of his blankets and stood. He didn't step off the bed because he was barefoot but if Chuck or Bo didn't show up soon, he'd just rejoin Faith.

He was facing the sand dune that hid the wagons from view and felt a bit foolish for standing there with his Colt in his hand and his boots and socks on the blanket. He was about to replace his Colt and get under the blankets again when he heard a low voice on the other side of the dune.

Wally had just snapped, "He ain't here, Steve!" and Steve had shushed him even though he began to think he'd been wrong about the kid's location.

In a normal voice, Steve said, "Let's just climb that dune so we can get a better look. Okay?"

"Alright."

While Joe hadn't been able to understand most of the conversation he'd heard, he did realize who was talking. While he may barefoot, he wasn't about to put Faith in danger by staying close. He felt his mind take control as he stepped onto the dirt and began walking carefully toward the dune. He wasn't sure if they were armed or not, but he trusted his acute awareness to give him the advantage. They had stopped talking, but Joe was certain that they were just on the other side of the dune. He wasn't about to risk walking up the loose sand, so he just stopped short of the base and waited.

Wally and Steve were sliding as they made their way up the dune and had to use their hands to keep moving. They both reached the top at the same time and stood to scan for Joe's cart.

As soon as they appeared, Joe realized they were unarmed, so he just asked, "You boys going somewhere?"

Steve and Wally were startled and turned to make a break to the river. Joe had expected them to go back toward the wagons, but as soon as they ran along the sand dune, he followed a parallel path at the base. He was able to avoid any obstacles because there weren't any. He also had easier going and his long strides allowed him to use a fast walk to match their panicked run along the shifting sand. If it hadn't been such a serious situation, Joe would have laughed at their stumbling, clownish attempt to escape.

Steve kept glancing back at Joe and knew that they weren't going to make it to the river. Then he realized he had a chance if he shoved Wally over the dune to get in the kid's way. He slowed just a little and as Wally continued to run, Steve caught up on his left side then jammed his elbow into Wally's chest.

Wally grunted as he tumbled over the top of the dune and awkwardly rolled down the other side. Steve immediately changed direction and used the dune's downslope to his advantage as he raced toward the river.

Joe didn't know why Wally had fallen but couldn't let him get behind him, so as soon as Wally stopped tumbling, Joe slammed his Colt's barrel into his head. After taking just a few seconds to make sure that the deserter was unconscious or dead, Joe began to jog toward the river. He couldn't see the second one and knew he'd have to climb the dune sooner or later. But it was much lower already as it neared the riverbank, so Joe shifted to his right and began an angling climb up the dune.

When he was able to see the other side, he spotted the second deserter about fifty yards ahead. He was almost to the river and Joe couldn't hit him from this distance with his Colt, so he crossed the top of the dune and hurried after him.

Steve thought he had made it when he reached the riverbank. He was grateful that he knew how to swim but before he waded into the water, he turned to make sure the kid wasn't there. He was stunned when he spotted Joe running towards him less than a hundred feet away, so he turned and raced for the safety of the dark water.

Joe had cocked his Colt as he neared the bank when Steve dove into the river. Joe slowed but kept his eyes on the water. The deserter was wearing his dark blue uniform, so even with the moon overhead, it was difficult to spot him.

Steve may have known how to swim, but after the hurried run, he wasn't able to stay under the water for very long. His lungs were already screaming for oxygen, but he didn't dare surface knowing that kid was near the bank with his pistol.

Joe was waiting for him to gulp for air but knew that the current was taking him downstream. While he suspected that the deserter wasn't going to survive anyway, Joe didn't want to give him a chance to come ashore and create havoc with the sleeping folks in the wagon train. So, he began walking along the riverbank in his bare feet, feeling the mud squishing between his toes as he kept his eyes on the river.

Steve held out as long as he could and believed he'd been beneath the surface for almost a minute, but it had only been twenty seconds. He dropped his feet to the muddy bottom of the shallow river and burst into the life-giving air. As he took enormous, deep breaths he looked at the river bank and felt sick when he saw the kid scout pointing his revolver at him.

"You might as well come out of there, mister. I don't want to shoot you, but I will if you don't start walking this way."

Steve snapped, "You're just a damned kid!"

"A kid with a cocked Colt New Army pointed at your belly. Now do you want to see if I have the guts to pull my trigger?"

Steve didn't say anything as he began wading out of the river. He was only twenty feet from the bank, so he left the water just thirty seconds later. By then, Joe had stepped far enough away to keep him from making another attempt to escape.

As he followed the deserter back to the wagons, he was surprised that no one had arrived yet.

Steve's uniform was dripping as he asked, "Where's Wally?"

"He's sleeping or dead on the other side of the dune. I'll find out which it is after you're tied up again."

Joe still didn't see anyone moving as they neared the wagons. It was only when he was close to the flatbed that he spotted Ed Carlisle asleep in the driver's seat. Joe didn't bother waking him before he had Steve sit on the blanket. He had him bind his own ankles, the took the rope and wrapped it around his chest before holstering his pistol. After making a tight knot, he let the deserter lay down then walked to the flatbed.

He shook Ed's shoulder and when his head popped up from his chest, Joe said, "Your prisoners escaped, Mister Carlisle. I have that one tied up again, but he's a bit wet. I'll go check on the other one now and if he's okay, I'll bring him back."

Ed blinked, then looked at Steve Clinton and asked, "When did all this happen?"

Joe replied, "Just a few minutes ago. I'll be back in a little while," then headed back to the dune in his bare feet.

As he walked, his chest suddenly reminded him that the danger was over, and Joe smiled.

He soon crossed over the dune and spotted Wally who hadn't budged since Joe coldcocked him. Joe wondered if he'd really killed the deserter and was surprised when he felt a pang of guilt. But after he slowly knelt next to Wally, he felt a strong heartbeat. Now he had a new problem in trying to figure out how to move him. Before he could come up with the answer, he needed to put on his boots.

When he was close to the buffalo bed, he wasn't surprised to see Faith sitting on the hide with the blankets wrapped around her.

She asked, "What have you been doing?"

Joe stepped onto the buffalo hide and sat down before replying, "The deserters escaped, and I reckon they were coming here to take Bessie and Betty and my guns. I knocked out one and brought the other one back to the wagons and tied him up again."

Faith couldn't make out the deserter in the shadows, so she asked, "Is the other one still there?"

"Yes, ma'am. I need to put on my boots and figure out how to get him back to the wagons."

"I can help, Joe."

Joe was pulling on his socks as he said, "I'd appreciate it, ma'am. You're going to need to wear your shoes, though."

Faith smiled then turned to pick up her socks and shoes as Joe tugged on his boots. He wasn't about to lift him or have Faith do it either but figured he'd have Bernie just drag him back to join his partner.

As it turned out, he didn't even need to disturb Bernie when he heard Wally begin to moan before he even woke up the donkey.

He turned to Faith and said, "He's awake, so I'll just walk him back to his pal then come back. Okay?"

"Alright. Then you can give me more details."

"Yes, ma'am."

———

It was twenty minutes later when Joe returned to their camp after securing Wally as Ed Carlisle kept watch. Wally hadn't said a word after Joe had found him and not one other person in the wagon train even realized what had happened.

But when he was close to their bed, he found Faith already asleep under the blankets. He smiled as he sat down and pulled off his boots but left his socks on before slipping beneath the blankets. It was a little after midnight when he finally slipped away.

CHAPTER 14

The distant bell destroyed Joe's very pleasant dream and as he opened his eyes he wondered if all that had happened last night was just a vivid dream.

He quickly slid from under the blankets and was rewarded with a jolt of pain from his chest. He heard Faith murmur something but still pulled on his boots then hurried behind the cart.

When he returned just a minute later, he found Faith pulling on her shoes and smiled at her.

She said, "Sorry I fell asleep before you returned."

"It's alright. You needed the sleep, and I wasn't even sure anything really happened when I first woke up."

She stood then said, "I'll be right back," before hurrying to the other side of the cart while Joe began folding the blankets.

The sun still hadn't risen as Faith prepared their scrambled eggs and ham breakfast.

As she scraped the eggs with Joe's spatula, she asked, "Why don't you drink coffee, Joe?"

"My father thought the money was better spent elsewhere and I never missed it. Did you want to buy some in Dobytown?"

"No. I was just wondering. We'd need a coffeepot, anyway."

Joe grinned as he said, "I have the cash, ma'am."

"That doesn't mean you have to spend it, sir."

Joe handed her a tin plate as he said, "No, ma'am. I feel the same way."

"But thank you for the britches and especially the eggs and ham."

"You're welcome, and you can still pick out whatever you want when we visit Dobytown."

"But now please tell me what happened last night."

"Yes, ma'am. I couldn't sleep and I had my pistol in my hand when I heard something…"

―――

Wally and Steve were having their breakfast under the watchful eyes of Bo and Chuck as Ed Carlisle explained what had happened last night. Ed was embarrassed for letting them escape and was trying to minimize his mistake.

"They must have untied those knots after I nodded off, Bo. The first thing I knew, Joe Beck was tapping me on the shoulder and telling me he had to get the other one. Then he walked the second one back, we tied him up then he left. Arnie Emerson showed up a little while later and I went to sleep. I'm really sorry, Bo, but I was really tired, and I figured they weren't going anywhere."

Chuck said, "It's my fault, boss. I musta done a lousy job on those knots."

Bo nodded then said, "Well, there's no harm done. We'll get the rest of the story from Joe when he gets here. Let's get ready to roll."

Joe and Faith were ready to roll and while Faith wasn't wearing her new britches, she was wearing her Colt. After Joe explained what had happened, she was determined not to be unarmed while she was awake. She had also reminded Joe that he needed to teach her how to shoot the pistol.

As he took Bernie's halter, she said, "I wonder if Marigold will be in a better mood today."

Joe grinned as they began walking and said, "You'll find out soon enough. Just ask her about her new sweater and see where that leads."

UNWANTED

They soon passed the edge of the dune and the wagons popped into view, outlined by the brilliant light provided by the rising sun. The folks were busy harnessing their teams and Joe knew they'd start heading west within minutes.

As they turned the cart toward the train, Joe said, "I bet Mother Nature is setting us up for a really long, wet week just when we need to cross the Platte. We should have seen more rain by now."

"Maybe we're having a drought. We had a bad one two years ago."

"We should be so lucky," he replied, then noticed the wagon master walking their way and said, "I think Bo wants to talk to me about last night."

"Do you have to help put those deserters on their horses?"

"I don't think so. I reckon they're ready to ride already."

"Maybe we should just have kept them here until we met the soldiers."

"Maybe we should, but they'll be out of our hands in a couple of hours."

Chuck pulled Bernie to a stop when Bo was fifty feet away then turned him around just before he arrived.

Bo quickly asked, "What happened, Joe?"

"Nothing much. I heard them coming, then met them with my Colt. One pushed the other down the dune and ran off. I tapped the one who fell with my pistol then chased the other one. He dove into the Platte but didn't get far. I brought them both back and we tied them up again. Are they ready to go?"

Bo glanced at Faith before replying, "Yeah, they're ready. We made sure they can't get loose again. Chuck will bring 'em out shortly."

"Okay."

Bo nodded then looked at Bessie and asked, "Why are you packin' a saw?"

"Didn't Chuck tell you? There's a single pine tree about two hours ahead and a thousand yards south that I intend to cut down. I'll take enough to fill my cart, but the folks can split the rest."

"A single tree, and it's still there? That's odd. Anyway, I gotta get back."

Joe nodded as Bo turned and hurried back to his wagon to start the day's journey.

Faith kept her eyes on the wagons expecting to see Marigold but asked, "Are you going to ride to Fort Kearny this morning?"

UNWANTED

"Yes, ma'am. We'll probably be late coming back because we need to find out about the Indian problem. So, if we're not back for the noon break, don't get worried. We'll probably meet up with you just when you reach Dobytown."

Then he stuck his hand into his pants pocket as he said, "Oh, and before I forget, I remembered to make a withdrawal from the State Bank of Axle Grease."

He handed her a folded wad of currency and as she accepted the greenbacks, she asked, "How much is this?"

"Thirty dollars. I wanted you to have it with you in case you get there before I do."

She stared at the small fortune and quietly said, "I can buy some flour, baking powder and sugar. Maybe I'll be able to find a Dutch oven, too."

"That's fine, but don't neglect your wardrobe, Mrs. Beck. I won't have my wife looking destitute."

Faith turned her blue eyes to Joe and smiled as she said, "I like it when you call me Mrs. Beck."

Joe grinned and said, "It makes us sound like an old married couple; doesn't it?"

Faith's smile evaporated as she looked back toward the wagons. She didn't say anything but just stuffed the bills into her dress pocket.

Joe felt like an idiot for reminding her that they'd been legally married for days but still hadn't physically bonded.

He didn't dare try to rectify his blunder, figuring he'd only say something else equally or even more idiotic. But soon, it became a moot point as he spotted Chuck leading two horses with their sullen cargo. Marigold was walking just behind and off to the side to avoid stepping in a surprise morning gift. Joe noticed she was wearing her new sweater and already smiling.

Faith finally looked back at Joe, smiled and said, "It looks like she's forgiven Chuck."

Joe smiled as he asked, "But is it just the sweater that's making her smile?"

Faith laughed as Joe stepped to Bessie, untied her from the cart and mounted.

He looked down at Faith and said, "I love you, Faith Hope Charity Virtue Beck."

"I love you too, Joe Beck. And you don't need to buy me a sweater to make me smile."

Joe nodded then walked Bessie away from the cart to meet Chuck.

Chuck swung his gray gelding wide around the cart and didn't slow as Joe trotted Bessie beside him.

UNWANTED

Joe waved to Faith just as Marigold reached her then took a quick look at the two deserters. They were both glaring at him which was hardly a surprise. Soon, they wouldn't be his problem. And in a couple of days, they wouldn't be the army's problem either.

After they'd ridden for a few minutes, Chuck grinned at Joe and said, "I took your advice and I reckon buyin' that sweater didn't hurt, either."

"I noticed Marigold seemed pretty happy."

"She sure is. I wonder when we'll spot those soldiers."

"Pretty soon, I reckon. I assume that we'll follow them to Fort Kearny."

"Yup. Bo wants us to talk to their captain and hear about those Indian problems."

"Did he say what he's going to do if it's really bad?"

"Nope. He'll figure that out when we learn more."

"I did some calculations last night and I figure that we can fend off a war party of up to sixty Indians depending on how they're armed. That's only if the folks are fairly accurate with their rifles. You don't know how good they are; do you?"

"Nope. But in my first trip, we ran across a hostile batch of about twenty Crow. We didn't shoot any of 'em but they musta been impressed by the amount of firepower we showed 'em."

"How many fired?"

"I reckon it musta been more than thirty."

"All at once? How many held their fire to cover the others when they reloaded?"

Chuck hesitated before replying, "Me and Bo had our pistols to give 'em time, but the Crow were already runnin'."

Joe didn't express his opinion of what they should have done because he was just sixteen and thought that Chuck knew that it had been a mistake to fire a volley with all of the muzzle loaders.

They talked about other topics not involving either Marigold or Faith as they headed west, and Joe searched ahead for the hills that hid the single tree.

Twenty minutes later, they rounded a curve and spotted a squad of cavalry heading towards them. Chuck checked on their prisoners to make sure they weren't getting loose again and found their eyes focused on the men who had recently been their comrades.

He loudly said, "There's your escort to the gallows, boys."

Steve snapped, "Shut up, you bastard!"

Wally just continued to stare at the blue-clad riders knowing that the scout was right. Despite counting some of them as friends, he knew that they would soon be watching him and Steve hang.

Just a few minutes later, they pulled up and met the leader of the detail, Sergeant Jack McCoy.

He looked at Chuck and said, "We'll take the prisoners now. Captain Gillespie asked if you were gonna come along. He wants to talk to both of you, but especially your partner."

"We were plannin' on it."

He nodded then twisted in his saddle and waved the first two troopers forward and told them to take control of the prisoners.

After they had the deserters' horses in tow, they passed Joe and Chuck then when they reached the short columns, the other six riders trailed behind the prisoners.

As the enlarged two columns rode west, Sgt McCoy turned to Chuck and said, "We made sure that none of Clinton's or Venable's pals were included."

Chuck then said, "I thought a squad was bigger."

"We left with ten, but I found a pine tree off the road and had a couple of men cut it down and take it back to the fort. I couldn't believe that it was out there all on its lonesome."

Chuck looked at Joe and snickered but didn't say anything.

Sergeant McCoy didn't understand what was funny until he noticed the saw lashed to Joe's saddle.

Then he grinned as he looked at Joe and said, "Sorry."

"It's alright. It's my fault anyway. I should have cut it down yesterday."

The sergeant wheeled his mount around and hurried to get in front of the column as Joe and Chuck followed.

―――

Faith didn't even get a chance to ask Marigold about her new sweater before Marigold excitedly began a luridly detailed description of her night. Faith simply listened, knowing that she would have probably turned beet red and covered her ears just a month ago. Now she just smiled and let Marigold gush.

After she finally mentioned her new sweater, Marigold asked, "So, what happened last night?"

Faith thought she was asking if she and Joe had engaged in similar activity, so she replied, "Not much. We just talked for a while."

Marigold's eyebrows peaked as she asked, "He didn't tell you how he captured the two deserters?"

Faith stared at Marigold for a few seconds before she laughed then replied, "He did, but I thought…never mind.

Anyway, what he told me was that he was thinking about what might happen when we met the Indians, and he heard a sound…"

Faith took her time telling the story as they walked beside the cart in the hope that Marigold wouldn't ask any more questions about what hadn't happened last night.

———

It was two hours later when Joe had his first view of Fort Kearny, and it wasn't what he expected. He thought it would be surrounded by a high wall of pointed logs, but it looked almost like a settlement. There were some larger buildings and what really surprised him was when he saw some tipis perched nearby. He could even see some Indians talking to soldiers and felt incredibly ignorant.

Fifteen minutes later, he and Chuck followed the soldiers as they rode past the tipis without even giving them a glance and headed toward one of the larger buildings. It wasn't long before Joe saw the carved sign over the doorway that read COMMAND.

He was still scanning the post and making note of each of the buildings' functions as well as counting soldiers and horses. He noticed that the two largest buildings were the stables and the barracks. There was a sutler's store and he wondered why the four soldiers had used the store in Dobytown rather than buy what they needed here.

The troopers pulled up and dismounted in unison leaving only the deserters in the saddle. Chuck and Joe pulled up before the neighboring building with an INFIRMARY sign, dismounted and tied off their horses.

Chuck said, "I reckon we'll just stay here 'til the sergeant tells us where to go."

Joe nodded as he continued his visual tour of the post. Each small revelation reminded him of his ignorance and knowing how little he understood bothered him. It made him feel almost insignificant.

But even as he realized how much he had to learn, he reminded himself that he needed to try at least once to test his theory. Last night's confrontation was yet another example of his mind's ability to shut out the pain from his injury, so he knew he should be able to figure it out.

Sgt. McCoy soon exited the command building and turned toward Joe and Chuck while four of his men began to take the prisoners down.

The sergeant stopped and said, "I'll take you to see the captain while Major Tipple deals with the prisoners."

Chuck nodded, said, "Okay," then Sgt. McCoy turned and headed back toward the command building.

As they followed the NCO, Joe wondered why they were seeing the captain and not the commanding officer. He knew that Captain Gillespie would want to talk to him but had expected that the man in charge would want to hear about the capture of the deserters.

After they entered the command building, Sgt. McCoy led them to a small office on the left side of the hallway and rapped on the doorjamb before saying, "I've got those two scouts, sir."

Joe heard a voice reply, "Send them in, Sergeant," before Sgt. McCoy waved him and Chuck into the room.

Joe had Captain Gillespie's brother's hat in his hands as he and Chuck entered and found the captain standing. He was an almost shockingly handsome man in his mid-twenties and had an air of command about him.

He wore a warm smile as he said, "Have a seat."

Joe and Chuck sat on the two chairs before his small desk as the captain returned to his own seat.

"I have to thank you for catching those two and returning my horse and saddle. The horse isn't army property, so I was fit to be tied when I learned that they had stolen him. I wanted to take a few men and chase after them, but, well, I didn't."

Joe assumed just by his reluctance to say why he couldn't track down deserters that it had been the commanding officer who had ordered him to stay.

Chuck smiled as he replied, "You're welcome, Captain. We were in kinda a standoff when my young partner Joe here asked that Wally feller why he was ridin' an officer's horse. The other one got spooked and went for one of his pistols, but Joe had his Colt already cocked and aimed at 'em."

Captain Gillespie smiled at Joe and asked, "How did you know that?"

"It was just a guess because the horse seemed too nice for a private and I hoped that they'd do something to end the stalemate."

"That was a really smart trick. So, Corporal Jones told me that you have my brother's hat. Can you tell me how it came to be in your possession?"

Joe nodded and started telling his shortened version of the episode but not much beyond scavenging the rebels and finding the hat. He figured the captain only wanted to hear about the hat anyway.

When he finished, Captain Gillespie leaned back and said, "I'm not ashamed to admit that I feel a sense of satisfaction knowing that you killed those rebels."

Joe said, "They might not have been the ones who killed your brother."

"I know, but now I'll be able to write a letter to our parents to let them know."

UNWANTED

"Would you like to have your brother's hat, Captain?"

"I didn't want to ask, but I'd appreciate it. I'll give you another one to replace it."

"That's not necessary. I'll buy one at the store in Dobytown that doesn't make folks think I'm a deserter."

He set the hat on the desk and Captain Gillespie took it in his hands then turned it over to look at the sweatband.

Joe watched his dark brown eyes moisten as he read his brother's scrawl and was glad that he'd decided to take the hat from the dead rebel even if it had been a violation of his rule. Maybe there was a reason why he had decided to take it and then join the wagon train that would lead him to Fort Kearny.

As the captain continued to silently stare at his brother's hat, Joe shifted his thoughts to Faith and wondered if those same wheels of fate had brought them together. From almost their first meeting he felt as if he knew her. But now he needed to know her in the Biblical sense. He had to show her just how much he loved her, and they truly were husband and wife.

He was startled when Captain Gillespie said, "Thank you, Joe. This means a lot to me."

Joe nodded and replied, "You're welcome, Captain."

Chuck finally asked, "What can you tell us about the Indian problem further west?"

"We're just getting a trickle of information as it's too far away for us to send a patrol, even if we had a full compliment. What we learned is that the Arapahoe followed a herd of buffalo onto Pawnee lands…"

As the captain passed along what he knew which wasn't much more than the corporal had told them, Joe realized that he'd just passed his experiment without planning to do it. While Captain Gillespie had been inspecting the hat, he'd been thinking about Faith and blocked out his surroundings until he has been startled when the captain thanked him. So, despite, or rather because his chest now ached, Joe smiled.

When Captain Gillespie finished his short briefing, Chuck asked, "So, you figure it'll get worse the further west we go?"

"Probably. Even though the Union Pacific hasn't laid any tracks yet, the word of the transcontinental railroad is spreading through the tribes and they're not happy about it. They know what will happen once those trains start running and while the armies are killing each other back east, they might think it's time to get together and try to prevent those rails from crossing their land."

Joe said, "It's kind of ironic; isn't it?"

Captain Gillespie looked at him and asked, "What is?"

"I reckon that each of those tribes took that land from another tribe after they lost their land to a different one. It's always been that way and not just on this continent."

Chuck stared at Joe as the captain said, "You're right about that, Joe. We're just a much bigger and better armed tribe."

"But if the army doesn't learn to fight better than what I saw at Lone Jack, then it doesn't matter much."

"Even if they do figure out how to kill better, the tactics will be completely different, and I know that the army doesn't change very fast."

Joe nodded then said, "Maybe they should make you a general."

Captain Gillespie laughed then replied, "I'm surprised they made me a captain."

Then he stood and said, "You probably want to start back. When your wagon train reaches us tomorrow, stop by and see me again."

Chuck shook his hand as he said, "We'll do that, Captain."

As he shook Joe's hand, Captain Gillespie said, "Thank you, Joe. You're one helluva man, even if you're just a teenager."

Joe shrugged but didn't reply before he and Chuck turned and left the small office then crossed the large outer area before exiting the command building.

As Chuck pulled on his hat, he grinned at Joe and said, "You need a haircut, too."

Joe snickered as they walked to their horses, untied them and mounted. They turned south and rode out of Fort Kearny without ever meeting the commanding officer. Nor did they know or care where the two deserters were imprisoned.

It was almost noon when Chuck and Joe left Fort Kearny while just five miles from Dobytown, the wagons stopped for their mid-day break.

Marigold had returned to her family as soon as Bo rang the bell, so Faith was having a quick lunch as she leaned against the cart and looked west along the ruts hoping that Joe might return earlier than expected. After a couple of minutes, she looked back at Betty who was staring at her with her big brown eyes.

Faith smiled and asked, "Are you getting fat just walking back there, Betty?"

She laughed and tossed the last piece of raccoon meat into her mouth then walked to the mare. She was stroking the horse's nose and wondered if she should put on her new britches and ride alongside Bernie rather than walk. It wasn't as if she was tired or sore but knew it would give her a much wider view. Maybe she could even convince Joe to let her ride with him and Chuck and let Russ or Jimmy take care of Bernie.

UNWANTED

Faith sighed knowing what he'd say then turned and walked back to Bernie and took his halter. Soon she was walking along the trail even though the wagons still hadn't budged. She wanted some time alone just to think. She knew she should be patient but still felt frustrated. Maybe if Joe hadn't kissed her and held her close before he was shot, she wouldn't feel this way.

But he had, and Faith had discovered sensations she never dreamt existed. As she walked leading Bernie west along the Trail, Faith believed she wouldn't be so impatient if Joe would at least hug her. After ten minutes, she decided that she'd confess her frustration and ask him to hold her, even as gently as she knew he must. Knowing that he couldn't do much more was almost like a safety net.

When Marigold left her family's wagon, she spotted Faith in the distance and knew that there was no possibility of catching her. So, she walked to the first wagon and climbed into the driver's seat to wait for Chuck to return.

Bo returned from talking with Ed Carlisle and the other leaders and asked Marigold to take the reins as long as she was in the driver's seat.

———

As Chuck and Joe approached Dobytown, Chuck asked, "Do you want to stop to buy a hat or press on? The wagons should be around four miles away by now."

"Let's keep riding. I'll pick up a hat when Faith and I do our shopping."

"It's gonna be crowded in that place if they make it before it closes."

"I reckon so."

Joe was looking east along the Trail hoping to see the roof of his tent-cart with only a blonde head bobbing nearby. He wanted one final confirmation of his theory and would rather test it without Marigold watching.

―――

Faith had kept a fairly rapid pace considering she was leading a donkey-drawn cart and a horse. She was anxious to talk to Joe and had extended her gap over the slow-moving wagons by more than a mile. She wasn't worried about being so far out front despite being alone. The first time she'd looked back, she saw Marigold in the distance and was relieved when she didn't follow but just returned to Mister Ferguson's wagon.

She continued adding distance between her and the lead wagon for the next twenty minutes when she saw two riders appear less than two miles away. Faith felt her heart skip a beat when she recognized Joe astride Bessie. She smiled at the instant recognition because her husband was so tall and not nearly as thin as he believed.

UNWANTED

She kept her eyes on Joe and was waiting for him to wave his blue hat over his head but soon noticed that he wasn't wearing a hat. So, she picked up her walking stick and wagged it over her head. A few seconds later, Joe pulled his Henry from his scabbard and waved it over his head. Faith laughed then slipped her walking stick into the cart and asked Bernie for a little more speed.

As he slid his Henry home, Chuck said, "Faith's gotta be a good mile ahead of the wagons. I reckon she's anxious to see you. I wonder why Marigold isn't with her."

"I can't imagine that they had a fight, so maybe Faith wants to tell me something, but I don't know what it could be."

Chuck snickered then said, "I don't reckon it's that you're gonna be a father."

Joe glanced at Chuck and knew he was just joking, so he replied, "Maybe Marigold already has morning sickness."

Chuck grinned as he said, "Maybe."

Joe kept his eyes on Faith and was pleased to see her so far ahead of the wagons and alone, not counting Bernie and Betty.

As they drew closer, Chuck said, "I'll see you later, Joe," then sent his gray to a canter.

Joe watched Chuck accelerate and wave as he passed Faith. He still slowed Bessie as he prepared to slip into his elevated state. He had figured out that it wasn't just wanting it to arrive, but simply letting it take over by focusing on one thing. In this case, it wasn't difficult at all as he kept his eyes on Faith.

Faith was growing more anxious after Chuck passed by and she had her blue eyes locked on Joe's browns as he pulled Bessie to a stop thirty feet in front of her.

As Joe stepped down, he kept his focus on Faith, and the mid-afternoon sun made Faith's blue eyes almost dance. He didn't bother taking Bessie's reins as he stepped closer to Faith.

As they drew closer, Faith wasn't even smiling as she gazed into Joe's eyes seeing something different. She was prepared to ask him to hold her just before he dismounted, but now she felt as if it wasn't important. She stopped and let Bernie keep walking as she waited for her husband.

Joe stepped close and without saying a word, wrapped his arms around Faith and kissed her even more passionately than he had before.

Faith was overwhelmed and without thinking, put her arms around his chest and pulled him tightly. She suddenly remembered his injury, but when he hadn't reacted to the pain, she let her own passion flow and her nagging concerns melted away.

The kiss lasted just fifteen seconds or so, but when it ended, Joe smiled and said, "I love you, Faith."

Faith sighed then asked, "Does it hurt, Joe?"

Joe pulled his arms back as he replied, "It will later. I'll explain after I tie Bessie to the cart. Okay?"

Faith nodded then released her grip before she and Joe had to trot to catch up to the still-moving cart. Bessie had already taken her place beside Betty, but when they reached the cart, Joe still tied her reins to the other tent brace.

Once they were in their normal position walking beside Bernie, Joe asked, "Remember how I told you that time kind of slowed down and everything became so vividly sharp when I was shooting those rebels?"

"Yes. And you said it was the same when you saw Mort about to shoot the Indian and again when he was going to shoot Chuck."

"That's right. I thought I had to be in a dangerous situation for that to happen, but I was wrong. Do you know how I made that discovery?"

Faith shook her head before Joe said, "Yesterday, when I was riding beside Chuck, I was thinking about you, as I do quite often, by the way. Anyway, I was engrossed in the image of you as you were taking your bath when Chuck startled me with a loud comment. Then I noticed that I hadn't felt the stab of pain when I flinched. I wondered if all I had to do was concentrate on one thing, so I tested my theory a couple of time and figured out how to do it. I can't force myself to go into that enhanced state, but I know how to let it happen. Does that make sense?"

Faith smiled as she replied, "No, not really. But does this mean that we'll be able to, um, you know…"

Joe grinned and said, "Yes, ma'am."

Faith took his hand as they continued to walk and asked, "You and Chuck returned pretty early, so are you going back out again?"

"Nope. We're probably not going out tomorrow morning either because we're so close to Fort Kearny. We should reach Dobytown in a little over an hour, so we can do our shopping then find ourselves a secluded campsite."

"That sounds like a good plan. What happened when you dropped off the deserters? And what happened to the tree you were going to cut down?"

"The tree was already gone because the soldiers spotted it and already cut it down and sent it back to the fort. But the short time at Fort Kearny was interesting. When we reached Fort Kearny, we were escorted into the command building…"

UNWANTED

As Joe told Faith about meeting Captain Gillespie, she felt the same sense of fate that Joe had experienced. *What were the odds that Joe would find the hat that belonged to the brother of a man stationed hundreds of miles away then meet him?*

When he finished, she said, "It seems as if one Yankee captain almost sent you to meet the second."

Joe looked at her as he replied, "I know. Speaking of the first Yankee captain, I have to get something."

He pulled Bernie to a stop, then dropped to his heels and unhooked the grease can from under the cart. After removing the money jar, he returned the can then stood and walked to the back of the cart as Faith followed.

Joe opened the jar then took out the rag that had been part of the shirt he'd been wearing when Mort shot him and used it to clean his hands. After they were clear of grease but still slippery, Joe reached inside and took out the remainder of the currency then handed it to Faith.

"Why are you giving me this, Joe?"

"I just want you to hold it for a few minutes."

She nodded as Joe rummaged around in the cart and pulled out his heavy coat but didn't put it on. Instead, he flipped open one side and reached into an inner pocket and slid out a nice leather wallet.

After returning the coat to the cart, he opened the wallet and pulled out a folded sheet of paper.

"This is the letter that Captain Chalmers sent along with the duffle bag of gifts. I'll read it to you after I put the currency back into the wallet."

Faith traded the cash for the letter then just stared at the words, annoyed with her inability to read. But she was able to recognize some of the words and smiled knowing that Joe would teach her to read. She wanted to learn to read even more than how to shoot her pistol.

She gave him the letter again and Joe read it to her. As she listened, she matched the spoken words to those she had recognized and added a few new ones.

When he finished, he folded the letter and slid it into the wallet's other pocket then said, "I hid the money in the jar because I was alone when I left Missouri. I'm never going to be alone again, Faith. I'll always be with you."

"I wasn't alone but felt as if I didn't belong. Now I know that I belong to you."

"And I belong to you, Mrs. Beck. I'll store this in Betty's saddlebags then let's start moving again. We don't want the wagons to catch up."

Faith smiled as she watched Joe lift the saddlebag's flap and after putting the wallet inside, he walked to take Bernie's halter when he suddenly turned, dropped to his heels again and removed the gutta-percha wrapped pouch and carried it back to Betty and added it to the saddlebag.

He smiled at Faith and said, "Now that we have horses, I don't have to worry about crossing creeks and rivers as much."

As they walked to the front of the cart, Faith asked, "How will we keep the clothes from getting soaked?"

Joe started Bernie walking again before replying, "I had a plan for that but was too busy to get it done. I'll make that modification before we reach the Platte River crossing."

"Can you tell me what it is?"

"I should have done it when I found Bernie. What I'll do is run two pairs of cord between the tent supports, then…"

Faith listened to Joe explain his new modification but was finding it difficult to pay attention. Her mind was occupied by thoughts of the buffalo bed. She had convinced herself that she would have been satisfied with just a gentle hug but after their long, passionate kiss, she wanted much more. She had finally shed any doubts that Joe had been right, and her mother was wrong. Now she just hoped that Joe's ability to block the pain would work. Faith failed to realize that once Joe was in his enhanced state, he would be concentrating on her and drive her into a very different enhanced state.

Chuck had taken the reins to the lead wagon after telling Bo about their visit to Fort Kearny.

Marigold asked, "So, she's not mad at me?"

Chuck laughed then replied, "Nope. I reckon she's just gettin' a bit anxious 'cause, well, you know."

"I thought I might have made her mad because I talked too much about us. I probably added too many details, too. When I saw her walking away, I believed that she might have thought that I was trying to make her feel bad because she's still intact."

"If she is, then that's between her and Joe. Now you can tell me what you said about us."

Marigold rubbed Chuck's thigh as she repeated the same lurid details that she'd told Faith.

Joe and Faith turned Bernie into Dobytown and soon pulled up before the dry goods store.

Joe said, "I'll let you pay for our supplies, Mrs. Beck, but I have another eight dollars and change in my pocket if you go crazy."

UNWANTED

Faith laughed before she and Joe entered the store. There were windows that gave them a good view of the cart and their horses, but Joe wasn't concerned. He and his wife were both packing iron.

The store didn't provide carts like the one in Kansas City had, but it wasn't a problem. After Joe picked up a fifty-pound sack of flour, Faith grabbed a twenty-pound bag of salt. They let the proprietor mark them down and carried them to the cart. They returned to the store and began adding the lighter items. Faith bought three dresses, some new bloomers and a pair of boots while Joe added a new hat that looked nothing like one that a soldier would wear.

Faith added two tins of baking powder then decided to buy a ten-pound bag of coffee, a coffee grinder and a coffeepot. They still had money to spend, so Faith was able to find a Dutch oven and picked up two more wooden spoons. Joe added two books to their stack: a copy of McGuffey's Primer and a Bible. Faith noticed but didn't comment. After paying for the order, Faith still had three dollars and fifteen cents in her dress pocket.

When they left the store, Faith looked at Joe and said, "Mister Moore complained that prices were too high at the store in Kansas City and said that he heard the store owners charged even more on the Trail. But that didn't seem to be true. Was he wrong?"

"No, ma'am. I heard those same things, but when I bought your britches and the eggs and ham, I learned that the proprietor has three different prices. The lowest is for U.S. banknotes, the next is for local banknotes and the highest is for Confederate money. He used to charge more but after they pulled most of the soldiers out of Fort Kearny, he had to drop his prices just to sell his stock. That's why those soldiers were buying some supplies here rather than in the sutler's store."

"Oh. Maybe the other stores will have the same problem."

"If we're lucky."

Faith then smiled as she said, "It'll take me a while to get used to that new hat."

"It will for me, too. It's flatter and a bit tight, but I'll break it in."

"At least it's not blue or gray."

"Some of those rebels had tan-colored hats, Mrs. Beck."

"The you'd better hope that none of those Yankee soldiers at Fort Kearny shoot you."

Joe laughed as he took Bernie's halter and turned him south to leave the town. Before they started moving, they saw the wagons approaching less than a half a mile away.

Faith asked, "Which way will we go?"

UNWANTED

Joe replied, "West," then removed his new hat and waved it over his head before pulling it back on.

He saw Bo and Chuck both wave back and then Marigold waved a few seconds later. Faith added her own wave to let Marigold that she wasn't angry, especially as she wouldn't be seeing Marigold again until tomorrow morning. No matter what happened tonight, Faith wasn't about to gush about it to Marigold tomorrow.

They turned west on the river side of the ruts and Joe began searching for a good place for their campsite. They walked for another ten minutes before Joe found a small feeder creek and turned Bernie off the Trail.

Before he even stopped, Faith said, "I'll make the bed, Joe. I don't want you to risk taking that buffalo skin down."

Joe grinned as he said, "We could use the raccoon pelts instead."

Faith just shook her head before Joe pulled Bernie to a stop. As he began unharnessing the hard-working donkey, Faith slid the buffalo hide from the top of the tent and then began gathering bedrolls.

―――

The sun was setting, and Faith was cooking supper when Joe slowly sat next to her.

She looked at him and noticed he had the new Bible in his hands, so she asked, "Are you going to start teaching me to read?"

"We'll start with the McGuffey's Primer, but I wanted to tell you the other reason why I decided to buy it."

He opened the Bible to the back pages and Faith understood his reason when she saw the blank lines.

"When we stop at Fort Kearny, I'll buy a pen and ink. Then I'll record our marriage. Then when each of our children are born and baptized, I'll let you add the information."

Faith softly asked, "Do you really think I'll be able to write by then?"

"Yes, I do. But I'm going to put the letter from Captain Chalmers inside rather than keeping it in the wallet. If the wallet is stolen, we'll just lose some money. I don't think any thieves would steal a Bible."

"I hope not."

Joe had already removed the letter from the wallet, so he turned the Bible to the first page of the Book of Revelations, inserted the letter and slowly closed the good book.

"I'll store this in Betty's saddlebags and be right back."

Faith nodded and watched Joe walk away. While she had expected him to tell her that he'd be entering their marriage in the Bible, she had been deeply touched when he said that she would be the one to enter their children's births and baptisms. It almost eclipsed her thoughts of the first step they would soon take to make those entries.

Faith found that she was surprisingly nervous as she lay beneath the blankets watching Joe pull off his boots. Outwardly, it was no different than it had been last night when they just talked, until she fell asleep. But once Joe joined her in their bed, everything would be different. Faith suddenly felt so incredibly awkward and tried to remember the excitement she'd felt each time Joe had first kissed her, but it was difficult to overcome her unexpected nervousness.

Joe hadn't noticed Faith's anxiety because he was already worrying about failing to suppress his pain. Unlike his tests, he couldn't afford to fail now.

He pulled up the blankets then slid close to Faith and rolled onto his right side. Faith then slowly turned onto her left side to face him.

The two young people looked in each other's eyes for almost a minute before Joe asked, "This is strange; isn't it?"

Faith smiled as she replied, "I'm really nervous and don't know why. It seems as if all I've been thinking about is making love with you. Now that it's about to happen, I feel like a silly girl."

"You've never been silly since I met you, Faith. But I can understand why you feel that way. I feel a bit awkward myself."

"You do?"

"Yes, ma'am. I'm pretty sure that I'll be able to focus all my attention on you and not even notice my wound, but there's that nagging concern that I'll fail. And the last thing I want is to disappoint you."

Faith whispered, "We can wait, Joe."

"For another month, Faith? I can't wait that long, and I doubt that even your patience would last a week."

Faith didn't say anything as she looked into Joe's eyes and waited.

There was another thirty seconds of tense silence before Joe lifted his right hand and slid his fingertips gently across Faith's cheek.

She placed her hand over his as he said, "I love you, Faith," then leaned forward and kissed her.

Faith's nervousness vanished as she her stored passion exploded.

Joe's sense of heightened awareness engulfed him even more completely than it had when he'd faced those eight rebels. As he kissed Faith, he nudged her onto her back then slid his lips to her neck.

UNWANTED

Faith gasped and tilted her head to her left to let him continue and felt her toes curl. She was overwhelmed and close to ecstasy already, yet they'd just begun. She couldn't imagine being more excited but wanted more. As Joe kissed her neck, she pulled his hand onto her right breast and shuddered when his fingers began a massage.

Joe took a moment to toss off the blankets then thought he'd be too clumsy to unbutton Faith's dress but didn't fumble once as he worked his way down the front. As he kissed her on the lips again, he was pleased and excited when his fingers told him that Faith wasn't wearing her camisole. He felt her tremble as a crop of goosebumps erupted on her naked skin then discovered that she wasn't wearing her bloomers either.

Faith wanted to do more but was lost as Joe continued to kiss and caress her. She felt the front of her dress open and spread her legs expecting that Joe would soon take her. She wanted it so badly that she forgot that he was still dressed.

Joe still didn't start unbuttoning his own shirt as he concentrated all of his attention on his wife. In the light of the almost full moon, he could see her thin but perfect body as if it was high noon. He was more aroused than he thought possible but was determined to keep his focus on Faith.

Faith was going mad as she waited for Joe to take her but when he began kissing her inner thighs, she cried out in an explosion of pleasure. She suddenly began to beg him to touch her, to kiss her and then started to loudly demand that he take her.

Joe had been startled when she had first cried out and thought he'd hurt her but just a heartbeat later, he realized that Faith was far from being hurt.

He didn't want to stop exciting Faith but still needed to rid himself of his shirt, britches and underpants.

Faith's eyes had been closed since Joe had started kissing her neck, but now she so intensely wanted him to take her that she opened her eyes to let him see the overpowering lust he had created. As soon as her eyelids parted, she realized that he was still dressed and immediately began to end that condition.

Joe felt Faith's fingers working to pop his buttons, so he slid back to where his head was close to hers and let her undress him while he continued to kiss and caress her.

Faith almost ripped his shirt off in her haste but after his last shirt button was free, she hurriedly began working on his britches.

She let her fingers slide across his chest and suddenly crossed over the rough, bumpy skin of his wound and expected him to jerk back, but he didn't. She then began to peel his shirt away.

UNWANTED

She managed to get his shirt free before she shouted, "Take off your pants!"

Joe rolled onto his back and in one swift motion, yanked off his britches and underpants then tossed them aside before rolling against Faith and resumed kissing and touching her.

Now that Joe was naked, Faith assumed he would take her but still let her hands explore her husband and was surprised that it added to her own excitement. But her belief that Joe would finally consummate their marriage was very premature.

When Joe felt her touching him, it immediately pushed his own desires to incredibly heights but also made him even more determined to focus on Faith. He tried to ignore her loud and repeated demands that he take her as he kissed and touched her in every conceivable spot.

Faith thought she might pass out as Joe pushed her to ever higher levels of arousal. Each touch and kiss made her gasp or moan and as much as she wanted him, she hoped that he didn't stop.

Joe was so far into his enhanced state that he thought that he'd first kissed her just five minutes ago when it had already been more than thirty. That misplaced timing only added to Faith's growing loss of control.

Faith Hope Charity Virtue didn't even notice the chill night air or the moon overhead as Joe continued to fire her passions. She wasn't the innocent girl who stood with a sign hanging from her neck just last month. She was a lusty woman who wanted her husband to make her his wife in every sense and was demanding that he fulfill his duty…now!

Joe was almost ashamed that he'd only lasted ten minutes when Faith finally grabbed hold of his hips and screamed at him to take her.

Before that first kiss, one of Faith's hidden anxieties was when she recalled that her mother and Marigold had said that the first time was painful. But as she demanded that Joe end their almost hour-long session of lovemaking, she no longer cared.

Then suddenly, Faith's loud demands were answered, and her mind erupted to an even higher level of ecstasy making her scream in utter joy. Her back arched and she felt a powerful urge to move as she and Joe joined in the last act of their consummation. Her eyelids fluttered as she grasped Joe's lunging hips and didn't know how long she'd be able to keep going. Suddenly, she wailed like a banshee as she experienced a burst of fireworks explode throughout her body and soul.

Joe was still so focused on Faith that when they reached that pinnacle of passion, it almost startled him. But even as he realized his own massive pleasure that hadn't diminished since he'd first kissed Faith, he didn't feel any pain from his chest.

UNWANTED

When he rolled onto his right side, he pulled his heavily breathing, sweat-covered wife close, then slid the blankets over them before he kissed her softly.

Faith was still disoriented as she opened her eyes and smiled at her husband then asked, "Does your wound hurt?"

"I don't even feel it, sweetheart. I'm sorry that I didn't last very long. Were you disappointed as Marigold was?"

Faith looked at him curiously and asked, "How long did you expect it to last?"

"At least twenty minutes."

"Joe, where were you? I think it was more than an hour and I was ready after ten minutes."

Joe stared at her for a few seconds before saying, "I guess I lost track of time because you were so exciting."

"I'm just pleased that I didn't disappoint you. You weren't disappointed; were you?"

Joe smiled as he replied, "Terribly. I think I need to visit Becky Witherspoon."

Faith laughed then kissed him before snuggling close.

She rested her head on his right arm and asked, "Will it always be this exciting, Joe? Even when I get fat after I start having our babies?"

"It will always be that way because I'll always love you."

"I love you so very much, Joe. I can't believe how much my life has changed since we left Kansas City."

"I can't either. Just a year ago, I was sent away because I wasn't wanted. Then after living by myself for all that time, I began to believe that I'd always be lonely. But then I met you and now I know that for the rest of my life, I'll have someone who wants to be with me."

Faith sighed then whispered, "And I was unwanted by my parents, but it was only a few days before you found me. Now I know that I'm loved and wanted."

Joe kissed her forehead and watched as she closed her eyes. He may not know where they would go or what would happen, but he knew that he now held his future.

TRANSITION

The next morning, Joe and Faith continued their journey as if nothing had changed, but everything had.

They stopped at Fort Kearny and met with Captain Gillespie who gave Joe his home address which he added to the Bible which now had its first entry: Joe Beck married Faith Hope Charity Virtue Goodchild, May 2, 1862 in Nebraska Territory. Captain Gillespie didn't offer him a hat again but did give him a nice army compass. Joe thought it wasn't necessary as they'd be following the ruts all the way to Oregon but still gratefully accepted it. Before they left, Joe also wrote and posted a thank you letter to Captain Chalmers and addressed it to the captain and his wife just in case her husband didn't survive more of the battles or disease.

Two days after leaving Fort Kearny, Mary Moore had no difficulties when she gave birth to another boy whom they named Oscar. Becky Witherspoon then moved in with the family to mind the other boys and help Mrs. Moore with the baby.

Joe began teaching Faith to read as well as use her pistol. While she wasn't a great shot, she learned how to read and write very quickly.

Before they reached the split in the Platte River, Marigold confided in Faith that she'd missed her monthly and Faith congratulated her. While Faith had told Marigold that she and Joe had consummated their marriage, she hadn't mentioned the extended length of each of their couplings as she didn't want to appear to be bragging. But she did look forward to those nights with her husband and doubted if Marigold had a husband who paid so much attention to her.

The long-delayed rains began falling the day after the newest member of the Moore family arrived and the week of constant precipitation slowed the wagons even more. Joe's newly modified tent-cart kept their clothes dry when they crossed a swollen creek and Faith appreciated his homemade tent that kept the water away from their buffalo bed.

As the wagon train approached the Platte River ferry crossing, Joe longingly looked south knowing that Colorado Territory was just a few days travel. But he was a scout for the wagon train, and they depended on him now. He may have been somewhat disappointed to be heading northwest, but wherever he found a place to settle, it would be a home because he found Faith.

Author's Note

I need to apologize for a few things. The delay was for a combination of health issues and a desire to edit my older books. I'm also sorry for the length of his one as it's really not finished yet. I knew when I first started that it was going to be long, which was unusual for me. Usually, when I start a new book, I figure that it'll be around 80,000 words, but then it keeps going. This one I knew would be longer, but by the time I was halfway through, I realized that it was going to be a beast. So, I decided to tell the story of Joe and Faith in parts, which is why it ends with a transition and not an epilogue. The number of parts will depend on what they decide to do by themselves. I'm just telling their story.

For those who aren't familiar with the history of Nebraska, you may believe that I misspelled Fort Kearny. It was named after General Kearny and when the nearby settlement of Dobytown changed its name to Kearny, the mapmakers were the ones to misspell the name by adding an 'e'. So, it's Kearney, Nebraska now and I'm sure that the folks who live there are well aware of the bureaucratic snafu. I'm sure that they're much happier with the new name too, despite the misspelling.

C.J. PETIT

BOOK LIST

1	Rock Creek	12/26/2016
2	North of Denton	01/02/2017
3	Fort Selden	01/07/2017
4	Scotts Bluff	01/14/2017
5	South of Denver	01/22/2017
6	Miles City	01/28/2017
7	Hopewell	02/04/2017
8	Nueva Luz	02/12/2017
9	The Witch of Dakota	02/19/2017
10	Baker City	03/13/2017
11	The Gun Smith	03/21/2017
12	Gus	03/24/2017
13	Wilmore	04/06/2017
14	Mister Thor	04/20/2017
15	Nora	04/26/2017
16	Max	05/09/2017
17	Hunting Pearl	05/14/2017
18	Bessie	05/25/2017
19	The Last Four	05/29/2017
20	Zack	06/12/2017
21	Finding Bucky	06/21/2017
22	The Debt	06/30/2017
23	The Scalawags	07/11/2017
24	The Stampede	08/23/2019
25	The Wake of the Bertrand	07/31/2017
26	Cole	08/09/2017
27	Luke	09/05/2017
28	The Eclipse	09/21/2017
29	A.J. Smith	10/03/2017
30	Slow John	11/05/2017
31	The Second Star	11/15/2017
32	Tate	12/03/2017
33	Virgil's Herd	12/14/2017
34	Marsh's Valley	01/01/2018
35	Alex Paine	01/18/2018
36	Ben Gray	02/05/2018
37	War Adams	03/05/2018

UNWANTED

38	Mac's Cabin	03/21/2018
39	Will Scott	04/13/2018
40	Sheriff Joe	04/22/2018
41	Chance	05/17/2018
42	Doc Holt	06/17/2018
43	Ted Shepard	07/16/2018
44	Haven	07/30/2018
45	Sam's County	08/19/2018
46	Matt Dunne	09/07/2018
47	Conn Jackson	10/06/2018
48	Gabe Owens	10/27/2018
49	Abandoned	11/18/2018
50	Retribution	12/21/2018
51	Inevitable	02/04/2019
52	Scandal in Topeka	03/18/2019
53	Return to Hardeman County	04/10/2019
54	Deception	06/02.2019
55	The Silver Widows	06/27/2019
56	Hitch	08/22/2018
57	Dylan's Journey	10/10/2019
58	Bryn's War	11/05/2019
59	Huw's Legacy	11/30/2019
60	Lynn's Search	12/24/2019
61	Bethan's Choice	02/12/2020
62	Rhody Jones	03/11/2020
63	Alwen's Dream	06/14/2020
64	The Nothing Man	06/30/2020
65	Cy Page	07/19/2020
66	Tabby Hayes	09/04/2020
67	Dylan's Memories	09/20/2020
68	Letter for Gene	09/09/2020
69	Grip Taylor	10/10/2020
70	Garrett's Duty	11/09/2020
71	East of the Cascades	12/02/2020
72	The Iron Wolfe	12/23/2020
73	Wade Rivers	01/09/2021
74	Ghost Train	01/27/2021
75	The Inheritance	02/26/2021
76	Cap Tyler	03/26/2021

77	The Photographer	04/10/2021
78	Jake	05/06/2021
79	Riding Shotgun	06/03/2021
80	The Saloon Lawyer	07/04/2021
81	Unwanted	09/21/2021

UNWANTED

Manufactured by Amazon.ca
Bolton, ON